"I brought my bathing suit."

"Won't need it," De

Her arms, both   eze and a slight shake.

"Jacob, honey,   want to go swimming and   al duty to use that pool as   sting so much energy to heat it."

He looked down at her. "I didn't say we weren't going swimming. I said you won't need your suit."

Her face changed, her eyes drifting half closed and he felt her body shiver.

"And I also didn't tell you, murgh makhani comes with my personal label ale and leads into turtle sundaes," he continued.

At that, her body melted into his side.

"Awesome food, homemade beer and skinny-dipping," she whispered. "Have I told you I like you today?"

"No. You told me you *really* like me," he contradicted.

She melted deeper into him, tipping her head back. "You're right. That's what I said because that's what I meant."

Her body, the invitation of her mouth, her words, he didn't let it slide.

But when he bent his neck to take her mouth that time, it wasn't quick.

Kaleidoscope

KRISTEN ASHLEY

FOREVER

NEW YORK   BOSTON

Copyright © 2013 by Kristen Ashley
Excerpt from *The Gamble* © 2012 by Kristen Ashley
All rights reserved. In accordance with the U.S. Copyright Act of 1976, the scanning, uploading, and electronic sharing of any part of this book without the permission of the publisher constitute unlawful piracy and theft of the author's intellectual property. If you would like to use material from the book (other than for review purposes), prior written permission must be obtained by contacting the publisher at permissions@hbgusa.com. Thank you for your support of the author's rights.

Forever
Hachette Book Group
1290 Avenue of the Americas
New York, NY 10104

www.HachetteBookGroup.com

Printed in the United States of America

Originally published as an ebook

First mass-market edition: December 2014
10 9 8 7 6 5 4 3 2 1

OPM

Forever is an imprint of Grand Central Publishing.
The Forever name and logo are trademarks of Hachette Book Group, Inc.

The Hachette Speakers Bureau provides a wide range of authors for speaking events. To find out more, go to www.hachettespeakersbureau.com or call (866) 376-6591.

The publisher is not responsible for websites (or their content) that are not owned by the publisher.

In Memory of Jená Kelly
*I'd give anything for just one more chance to curl up on the
couch with you and right the world's wrongs.*
Seems I'll have a wait.
So until that time comes for me, I'll hold you in my heart.
Then again, you've always had your place there.
And you always will.

Acknowledgments

To my girls, Erika Wynne, Chasity Jenkins-Patrick and Emily Sylvan Kim, it bears repeating, well...*repeatedly*, thank you for taking my back. Always.

To Amy Pierpont, thank you for caring so much about my work and for giving me the freedom to tell my characters' tales the way they need to be told. You rock!

And to Jill Shalvis, thank you for making me laugh (frequently) and for sharing your wisdom (even more frequently).

Kaleidoscope

CHAPTER ONE

Dimple

"Jacob Decker!"

Deck turned at hearing his name called in a voice he knew but hadn't heard in years. A voice he liked.

A voice he missed.

A voice that made his blood run hot.

He scanned the relatively busy lunchtime wooden sidewalks of Gnaw Bone and couldn't spot her.

What he could see was an amazingly beautiful woman walking his way. She was in tight dark-wash jeans tucked in stylish high-heeled brown leather boots that went nearly up to her knees, a distressed, feminine, brown leather modified motorcycle jacket with an expensive-looking scarf wrapped loosely around her throat. Her long, gleaming dark brown hair shone in the cold winter Colorado sun, subtle red highlights making an attractive feature stunning. From under a knit cap pulled down to her ears, her hair came out in sleek sheets flowing over her shoulders. Covering her eyes were huge, chic brown-framed sunglasses.

Her full rosy lips were tipped up in a grin.

She stopped two feet in front of him and he stared down at her with surprise as, even in her sunglasses, her face showed fond recognition, warmth and a fuck of a lot more.

But he'd never seen this woman in his life.

And Deck never forgot a face.

Never.

But if he did, he would never forget that face.

Or any other part of her.

Then her grin turned into a smile, a dimple he remembered vividly depressed into her right cheek, his surprise switched to out-and-out shock and she leaned into him. Lifting a hand and placing it lightly on his shoulder, her other hand she rested on his chest, she rolled way up on her toes and pressed her cheek to his.

"Jacob," she murmured, and he could feel her fingertips dig into his shoulder even through his coat.

Jacob.

That name, a name he allowed very few people to use, said in that voice, a voice he missed, sliced through him.

Deck tipped his chin and felt her soft hair slide against the skin on his cheek. His blood was still running hot but his chest now felt tight.

"Emme," he whispered, lifting a hand and wrapping his fingers around the side of her trim waist.

She pulled her head back; he lifted his and their shades locked.

She was still smiling that smile, that cute dimple shooting a flood of piercing memories through his skull. Memories he'd buried.

Memories about Emme.

"It's been a long time," she said quietly.

"Yeah," he agreed.

And it had. Years. Nine of them.

Too long to see Emme again.

"How are you?" she asked, still not moving away.

"Alive," he answered, that dimple pressed deeper and he knew, if she wasn't wearing shades, he'd see her unusual light brown eyes dance. He'd made her eyes dance frequently back then. And he hadn't had to work for it. She just gave it to him. And often.

"Em!" a man's voice snapped.

Deck's head came up and Emme moved slightly away, dropping her hands from him as she turned. They both looked at a tall, good-looking, well-built blond man wearing a mountain man uniform of flannel shirt, faded jeans, construction boots and jeans jacket standing three feet away, scowling.

Emme shifted to the man, her dimple gone but her lips still tipped up. She wrapped a hand around his bicep and leaned into him in a familiar way that said it all about who he was to her.

Deck felt that slice through him, too, but this time in a way that did not feel good.

"Dane," she began, "this is an old friend. Jacob Decker." She threw a hand out Deck's way as she lifted her sunglasses to his face. "Jacob, this is Dane McFarland. My, um...well, boyfriend."

Again, shocked as shit that Emmanuelle Holmes had a boyfriend, but not shocked this slim, stylish, stunning Emme had one, Deck opened his mouth to offer a greeting but McFarland got there before him.

"An old friend?"

Deck felt his body tighten at the man's terse tone as he watched Emme's head turn swiftly and her shades lock on her boyfriend's face. He also noted her grin had faded.

"An old friend," she stated firmly.

McFarland, not wearing sunglasses—his were shoved up in his hair—took Deck in top to toe through a glower.

He had the wrong idea.

McFarland's eyes sliced to Emme and what he said next proved Deck right.

"What kind of old friend?"

It was the wrong thing to ask. Deck knew this because, even if a man had suspicions his woman just introduced him to an ex-lover, he should wait until they were alone to call her on it. He also knew this because Emme's smile was not only gone, her face had grown slightly cold.

"The kind I'd introduce to my boyfriend?" she replied

on a question that didn't quite hide its sarcasm, her smooth alto voice—something among many things he'd always liked about her—having grown nearly as cold as her face.

Emme didn't take shit from her man.

Another surprise.

Dane's glower subsided, he started to look contrite, but none of the cold left Emme's face and Deck decided to wade in.

"Let's start this again," he stated, offering his hand. "Dane, like Emme said, I'm Jacob Decker. An old friend of Emme's, just a friend from back in the day. Everyone calls me Deck."

McFarland's eyes came to him, dropped to his hand then back to his face when he took Deck's hand. He squeezed and he did it hard, a challenge, a competition. His ludicrously strong grip saying either he didn't like his girl having men friends no matter how they came or that he'd noted Deck had three inches on him and likely forty pounds, but he felt he could still take him.

Or it said both.

This guy was a dick.

He was also a moron. Just with the difference in their sizes, any man would be smart enough not to issue that kind of challenge or think he could best Deck. But the fact that those forty pounds Deck had on him were all muscle and McFarland couldn't miss it made him more of a moron.

And Deck did not like that for Emme.

Unable to do anything but, he squeezed back, saw McFarland's flinch, felt his hand go slack in reflexive self-preservation in order to save his bones getting crushed, and his point made, Deck let the man's hand go.

McFarland flexed it twice before shoving it into his pocket.

Emme missed this. She was looking up at Deck.

"What are you doing in Gnaw Bone?" she asked.

"Could ask you the same thing," he returned.

"I live here now."

Another shock. Her family was in Denver and they were tight. She didn't have a shit ton of friends but they were in

Denver too. And she was the kind of woman he thought would settle early in a life she found comfortable and stay forever.

Then again, he thought a lot of things about the Emme he knew including the fact she was sweet, funny, interesting, and no one but his best friend Chace Keaton gave better conversation. But even if it made him a dick for thinking it, she was always sexless. She made it that way. Worked at it. Her looking like she looked, dressing like she was dressed, having a man, meant her making the move to Gnaw Bone shouldn't be that big a surprise since she'd made a lot of changes.

But he didn't like that she lived in Gnaw Bone.

It wasn't her living there. It was that he had no idea how long she'd been there, but he couldn't deny the fact that knowing she lived close for however long it was, he found upsetting.

"Your turn," she prompted when he said nothing as to why he was in that town.

"Business," he answered, and the dimple reappeared.

"That's great," she replied. "Please tell me you're going to be around for a while. I've got to get back to work but I'd love to meet you for dinner."

He'd be around for a while. He didn't lie. He was in Gnaw Bone for business. But he lived in Chantelle, a twenty-minute drive away.

And he didn't have plans. So he definitely could make dinner.

He grinned down at her. "You're on."

"Uh, Em, I got shit on tonight," McFarland broke in, and both Deck and Emme looked at him.

"That's okay, babe," she told him, and Deck fought back his grin turning into a smile when McFarland's eyes flashed with annoyance. "Jacob and I can have dinner without you. And anyway, we have a lot of catching up to do and you probably would be bored seeing as you won't know who or what we're talking about."

McFarland did not like his woman making dinner plans with another man, or having history with him even if it was platonic. It showed clear on his face but he'd learned from moments earlier and kept his mouth shut.

Emme looked back at Deck.

"Do you know The Mark? It's just down the street." She pointed behind him but he nodded as she did.

"Know The Mark, Emme," Deck told her.

"Great." She gave him another dimple. "How's seven o'clock sound?"

"Works for me," he agreed.

The dimple pressed deeper even as unhappy vibes rolled off her boyfriend.

"Looking forward to it, honey," she said softly, words meant just for him, an endearment that made her boyfriend even less happy and that was reflected in the vibes rolling off him getting barbed.

But those words shifted through Deck like a razor blade through silk.

She'd always called him honey. Elsbeth had hated it. Then again, Elsbeth had eventually not been a big fan of Deck's friendship with her BFF.

In his surprise at seeing Emme here in Gnaw Bone, hours away from where he knew her to live. Seeing her as he saw her, completely changed, hair much longer, those highlights, becoming clothes, at least twenty, probably more like thirty pounds off her frame. Seeing her with a man. Fuck, seeing her at all after what went down, how things ended and the last thing she did the last time he saw her.

With all that, belatedly, he realized he should have taken more care. He should have kept his shit together. He should maybe not have agreed to go to dinner with her. He'd shut the door on her, literally, after things ended with Elsbeth. It had hurt her. And he'd been so hung up on Elsbeth, he'd never gone back to open it.

But he did make dinner plans.

And he did because she didn't look a thing like her, Deck wondered why, and Deck didn't like puzzles. He found a puzzle, he solved it. This colossal change in Emme was a puzzle he intended to solve.

He also did it because of the last thing she did the last time he saw her.

And last, he did it just because she was Emme.

He may have hurt her but if he was reading her current behavior correctly, she held no grudges.

"Me too," Deck murmured.

McFarland slid an arm around her shoulders, pulling her into his side and stating, "We gotta get back to work, babe."

She looked up at him and nodded. "Right." Her shades came back to Deck and she gave him another grin, no dimple. "Tonight. The Mark. Seven o'clock."

Because her boyfriend was a dick, and because it made sense, Deck suggested, "Give me your number. I'll give you mine. Just in case shit gets screwed, one of us is late, or whatever."

As expected, McFarland didn't like this and he gave Deck a hard look.

Deck ignored it and pulled his phone out of his back pocket as Emme moved out of the curve of her boyfriend's arm to dig in her purse.

"You first, or me?" she asked, head bent, hair shining in the sun. He had her profile and the elegant curve of her jaw was on display. Something he never noticed before. Something else that surprised him not only because he noticed it but also because it was elegant, alluring, inviting touch, even taste, and it also surprised him because he always noticed everything.

But he'd never noticed that.

And he didn't need to be thinking about how Emmanuelle Holmes's jaw might taste when she was standing next to her boyfriend.

"Me," he said. She nodded and he gave her his number.

She did the same when he was done and shoved her phone in her purse.

"Now we're good," she told him.

"We are," he agreed.

"See you at seven," she said.

"Yeah," Deck replied then looked up at McFarland. "Later."

McFarland jerked up his chin, said nothing, slid his arm around Emme's shoulders again and pulled his woman around Deck.

She wrapped an arm around McFarland's waist but still twisted to wave at Deck and give him another smile with dimple as she walked away.

Deck stood on the relatively busy sidewalk and watched McFarland load Emme up in a big, red, flash, totally pimped out, my-dick-is-small GMC Sierra.

Another reason to go to dinner with Emme. That was, find out what the fuck she was doing with that asshole.

He turned away, burying how seeing Emme again made him feel as he moved down the wooden planks toward the police station. All that shit went down a long time ago. It was over. He was over it. Finally. After nine years.

And the bottom line truth of it was, in the end he'd eventually learned that the biggest thing he lost in all that was Emme.

So, thinking on it, it didn't suck that maybe he could get her back.

He pushed into the police station, shoved his sunglasses back on his head and moved to the reception desk seeing the receptionist eyeing him.

The instant he stopped in front of her, before he could introduce himself, she stated, "You're Jacob Decker."

He wasn't surprised. There were men that were hard to describe. Deck, a few words, people would know him from two blocks away.

"I am," he confirmed.

"Mick and the others are waiting on you," she informed him, eyes going up, down, up and stopping every once in a while to get a better look at something, his hips, his shoulders, his hair.

This also didn't surprise him. Women did this often. At six foot four, there was a lot of him to take in. It wasn't lost on him that most of it, women liked looking at. And, if he liked who was looking, he didn't hesitate to use this to his advantage.

"Just go on around the counter, back down the hall, second door to the left. You want coffee, keep goin', get yourself some and backtrack," she finished.

He nodded, muttered, "Thanks," and moved.

He didn't bother with coffee. He had the means to have the finer things in life and therefore accepted nothing less. And from experience he knew police station coffee was far from the best. Deck ground his coffee fresh first thing in the morning. He bought it on the Internet. It cost a fucking whack. And it was worth it.

He went to the second door to the left. It was closed. He gave a sharp rap on it with his knuckles and entered when he heard the call.

The gang was all there, as Chace had told him it would be.

Mick Shaughnessy, captain of the Gnaw Bone Police Department, standing by his desk.

Jeff Jessup, one of Gnaw Bone's detectives, standing by the window.

Henry Gibbons, captain of the Carnal Police Department, leaning on a table across the messy office.

Carole Weatherspoon, captain of the Chantelle Police Department, standing close to Gibbons, arms crossed on her chest.

Kenton Douglas, County Sheriff, standing shoulders against the wall.

And last, Chace Keaton, Deck's best friend since school and a Carnal detective.

It was Chace Deck was watching as he closed the door behind him, and he was watching Chace because he knew the man well and he didn't like the look on his face.

But it was Shaughnessy who spoke first, taking Deck's attention.

"May be rude but I'll start by welcoming you to this meetin' but statin' plain, I don't like it."

"Mick," Chace murmured.

Deck ignored his friend and informed Mick honestly, "I'm a big fan of statin' shit plain."

"Good, then I'll state it plainer," Mick went on. "We talk this through with you, you take this contract, Kent deputizes you, you are not a maverick. Chace suggested your services and I looked into you, found nothin'. No man's got nothin' but a fully paid truck, a fully paid house, a credit card with no balance, taxes fair and square and a load of cash in the bank. Makes me nervous."

"I see that," Deck allowed, not annoyed by the check—he'd expect nothing less—but he said no more.

"So, before we talk this through with you, you know that if you take this on, you do this by the book. You're deputized, you report, you take orders and I'll repeat, you don't go maverick," Mick continued, and Deck drew in breath.

Then he stated it plain.

"My understanding of this meet is, if I wanna take this on, and seein' if I do, my usual charges will need to be significantly discounted considering you can't afford to pay them as I charge them, it'll need to be somethin' I really wanna do. And you got a reputation I admire, Shaughnessy, so I hope you take no offense but I don't take orders. I work a case how I feel it needs to be worked. I report what I feel is necessary. And last, I only do maverick."

Mick looked to the room and announced, "This isn't startin' good."

"Why don't we lay it out, see what Deck thinks and get the other shit sorted if it's somethin' he wants to do?" Chace suggested, moving to a wide whiteboard set at an angle in the corner.

No one said anything. Deck settled in but Chace's eyes came to him.

"You're gonna see somethin' you might not like on this board that probably will make Mick's warnings moot seein' as I figure you are not gonna want this case. I would have told you about it sooner, but if I did, you might not have come in, and, respect Mick," Chace glanced at Shaughnessy before he looked back to Deck, "with what happened a few days ago, we need you."

With that, he flipped the whiteboard and Deck's eyes scanned it.

Half a second later, his body froze solid.

This was because there was a picture of the man he just met on the street, top center of the whiteboard, his name in red marker written under the picture, "Boss" under his name. Coming off his picture were a variety of red, black and blue lines that led to smaller pictures with names and other information. And last, the reason he knew Chace knew Deck would not like what he saw was the blue line that led from McFarland's picture down to the bottom right corner where there were two pictures.

One, a color shot of McFarland and Emme making out at the side of his pimped-out truck. The one next to it, a black-and-white shot of Emme walking down the boardwalk, head turned to the side looking at something. She was wearing different but no less fashionable shades over her eyes, her long hair was unhindered by a hat showing she had a deep, thick, sexy-as-all-fuck bang that hung into her eyes, her body was encased in different jeans, coat and shoes but her outfit was no less stylish. Her lips were smiling, the dimple out.

Under the picture it said "Emmanuelle Holmes." Under that "Girlfriend/Lover." Under that it said "Partner?"

With practice and deduction, Deck knew that the black lines were definite alliances the team had confirmed. Red lines were hot, lieutenants or those with records, possible weak links. And blue were unconfirmed members of the crew.

"Doesn't look like it, but it's Emme, man," Chace said quietly, and Deck tore his eyes from the picture of Emme and looked at Chace. "Saw the name. Couldn't believe it until they showed me her trail. It all fits. That's her. Totally changed."

"Saw her outside, just now, with him," Deck told the room, watched Chace blink and jerked his head toward the top of the whiteboard. He then declared, "He's no boss. She's no partner."

"So you do have a history with Emmanuelle Holmes," Carole stated, but it was a question and Deck looked to her.

Shaughnessy ran his men his way and word was, Shaughnessy took his job seriously but he was as laidback as they come otherwise. Even his officers didn't wear uniforms. They wore jeans and tan shirts with their badges but that was as far as they got.

Gibbons was mostly the same, his two detectives dressed as they wanted. Officers wore uniforms, however.

Weatherspoon, who oversaw Chantelle, a town with more money, coming in top of the heap of the trinity it held with Gnaw Bone (second runner-up, a town that depended a great deal on tourist trade and took that seriously) and Carnal (not even close, it was a biker haven, mostly blue collar, definitely rougher), was in full uniform. Her officers wore full uniforms. Her detectives wore suits or sports jackets and trousers. Her elite citizenry would expect nothing less.

Deck's eyes shifted to Kenton Douglas.

That man was a wild card. Recently voted sheriff, he came out of the blue, young, attractive, African-American, in the Sheriff's Department only ten years, and he'd wiped the floor with his opponent who held that spot for twenty-five years. The old sheriff also held it while a serial killer hunted his patch and a police chief in his county got so dirty he was foul. The county was ready for change. Douglas was smart enough to know the time was ripe and slid in on a landslide.

Then he made sweeping changes.

And one of those changes was taking his sheriff's police out of uniform and giving them the Mick treatment. Tan shirts. Badges on belts. Jeans. Boots.

It was a smart move. His county was a rural, mountain county. His residents liked easy and familiar, but they were scared after all that had gone on and many of them had learned not to trust the police. Easier to trust a badge wearing jeans and boots than one kitted out in full gear.

It wasn't only smart, it was subtle. And so far, successful.

Change wasn't easy and it wasn't easily accepted.

Douglas breezed his through, didn't take a breath, and kept on keepin' on.

Deck didn't know what to make of him. He was handsome. He was slick. He was personable. He was sharp. And he had balls. So Deck was leaning toward admiration.

"She's an old friend," Deck answered Carole's question about Emme.

"What kind of old friend?" she asked, and Deck tamped down his annoyance at going through this again.

"My ex's best friend," he answered. "That kind of old friend."

"How do you know she's not involved?" Jeff asked and Deck looked to him.

"I know Emme. She wouldn't do this shit," Deck stated.

And she wouldn't. He knew what was happening. The whole county knew. It was bad shit that, four days ago, got a hell of a lot worse. With all the shit going down in that county over the last few years, they wanted this nipped in the bud and they wanted that three months ago.

Problem was, they had a multi-department task force set up to do it and they still were finding fuck all.

This was why Chace suggested Deck. Deck would find everything they needed to end this and he wouldn't dick around finding it.

"How well do you know Emme, son?" Henry asked, and Deck's eyes went to Chace's boss.

"Well," he answered.

"They spend a lot of time together," Jeff noted. "Holmes and McFarland."

"She's his girlfriend. They would," Deck told him. "But this shit?" He shook his head. "No way."

"Sometimes," Chace started, and his tone was cautious, "girls like her, girls like she used to be who turn into girls like she is now, get a guy's attention, a good-lookin' guy like that, and they can go—"

Deck cut him off. "Chace, you know Emme. You know that's bullshit. She's always known her own mind. And she's always been cool. Even when she wasn't a knockout, she wasn't that kind of person."

"It's been years, Deck," Chace reminded him. "A lot of them. People change, and it isn't lost on either of us she has in a big way."

"Yeah, and I just met her on the street. I'm havin' dinner with her tonight and she looks good, man, but she acts the same. And her man is a dick but he's also a moron. So he's no boss," Deck declared and looked at Shaughnessy. "And you just got yourself a maverick."

The mood in the room shifted. It had been alert. Now it was relieved.

Shaughnessy was the only one who didn't want Deck stepping in.

The rest of them, after all they'd seen for the past few years, wanted this done, and they were willing to take risks to get that.

"Terrific," Shaughnessy muttered, his eyes moving through the room.

"Decker, this needs to be discussed," Douglas stated, and Deck looked to him.

"You want me on the team, we talk money. I'll give a discount, see this shit sorted. I'll want a full brief. I'll want the entire file. I won't take orders. I'll keep you in the know of what I do and what I find. But, just sayin', that woman means something to me." He threw out a hand toward the whiteboard. "So even if you don't put me on the team and pay me, I'll still be seein' her clear of this shit."

"You can't let her know we're investigating her boyfriend," Carole said swiftly.

"This isn't my first rodeo," Deck returned. "What's goin' down, I wouldn't fuck your investigation. But she's still clear and she's clear in no more than a week. Not months. Not as long as it'll take you to track this crew, the way you're goin', and stop their shit."

"As contract to this task force, you cannot engage in illegal activities. We can't prosecute with fruit from the poisonous tree," Douglas told him.

"Again, not my first rodeo," Deck replied.

"You have a crew or do you work alone?" Henry asked.

"This, I'll be bringin' in my crew," Deck answered.

"They'll all need to see me," Douglas stated. "Contract is signed, you all work for my department until the case is done."

Deck nodded and his eyes went to Chace. "Want a picture of that board, want the file."

"Deck, not sure this is a good idea. You got a conflict of interest with this—"

Deck again cut Chace off. "This is Emme."

"I know it's Emme," Chace shot back, concerned for Deck and losing patience because of it. "Until just now, I had no idea you'd react the way you have when you saw it was Emme. So *Emme's* the goddamned conflict of interest."

"You know her," Deck whispered, also losing patience, and he watched his friend's face. Definite concern but also indecision.

He knew Emme.

Chace went from the academy into Carnal's Police Department and stayed there but that didn't mean Deck didn't spend time with Chace throughout all Deck's travels. Chace had met Elsbeth. Chace had spent time with her. And with Elsbeth came Emme. So Chace had spent time with Emme too.

"Her change is remarkable, Deck," Chace noted again. "That's something to take into account."

At his words, Deck felt the ghost of her fingers digging into his shoulder through his coat. Saw the dimple. Heard her call him honey.

And he knew her history. Elsbeth told him. He knew what she'd survived. He knew what made her what she was.

He didn't know what made her what she was now, but he was going to find out at dinner.

Last, he knew Emme would not be a part of a crew who burgled homes across an entire county and recruited high school students to do it. Not for the attention of the likes Dane McFarland. Not for money. Not for power. Not for anything.

"She's up first. I investigate her. Clear her. Then clear her of this shit," Deck stated.

"You work that with me," Chace returned.

"Suit yourself. But dinner with Emme tonight is just her and me."

Chace studied him.

Deck took it then looked to Douglas. "You got a file for me?"

"It'll be delivered to your house by three thirty," Douglas replied.

"Contracts will be emailed to you by then. My crew will be in tomorrow at eight to be deputized," Deck replied.

"You gonna be with them?" Douglas asked.

"Wouldn't miss that shit for the world," Deck answered, cut his eyes through the people in the room, noting Henry Gibbons looked amused, Mick Shaughnessy looked annoyed, Carole Weatherspoon looked reflective and Chace still looked worried.

Then he walked out of the office, out of the station and to his truck.

CHAPTER TWO

Kaleidoscope

DECK STOOD AT his dining room table, chin tipped down, eyes scanning the carnage in the photo on top of the mess of papers that was spread out across his table that had once been three thick but organized police files.

A kid. Boy. Seventeen years of age. Hair too long. Clothes ill-fitting by design. Top of his head blown off since he put the barrel of a gun under his chin and pulled the trigger.

He'd been bonded out two hours before. They were pushing to try him as an adult. They were doing this because, in the six months the burglaries had been occurring with increasing frequency across the county, he'd been the first one they caught.

Not the first one who was seen. There were two others, both boys, described as young, but since the burglaries occurred in the dead of night, the vehicles used stolen and later dumped and no fingerprints, no IDs had been made. But both the others seen were noted as no older than eighteen.

They were hoping the one they caught would run scared and talk. He'd lawyered up, his family bonded him out, but the cops made it clear that things would go smoother on him, he turned rat.

Two hours later, he'd got his dad's gun and, instead of talking, took his own life.

Bad shit.

Dark shit.

Pitch.

And no way Dane McFarland would make a kid run that scared he'd blow the top of his head off instead of talking. And no way the likes of Dane McFarland could make a kid follow him to the dark side.

He shoved papers and pictures aside and found a messy stack he'd made. He flipped through them, examining them closely even if it made his throat prickle.

Emme. The new, beautiful, stylish Emme with McFarland.

He couldn't get used to seeing her like that, even as long as he studied those photos. If the dimple wasn't there, he wouldn't believe it was her. And if there weren't shots of her without sunglasses so he could see her eyes. Eyes he always thought of as exotic. Perfect almonds coming to points at the sides that tipped up, back then her most attractive feature (outside the dimple) by far. Now it was debatable.

Jeff was right. She and McFarland spent a lot of time together. And McFarland wanted it known she was his. He did this by touching her all the fucking time. Hand to her hip, her waist, the small of her back. Arm around her shoulders. Her in both his arms, his mouth locked to hers. PDA and lots of it.

If Deck didn't know her and he had that dimple in his bed, those light brown eyes he could make dance, he'd likely do the same.

But he didn't like it with McFarland. It wasn't just possessive. It wasn't at all protective. It was a statement and it was borderline creepy.

He couldn't see Emme putting up with that.

And he didn't like that she was.

He had to get her shot of this guy.

What he could see was what Chace said. Whatever made her make the change, grow her hair, get her style together, take off weight, could mean she was finally moving beyond what happened to her and looking to enter the game, find a man.

And maybe after not having one for as long as he'd known her, before (if what Elsbeth said was true) and likely for a while after, it could make her think she struck gold with a tall, good-looking, built guy who showed her a fuckload of attention. This might make her put up with a load of shit that might send up red flags she'd ignore just to get that attention, the kind she'd never had.

His eyes drifted to his mantel and the long, polished, handsomely carved wooden box sitting there.

Seeing that box, he again couldn't see Emme doing that.

Further, McFarland had tried that possessive bullshit with her in front of Deck and she ended it in a second.

He was whipped. She was not the one having the wool pulled. He had her and he was still gagging for more.

This made Deck's throat prickle further due to the fact that, he didn't know Emme, he saw what he saw, he'd be switching pictures on that whiteboard. McFarland bottom right corner, Emme, top center.

But, his eyes aimed to that box, he knew her.

That shit couldn't be.

He looked back down, shoving the pictures aside and scanning the reports.

He got why they pinpointed McFarland as boss. He had a sister who was a high school chemistry teacher in Carnal. He had a brother who was a high school history teacher in Gnaw Bone. The dead kid's history teacher. Black lines from McFarland to both of them. The sister had a red line between her and her boyfriend, a known dealer who worked the Carnal/Gnaw Bone/Chantelle triangle. Another red line from that dealer to McFarland since they'd been best friends since high school.

But Emme was clear on paper. Copious recognizance showed she spent the night with McFarland but mostly he spent the night with her. Her father bought the local lumberyard a couple of years after the last owner got put away for murder. Emme ran it for him.

She also bought a place called the Canard Mansion.

Deck had looked it up on the Internet and it was a summer home built for Denver-dwelling silver boom millionaires in 1899. It was purchased from them by different kinds of millionaires in the 1920s. Throughout the '20s, it saw a variety of rip-roarin' good times but fell on hard times, as did the rest of the nation, when its owners were cleaned out by the Depression. A number of subsequent owners did their best with the twenty-room house but eventually it fell out of glory to become a bed-and-breakfast and stayed that way through the '70s and '80s. The owner lost his wife, grew reclusive, lived in that big pile the next two decades and died without a will. His family fought over it for half a decade before Emme bought it for a song.

It was likely a wreck.

He figured this from his Internet research and the fact that reports stated, when Emme wasn't working, getting her hair done, going to Denver to visit family and friends or fucking McFarland, she was working on her house.

On her own.

She didn't have time to work in or lead a burglary crew.

McFarland, however, frequently disappeared, shaking a tail in a way that the task force was relatively certain he knew he had one. Which meant he had a reason to have one and shake it.

Emme didn't. If she noticed a tail, she didn't try to shake it. She lived open.

His eyes went back to the box on his mantel just as his phone rang.

He pulled it out, saw the display and took the call.

"Yo, man," he said to Chace.

"I'm guessin' you aren't gonna delay in seein' to Emme," Chace noted accurately.

"Her and me dinner, after, we stake out her house. McFarland takes off late to do whatever it is he does, you tail him and try not to lose him. I go in and search her house."

"Jesus, Deck, you can't break into her house and search it. Not at all but not when she's fuckin' there," Chace clipped.

"I'll wait 'til she's asleep," Deck told him.

"You won't go in at all. I've tried to tail McFarland. He's lost me twice. You're new to the team and not a known officer of the law. In the dark he might not make your vehicle. You're on the tail. I stake out the house."

"I'm searchin' her house, Chace, and I'm not waitin' for a warrant."

"You're not goin' in at all."

"She's clear of this shit and soon. I clear her house, we won't need a warrant."

"Jesus, Deck, listen to me, man. You are not *goin' in at all.*"

"She's clear," Deck growled, losing patience.

Chace was silent.

Then he stated, "I looked into her."

Deck wasn't surprised and he knew what Chace found.

"That wasn't buried," he told Chace.

"So you know," Chace replied.

"Elsbeth told me."

Chace again fell silent for a long moment before he remarked, "This is not bringin' up good shit for you."

"Elsbeth is gone. Emme is not. Best part of all that was Emme. Took me a while to realize it. Now I got my shot to get her back. But yeah, I knew about her history. And yeah, part of gettin' her clear of McFarland and fast is that she doesn't need more shit in her life. Not after that."

"You figure that's why she was the way she was?" Chace asked.

"Absolutely," Deck answered.

"Now you've seen her and you notice she was the only one worth your time in that mess, you rabid to get McFarland clear so you got your shot?"

That dimple in his bed.

Those dancing eyes.

That hair, now long and gleaming, not bobbed up to her

chin and unappealing, doing nothing for a face with those eyes and that smile.

Her body was arguably better before. He was relatively certain she had curves. She just hid them under shit clothes.

She still had curves, just not as many of them. Something easily taken care of with a shitload of frozen custard turtle sundaes and Reese's Pieces, her weaknesses.

Fuck.

"No," he replied.

"Bullshit," Chace whispered. "Not only seen pictures, man, but I've been on this case now for months. Seen her in action. She's your type from top to toe."

"We'll talk about you keepin' the fact that Emme lives local to yourself later. For this conversation, she's Elsbeth's best friend, and I reckon neither of us will wanna go there. But that doesn't mean I can't have her like I had her and I'm gonna have her like that. I shouldn't have waited this long to reconnect. Fuck, it was pure luck I ran into her at all. I don't squander luck, man, and you know it."

Chace was silent. He knew it.

Chace ended his silence. "You're not goin' in without a warrant."

Deck dipped his voice low. "You know I am. You want me to tail him tonight, I will. But you know I'm goin' in sometime and that sometime will be soon seein' as you also know I don't fuck around. So you take my truck, tail him, less chance you'll get made. I do what I gotta do, which is what I'm gonna do no matter what. I'm not deputized yet. Tomorrow, we'll see about me playin' by the rules."

He heard his friend sigh.

Then Chace stated, "We didn't have this conversation."

Deck grinned at his phone and muttered, "Right."

"He usually goes to her," Chace told him something the reports already did. "That place is a fuckin' nightmare and he lives in a nice condo outside town but he'll go to her."

"I'll text you when we're done with dinner. I'll go in through the woods. You get my truck, you take the lane."

"Copy," Chace murmured then, "Be careful, Deck. Emme was never stupid."

No, Emme was never stupid. Though she made bad choices in friends, but women did that shit all the time.

"Right," Deck replied.

"Later."

"Later, man."

They disconnected and Deck looked back down at the reports, his eyes scanning them before the box on the mantel again called to him.

This time, it did it in a way he moved to it.

He'd had it for nine years. Took it everywhere with him. Treated it with care because what it held was fragile and for other reasons besides.

He didn't study it. Instead, he picked it up, flipped open the lid and carefully pulled out what was inside.

A long triangular tube of exquisite stained glass leading to five disks also made of stained glass.

A kaleidoscope.

If you put it to your eye, aimed it at a light and dialed the disks, an array of beauty so stark it made your breath stop could be found at the other end.

You think you lost beauty, Jacob, but you didn't. That dimple. That fucking dimple. This time coming out under sad eyes before she'd whispered, *Just turn the dial.*

Deck pulled in a breath. He reached up, flipped the lid shut on the box and carefully set the kaleidoscope on top, displayed now, not hidden as it had been for nine years.

After he did that, he reached into his pocket, pulled out his phone and made the call.

It rang twice in his ear before, "Nightingale."

"Lee, you want me to owe you a marker?" Deck asked Lee Nightingale, owner and top dog badass of Nightingale Investigations, the premier private investigations agency in Denver.

There was only a moment's hesitation before Lee invited, "Talk to me."

Deck talked and he said nothing about Dane McFarland and a lot about Emmanuelle Holmes.

When he stopped talking, Lee stated, "We're on it."

They disconnected. Deck moved back to his dining room table and looked down at pictures of Emme that did not sync with memories.

Then he looked to his watch, gathered up the files, securely stowed them in his safe and took off to meet her for dinner.

CHAPTER THREE

Listen to Your Gut

DECK SAT IN the far corner booth of The Mark, back to the wall, eyes to the doors so he saw her come in.

She hadn't changed clothes, and watching her spot him immediately, make motions and speak to the hostess as she made her way to him, he saw he'd been wrong at first glance. She hadn't taken off thirty pounds. Twenty, tops. Her hips were still full, a lot narrower than he suspected they used to be back when she'd covered up with huge sweaters or shirts that hung low, loose-fitting pants that made her look bulky, shapeless dresses or skirts that did nothing to attract attention to her figure.

He watched her pull off her cap, her hair flew out with it and she ran her fingers through it, that heavy bang falling into her eyes immediately.

Watching it, he noted her hair was the kind of hair a man wanted spread across his pillow. That thick bang shading her eyes, catching her eyelashes, making a man want to lift his hand and brush it away—for her, and so he could feel it on his fingers.

And those eyes. Her hair had never been glossy like it was now, dark, but not glossy. But with that gleam, those highlights, that bang, those eyes were fuck-me eyes.

No, they were fuck-me-all-night-and-do-it-hard eyes.

Fuck, he was thinking this shit about *Emme*.

He needed to get her shot of McFarland. He just, at that moment, was not going to think about why he needed that so badly.

He buried those thoughts, slid out of the booth and gave her a grin.

She moved right into him and gave him a hug.

Now that was pure Emme, and he wondered why he hadn't remembered that before.

She touched and she liked to be touched so McFarland touching her and her allowing it was not outside her norm.

Even so, the way McFarland did it was still not right.

Emme wasn't social and there were few she was tight with. She was mostly a loner. But if she liked you, she hugged. She touched. She grabbed your arm or hand. She sat close with her knee touching yours and leaned in, holding your eyes and doing it steady. Giving you her full attention. Making you think what you had to say was important and she really wanted to hear it.

Elsbeth ended up hating that as she did a lot about Deck and Emme. She also ended up sharing it and demanding he stop doing it. Something he did that he regretted, since Emme felt it, he saw it. He also saw the hurt it caused her and he didn't like that. But he was in love with Elsbeth and he was young. He reckoned you did shit like that for your woman so she wasn't uncomfortable and you could avoid fights about stupid shit your woman was uncomfortable about.

The problem was, Emme was never stupid shit.

At first, Elsbeth knew, with her extreme beauty, Emme was no competition. But she wasn't dumb either. She knew for some men, it might start with the way you look but it ended with the way you were.

Emme was smart. She watched the news. She went to see movies. She read a shitload of books. She gave a fuck about what was happening around her, in her community, and she got involved.

She traveled too. She had a strict rule. One week vacation a year, relaxation on a beach. The other week of vacation, adventure. Going somewhere she could learn, see, taste, experience.

Therefore, since Deck traveled a lot too, and paid attention to what was going on in the world, Emme and Deck talked as well as argued all the time about politics, current events, historical events, whatever. The good-natured arguing that got your heart pumping, made you think, made you listen, made you feel just that bit more alive.

Elsbeth couldn't do that. Elsbeth knew Deck had an off-the-charts IQ. Elsbeth knew she could never challenge his mind. She could suck his cock great, ride it like a pro and look phenomenal doing both, but there was an important part of his body she'd never challenge, never pleasure, and she grew to know it.

Looking back, Deck understood she also grew to know that Emme could.

And being a woman, she probably saw what Emme was now under what Emme was then and she didn't want Deck to see it.

He'd learned, after last summer when he saw Elsbeth for the first time in years, doing it by design, that what he thought he had and lost in Elsbeth was not what he'd built it up to be after it ended.

It wasn't what Chace had after living through years of hell then finding the woman who was made for him.

It wasn't a turn of a dial on an extraordinary kaleidoscope to find something beautiful.

It was him being young, stupid and led around by his dick.

He lost Emme through that even before he really lost her after he lost Elsbeth. It hurt her. But she never said a word. Not before. Not after. She took him as he came.

He took himself away.

And for him, she'd allowed that.

Ending his thoughts but not their embrace, Emme pulled away but slid her hands up his chest and left them there, tipping her head back and grinning at him.

"I'm so glad I ran into you," she told him. No shades, he could see her exotic eyes lit and happy. "I've been looking forward to this all afternoon. I almost called you and asked if you could meet at five thirty, that's how much I was looking forward to it."

Again, pure Emme.

Not a bullshit artist. Straight up. She bared all. If she cared about you, she let it all hang out.

She had no clue McFarland was into dirty dealings. If Deck didn't already know, these reminders solidified that in his head.

"Should have done that, babe. I would have come early," he replied, his arms loose around her waist and he didn't let go.

"Well, I'm driving, and if we met earlier, I'd probably be tempted to have too many beers which would require a taxi ride which would be money I couldn't dump into my house which would be bad," she returned.

On another smile, she pulled out of his arms in that natural way that he also forgot about or more likely buried. Not like she was pulling away but like she was taking you along for her ride, wherever that would lead.

This time, she led them into the booth, Emme sliding in her side and he followed on his. She shoved aside the menu the waitress had set in front of her seat before she dumped her purse in the seat, unraveled her scarf and took off her jacket to expose a form-fitting sweater that showed plainly she also didn't lose much of her tits.

She did this talking.

"So, what business are you in town doing?" Her head tipped to the side and she grinned as she shrugged off her coat. "Or can you tell me without killing me?"

"Live in Chantelle, babe. Had business at the police station here and no, I can't tell you. Though if I did, I wouldn't have to kill you. But I would lose a contract."

She dropped her coat by her side and her eyes came back to his, brows raised. "Chantelle?"

"Yep."

"How weird," she muttered. "You there, me here." She settled more firmly into the booth by tipping to the side, shifting up a calf to sit on it then sitting back and focusing on him again, and he forgot that too.

She always sat on her leg or cross-legged or with her knees up, arms around her calves or with both legs twisted under her, folding herself up, tangling her limbs. She also talked with her hands and body, moving, twisting, flicking, gesturing. She was rarely sedentary, even during a conversation. He had no idea why but he'd always found all that appealing too. It was like her personality was so lush, so interesting, it spilled out in everything she did.

When she finished, her eyes flashed and she murmured, "Chace."

It was a guess as to why he lived there. And if she'd been around awhile, she'd know Chace was close. He'd made the papers. Repeatedly.

"Part of it, yeah," he told her. "Other part is, view doesn't suck around here."

She tipped back her head, exposing the elegant vulnerability of her jaw in full force and laughed her smooth, low laugh.

He'd buried how much he'd liked watching her laugh too.

And seeing it, he was reminded how much he really wanted to taste her jaw.

Fuck.

Maybe dinner before getting her shot of McFarland *wasn't* a good idea.

She stopped laughing and again looked at him. "You are not wrong. The view out here doesn't suck. Grew up in Denver, always proud my city had a backdrop of the Front Range." She leaned in. "Better being *in* the mountains." She leaned back. "Anyway, please, God, tell me you're after those jackasses who're targeting high school kids to commit felonies."

Jesus. Straight to it.

And Emme, so smart, she'd figured it out.

"Can't talk about it, Emme," he said quietly, studying her as she studied him.

"Well, let's just say, I hope you are. You're on the case," another grin, "their days are numbered."

Deck said nothing but he knew one thing. If she was full of shit, he was retiring.

Suddenly, her face changed, her chin dipped and she became engrossed in unwrapping her silverware from her napkin and she did this saying, "I hope you're here because you want to be here and not here because you feel you have to be out of some old-acquaintance duty." Her eyes slowly lifted to his. "I was so excited to see you, I didn't think about—"

Deck cut her off, "I'm here 'cause I wanna be here."

"Good," she said softly.

"Long time ago, Emme."

She nodded. "Yeah." Her eyes moved over his face. "Glad that's . . . well, time heals."

It didn't until last summer.

Now it had.

He was saved from commenting when the waitress showed. Emme, not looking at her menu, ordered a Guinness, fried mozzarella sticks to start, followed by cheesy Texas toast and pork chops.

At her order, Deck was vaguely disappointed. It appeared she'd turned into one of those women who pretended she didn't give a shit about food when she was in company, therefore, to keep her slim figure, she likely starved herself when she wasn't.

He couldn't recall paying much attention to how she used to eat, though she put on a great spread at her frequent dinner parties, but he also didn't recall her having issues with food or Elsbeth mentioning it. And the way Deck's brain worked, he recalled everything.

Deck ordered a Newcastle and the meatloaf dinner and the waitress moved away.

"Right, so," Emme started the minute she left. "Tell me everything."

He cut to the chase immediately.

"My line," Deck replied, and her brows drew together.

"Pardon?"

"Babe," he said low, "not lost on me and you can't think it is that you are not the you I used to know. Act it, yeah. Look it, no."

She waved her hand in front of her face before dropping it to the table and stating, "It's not a big deal."

"Emmanuelle, I didn't recognize you until you smiled."

She blinked. "Really?"

"Really."

"You?" she asked, sounding stunned, knowing he forgot nothing, not a face, not a name, not a memory.

"Me," he answered. "Heard your voice call my name. Recognized that. You came at me, I had no fuckin' clue who you were until you smiled."

"Wow. I grew my hair, Jacob. And got some highlights," she told him. "Really not a big deal."

"And took off weight and got a new wardrobe."

"Well, that was...it was...well," she shrugged. "Necessary." Another grin. "And fun. The second part, that is."

At that he felt his brows draw together and his gut get tight. "Necessary?"

"It isn't a big deal," she replied.

"What isn't a big deal?" he asked.

She looked him in the eye, sighed then announced, "I was sick for a while."

His gut clenched and his chest got hot. "What?"

"It wasn't a big deal, honey," she said quietly.

"You keep sayin' that, sittin' across from you, watchin' you, *seein'* you, I'm wonderin' if you're tryin' to convince you or me."

He saw her mouth move as her eyes gave away that she was thinking about this before she admitted. "Weird. Maybe I am."

"Tell me," he ordered.

"Okay." She shifted in her seat then leaned on her arms on the table to get closer to him even as she held his gaze. "I'll admit, at the time, it was a little scary because the doctors didn't know what it was. At first, I was just fatigued. Then, so tired, Jacob, it was wild. It got to the point I could barely get out of bed and I couldn't wait to get back in. Then it got worse. I lost my appetite, and it's good we're talking about this now before the food comes, but I couldn't hold anything down. Eventually, it was so gross and made me even more tired, I quit eating in order to avoid vomiting. I went in to see the doctors again and again. They ran a bunch of tests. Nothing."

"And?" he prompted when she stopped talking.

"Well, they ultimately had to hospitalize me."

"Fuck," Deck clipped and she leaned in further, her hand moving out to grab hold of his.

"As you can see, I'm fine," she assured him.

"What was it?" he asked.

She gave his hand a squeeze and sat back but did it still leaned toward him.

"Just an infection, if you can believe that. Though a rare one. Actually, I'd lost even more weight than what you can see and was in the hospital for three weeks because, once they figured out what it was, they then figured out it was resistant to antibiotics so it kinda took a long time to beat it but I did. I got out. Started eating, sleeping, recovering, gaining back some of the weight. Took a while to get my stamina back but," she flipped out her hands and sat back in her seat, "here I am."

"How long ago was this?"

"Early last year it ended, started the year before." She hesitated before she told him, "It lasted about a year."

"Fuck, it took that long to find an infection?" Deck bit out.

"It was rare," she repeated.

"Jesus," he muttered.

"I'm fine, honey."

"Scared you shitless, Emme."

Her mouth shut.

"Keep sayin' it's fine. Keep sayin' it isn't a big deal. It wasn't the first but it was the last," he told her.

"You're right about that for the then. But it's okay now."

"I can see that," he returned. "And you say it but you aren't gettin' it since you were sick for a year, had no fuckin' clue what it was, which would scare anybody and it scared you. It ended well, but you don't deal, you don't get over it."

Her chin jerked back before she said in a tone that was an accusation. "I forgot how smart you are."

"Glad you're remembering."

"I also forgot how annoying it can sometimes be."

It was then he burst out laughing and when he was done, she no longer looked peeved but was grinning.

Their beers came. They both took a sip then set them aside.

"So, you got sick, why was a new look necessary?" he pushed, and she again shrugged.

"You're exhausted like I was, you're too exhausted to go out and get haircuts. Trust me, haircuts are the last thing on your mind when all you want to do is get to work, go home and go to sleep. And my hair grows fast, apparently. And I found I kinda liked it so I let it keep growing. Then, after it was done and I was getting better, but none of my clothes fit, my friend Erika...do you remember her?"

Deck nodded. Erika was one of her limited posse. Elsbeth didn't like Erika either. This was because Erika was beautiful and intelligent, both scarily so, especially for someone like Elsbeth.

"Well, she wanted to make me feel better, and have clothes that actually fit," Emme went on. "So she took me out on a day of beauty. She's a personal shopper and she'd been dying to get ahold of me for years anyway. She took me to have my hair done, had a makeup artist teach me how to do my face, took me out and we tried on a bunch of clothes. Most of them don't fit anymore because I put on twenty pounds since then but somehow, I got bit by the bug." She leaned and whispered conspiratorially, "Don't tell anyone in Denver. I put on my old clothes and wear a wig when I go home. I don't want them to know I've turned into a fashionista."

"Lips are sealed, baby," he said through a smile but

watched her blink again, surprise lighting her eyes before she cloaked it and sat back.

He let that go when she kept talking.

"Anyway. Now that super-smart, see-into-thoughts-with-the-power-of-his-mind Jacob Decker has made me think on it, I'm wondering if maybe being sick like that didn't wake me up somehow. Teach me to stop and smell the roses. And by that I mean pampering myself with visits to excellent stylists, spending mega bucks on salon-quality products for my hair, regular facials and way too many trips back to Denver to drop a load on clothes."

"Not a crime, Emme," he noted.

She grinned and replied, "Luckily, no."

"Elsbeth take your back?" he asked.

Another blink, this one more surprised, and she asked, "Pardon?"

"Elsbeth, through this shit, she take your back?"

She held his eyes and she did it a long time before, slowly, she said, "Jacob, honey, I haven't spoken to Elsbeth in nine years."

He felt that heat in his chest as he stared at her.

His voice was gruff when he asked, "What?"

"She, um…ended things with you, and I," she shrugged, "ended things with her."

"No shit?" he asked.

Her eyes unusually hit the table as she murmured, "I don't like stupid people."

Jesus Christ.

"Emme," he called, and it took some time but she lifted her eyes to meet his. When she did, all he could get out was, "Babe, you two were tight."

"She threw away something good. I know you know that, Jacob, because it was you she threw away so I don't want to bring it up and hurt you but I…well, I knew why. And like I said, I don't like stupid people. I don't have time for them. So I haven't seen her in years. She asked me to her wedding. I didn't go. Mutual acquaintances used to tell me about her but I moved up here about three years ago. I go home often but just to see my folks and friends, none of whom was really close with Elsbeth so," she shrugged again, "I have no idea what's happening with her and she definitely has no idea what's going on with me."

The waitress came and slid the mozzarella sticks in front of Emme, Emme murmured, "Thanks, Sarah," the waitress replied, "No probs," and was off again.

Emme shoved the plate to the middle of the table and offered, "Help yourself."

She took one.

Deck took one.

He ate it whole, swallowed and shared, "Elsbeth isn't happy."

Her head snapped up from looking at the sticks, she chewed, swallowed and asked, "You've talked with Elsbeth?"

"Fucked her in Denver last summer."

Her mouth dropped open.

Deck didn't know why he said it and he further wouldn't know why he kept talking.

Then again, he'd talked open and honest to only three people in his thirty-seven years of life. His dad. Chace Keaton. And Emmanuelle Holmes.

"Did it before I knew she was still hitched. Found out she was still hitched when I heard her talkin' on the phone to her husband even though she tried to hide it. Told her she was a piece of shit, walked out. Before I did that, I had to get dressed so I listened to her tell me how her life was in the toilet and her husband was an asshole. Still left. First time I saw her since back when, and, I'll admit, babe, I looked her up, she took me up on a get-together, chatted me up until we hooked up. Now I hope it's the last time I ever see her."

Emme continued staring at him with lips parted. It was cute. It reminded him of the old Emme when they'd talk politics and he'd say something ridiculously conservative in response to something she'd said that was ludicrously liberal and he did it just to get a rise out of her.

She finally got over her surprise and stated, "Okay, her husband being an asshole, not a surprise. He was that before she married him. He'll be that forever. He's probably trying to find ways to be that from beyond the grave, working with gypsies to do it or something."

Deck felt himself smile as Emme kept talking.

"But, she went for you?"

"Got played, Emme. She told me lettin' me go was the worst mistake of her life."

Her shoulders shot straight and she replied instantly, "It was. But cheating on her husband with you without you knowing you were doing it isn't the way to rectify that mistake."

And there she showed another something he forgot or buried.

Emme had fire.

It was cute. It had always been cute.

Women like her, it was hard to be cute. She was not small. Elsbeth had been five foot six but teetered around on high heels every day, even in jeans or shorts, so she could be five nine or ten. Emme was five nine; now with high heels she wore with more naturalness than Elsbeth who'd probably put on her first pair at age three, she was six foot at least.

Being tall, curvaceous, intelligent, women like that could be alluring, sexy, a lot of things, but not often cute.

Emme pissed, was cute. When she showed her fire, he always thought so. During a discussion. In defense of a friend.

Fucking adorable.

And no less now.

Shit.

"Got that right, baby," he muttered through his grin, her eyes again got that weird light before she hid it, shook her head and reached for a stick.

"She's whacked," Emme declared.

"Reckon she always was."

Her eyes lifted to his, held steady and she whispered, "She always was."

Deck stared into her eyes and his chest seized at what he saw.

Just turn the dial.

Jesus.

She gave him that kaleidoscope and told him to turn the dial, find more beauty.

And fuck him, she was standing at his door the day after Elsbeth dumped him for a rich man who could give her the life she grew up having and Emme had offered herself to him as friend, or maybe even lover. All he had to do was turn the dial.

And he'd been so fucked up by Elsbeth, the promise of her, the beauty he thought he'd lost by not doing what she wanted and losing her, that he didn't see it. He didn't see he had something even more beautiful right in front of him.

Until nine years later.

Fuck.

Him.

Before he could capture that moment, she looked away, shoved more mozzarella stick in her mouth and grabbed her beer to wash it back.

She didn't want that moment. Maybe back then. Now she had a man. Her mind might not be going there. He might be wrong and it might never have gone there. Not where Deck's seemed to be going every other second, her sitting across from him. But she had a man and fucking him over like Elsbeth fucked over her husband by using Deck last summer would never enter her mind.

Which meant the next week would suck for her because, picture proof, McFarland was into her in a big way. He didn't know how into McFarland she was, but in cases like this, she wouldn't have a man on a string and keep casting her lures.

She'd be loyal.

But McFarland was also a dick, a moron and a criminal. And he was going down.

He just wasn't going to take Emme with him.

"Babe," he called, she put her beer down and looked at him. "You can't drink too much beer because you gotta sink all your money in your house?"

Again, her eyes lit, this time with excitement. She leaned into her arms again and smiled so huge, her dimple pressed deep.

"Jacob, honey, I bought this house that...is...the...*absolute...bomb*!"

"Yeah?" he asked.

She nodded.

"Oh yeah. I'm fixing it up. Of course, I have no clue what I'm doing but I did manage to get broadband out there so I have YouTube and I work in a lumberyard...by the way, Dad bought the local lumberyard and I'm running it for him. Which proves what he always said. I could run a ship with a manual just as long as I can convince the men to go about their duties and that I know what I'm doing when I don't."

She grinned and the dimple came out. Deck was dealing with how much he liked that dimple when she went on.

"But, anyway, they also tend to know how to plumb stuff and fix stuff and other stuff so I pick their brains if I can't learn on the Internet. It's awesome. I'm having so much fun doing it. I can't wait until it's done. Which, if the current work-load and schedule continue, should be sometime in the next decade and a half."

She shot back in her seat and her eyes lit even more.

"You have to come up and see it," she invited.

"I will, babe," he told her. "Soon," he promised, though she wouldn't know just how soon that would be—in other words, that night.

"We'll set it up," she said, going for another stick.

He let her eat it and take another sip of beer before he went for it.

"Emme, that guy, McFarland, what's up with him?"

She tipped her head to the side. "What's up with him?"

"Where'd you meet him? How long you been seein' him?"

"He works at the lumberyard so I met him three years ago. But we've only been seeing each other for about four months."

That coincided with the reports.

"Why do you wanna know?" she asked.

He studied her before he asked back, "Straight up?"

He watched her face grow wary even though she answered, "Yeah."

"Don't got a good feelin' about that guy."

"Why?" she queried, her voice lower, softer but her eyes never leaving him.

He couldn't tell her why.

All he could say was, "Got a feelin' in my gut, Emme, I always follow it. He doesn't give me good vibes. Four months, you must be into him. I'm sorry, babe. But I gotta tell it like it is."

"We aren't serious," she shared.

At least there was that, and Deck didn't allow himself to process how much relief he felt about it, and not just because of the investigation.

"You exclusive?" he asked.

"Well," her eyes slid away, not embarrassed, evasive. She looked back to him. "He is. I'm unsure. Though, that said, that doesn't mean he isn't the only one. He is. It's just that I'm not sure I want to make that official."

And there was that. She was loyal but she was unsure.

More relief.

"Promise me, keep thinkin' on him 'til you come up with the right answer."

After that, she held his gaze and again did it direct and steady. "Okay, Jacob. I'll keep thinking on him."

He hated doing it, and she found out he was working this, she'd be pissed he did it but he had to do it. For her and for the job.

"Is there a reason you wanna share why you're unsure?" he asked.

Her eyes again lit with activity. She was thinking on this.

Then she stated, "No. I . . . well," she grinned, "I think it's my gut too."

Dead end with that, McFarland was giving her bad vibes but nothing to pinpoint. But at least, when they brought McFarland and his crew down, she hadn't shared anything with him not knowing why he was asking and he hadn't pressed her to do it.

Better, she was sensing the red flags and didn't like them.

"Always listen to your gut, Emme," he advised.

"Right, Jacob," she said, still grinning.

"No joke. Can't say this guy is bad news, not for sure. But can say, I don't like him with my girl. He's yours. I been in his presence not five minutes. You gotta make your choice and I hope, tonight, us findin' out we're near, this won't end."

He gestured between them and saw her eyes warm, her face get soft, the dimple come out even just through a grin so he knew, thank fuck, this wouldn't end.

He kept talking.

"So you like the guy, your gut gets sure, he'll never know I didn't like him for you. That's your choice. Just sayin', careful."

"I'm always careful, honey," she told him, and what was done to her at the age it was done, she would be. Maybe too much.

He just hoped she stayed that way.

For at least another week.

"Good," he murmured.

She dipped her head to the plate between them. "You gonna eat the last stick?"

"All yours," he told her and she went for it.

When she was done chewing, swallowing and sipping more beer, he again went for it.

Leaning into his arms on the table, he grinned and demanded, "Now, Emmanuelle, tell me about this house you are no doubt totally fuckin' up seein' as you have no clue what you're doin'."

Her entire face lit with her low chuckle, she leaned toward him into her arms and she complied.

CHAPTER FOUR

Two Days

HIS FLASHLIGHT LIGHTING the way, Deck moved through the snow, dense pine and aspen. He had his gun at his hip, his flashlight in hand and a canister of Mace at his other hip.

There were bears in those woods and if he encountered one, he wouldn't want to put bullets in it. Not because he didn't want shots heard, but because it would be a crime against nature to bring down such a magnificent beast.

A bear would, however, survive a dose of Mace.

His phone vibrated at his ass, he pulled it out and looked at the display.

In place.

Chace was set.

He'd picked Chace up in town. Chace had dropped him at the road down from Emme's place and taken off in Deck's truck. They left Chace's Yukon in town because they didn't want to leave a vehicle on a road close to Emme's house. If Chace managed to keep the tail, he'd send a car to pick up Deck when Deck finished his business.

Deck's thumb moved over the screen and he sent back, *Copy.*

He was about to put his phone back in his pocket when it vibrated in his hand and he saw the display said "Emmanuelle calling."

Seeing her name on his phone sent warmth through his gut.

Seeing it on his phone after ten at night when he'd left her about half an hour ago and with all the shit going down around her made his warm gut tight.

Fuck.

He stopped, took the call and put the phone to his ear.

"You okay?" he asked as greeting.

"I forgot about Chace," she replied.

At her words, his body got tight.

"What?" he asked.

"In all the talk about life, my house, your house, which, by the way, if I don't get an invitation to see it and drink your homemade beer, and soon, I'll be peeved, and you giving me stick about my Bronco, I forgot to ask about Chace." Her voice dipped lower. "Been around these parts a while, honey. I heard what happened to him and his then girlfriend, now wife. Are they good?"

His body loosened.

"Since they're good and the proof of that bein' the fact that Faye's heavily pregnant and Chace is actin' like he's the first man who's ever gonna be a daddy on this earth—in other words, he's over the goddamned moon he knocked up his wife—givin' you stick about your desecration of God's vehicular gift to all mankind, the operative part of that word bein' *man*, took precedence over discussing Chace and Faye."

He heard her low, alluring chuckle, grinned at the phone and continued to make his way through the woods but did it slower, thus quieter. He didn't want her to hear crunching snow or breaking twigs.

His focus on several things, with ease, he kept it and called up the recent memory of standing outside the opened driver's-side door of her Bronco after walking her there when they'd left The Mark, teasing her and making her laugh.

He was not wrong in teasing her. A Ford Bronco was a man's car, no doubt about it. The fact that her bronze 1995 Bronco had ponytail holders shoved down the gearshift, a glittery butterfly hanging from her rearview mirror that had the words "Free to Fly" in script under it and a marketing shot of

Raylan Givens from the TV show *Justified* lounging back in a chair, one leg bent, one cowboy-booted foot stretched straight out, gun up, cowboy hat tipped low on his brow, this taped to the ceiling of the truck over the rearview mirror was Bronco Sacrilege. Not to mention, the truck was clean as a pin.

Some men, seeing that, might be moved to rip that shit out and take it four wheeling, getting it as muddy, dusty and dirty as humanly possible.

Some men, seeing Emme and knowing that was her truck, might be moved to do that either before or after they turned her over their knee for committing such blasphemy.

Deck was finding he was the latter.

Her words cut into thoughts that were making even Deck lose focus.

"Chace's wife is pregnant?" she asked.

"Heavily," he answered.

"That's good," she said softly. "I . . . well, after all that went down, you know, after she was rescued and it made the news she was buried alive and Chace was again in the papers, I went to the library to check her out."

Chace's wife, Faye, was the librarian at Carnal Library.

Deck said nothing. He still found it difficult to think about that night. A night he spent with a friend who had endured torture, knowing his woman was buried under dirt. So he held on to the fact that they pulled Faye out of that box breathing, a year later he watched her tie the knot with his boy and now they were building a family of more than them and two serious-as-fuck ugly cats that Faye adored.

"She's really pretty," Emme told him.

"Yeah," Deck agreed, still moving.

"Perfect for Chace."

"Yeah," Deck repeated, this time with more feeling.

"Knowing he was around, I thought of, you know, doing an approach, letting him know I lived close. But I didn't know, what with all that went down, if I should. I mean, not only with Elsbeth and how that might reflect on me but also with Chace."

His boy had had it rough. And Deck was tight with his boy so Emme would know Elsbeth ending things would not make Elsbeth or anyone around her Chace's favorite people.

It was again pure Emme she'd have a mind to that. All of it.

"Sure he'll be glad to reconnect."

"Good, then maybe he and Faye can come over to your house when I'm there drinking your homemade beer. Though Faye obviously can't drink it."

He again grinned at his phone as he saw light coming through the trees. He switched his flashlight off and kept up his approach to her house.

"I'll arrange that. And soon," he told her.

"Right, great," she replied. "Then, I was so busy taking your guff about my girl I forgot to ask you over for dinner tomorrow night."

Pleased she was asking him to dinner, still, Deck moved toward the light but addressed the more important part of what she said, "A Bronco is not a girl. A Bronco is definitely a guy."

"Her name is Persephone."

Jesus.

Deck bit back laughter and returned, "I've just re-anointed him Elrod."

"Persephone," she shot back.

"You don't like Elrod, you can pick Cletus."

"I'm not renaming Persephone!" she snapped, but there was humor in her tone.

"All right, baby," he muttered, smiling at the phone, keeping to the shadows but moving toward the lit clearing he spied through the trees.

He got silence. Complete silence.

So he called, "Emme?"

There was another moment's quiet then, "Are you coming over for dinner tomorrow night or what?"

He had work to do, that work important, work that would mean getting her clear of that asshole.

"Yes," he replied.

"Good. The yard is open until six but I go in early and leave early. So I can have dinner on the table by six. But I'll have beer available from five o'clock on."

"Then my ass'll be at your door at five o'clock," he told her, stopped in the shadow of a tree and trained his eyes on her house.

His back shot straight and he stared.

Jesus.

Fuck.

It wasn't a money pit.

It was what Chace described it as being.

A nightmare.

He could see under all that dilapidated mess that there was beauty. Amazing beauty.

But she had a long way to go before she got it back to that state. This wasn't only because it was a nightmare. This was also because it was *huge*.

As his eyes moved, he decided, first and foremost, his girl needed new insulation. They'd had sun that day, it was cold but Colorado sun could burn snow off a roof. But there were tall pines all around the house, short days in February, limited sun and the shade those trees would bring would mean the snow they had yesterday should still be on her roof—if her insulation was good.

The snow was gone.

Her insulation was shit and she was losing heat.

She was also probably losing heat through some of those boarded windows.

Fuck.

"Five o'clock," she said in his ear, again taking his attention. "Now, I'll expect you to get on your knees before going to bed tonight and pray my oven works tomorrow or we're going to be reduced to ordering pizza."

Looking at her house, if the inside was anything like the outside, Deck had no doubt every time she turned on her oven, it was a crapshoot.

"I'm multi-tasking, talking to God right now," he told her and got another chuckle.

"Good, honey. I'll see you tomorrow night."

"See you then, babe."

"'Bye."

"Later."

He disconnected, his eyes scanning her house, automatically prioritizing. Insulation. Inspection of the roof, probably reshingling. Definitely windows. Double-paned but wood framed so they would work with the look of the house but hold in the heat.

That was just a start.

And that would cost a small fortune.

Fuck.

The investigation notes said she'd been living there for near on three years. One of those years she'd been ill. Still, that left two others, and it looked like the place hadn't been touched.

He set aside thoughts of her house, bent his head to his phone, texted Chace with *In position*, got back a *Copy* and he shoved his phone in his back pocket.

Five minutes later, he got a text that said *Incoming*, and a minute after that, the pimped-out Sierra made the approach, parked outside by Emme's Bronco and McFarland climbed out.

Deck's throat prickled as he watched the familiar way McFarland approached the house.

The prickle eased when he didn't walk right in but knocked, waited, and Emme opened the door to him.

It came back when he watched McFarland round her waist with an arm, smile down at her and back her inside.

The door closed.

Deck instantly revised his schedule.

Emme would not be shot of this guy in a week.

He was thinking more like two days.

His phone vibrated and he got a text from Chace.

Man's in.

Deck texted back, *Saw that. Doing a perimeter check.*

Chace sent back *Copy* and Deck moved stealthily around Emme's property.

As he did, he began to see it. Why she picked this place. He'd even consider it, but only if he viewed it on a day when he felt like taking on a challenge.

There was an outbuilding, built after the main house and not well, and it looked like it was meant to store cars at one point but with Emme's Bronco out front, it was not used for that now and he could see why. It was in worse shape than the house.

The back had a remarkable garden, terraced up the mountain, incorporating the aspen and pine, this leading down to a patio made of flagstone arrayed in an extraordinary starburst design. All this had been cleared, patio furniture on the flagstone that was probably very nice since it was now covered for the winter. She'd done work here. The garden looked good covered in snow. He figured it'd look amazing in spring and summer.

As he moved around the house he saw there were bay windows, turrets, attractive stone carvings in the façade, even gargoyles in the corners. It had personality. It had been made with a mind to craftsmanship and no expense spared.

But it was over a century old, the last five or six decades not well tended and it showed.

He made it back to position and saw only one light through the windows not boarded. Three floors in the house, second story, left of the front door.

The prickle came back because Deck reckoned it was her bedroom. Usually masters were at the back of the house to avoid street noise. But here, this house being the only one up her lane, no street noise, so the master would be at the front. This was because the back had a view to close-up mountain and trees. The back might have a spectacular garden as well but the front had a panorama of the Rockies, the valley and Gnaw Bone. Anyone in their right mind would want that view from their bedroom window.

So they were in her bedroom.

He waited, he watched. They stayed in her bedroom, the light on.

His throat burned.

The light went out.

Deck took in a deep breath through his mouth, letting the cold mountain air ease the burn.

Two days, he'd get her shot of him.

No more.

Definitely.

Ten minutes later, the front door opened. Deck went alert, pulled out his phone and watched McFarland move to his truck.

He texted *Man's on the move* to Chace.

Got it, Chace sent back.

McFarland drove through the circular forecourt of Emme's house and away.

Deck's eyes moved over the front of the house. No lights except the outside one. Not even a dim one coming from her bedroom.

He gave it time, not too much, that monstrosity, he'd need a lot of it to do a search and he had no idea if or when McFarland would be back.

The investigation notes said McFarland often took night trips to places unknown, leaving Emme but returning. This probably being one of those red flags Emme couldn't quite put her finger on if McFarland was cagey about where he was going.

But Deck didn't want to enter until he knew Emme was asleep.

He looked to his watch. She said she was at work early, left early. Which meant she'd go to sleep early. It was just past eleven.

Their dinner finished around ten. He was trekking up the mountain to her house after ten, talking to her on the phone. This meant McFarland came and left, the first probably in two ways, in under an hour.

Which made Deck wonder, even if he didn't like wondering

it, if McFarland had given himself enough time to give Emme what she needed.

That amount of time, he doubted it. A woman like Emme, unless you didn't have the time and were forced to fuck fast, but good, you took your time.

And lots of it.

He pushed these thoughts aside, moved through the woods surrounding the house, made his approach and picked the lock at a back split farm door he figured would lead to the kitchen.

Turning his flashlight to low beam, he entered and was not surprised to find the kitchen an avocado nightmare. Clearly updated in the '70s—poorly—it had been left that way, and even with the low beam, its sheer ugliness hurt his eyes.

That was all the ugliness to be found.

After searching the kitchen, as he moved through the house, Deck saw nothing but beauty.

Extreme beauty.

Seeing it, he finally got it, why she chose this place, what urged her to restore it, bring back that beauty, show this house it was loved.

It was not a mess in the middle of restoration. It needed work but it was clean, tidy, what seemed like acres of handsome wood glowing.

There was another starburst, this one spectacular and fashioned by varying woods in the floor of the massive circular entryway over which hung a huge chandelier and around the walls a sweeping rounded stairway.

She had work to do, definitely, and he saw she was in the middle of several projects.

But he was pleased to see long gaping holes in the walls that exposed she'd already had the entirety of the electrical rewired but hadn't yet replastered. New light switches. New outlets. Dimmers.

She needed to do some sanding. Painting. Plastering. And he saw she was in the middle of cleaning the chandelier in the great room at the front. The floors, woodwork and walls had all been done, furniture covered in sheets, the chandelier all that was left to do. It was down, sitting on a sheet on a table, but the hundreds of crystals had been removed with great care, keeping their array intact even if they were arranged on another sheet on the floor. This so, after they were cleaned, she could reattach them where they were meant to be.

His Emme. Smart as a whip.

But as he moved around inside, even with the walls not re-patched after electrical work, it was a home. It was furnished in a mix of antiques and modern that worked beautifully, albeit it was furnished sparsely. But in that place, it'd take years to fill it with furniture.

Upstairs, more of the same except many of the rooms were closed, draft protectors at their bases, radiators off inside, rooms freezing cold, no furniture or even boxes in those rooms.

Except one room, a guest room, was entirely refinished. Its bathroom the same. The only rooms he saw that were complete. All in keeping with her décor, but in those rooms, mostly antiques, black-and-white mosaic floor in the bathroom, claw-foot tub, beveled mirrors, heavy wood queen-size bed with lots of pillows and understated but attractive bedclothes.

He kept moving through the house.

No stolen property.

No burglary gang command center.

Just a home. A big one. A fucked-up one that would one day be sheer beauty. But a home.

The last room he went to was the room he knew to be her bedroom. It was unlikely he'd find anything there, but Deck was always thorough.

But there was something outside of being thorough that drew him there. Something he'd contemplate later, after he got her shot of McFarland.

Cautious, silent, he turned the knob to the closed door and hoped it didn't creak. Then again, not a floorboard or a door creaked as he moved through the house so someone knew how to use WD-40.

The door opened silently.

He turned out his flashlight, moved in and stopped dead.

The large windows were covered but with sheers, the curtains were opened. The room was warm.

And the moonlight illuminated Emme in bed.

She was on her side and had her back to him.

Her bare back.

The covers were pulled up to her hips but not high. He could see the curve of her hip, the top of the round of her ass.

No panties.

Just all that sleek skin of her back, shoulder, side, her hair splayed dark against the light of the sheets.

Fuck.

Fuck.

His body reacted, his mind engaged, and seeing her, remembering all she was to him, knowing that had not changed, not ever, spending time with her that night, Jacob Decker made an instant decision.

He also began to back out of the room.

He tore his eyes from a naked, just-fucked-by-another-guy Emme in bed. His mind consumed with what he'd decided and all he felt knowing fucking Dane fucking McFarland had his hands on her, his mouth on her, his dick inside her, when he spied the small, opened jeweler's box on her nightstand, he almost missed it.

But he saw it, stopped and his eyes narrowed on it.

Furtively, he moved to the bed and stared at that box, the ring inside.

Quickly, he picked it up, moved quietly out of the room, down the hall and tugged out his phone. He took a picture of the large oval ruby surrounded by diamonds and set in white gold.

Just as quickly, he went back, replaced it, backed out of the room and closed the door.

Then he got the fuck out of the house, throat now burning, gut tight, shafts of piercing pain driving through his brain.

He pulled out his phone and texted Chace, *I'm out. You lose him?*

No. I'm on him. He's taking a meet. I'll send a car.

Copy, Deck typed in.

New guy. Don't know this guy. Got pictures, Chace texted back.

Good, Deck replied but didn't share about the ring. He'd do that in person tomorrow when he could state plain to all involved how they were going to proceed.

He shoved his phone back in his pocket and moved through the woods.

He stood and waited, hidden by a tree, and only came out when Jeff Jessup rolled up in his SUV.

Jessup took Deck to Chace's Yukon and while he did, Deck did not invite discussion. Jessup, not stupid by a long shot, didn't push it. Jessup also had a very pretty wife and a new baby so he didn't have time to shoot the shit. Deck knew the man just wanted to get home.

Jessup dropped him at the Yukon and Deck swung into Chace's vehicle. Chace and Deck would switch trucks tomorrow.

Deck drove home.

When he got there, he pulled out the files, flipping through, finding it.

A picture taken for an insurance company.

He got out his phone and pulled up the shot of the ring.

He looked between his phone and the picture.

McFarland had given Emme a stolen ruby ring.

Dumb fucking moron.

And they had the dumb fuck but they had him with fruit from a poisonous tree. He'd got the photo searching Emme's home without a warrant and Deck not yet being deputized.

It was inadmissible evidence seeing he got it essentially while breaking and entering.

They couldn't use it.

"Fuck," Deck hissed.

With no choice but to wait until the next day, he put the file back, got ready for bed and slid between the sheets.

He did not find sleep.

This was not unusual. Since he was a kid, he slept deep but he never slept long. For as long as he could remember, he needed four hours a night, no more. It drove his mom and dad 'round the bend. Elsbeth hated it, bitched about it all the time and refused to entertain the idea of keeping him close so he could read, or do other things, when he woke early. So when he woke, he left her in bed and spent his early awake hours elsewhere.

But he wasn't finding sleep that night because this was the norm.

He wasn't finding it because, thirty miles away, Emme, *his* fucking Emme, was lying naked in a bed in a ramshackle mansion that looked good but needed a shit ton of work that, on her own, would take a fuck of a lot longer than a decade and a half, a bed where she'd been fucked by a criminal, a stolen ten-thousand-dollar ring sitting on her nightstand.

"Fuck," Deck clipped and rolled.

An hour later, still not finding sleep, he knifed out of bed.

Not knowing why, he went to the kaleidoscope on the mantel. He nabbed it, its box and took them to his bedroom.

He put them on his nightstand and stared at its shadow in the dark.

Five minutes later, he found sleep.

CHAPTER FIVE

Where I'm Takin' Us

I LOOKED OUT my office window, down to the yard, my eyes to the bustling activity, and I did this tapping my phone on my desk.

I should be working but I wasn't thinking about work.

I was thinking about Jacob.

More precisely, I was thinking about calling Jacob, had an overwhelming urge to do so.

I was also trying not to do so because I had a boyfriend, even though he was a boyfriend I wasn't all that sure about. He was sweet, he was into me, but he was just . . . off.

Then again, I didn't have a lot of experience so what did I know?

Additionally, after my dinner with Jacob last night, within an hour, I'd called him after ten at night and now it was only eleven thirty the next day.

I didn't want him to think I was psycho, and calling him would imply psycho behavior. Further, when I called him last night, I'd asked him to dinner, which was dinner two nights in a row with a woman he hadn't seen in nine years, a woman with a boyfriend, and that was semi-psycho.

Okay, maybe it was totally psycho.

I didn't want Jacob to think I was psycho.

Ever.

But I wanted to hear his voice. I wanted to connect with

him on the phone. I'd missed him and I liked having him back. I liked it a great deal.

I also missed him a great deal.

And I needed to ask him something. Further, he was the only one I could ask.

I looked from the yard to my phone. My mind telling my thumb not to do it, my thumb not listening, I found Jacob's contact and hit go.

I put it to my ear.

"I'm a psycho," I whispered and luckily finished whispering two seconds before Jacob's voice sounded.

"You okay?" he answered.

He kept asking that mostly, I figured, because I kept calling when I didn't need to so he probably thought something was wrong.

Or that I was a psycho.

"I need to know if you don't eat anything," I lied.

Actually, it wasn't a lie. Although I remembered a lot about Jacob (most everything, in all honesty), I couldn't recall if there was something specific he didn't like to eat.

I could recall how beautiful he was, how tall he was, how strong he was. I could recall how smart he was and how funny he was. I could recall how cool he was with me. I could also recall how much I missed him. But I couldn't recall if he didn't like chicken.

But that wasn't the only thing I needed to know. I needed to know something else too.

Much like last night, when he didn't make me feel like a psycho, in fact, the opposite and sounded like he was happy to hear from me and would be willing to talk all night, he again sounded like me psychotically calling him yet again in a pre-cursor to stalker way was no big deal.

"I don't eat it, I'll pick it off."

"You can't pick it off if I cook with it *in* it or if the mainstay of dinner on the whole *is* what you don't eat," I informed him.

"You makin' Indian food?" he asked.

"No. Don't you like Indian food?" I asked back.

"Love it," he answered.

"Then why'd you ask if I was making Indian food?"

"'Cause I hoped you were."

I burst out laughing.

No, Jacob definitely didn't make me feel like I was being a psycho.

When I quit laughing, I told him, "Sorry, honey, I don't know how to make Indian food."

"Shame," he muttered, a smile in his deep, attractive voice, and if I was on an infrared scanner, specific parts of me would have shown up hotter.

You have a boyfriend, Emme! I told myself.

For a while, I answered myself.

Jacob is also your ex–best friend's ex-boyfriend, Emme! I reminded myself.

So? I asked myself.

I shoved those thoughts aside, thoughts that, if anyone knew I was talking to myself in my head, might prove I was indeed a psycho, and pointed out to Jacob, "You haven't actually answered the question."

"I'll eat what you cook, Emme. Cook what you like."

He was *such* a nice guy.

He always was.

Nice. Tall (*very* tall). Handsome (unbelievably handsome). Smart (so damned smart). Funny. Interesting. Gentlemanly. And a repeat of nice because it was worth a repeat since he was just that nice.

I liked all that about him. I liked that he wore his dark hair way too long. I liked that sometimes a thick hank of it fell over his forehead and into his eye. I liked that he was who he was and didn't wear designer jeans or put gel in his hair. I liked that, even considering he was extortionately intelligent, in fact, a genius, he never made anyone feel less than him because they weren't as smart. I liked that he never acted superior or arrogant and with all that was him, looks, body, brains, he was one person who could. And I liked that he liked to do what he liked to do, he did what he liked to do and wouldn't get pushed into doing something he didn't want.

Like Elsbeth tried to do.

He'd lost her to that and he'd accepted it. I knew it killed. He'd loved her to distraction. But he refused to be the man she wanted him to be and instead was the man he was.

She should have seen she had it all even if he didn't make bucketloads of money and thus couldn't give her the life she was used to getting from her daddy. Country clubs, tennis lessons, vacations in villas in Italy and beaches in Thailand, fabulous homes kept by maids and fabulous meals cooked by cooks.

She didn't see all she had.

Stupid.

"Are we done?" Jacob prompted when I fell silent.

We were. Or at least we should be.

But we weren't.

"Okay, well, I could obviously talk to you about this tonight but it's preying on my mind so much I can't get any work done. So do you have a second?" I asked.

"For you, anytime, babe," he answered.

Really, *such* a nice guy.

I took in a breath and started, "Okay, you're a guy—"

There was laughter in his voice when he interrupted with, "Glad you noticed."

Oh, I'd noticed. Any woman who was breathing noticed Jacob Decker. Hell, it was possible he could walk through a graveyard and his very presence would call up the dead females as zombies rabid to get just an undead glimpse of him, he was that noticeable of a male.

"Shut up, Jacob, and listen, will you?" I asked, a smile in my voice.

"Right. Out with it," he invited, a smile in his.

"So, you're a guy and say you've got a girl. You've known her for a while but you've been dating her for a short period of time. You like her and she knows this. You also know that she's holding herself back like she did the fifty times you asked her out before she finally said yes."

I paused.

Jacob said nothing while I did and when I didn't continue, he prompted patiently, "Right, Emme, got that part."

I knew he did. I knew he knew I was talking about Dane. I didn't know why I was beating around the bush. I just felt I had to, maybe to protect Dane, maybe to protect me from Jacob thinking I was an idiot.

"Okay, you got that part, so you're a guy, say you're *that* guy and no vows of love have been exchanged. No commitments, not even to be exclusive. Would you, um...say, buy her an expensive gift to maybe get the ball rolling in your relationship?"

This question was met with silence that stretched so long I had to call his name.

When I did, he spoke.

"What kind of expensive gift?"

"A very expensive gift," I told him.

"What kind, Emme?" he pushed.

I closed my eyes, opened them, looked to the yard, saw Dane was now there talking to a customer and I looked away.

"A ruby and diamond ring," I answered quickly.

This was met with more silence that lasted longer.

I spoke into the void and I did it semi-babbling. "Jacob, honey, I don't know. It's weird. I mean, it isn't an engagement ring or anything. More like a cocktail ring. Which is weird in and of itself because I run a lumberyard. I wear jeans to work. They're nice jeans but it's not like I go to the opera on weekends and hobnob with society. But more, the ruby is very big and you don't have to be an expert jeweler to know it's expensive. Like *very* expensive. Even the box it's in is really nice."

I was quiet a moment then my voice dipped low.

"It's kinda creeped me out."

I was quiet another moment then my voice dipped lower.

"It's actually kinda made me make my mind up about Dane."

Through this, Jacob said nothing.

"Jacob?" I called.

"And what's your decision about Dane?" he asked.

I shook my head like he could see me and didn't even consider how weird this was, talking to Jacob about this, talking to him like there wasn't nearly a decade between meeting him in town yesterday and the last time I saw him.

Then again, I'd talked through a lot with him, none of it really personal because, back then, I really didn't have a life. But the personal part of my life, when he was in it, he knew. What movies I went to. What candidates I was voting for. The specifics (in detail) of where I was going on my next vacation and what I intended to do. That all was personal to me and very few people knew it, except family, my few friends and Jacob.

So it seemed natural, having him back, having him happy to see me, having him say it straight then act on the fact that he wanted us to stay connected this time.

We just, both of us, slid right into where we used to be.

Like real friends. Like the friends we once were.

So I answered, "I talked to him this morning, said I needed a bit of space but I wanted him to come over on the weekend. Then I'm breaking up with him."

A moment, before, "How'd he feel about the space comment?"

"He didn't seem pleased," I gave him my understatement.

"I bet," Jacob muttered, knowing it was an understatement.

We were conversing but he wasn't giving me anything.

So I pressed for it.

"Okay, I laid that out and you haven't said anything. You're a guy. Is this something you'd do? The ring thing. I mean, is he being sweet and I'm just being weird?"

"Guy's a dick and he's a moron and he's into you, Emme, too much. That feels wrong, smothering, creepy, you get the fuck out," Jacob answered.

There was no way to misinterpret that and he was right about the last part. The first parts, I felt it necessary to say something.

"He's actually not a dick or a moron, Jacob. But he is kinda into me, well...too much."

That also was an understatement.

"Thought I was somethin' else when he met me yesterday, called you on it right in front of me. Didn't shake my hand, tried to break it. That's a dick. That's a moron."

I didn't know about the hand-shaking thing but I wasn't surprised. That seemed a Dane thing to do.

But when Dane went weird about Jacob, that ticked me off.

Then again, Dane going weird around guys tended to happen a lot so I tended to get ticked off a lot which was one of the reasons why, even though he was usually sweet, not hard on the eyes and it felt nice that he was way into me, I wasn't so sure about him.

That and him being...off.

I put my elbow on my desk and my head in my hand, mumbling, "Oh God, now I have to break up with him."

"Do it on neutral ground then walk away. Or have me over, open your door to him, tell him it's over, close the door. He knocks again, I answer."

I blinked at my desk. "You'd do that?"

"Fuck yeah, Emme. Guy's a moron and a dick. No tellin' what he'll do. So you break the news on neutral ground with people around and then get the fuck away from him or you do it when I'm over."

"I can't...I mean...." I stammered. "I can't believe you'd do that, honey. That's so nice."

"Today's Thursday," Jacob declared. "I got a lot of shit to do, put him off 'til Sunday and I'll be sure I'm around."

So, *so* nice.

But, this brought me to my next problem. I'd done what my father would call shitting where I lived. This was one reason I'd put Dane off since he'd asked me out the first time about three days after I got back to work after I'd been hospitalized. Now I had to work with him after I broke up with him. Work with him as in be his boss.

"Emme? Baby?" Jacob called.

Thoughts of breaking up with Dane exited my head instantly.

Baby.

What was that?

Jacob had said that several times since we reconnected and each time he said it, it felt like a physical touch. A good one. An affectionate one.

A sexy one.

Jacob had never been sexy toward me.

Ever.

He was my then–best friend's boyfriend, of course. But he'd never even flirted in a casual way.

He'd called me "babe" before, a lot (even though Elsbeth didn't like it). He'd also called me "honey" sometimes (and Elsbeth didn't like that either).

But *baby*?

"Emme," he growled, his voice rougher and getting impatient.

He'd also never growled at me.

It was hot.

I didn't need to think of Jacob as hot, or not hotter than he naturally exuded simply being Jacob.

"I'm here. I'm freaking but I'm here," I told him.

"It'll be okay," he assured, growl gone, his deep voice was again smooth.

"I work with him, Jacob."

"Yeah, that probably wasn't your usual smart," he murmured.

I closed my eyes, plopped back in my desk chair and groaned, "Ugh."

"You're an adult, he's an adult. You both suck it up and act like adults. I know you can do that. He can't, you find a reason to fire him."

I shot up and cried, "Jacob! I can't do that. This is his livelihood."

"He shoulda thought of that before he asked out the boss then creeped her out."

This was true.

I straightened my spine and declared, "Okay, I've just decided I'm taking this one step at a time. I'll tell him to come around Sunday. I'll break up with him. I'll ask him if we can behave like adults at work. And then I'll call you for another strategy session if he's unable to do that."

He had another smile in his voice when he replied, "Sounds like a plan."

"Yeah," I agreed then I called his name like we weren't talking on the phone.

"I'm here, Emme."

My voice had dipped low again when I shared, "This is cool, having this back. Having *you* back. Thanks for making it easy and taking us right back to where we left off."

That got me nothing and that was unusual. Jacob could be verbally and physically affectionate, and after I said what I just said, the Jacob I knew would say something gruff or funny, but whatever it was, he'd say something to make me know he liked what I said.

Therefore, I asked, "Have I lost you?"

"We'll talk tonight about where I'm takin' us," he said as answer and I froze solid, staring unseeing at my desk blotter.

Where I'm takin' us.

Us.

What on earth did that mean?

Were we an us?

"Now, babe, gotta go. I'll be at your place tonight at five," he said.

"I...okay," I replied, still reeling from what he said before. "Do you need me to text you directions?"

"Everyone in town knows your pad but a big giveaway of how to get to it is that it's called Canard Mansion and it's on Canard Lane and there's only one house on Canard Lane, your house, so I reckon I can find my way."

That erased the weirdness of before and I laughed quietly as I replied, "I forgot about your awesome mental powers so I'll let them lead you to me."

He had quiet laughter in his voice too when he said, "Right. Later, Emme."

"'Bye, Jacob. And thanks for your guy advice."

"Anytime, baby."

Baby.

I was still dealing with that when he rang off.

I looked back out the window into the yard.

Dane was gone.

I sighed.

Things Jacob said last night made me realize that I'd said yes to a date with Dane because I'd been sick, I'd unconsciously reflected on my life and how I was living it, and I decided to live it differently.

I'd always liked my life and tended to gravitate toward solitude. I was close to my family, had a small cadre of friends who were all real, true friends, even Elsbeth had been a true friend (just, in the end, a stupid one). But I didn't mind being alone.

It was being sick alone that made me feel lonely.

I'd felt loss before. When Elsbeth broke up with Jacob then I broke up with her because she did. I hadn't realized what a big part of my life they were, including Jacob. How I'd have them over to dinner just to get a chance to talk to him. How I'd pop by their place on the off chance I'd see him. How I'd be the first one to their parties and the last one to leave because I liked spending time with him.

When he was gone, and even before, when he got distant (and I knew that was Elsbeth, I didn't know why, but she could be weirdly jealous), I felt that loss.

Acutely.

But nothing was worse than being sick, really sick, and going it alone.

Not that I wanted to share my exhaustion and vomiting with someone I loved.

Just that it highlighted how really alone I was. Especially up here, away from family and friends.

I loved the mountains, jumped at the chance to move here, something new, a change. I didn't know why I did but it just came when I was ready for it.

And it seemed I'd found my calling, not the lumberyard, where I had to admit I enjoyed working. Being the boss didn't suck and my dad being my boss didn't suck either, seeing as he loved me and always believed I could do just about anything.

My calling was my house, which I took one look at, saw what was under all the mess and fell in love.

But after I was sick, I made changes I hadn't really even noticed were changes. They just came naturally. New hair because I'd gone so long without a cut. New clothes because I'd lost so much weight.

And a boyfriend because he was cute, sweet and into me and it meant I might not be so alone.

Now I'd screwed the pooch.

I sighed and turned back to my desk to get some work done, thinking people lived through worse, me being one of them. And at least I had Jacob back. Better, it seemed like Jacob was happy to be back.

So it would probably suck for a while.

But that was life.

Then everyone would move on.

One way or another.

*   *   *

"Jesus, Emme, baby, this place is a heap."

This was what Jacob said upon me opening my door to him at five-oh-three that night.

I stared up at him a second then asked, "Are you kidding?"

He put a hand to my stomach, shoved me inside, came in with me and pulled the door out of my hand to swing it closed with a flick of his wrist.

My door was twelve feet tall, solid wood. It weighed a ton. Maybe not literally but it felt like it.

And Jacob threw it to like it was a flimsy screen door.

This was hot and I'd forgotten how Jacob doing super-human things with his big-guy strength gave me a little tingle.

Back then, I wasn't allowed to really feel that tingle because he was Elsbeth's.

Now he wasn't so that tingle struck full force.

I was dealing with the tingle as he walked into the entry-way, looking around and talking.

"Fuck, don't know whether to pack you up, take you to my place and save you from this nightmare or move in here and start work tomorrow…" he turned, locked eyes with me and finished, "and save you from this nightmare."

I fought back the tingle and put my hands to my hips. "It's not that bad."

"You don't have any snow on your roof."

I rolled my eyes. I knew what that meant. Dad had been on me about insulation since about three hours after I moved in. I didn't need the same from Jacob.

I rolled my eyes back to him and declared, "It's fine."

"You're heating the mountain, Emme, and payin' for it. It isn't fine. And you need new windows."

"Tell me something I don't know," I returned. "They're after the kitchen."

He shook his head and moved to me. "Before the kitchen, babe. Heat *and* safety. Windows may seem more fragile than boards but some asshole who wants in will balk at breakin' a window. He won't balk at pryin' open a board."

I hadn't thought of that.

"But insulation before that," he went on to announce.

"I'll get to it," I told him.

"When?" he asked.

"When I have the courage to go up in the attic," I shared, and he stared.

Then he asked, "What?"

"The attic creeps me out. Spending a lot of time up there…" I shook my head then informed him, "This is an old house. It's seen a lot. There might be ghosts. And ghosts congregate in attics."

Jacob said nothing but he did this continuing to stare at me, now like he thought he might need to take my temperature.

So I kept talking.

"I'll give on the windows before the kitchen, which sucks since I'm about saved up for the kitchen and my kitchen sucks and I really was looking forward to a new one. But the insulation, I'll wait until summer when the days are longer and, incidentally," I leaned toward him and finished, "brighter. Ghosts don't like bright."

Jacob kindly ignored my comment about ghosts and stated as a question, "You're gonna install insulation in the summer, when you don't need it, instead of the winter, when you do?"

"I've lived here three winters, Jacob, I've been fine."

"And your heating bill has probably been astronomical."

I couldn't debate that because it was true, so I shut my mouth.

He watched my mouth close.

"Fuck," he muttered, shaking his head. "I'm already planning to be here on Sunday. You break up with your moronic dick, I'll install insulation."

It was my turn to stare. "Are you serious?"

"Didn't hear the beat of the drum to announce the end of the joke, babe."

At his quip, I grinned at him but shook my head. "I couldn't ask that. That's a big job. I have a big roof."

"And I'll bring Chace. Got some other buds. We'll see to it."

I held his gaze.

He actually thought he was going to see to it.

"I don't know what to say," I said softly, still holding his eyes.

"Say you'll be here on Saturday when I'm gonna have the insulation delivered."

I waved my hand in front of my face. "Don't worry about that. I'll order it tomorrow."

"Installin', Emme, and payin'," Jacob declared, and my

mouth dropped open. "You need your money to order new windows."

"I . . . you . . . I can't . . . you can't pay for that," I blathered.

He turned away, mumbling, "Late housewarming present." Then he started walking toward the back of the house asking, "Do I gotta wait until work's done Sunday to get a beer?"

I didn't answer.

I was standing there, speechless, staring at him disappear.

When I got over being speechless, I rushed after him to get him a beer.

* * *

"Leave it to a woman to put a guest room and kitchen before insulation and windows," Jacob remarked.

It was after dinner. We were in my somewhat-habitable (Jacob's words) family room at the back of the house. Jacob had started a fire in the fireplace, doing it mumbling under his breath about the state of the chimney and how he hoped he wasn't creating an eventual smoke out.

Earlier, he'd had beer. I'd had beer. I'd given him a tour of the house. Through this, he'd verbally lamented my choice of dwellings and feared for my safety. He did this teasing so I only got mock upset. We had dinner and conversation, which, as always with Jacob, was titillating. Talking with Jacob, as I remembered and as I again experienced over our back-to-back dinners, was like foreplay except the mental kind.

And way better than any of the real kind I'd ever had.

Now we were in my family room with more beers and Jacob was back to teasing me.

He was lounged in one corner of my couch, his long, *long* legs stretched out in front of him, his long, *long* arms curved around the arm and back of the couch, a beer in one hand. I was in the other corner, sitting on a calf I'd folded under me, my chin on my opposite knee that I had bent and I'd wrapped an arm around, my fingers curved around a beer in my other hand.

"Considering the fact that every time I flipped a switch, a

fuse blew or sparks flew, I've had the entire house rewired too," I pointed out, trying to be funny but failing when I noticed my words made Jacob's hazel eyes flash and his jaw go hard. So I hurried on. "And I have a new boiler. Hot water heat can't be beat. And I redid the master, the master bath." I reminded him then continued, "And the garden. Honey, in summer...wait until you see. It's magnificent."

"Gotta have somewhere to sleep, somewhere to shower," he replied, his eyes moved the truncated length of me in a way that made my skin feel warm, "and you did a good job with that, babe. Looks phenomenal. But now you gotta stop lookin' at this as a whole project. You gotta break it down and prioritize."

"I know that," I told him.

"Then why do you have the chandelier down in the front room, cleanin' it, at the same time you're reskimmin' the walls in the dining room, at the same time you're refinishing the floor in the conservatory?"

Unfortunately, he had a point. It seemed I had a schizophrenic style when it came to my restoration efforts.

"I see something, I get the urge to fix it and give in to the urge," I told him.

"Emme, in this heap, everywhere you turn, you'll see something to fix. You gotta have a plan. And that plan is, Sunday, insulation. You get contractors in here to give you bids on the windows. Next up, repointing the brick so the place doesn't fall down around your ears. After that, outside lighting updated so you cut through that dark and give yourself more safety. *Then* you focus on the inside, one room at a time, starting with that avocado nightmare that's your kitchen."

That was the fourth time he called my kitchen "that avocado nightmare." An apt description that meant that was the fourth time I grinned at him when he said it.

Then I informed him, "The work outside is work I can't do, Jacob. The work inside is stuff I can do, outside the electrical, which cost a small fortune and I narrowly avoided five years indentured servitude to get it done. If the project is contracted out, it's a case-by-case basis and you know, those windows are going to cost thousands because it isn't just the broken ones that need replacing. All of them do."

"So bid it out," he returned. "And I'll ask around. Been in Chantelle a few years, know a few guys. We're comin' out of a recession but all of them felt that sting so they'll be happy for the work. I'll see if I can swing you a deal for a marker or your promise of a discount at the yard."

This kind of brought us around full circle so I rolled with it.

"I'd appreciate you doing that, honey," I told him quietly, holding his eyes, lifting up and taking my chin from my knee. "But this reminds me we have to finish our conversation about you paying for the insulation."

He shook his head, saying, "I'm payin'."

"Jacob—"

"Emme," he cut me off, leaning toward me, "I'm paying."

I unwrapped my arm from my leg to throw it out to the side. "That's crazy."

"Nothin' crazy about it," he replied.

God, his thinking it wasn't crazy was also crazy.

I dropped my leg so I was sitting cross-legged in the couch and leaned into him. "Honey, you remember everything so I don't have to remind you I haven't seen you in nine years. I dig it that we reconnected and I love having you back." I again threw an arm out, this time toward him and back to me. "This is great. You and me spending time together, shooting the breeze. I missed that. And I get it that friends make gestures, but this is too much."

His eyes warmed during this speech and he took his arms from the couch, bent his legs, leaned into them, and me, and put his elbows to his knees, never releasing my eyes.

"Baby, I want you warm and liquid. The first bein' physically, the second bein' financially. You stop payin' so much for heat, you'll have more money for the rest of the shit you gotta do."

This made sense.

But he'd again called me "baby."

And I needed to address that.

So I asked, "What is that?"

His head cocked and his eyebrows drew together. "What's what?"

I drew in breath and on the exhale, stated, "You calling me baby." Then I went on quickly, "Not that I don't like it. It's sweet. It's just not..." I hesitated, *"us."*

Something happened to his eyes, his face, his whole big body and that something made me brace at the same time it made my heartbeat escalate.

"You know what it is," he said softly.

I didn't.

"I don't," I shared.

His eyes stayed locked to mine and I knew him relatively well, or I used to. But even if we hadn't been separated for years, I still would not have been forewarned to the fact he was about to blow my mind.

"Before, we had Elsbeth between us. My head was fucked about that, about her, and it took almost a decade to get it unfucked. Lookin' back, havin' you back, I now know and I reckon you know, that's the way it was. She was between us. She knew it too. And she didn't like it. But it didn't matter. My head was fucked so I couldn't see clear of her and not doin' that, I didn't see you."

I knew my lips had parted. I also knew my eyes got big. And last, I had no clue what to say.

So I said nothing.

"Now she isn't between us," he finished.

It was then I knew what the "baby" business was.

I just had no idea how to react to it because I never considered it. He was beautiful. He was kind. He was smart. He was funny and interesting and affectionate.

But he was my best friend's boyfriend.

That didn't mean my mind didn't go there in vague ways, not stupid enough to wish for something I could never have, just silently covetous of what Elsbeth had. And, because of all that he was and that Elsbeth had it, in the end, infuriated she threw it away. Angry enough to end an important friendship because of it.

Sitting there, all that was Jacob, and all that being spectacular sitting across from me, holding my eyes, I finally understood that the reason I was angry at my friend was because, in throwing Jacob away, she took him away from me.

And now I had him back, but also, he was saying I'd always had him a different way, we just didn't go there and he was going to take us there.

Yes. I had no clue what to say but my body had a clue how to feel. Warm and there were a lot more tingles.

"Jacob—" I started on a whisper.

But he interrupted again.

"You saw me, asked me out to dinner that same night, no fuckin' around. Since then, you've called twice for no reason except to connect, and, baby, before you freak that I noticed that and what it said, I'll tell you, I'm fuckin' glad you did and I'm also fuckin' glad about what it said. The boyfriend you were on the fence about, you got off the fence in less than twenty-four hours after seein' me again and decided to get shot of his ass. And you didn't waste any time gettin' me right where I am tonight. That is not friends reconnecting. You know it. So do I."

"I—"

"Don't deny it."

I shut my mouth.

When I did, the skin around his eyes got soft and his mouth twitched and I'd seen that before but not during an intense discussion where Jacob Decker was essentially telling me he was into me. So although before I liked it, now it made my hands start shaking. Therefore, I clasped them both around my beer bottle in my lap.

"Now, layin' this shit out for you, I fucked up," he continued. "In a big fuckin' way that I been dealin' with since summer. Hung up on a bitch, and Emme, honey, I know you two were once tight and women don't like men referrin' to women as bitches but there's no denyin' what Elsbeth pulled this summer exposed her as just that. I thought she was what I wanted and my only shot at gettin' it and to be the man I felt I needed to be, I'd selfishly let that go. I been kickin' my own ass about that for fuckin' years then kickin' my own ass when it hit me I shouldn't have been."

He stopped and it appeared he wanted a response from me and the only one I had was to nod, which fortunately was all he needed for he kept talking.

"But I got a kaleidoscope that I've been carryin' with me everywhere I go for the last nine years that I was too blind to see until very recently that holdin' that thing with me proves that shit irrevocably wrong."

At the mention of my gift to him, my pulse started beating so fast I could feel it in my fingertips.

This was because that kaleidoscope was something it took a lot of courage to seek him out and give to him. It also was something that meant the world to me to give, most especially the message I gave with it. I still figured he'd kindly taken it from me because he was that kind of guy. I also figured he then gave it away because it wasn't his type of thing.

But knowing he took it everywhere threw me.

It also delighted me.

Beyond belief.

Therefore, I whispered, "Everywhere?"

"Been to some interesting places, Emme, baby, and that has always been with me."

My breath started escalating and I knew Jacob didn't miss it when his eyes dropped briefly to my chest before cutting back up to mine.

"Now," he said gently, "unlike your very-soon-to-be ex, I'm not a dick. You gotta sort that and I gotta give you the space to do it. So tonight is not gonna end where I'd wanna lead it."

My breath quickened even more.

He wasn't done.

"But one thing I did learn from Elsbeth that you're gonna get the benefit of, honey, and that's that a man looks after his girl. That means I'm payin' for your insulation and I'm installin' it. And that means you're gonna let me."

"Your girl?" I asked, my voice coming out in a near on squeak.

"Yeah," he answered, his voice deep, low and firm.

"This is, well . . . kinda weird." Understatement! "And fast." Extreme understatement!

"Met you fourteen years ago and we're just gettin' here. I don't call that fast. I call that a waste of fuckin' time I'm about to rectify."

Again, I was speechless.

Jacob wasn't.

"So, summin' up, you got until Sunday to get your head together about McFarland. On Sunday, you scrape him off. On Sunday night, the boys are gone, you learn the true meaning of me callin' you 'baby.' "

I could no longer feel my pulse beating just in my fingertips. It was beating somewhere else, somewhere special, somewhere private, somewhere *awesome*.

"Jacob—" I began again but his head cocked again.

"You don't want that?"

I shut up.

"You want that," he murmured, his gaze on my mouth, the skin around his eyes again going soft but his mouth didn't twitch because the look in those eyes was hot and intense and I could tell he wasn't finding anything funny.

The pulse radiated out from that awesome place and I felt my entire body get warm.

His gaze lifted back to mine and he unfolded from the couch, putting his beer bottle on my coffee table. It was then my entire body got stiff as he moved toward me and leaned in. That was, my entire body but my neck, which bent back to hold his eyes.

Then I held my breath as he slid the tips of his fingers along my forehead, sweeping aside my bangs, before they went back until his fingers were tangled in the strands and cupping the back of my head.

That felt unbelievably nice.

He dipped closer.

I started breathing again only to hyperventilate.

"He's been jacked by a woman," he said quietly, "a smart man learns. And, baby, you know I am not dumb. And what that man learns is not to waste time on bitches. But more, not to waste time when he finds one who he knows is worth it. Now, you got until Sunday. You with me?"

He stopped speaking and I knew he wanted a response but I just didn't have it in me. I couldn't cope with this, this massive shift, this incredible gift, the offer of all his beauty.

He got so much closer all I could see were his hazel eyes. And that close I noticed that, although his lashes were dark, short and spiky, there were a lot of them. So dense, they were fascinating, and I found myself wanting to take up the challenge of counting each and every one.

"Emme," he whispered.

I blinked and focused.

"You with me?" he repeated.

"I think our conversation about insulation took a very weird turn," I replied.

His eyes lit with warmth and humor and I lost my fascination with his lashes because I'd seen that look in his eyes frequently when he was with me but I'd never seen it that close and it was so beautiful, I wanted to hold on to that moment for eternity.

"Right," he said. "You got until Sunday. You feel like pickin' up the phone, I'm busy but I always got time for you. You need space from me 'til then, you got that too, baby. Yeah?"

I decided my best bet was to nod.

So I did that.

"Okay," he murmured. I felt his hand in my hair pull me

forward and I felt my breath stick in my throat before I felt his lips touch my hair and there he kept murmuring to say, "Strawberries."

My hair did, indeed, smell like strawberries. That was what the shampoo smelled like that cost an arm and a leg and a vague promise to the devil I'd bear his children to populate the earth with devil's spawn in order for my hair to get this soft, sleek and shiny.

But Jacob murmuring that word against my hair, I decided to make that promise not at all vague. I'd produce demon spawn to hear him say it again and again.

Alas, he did not say it again.

But what he did was a whole lot better.

His hand at my head pulled me slightly back, his fingers drifted through my hair to my temple then curled so the backs could glide lightly across my cheek and down, touching the side of my lip in a way that was a promise I felt sear through me from my lips, through my heart, straight between my legs.

Was this happening?

"You can shake and bake with the best, Emme," he told me, his hand settling cupping my jaw, and at words that were so far out of the moment, I stared.

Then, at the reminder of the dinner I served and that it might be good, but it was a far cry from gourmet and it was *so* Jacob to mention it, tease me about it, and it was also *so* Jacob to go out of his way to take us out of intense and put me at ease, that suddenly a feeling I didn't quite get but I really liked stole through me and I felt my lips smile.

"Gourmet all the way with me, honey. That's why you got the buffalo-flavored Shake 'n Bake."

"I cook next time," he declared, and Jacob was an excellent cook. Amazing. And he didn't shy away from anything, even gourmet.

And what he said meant he intended to cook for me.

That stole through me too.

"I expect Indian," I told him and something about him

shifted, relaxed, and I knew, in sharing I was going to be eating with him again, I'd also shared I was "with him."

My breath started coming faster again.

"You got it," he replied, leaned in, kissed my forehead, leaned back and caught my eyes. "Later, Emme."

"Drive safe, Jacob."

He grinned.

My heart jumped.

His hand slid away from my jaw and I watched him saunter out of my living room.

Then I sat immobile and listened to the front door open and close.

And last, I listened to the distant sounds of his truck growling out of my drive.

Been to some interesting places, Emme, baby, and that has always been with me.

I sat unmoving and remembered standing outside the door to the hotel room he was staying in since he left the apartment to Elsbeth. I stood there heartbroken for him, heartbroken for me, and I gave him that kaleidoscope. I remembered what I said. I remembered his eyes got warm and surprised and he took the box and opened it, pulling out the piece of beauty within and holding it like it was precious.

I also remember he didn't let me into his room.

He just kissed my cheek and whispered in my ear, "I'll always remember you, Emme," before he pulled back, gave me a smile that got nowhere near his eyes and backed into the room, closing the door on me.

Taking the kaleidoscope with him.

At the time, I got it, why he had to close the door on me. At the time, I was distraught at what his breakup with Elsbeth meant to him.

And to me.

So I'd walked away and let him go.

But at the time, I also was dealing with things, things I didn't share with anybody, not Elsbeth, definitely not Jacob.

I still had that secret.

Words came to me. Words said in a man's voice, a man no one knew was in my life. A man who was special to me in a way I knew no one would get. A man I shared with nobody.

I hope this wakes you up, sweet Emme.

I closed my eyes and called that moment up in my mind.

It was a month after I got out of the hospital. I'd visited him. He could not visit me. He'd been concerned. Eaten up with it, it was plain to see. But he could not come to see for himself I was all right.

He had to wait for me.

We were sitting in his kitchen, drinking coffee.

I hope this wakes you up, sweet Emme.

It did. Being sick like that, it did.

I didn't get it then. I didn't get it when he said that to me. I only got it when Jacob pointed it out.

I opened my eyes and looked to Jacob's beer bottle on my coffee table.

You can shake and bake with the best, Emme.

I knew right then that Jacob saying that meant that he intended to keep the goodness, the easiness, the familiarity of what we had safe.

He just intended to add really great things.

I hope this wakes you up, sweet Emme.

I took a sip of the beer that I held until then forgotten in my hand.

And when I was done, I whispered, "I think I just woke up, Harvey."

And when I did, pure joy flowed through me.

So I smiled.

CHAPTER SIX

Weird

One hour, two minutes later...

I LAY ON my back in my bed, staring unseeing at the ceiling and going over the last two days in my mind again and again.

No way I could sleep.

No way.

So I rolled, turned on my light and saw the ring Dane had given me the night before on my nightstand.

The box was open.

I flipped it shut and put it in the nightstand drawer.

Dane giving me that weirded me out, but it was the kind of gesture that you didn't make an "euw" face and throw it across the room.

So, after I'd tried to refuse it, gently saying it was too much, and he'd refused my refusal, adamantly and repeatedly, I'd given up, thanked him and kissed him.

He'd done what he always did when I kissed him. He escalated things and made love to me.

I'd had two lovers in my life, and to say Dane was better than the first one was a massive understatement.

Still, I read enough, watched enough TV and movies, heard enough girlfriends talking about it, I knew I was missing something.

Even from Dane.

I knew this because I'd never had an orgasm with a partner. Not once.

I faked it.

It wasn't a good thing to do but eventually things just kept going, it got tedious, and I had to do what I had to do to end it so I could get some sleep.

Thinking on this brought me to the memory that Elsbeth had not shared often, but she had shared. And what she shared was that Jacob had no problems in that department. They'd started their relationship young and had been together for five years. Elsbeth and I were the same age and she'd been twenty when they started out. He'd been twenty-three. She had not been a virgin but she'd been an orgasm-during-sex virgin.

According to Elsbeth, Jacob had taken that particular virginity and done it spectacularly then went on to give that to her frequently and unfailingly.

Now I was thirty-four and had two lovers and no orgasms that had been given to me by anyone else but me.

And I had sexual knowledge of the man who that night told me he was interested in me and intended to do something about it.

So even though it was late, I was me, he was Jacob and I was psycho.

Not to mention, these thoughts were tamping down the joy I'd felt earlier, and I didn't like that much.

So I got out of bed, wandered through the dark to the kitchen and nabbed my phone.

I called him wandering back to my room through the dark.

"You okay?" he answered.

"Just to say, if I wasn't, although you have superhuman strength and an off-the-charts IQ, I'd still probably call 911."

"Babe," he replied.

I waited but he didn't follow that up.

So I asked, "Babe, what?"

"Babe," this time there was a smile in his voice, "get on with what you're callin' about."

"Right," I muttered as I walked up the rounded stair-case that was reason three I bought this house. Reason one being the view I saw from the circular drive. Reason two being the extraordinary wood starburst inlaid in the entryway floor.

"Emme," he called.

"Sorry," I replied. "I was thinking about my starburst."

"What?"

"Nothing," I said quickly. "Is this too late to call?"

"No, but just to say, no time is a bad time to hear from you."

Good answer. So good, it made me feel mushy inside.

Safe in that feeling, I admitted, "I can't sleep."

"Emme—"

There was concern in my name and a hint of Jacob being what Jacob had been recently. Determined to go full steam ahead, do most of the talking and the talking he did blowing my mind.

So I interrupted him.

"No, please, Jacob, hear me out."

He said nothing.

I walked down the hall toward the light coming from my room trying to find the courage to say what I needed to say.

Walking into my room and seeing the pretty I'd wrought with my own two hands, some YouTube videos and a lot of elbow grease, I found the courage.

"This is weird," I said softly, making my way to the bed. "I know things about you."

"Girl talk," he murmured, and I knew he knew what I was saying.

"Yeah," I agreed, climbing into bed and sitting cross-legged on it.

"Bad shit?" he asked and I felt my head jerk.

"Bad shit?" I repeated.

"She bitch about me?"

She hadn't. Ever. I didn't even know if they ever fought.

God, she was so stupid.

"Was there bad shit?" I asked hesitantly.

"I didn't think so until she dumped me," he replied and I felt my lips smile.

"That came out of the blue for everybody, honey," I told him. "Not just you."

"Right," he replied, that word clearly a prompt to get on with it.

So I did.

"Just us having this conversation is weird, Jacob."

"Why?"

"You were once my best friend's boyfriend."

"So?" he asked.

"So, this isn't a thing girls do."

"You haven't spoken to her in nine years, and, I'll point out, Emme, it's been fuckin' nine years, which is a long time."

"You hooked up with her this summer."

"So?"

I didn't have an answer to that "so."

When I said nothing, he asked, "What'd she say?"

"Pardon?"

"Elsbeth. Girl talk. What'd she say?"

I was not a psycho. I was an idiot.

I couldn't tell him that.

Thus I should never have called him.

I didn't even know why I did, except he was Jacob and I'd always been able to talk to him about anything. The problem with that was, back when, I'd never really had anything deep and personal to discuss.

Now I did but that deep and personal involved him.

I wasn't an idiot. I was a psycho idiot.

This called to mind the fact that I'd left all my girlfriends in Denver and had not replaced them in Gnaw Bone. It also called to mind the fact that all my somewhat friends in Gnaw Bone were guys who worked at a lumberyard. And this called to mind the fact that not one of them was a candidate for a conversation about a potential new boyfriend I was getting *before* getting rid of my old one who happened to be one of their brethren, and all the things I needed to discuss.

Primarily, that I'd never had an orgasm during sex and I was worried that was on me, not my partners.

And I didn't want to disappoint Jacob. Because if I did, that would be an end to him and me. Not the new good stuff we might have. The old great stuff we just got back.

I needed a girl posse.

I didn't share this with Jacob either.

"It doesn't matter. It's just that this is..." I paused then finished, "I don't want to lose what we have."

He was losing patience at my evasiveness and I knew this with how he asked, "Emme. What. Did. She. Say?"

"I—"

"Okay, honey," he cut off my protest knowing that was what it would be. "I know I dropped a bomb on you tonight, you didn't hide it. You also didn't try to escape it. And what we got started from me meetin' you through her. Neither of us can escape that. But I think, you dig deep, back then you know what was growin' between us. I don't know if you felt it. I just know I didn't. I also know Elsbeth did and put a stop to it. Now I see it, I feel it and I'm gonna explore it. So I dig that this is a shift and you need to talk shit out, this change, how we started. And I'll give you that, late at night, first thing in the morning, anytime. But to talk it out, just sayin', baby, you actually gotta talk."

"I know personal things about you," I told him.

"Like what? That I snore?" he asked, and my heart plummeted because Dane snored and I hated it.

"Do you snore?" I asked.

"Not that I know of," he answered.

"So why would you ask that?" I pushed.

There was laughter in his voice when he replied, "Because you aren't givin' me shit, babe, so I'm tryin' to pull it out. Have no clue what she said to you, so I'm guessin'."

"It wasn't that you snore, and just so you know, I wouldn't

call late at night to talk to you about snoring. Though, also just so you know, I really hope you don't."

"I hope you don't either," he returned.

"I don't snore!" I snapped.

More laughter with his, "Good we got that straight."

"Jacob—"

"Talk to me, Emme."

"I can't—"

"Emme, I'm lying in bed lookin' at your kaleidoscope sittin' on my nightstand, knowin' you've been with me every day for nine years. Which means I wanted you with me every day even when I didn't realize it. Which means you mean something to me and not a little something. You think I'd make that play tonight if I thought makin' it would fuck us up?"

"No," I whispered because I didn't. He wouldn't do that. Ever.

And he was lying in bed and my kaleidoscope was there.

Have mercy.

"So, I made a decision and carried it out but I know what's at stake here and I'm gonna bust my ass to lead this careful, gentle so it doesn't get fucked up. I know this is fast, but from here we don't have to go fast. We just gotta go forward. And we gotta do it honest. So talk to me."

"I know you're a good lover," I blurted.

Jacob said nothing.

So I called, "Jacob?"

"And you're wound up about me bein' intimate with Elsbeth," he said.

"No," I contradicted.

"No?" he asked.

"Well . . . no."

More nothing from Jacob then, "So, fill me in here."

"It's just weird," I shared.

"It's weird," he said.

"Don't you think so?"

Again, nothing until a murmured, but it was a very intensely murmured, "Fuck me."

"What?" I asked.

"Nothin', baby," he said quickly. "You're right. It's weird. I don't know how much she shared, but yeah, you hearin' that from her is weird. But this isn't me and her. This is me and you. And we haven't even kissed, Emme. So, honey, don't get wound up in this shit. You said one step at a time with McFarland, that's the way we're gonna take it. I'll lead but you tell me the speed. You want slow, that's how we'll go. That work for you?"

"I don't want us to get screwed up," I told him.

"So we'll take it slow," he told me.

"I don't want to lose you again."

Jacob fell silent.

"I missed you," I whispered.

"How bad?" he whispered back.

"I wouldn't allow myself to think about it, that bad."

"Baby—"

"Maybe we should just be us," I suggested.

"And maybe this was the us we were always meant to be and we should be that."

At his words, words that spoke to me deeply, my shoulders jerked forward with the force of my lungs hollowing out.

"Emme, you with me?" he called.

I closed my eyes tight, put my forehead in my hand, my elbow to my knee and I whispered, "What if you don't like the way I kiss?"

"I'll like the way you kiss," he whispered back.

"What if you don't?"

"You're the smartest woman I know, baby, you'll learn to give me what I like."

That was an excellent answer.

"What if you don't like the way I do other things?" I pressed.

"I will."

"Ja—"

"You'll learn, and just sayin', honey, so will I. That's the way it goes."

Not in my experience.

"This is an important part of us takin' it slow," he carried on. "Said it before, I'll promise it now, Emme, we'll go at your speed. But I want us finally to go where what we got has always been leading."

"Do you really think so?" I asked.

"Babe, would we be having this conversation if I didn't?"

We wouldn't. Absolutely.

I opened my eyes, sat up and admitted, "I'm a psycho."

"You care about me, have for a while, don't want to lose me. That's not psycho, Emme. That's real. And it's smart. And it means a great deal to me. What you need to get from all I'm sayin' is, because it means that much to me, I'm gonna handle this with care. You just gotta believe in me."

"Do you believe in me?" I asked and got nothing so I felt my heart squeeze.

Then I got something.

And it was huge.

"Emme, what you're worried about, I get. I like it. It's sweet. It's you. But outside of us makin' our way in that, discovering that part of the relationship we're gonna have, nothin' else about you makes me think for even a second I don't believe in what I could have with you. That's somethin' else you gotta get. I missed it. For years. There are three people in this world I trust with everything about me: my father, Chace and you. And I finally figured out I don't give you that because you're my girl but because you've always in a way been *my girl*. I felt it again last night. You feel it too. You just gotta admit it then we'll sort the rest out."

It was my turn to say nothing.

"Emme, baby, talk to me."

"I want this," I whispered.

And I did. Badly. And I might have done for a very, *very* long time. I just wouldn't let myself think about it when he was with my friend and definitely not after I lost him.

"Good. You got it. Starting Sunday," he replied immediately.

"There's things to know about me," I admitted.

"You'll tell me and you'll do that at your pace too."

God, he was *so nice*.

"Okay," I agreed.

"You gonna sleep now?" he asked.

No way.

"Yeah," I answered.

"Bullshit," he muttered, a smile in his voice.

"Uh, reminder, Jacob, it's just over twenty-four hours since we met in town and things have progressed at light speed. Since I'm the first human being in history to travel at that speed, I think it's okay that I allow myself a moment to process the feeling."

"I get you but I don't want you losing sleep over this."

So nice!

"Not sure you can do anything about that," I told him. "But I'll be okay."

"Faye's having a boy," he announced, and I blinked.

Then I asked, "Pardon?"

"You in bed?" he asked back.

"Yeah, kinda. Sitting on it."

"Get under the covers, Emme."

His deep voice saying that started that pulse beating in that awesome place and I did what I was told.

"Light out," he ordered.

I did that too.

"You in?" he asked.

"Yeah, but—"

"They're namin' him after me."

"Oh God!" I cried. "That's so sweet."

"Yeah," he replied.

And that was when Jacob talked to me about a lot of things, none of them taxing, none of them earth shattering, all of them how we always used to be except sweeter, and he did it for a long time. He did it until he heard my voice get sleepy.

Then he said softly, "Gonna let you go now, baby."

"Okay, honey."

"Sleep good."

"You too."

"'Night, Emme."

"'Night, Jacob."

I disconnected, put my phone to the nightstand and stared at it in the dark for three seconds.

Then my eyes closed and I fell asleep.

*   *   *

Twelve hours, seven minutes later...

I hit Jacob's contact button and hit go.

It rang once.

"You okay?"

Feeling weird when I called him, at his question, I felt weird no more and laughed.

"Yeah, honey. Just that, you're bringing boys over, I need to know how many and what they want to eat."

"Manual labor. Beer, chips and brownies."

"I was thinking more along the line of homemade burritos."

"You'd be thinkin' wrong 'cause, one, you lucked out on the Shake 'n Bake, but it'll be important to keep those boys fed, and your stove gives up the ghost, I'm not gonna wanna take a break to try to fix it or go out and buy a camp stove."

I started laughing softly again and Jacob kept going.

"Two, they need to expend their energies rippin' out insulation, haulin' it down, luggin' new up and staple-gunning it to beams. Food that requires silverware is an unnecessary expenditure of that energy."

"Got 'cha," I murmured. "Beer and munchies."

"Right. And now that I got you, insulation is ordered. Delivery window is one to four tomorrow. That good for you?"

I blinked at my desk. "You ordered it?"

"Yeah."

"Already?"

"Babe, need it Sunday. No time to fuck around."

"But you didn't measure," I reminded him.

"You gave me a tour, didn't you?"

I sat up straight as it hit me, like it sometimes did, how very sharp he was. I knew without a doubt he'd ordered enough, not too much. And he calculated the amount of insulation I'd need by walking through my house.

"Yeah, I did," I answered. "And I'll be there for delivery during the window."

"Good," he replied then asked the question I'd hoped he wouldn't ask, "McFarland being cool with you?"

He was. And, in Dane's way, he also was not. And I figured Jacob wouldn't see the part where he was, only the part where he wasn't.

I had to answer so I decided it was safe to share some of it, but not all of it.

"He came up to the office and asked if we could talk. I told him to come by the house at one on Sunday and I'd say what I had to say then."

"And?" Jacob prompted.

"And, well..."

Crap!

I didn't know whether to tell him or not.

Because I was psycho, I told him, "Then he asked who owned the black Dodge Ram that was outside my house last night."

Silence.

I shouldn't have told him.

"Ja—"

"He was at your house last night?"

I'd never heard him use that deep, rumbly, controlled-but-barely tone of voice and I wished I'd still never heard it because it was more than a little scary.

"He, well...does that sometimes when he's, well, we're not...when we don't have plans," I stammered. "He does it because I live up there alone and he wants to check on me. Make sure I'm good."

"He does it because he's creepy into you, Emme."

I was getting the feeling that might be true so I said nothing.

"We need to get around to having a conversation about this guy, babe," Jacob told me.

"It'll be over Sunday, honey," I told him.

"Yeah, but evidence is suggesting he's not gonna like that and he's also not gonna like you movin' on, and you work with him. So we're gonna have a conversation about him and soon. What'd you say about my truck?"

"I told him you were over."

More silence then, "Straight up?"

"Well, I didn't share about your earth-shattering shift in the path of our relationship but, yeah. I said you came around for dinner. Why?"

"And how'd he react to that?"

"He's always been weird about me with guys," I admitted.

"Creepy. Fuck," Jacob murmured.

"He gets over it," I told him.

"No he doesn't, Emme. He hides it. And Sunday, after the boys go, we have that conversation. Yeah?"

"Okay," I mumbled.

"I also want you spending the night at my house tonight and tomorrow night."

My entire body spasmed.

"Pardon?" I breathed.

"I got work, I won't be there. I'll drop the keys at your office with directions. But, he's doin' drive-bys, you're not gonna be there."

"Jacob, you said we'd go slow," I reminded him cautiously.

"Babe, job I'm on, I'm not gonna be in my bed until Sunday night."

At the mention of his bed, I got another full-body spasm.

I ignored that and asked, "What job are you on?"

"Emme, honey, can't say, and with my work, you gotta know, I'm never gonna be able to say. As we're takin' this forward, you'll get everything you want from me, anything you ask, just not that."

I knew this. I knew this because, even back when, Elsbeth couldn't say. Considering his mind and the company he kept, I'd been fascinated by his work and asked her once what he did.

Her response was uttered on a shrug, "No idea. I just know he busts his hump, doesn't talk about it and doesn't get paid much for doing it."

That said, it didn't take a genius the caliber of Jacob, what with the policemen, private detectives and bounty hunters that came to their parties, to know it had something to do with the things they did. It just seemed that whatever it was was a lot more secretive.

Which, of course, made it a lot more fascinating.

"So, I drop the keys, you pack a bag," he ordered.

"Honey, honestly, I'll be okay at home."

"Baby, honestly, I'm a town away from your creepy soon-to-be ex and I got a security system. You'll be more okay there and that's where you're going to be."

This was something else I knew but had never experienced directly. Elsbeth had told me Jacob could get bossy.

"I think you're worried about nothing," I told him.

"And I think I got a dick," he told me and I blinked at his words. "And havin' a dick, I know how other guys who got one think. I also know you dress great. You got great hair. You got unbelievably beautiful eyes. You got a winning personality. You're funny. You're smart. You got that thing goin' on where you state plain with pretty much everything you do you don't need anybody, and a man falls for all that the wrong way, you also got problems."

I was feeling so mushy-happy at these words I didn't have the ability to speak.

"Pack a bag. I'll drop the keys," he repeated his order into my silence.

"Okay," I gave in.

"You get in, make yourself at home. I'll call Donna and tell her she doesn't have to worry about Buford for a couple of nights."

"Buford?"

"My hound."

"Your...what?" My second word was pitched higher.

"You don't like dogs?" he asked but before I could answer, he stated, "I thought you liked dogs."

I loved dogs. I wanted a dog. I just wanted to start with a puppy and I didn't want a puppy chewing on exposed wiring and getting electrocuted so I'd start my first tenure as Puppy Parent by digging a Puppy Graveyard in my garden.

"Yeah, I like dogs," I confirmed.

"Good. Thought so," he muttered, then, "Buford is a blood-hound. He's sweet. He loves everybody, but, just so you know, he hogs the covers."

I started giggling.

Then I asked, "Donna?"

"Neighbor. She looks in on Buford when I'm out."

"Oh," I mumbled and stopped giggling, thinking about Donna, neighbor to a man that was all the man that was Jacob and how I'd also look after the unknown Buford while Jacob was out, and even offer to do it when he was in.

"She's also married to an ex-Bronco defensive lineman," he went on, telling me he knew why I quit laughing.

The giggle came back and through it I repeated, "Oh." Then, "You named a bloodhound Buford?"

To that, smile in his voice, I got, "You name a Bronco Elrod or Cletus. You name a bloodhound Buford. It's the law." That got him another giggle and I could still hear the smile when he said, "Now I gotta go. I'll be around this afternoon with the keys, directions and my security code."

"Okay, Jacob."

"Stay away from McFarland," he demanded.

That wouldn't be hard to do. That was already on my itinerary for the day.

"You got it."

Another smile in his voice when he said, "Later, Emme."

"'Bye, honey."

We disconnected. I put my phone down and grabbed the piece of paper I'd been scribbling on before I called him. I crossed off tortillas, cheese, ground beef and refried beans and added munchies and brownie mix.

Then I went back to work.

*   *   *

Seven and a half hours later...

The black and tan bloodhound Buford following me, I wandered Jacob's living space.

I did this lips parted, eyes big, shocked to the core.

I stopped in his sunken great room, the view from his two-story panoramic windows awe-inspiring. And not just the unhindered vision of the purple mountains majesty I could see silhouetted in black against the midnight blue of the starry sky. But also the pool that was heated if the steam coming up from it was anything to go by, and it had a light that gave its tranquil waters a slow shift through a variety of colors including purple, blue, green and pink.

And that wasn't even getting into the flagstone patio and awesome patio furniture.

It was amazing.

Jacob might not have been paid much before for whatever mysterious dealings he dealt, but he clearly moved up the food chain.

High up.

Buford's wet nose touched my hand and I looked into his adorable black and tan droopy-eared, droopy-skinned face with its lolling pink tongue.

Then I told him, "You didn't know her but, trust me, Elsbeth was really, *really* stupid."

Buford's tail wagged.

I gave him a head scratch for doggie-agreeing with me.

My phone in my purse rang.

I dug it out and saw the display said "Jacob calling."

I took the call by proclaiming, "You live in a showplace."

"What?" he asked.

"Your house is huge and beautiful."

"Babe—"

"And you have an unhindered view of the mountains."

"So do you."

I ignored that and carried on.

"And you have a heated pool."

"Em—"

"With a wheel of pretty lights."

"Baby—"

"You failed to tell me I should bring a bathing suit."

"You're sleepin' in my bed the first time without me. You do not get in that pool for the first time without me."

And another full-body spasm.

"Jacob—"

"I take it you're in and you're settled," he remarked, explaining the call.

"Buford has a droopy face and it's cute," I said as confirmation, looking down at his dog who again wagged his tail.

"You're in and settled," he muttered, then, louder, "I gotta go."

"Okay, honey."

"Eat what you want. Got lots of DVDs. Whatever. Yeah?"

"Okay."

"Sleep good."

"Okay, be safe."

"Right. Later, Emme."

"Later, Jacob."

We disconnected.

I looked down at Buford.

"Let's check out Jacob's bedroom," I suggested.

He got up from sitting like he knew what I was saying.

We checked out Jacob's bedroom.

It. Was. *Awesome.*

I stood in the middle of its awesomeness, bent slightly, scratching Buford's head, staring at the (unmade but still fantastic) huge bed with its cream comforter cover with black piping, black sheets and cream shams (with black piping). This color scheme was used throughout the room, giving it not a small amount of seriously classy masculine appeal.

My eyes fell on the kaleidoscope on his nightstand.

He *did* keep it by the bed.

I felt my lips tip up.

Then I commented to Buford, "I think you're good. No way you could hog all those covers."

Buford had no reply.

Five hours later, I'd find out I was wrong.

*   *   *

Nineteen hours later...

"You okay?"

I burst out laughing.

"Babe," Jacob called through my laughter.

I got control of it and when I did, I saw the piles of rolled insulation that now filled two of my upstairs rooms, one of which I was standing in the door of.

"Just calling to confirm delivery," I told him.

"Good. Now go back to my house," he ordered.

"Jacob—"

"No bathing suit."

"Ja—"

"Gotta go."

I stopped trying to get out his name seeing as it seemed he was in the middle of something important and said, "Okay, honey. See you tomorrow."

"Text me when you get to my house," he replied, then, "And yeah, babe. Tomorrow. But, way things are going, good chance I'll be home tonight."

Tonight?

But I'd be at his house tonight.

With him there!

Before I could begin a discussion about this, Jacob said, "Later, Emme."

I knew he was in the middle of something important (or guessed), so all I could do was say, "'Bye."

I disconnected and wandered to the stairs, looking forward to spending more time with Buford and lounging around Jacob's big house where you could search for hours and find nothing that needed working on.

I was also freaking out because Jacob would be in that house with me (maybe) and we'd be together for the first time as a different kind of us (except for his hurried fly-by at my office to give me his keys, which included him kissing my forehead again—which was very nice—but that was all it included) and I didn't know if I was ready for that.

I was. I was looking forward to it. Anxiously. Excitedly.

I just also wasn't. Mostly because I was thinking on it, panicked.

I was walking down the stairs, thinking these thoughts, when I saw the police cruiser through my own not-so-panoramic but nonetheless fabulous etched windows that luckily had never been broken that flanked my huge front door.

So I would not be going over to Jacob's house imminently.

No.

But I had no idea that things were going to change dramatically in ways no one would expect.

Even when they were watching a police cruiser pulling up their drive.

CHAPTER SEVEN

More

Five hours later...

"DECK," CHACE WARNED low, his hand in Deck's chest, holding him back from Kenton Douglas.

"Tell me you're shitting me," Deck demanded, his eyes locked to Douglas.

"She was in the possession of physical evidence that linked Dane McFarland to a crew of thieves who have been working this county for six months, recruiting vulnerable high school students to do their dirty work," Douglas replied. "That evidence had to be collected, as did her statement. Jesus, Decker, you told us about the ring yourself. And I took her statement with a deputy, and you're right. She corroborated your report that she thought it was a gift he purchased and was visibly stunned by the news it wasn't. It's clear she has no knowledge of what's going on. So clear, we didn't even ask her to go to the station."

The news Emme was "visibly stunned" made Deck, already unhappy, seriously fucking unhappy.

"You approached her without telling me," Deck shot back. "And I told you when I told you about the ring that in any dealings with Emme, you don't do shit without telling me."

"You're not running this investigation, Decker. We can't sit on evidence," Douglas returned.

"An hour after you visited her, I handed you enough to bring them all in without that fuckin' ring," Deck snarled.

"She can't keep stolen property," Douglas retorted.

"I didn't say she'd keep it," Deck gritted. "Fuck, she didn't even want it when she thought it was a gift McFarland bought her. But I wanted to be the one to tell her her ex-boyfriend was involved in that mess."

"I'm thinking maybe you should have divulged how deep your link to her was before you signed the contract," Douglas fired back, watching him closely.

"That wasn't pertinent to the investigation," Deck replied.

Douglas's brows shot up and Deck knew why. That was bullshit and they both knew it.

He just didn't give a fuck.

Deck continued, "I told you I wouldn't blow your investigation. I also told you I'd clear her. I didn't say smack about the investigation and I cleared her within twenty-four hours. You yourself questioned her and you know she's an innocent in this whole gig or she'd be being booked like the rest of them are right now. You have not one material or circumstantial piece of evidence that ties her to that fucked-up shit. But she was mine to handle. I made that clear and you visited her at her goddamned house."

"You're right. We don't have any evidence and that's why she's not one of the five people arrested tonight," Douglas returned. "But that ring is evidence and it needed to be procured, today, not whenever you got around to it."

Deck growled.

Chace said, "Kent, give me a minute with Deck, will you?"

Douglas looked to Chace then to Deck. He jerked up his chin and walked out of Shaughnessy's office, leaving the two men alone.

Chace dropped his hand and stepped away but held Deck's eyes.

"What the fuck is goin' on?" he asked low.

"Emme's mine," Deck answered and watched Chace's head jerk.

"Yours?"

"Mine," Deck bit out.

Light dawned so Chace started, "I thought you said—"

Deck cut him off. "Things changed."

Chace's brows went up. "In seventy-two hours?"

Deck moved to the whiteboard, ripped off the black-and-white picture of Emme and threw it at Chace. It sliced through the air and landed on the floor, faceup.

"That," he pointed to the picture, "comes with all that's Emme, and all that's Emme has fuckin' *been* Emme for fuckin' *years*. Had dinner with her twice. Talked to her on the phone a lot more than that. So, yeah, in seventy-two fuckin' hours, and I wish I had seventy-one of them back."

"She's not arrested, Deck," Chace said carefully. "She's cleared. She isn't even a suspect. Douglas and his deputy talked to her less than an hour. You said she wasn't tight with this guy and that she's even breakin' up with him. This is done for her. What's the big fuckin' deal?"

"The big fuckin' deal is, she's supposed to be at my house and she was supposed to text me when she got there four and a half hours ago. She didn't. I called. She picked up and then she hung up on me without even sayin' hi. This happened five fuckin' times. That's the big fuckin' deal."

"Oh shit," Chace muttered, knowing what that meant.

"Yeah. Douglas shared and she's got ideas seein' as me and McFarland are probably the only two who knew about that ring. She doesn't know about my work, but she isn't stupid. Even not knowing, she knows. I asked Max to go to her place to check she's okay, she wasn't home. No Bronco. Made calls. Got boys lookin' everywhere, not hard to spot a bronze Bronco with a fuckin' glittery butterfly hangin' from the rearview. Hours. Nothing."

"You told me things changed, I could have finessed that for you," Chace told him.

"Sorry, man, I was too busy solving a case in three days you and a task force of your brethren couldn't solve in six months. Should have kept you up to speed on who I decided I'm gonna take to my bed. I'll do that next time."

"Don't be a dick," Chace clipped. "You know your relationship with someone involved with someone involved in an investigation is pertinent to that investigation. You also know it's seriously pertinent to me partnerin' with you *on* this investigation and if you'd shared, I could have fuckin' finessed it."

Fuck.

He was right.

And that sucked.

Deck said nothing.

Chace studied his friend.

Then he murmured, "Jesus, she's it for you."

"Look at the picture, Chace," he pointed to the photo on the floor. "All that's been there fourteen years and I didn't see it. Fucked around, pinin' for fuckin' Elsbeth and I didn't see it. She kept it hidden from me. From everybody. Now, for some reason, she's let it out. But what's worse, she's been a town over and I didn't *know* it. I didn't know she took down the veil. Part of that, I'll add, is thanks to you not sharin' that info. Now I've had it without *havin' it* for seventy-two hours and she's disappeared."

"You'll find her."

"And what do you think I'm gonna find?" Deck asked. "You know her history. You knew her before. She tries it with Dane, finds out he's fucked. She was willin' to go there with me, not eager, freaked, but I got her there, and she thinks I played her. What am I gonna find, Chace?"

"Just talk to her, man."

"This kinda shit can take her right back behind that veil she's been hidin' behind since that shit happened to her when she was twelve."

His friend's eyes lit with understanding, Chace moved closer and his voice got lower. "Then find her and *talk to her*, man."

Deck held Chace's eyes then it occurred to him Emme was out there pissed, maybe hurt, and he was wasting time. So he jerked up his chin.

But he didn't move to the door.

He stated, "Kenton Douglas knew he didn't approach Emme. He knew she was mine. He's not stupid either so I reckon he also knows how she's mine. He's impatient to make his mark. I think he's got good in him. I think he'll do good things for the office. But you, Henry, Shaughnessy, Carole, watch out. Enthusiasm like that can turn bad."

"He jumped the gun and Emme's Mick's, Deck. You don't know Mick well but he considers every citizen of Gnaw Bone his personal responsibility. You weren't here when Douglas got back from talkin' to Emme, but Mick was not real pleased because Douglas didn't even tell Mick he was makin' that ride. Mick also understood you had a connection and he's the kind of man who would have told you he was rollin' out in a cruiser so you'd have a heads-up. So, what I'm sayin' is, this isn't lost on us."

They held each other's gazes for a moment before Deck murmured, "I gotta find my girl."

"You want my help?" Chace offered.

"You feel like cruisin' a few streets before goin' home to Faye, yeah."

Deck knew the answer before Chace gave it to him.

"I can do that."

Deck nodded. They moved out and Deck avoided Douglas as he did so.

No one stopped him. His file was thorough. Officers went out to pick up suspects after three pages were read. They were busy following leads Deck gave them and corroborating evidence he supplied.

But Deck's job was done.

So it was time to find Emme.

*   *   *

Four and a half hours later...

As Deck's truck moved down the street to his house, he knew why neither he, nor any of his boys, nor Chace, nor anyone he'd put a feeler out to could find Emme.

Because she was at his house.

He did not know if that was good or bad.

But he reckoned it was bad.

He hit his garage door opener, drove by her Bronco in his drive and parked in the garage.

Snow was being forecast for the night. He'd move her truck in after they had the conversation he figured they were going to have.

He found her in his great room, no jacket, no scarf, no purse. She'd lit out so pissed she likely hadn't grabbed anything but her keys.

She was sitting on one of his denim-covered sofas, Buford sitting on the floor by her side, his head on her knee, her hand scratching behind his ears. His dog didn't move anything except his eyes to Deck when he walked in, that was how much he liked exactly where he was. Hell, Deck reckoned this could have been their positions for the last seven hours, Buford liked to have his ears scratched that much.

He stopped moving, they locked eyes and before he could say a word, she started.

"You knew me for five years, didn't even mildly flirt. You," she lifted her hands and did air quotation marks, "*run into me* three days ago when I'm with Dane, after nine years of nothing, you've got all the time in the world for me."

"Em—"

She interrupted him, saying, "Don't even start. Whatever you've got to say will be full of shit." He took two steps toward her but she halted his progress by hissing, "Don't bother. I'm leaving."

She gave Buford one last stroke and rose from the couch as he spoke. "Emme, listen to me."

"No fucking way," she told the floor, eyes to her feet, feet moving fast.

Deck moved faster.

He cut her off and she tried rounding him so he shifted and cut her off again.

She took two steps back and squared off, eyes slicing back to his.

"Let me pass, Jacob," she demanded.

"Baby, you gotta—"

He didn't get that out. For some reason, his words tripped something in her and she advanced, fast. Shoving a palm into his chest, she pushed hard. He rocked back and caught her wrist in his hand.

"Emme—"

"I missed you."

Fuck.

"Em—"

She leaned into him and her hand. "You *played* me."

His hand tightened around her wrist and he growled, "I fuckin' did not."

"Bullshit," she snapped.

"Listen to me."

"Fuck that," she bit out. "This is for the birds. Next time I'm puking my guts out and so goddamned tired, I want to cry because I have to pull myself out of bed to get a 7Up to settle my stomach but I'm too fucking tired to even cry, I won't lie there and think how fucked-up shitty it is to be so goddamned alone and so fucking lonely. Scared I'll die, no one will care. No man. No kids. Fuck that. I'll lie there knowing all I had and all I ever had to depend on is me and that'll get me through."

Fuck!

"Emme, shut it and fuckin' *listen to me*," he ordered.

"No fucking way," she hissed. "Let go of my hand."

"Listen to me."

"Let go!" she yelled, twisting her wrist to get away.

But he took a step back at the same time yanking her with him. Then he took a step forward so she collided with his frame. Her other hand came up to break her fall so when he let her wrist go and clamped both arms around her, she was stuck, her arms caught between them.

She struggled.

His arms got tighter.

She stopped struggling and her head jerked back. "Let me go."

"I can't talk about my work."

"Yeah," she tossed back. "Bet that's even more so when it's a mark you're playing *for* your work asking *about* said work."

"Emme, you weren't a mark. Honest to God, I was as surprised as you when I met you on the street, and I didn't know you were involved in the investigation they were contracting me for until ten minutes after we made plans for dinner."

"Now I bet you were glad you made that date," she shot back with extreme sarcasm.

"Yeah, I was, babe, because," his arms grew tighter and his face dipped closer, "I missed you too."

"Well, you know, seeing as you lived not far away for a while and you have awesome powers, I figure if you did miss me so damned much, you could have done something about it. That was a door *you* had to open, Jacob, and we both know it. But you didn't. Not until I was dating a felon you were investigating. So forgive me if I find the coincidence too much to take. But I fucking," she got up on her toes, narrowed those fucking beautiful eyes, her fire dancing in them, and she finished, *"do."*

She wouldn't shut up and listen?

He'd shut her up and communicate a different way.

So he did.

He slid one hand up to cup the back of her head, tilted it and crushed his mouth to hers.

She struggled, opening her mouth to protest and he slid his tongue inside.

Fuck, she smelled of strawberries and tasted like them too. Fresh, cool and sweet.

At the touch of his tongue, Emme went completely still.

Deck pressed his advantage and deepened the kiss, drinking from her mouth, taking all he could get.

Christ. Unbelievable.

It became more unbelievable.

Because two seconds in, she...went...*wild*.

Fingers fisting in his shirt, pulling him to her even when he had nowhere to go, she rolled further up on her toes, tilted her head more, tangled her tongue with his and pressed everything she had deep, her whimper filling his mouth.

Not unbelievable.

Phenomenal.

Without releasing her mouth, Deck shifted back an inch to give her her arms and she instantly tugged them out but only to curl her fingers in his jacket and yank it down his arms.

He let her go and shrugged it off. Mouths still connected, after his jacket dropped to the floor, he walked her backward.

Her hands went back to his shirt at the sides, wrenching it up, pulling it out of his jeans then they dove in, skin against skin, her touch warm, light, slightly tentative, definitely searching, discovering.

He steadied her with an arm around her waist, bowing his back to keep her mouth, and walked her down the three steps to his great room before he angled her to the couch.

She pulled one hand out of his shirt and slid it up his chest, it curled around the side of his neck then slid up in his hair and she held his mouth to hers.

He twisted them and fell back over the arm of the couch, taking her with him.

She landed on his body and he rolled instantly, trapping her underneath him, all the while he kept at her mouth.

She didn't deny him, one hand roaming, losing the shyness, becoming confident, another little mew slid down his throat and her nails dragged down the skin over his spine.

He tore his mouth from hers to mutter, "Fuck, baby."

Eyes closed, she lifted her head and pressed her lips against his, this time her tongue slid into his mouth.

He growled and pressed her deeper into the couch. His hands moving to her sweater, he yanked up.

Her arms flew up and she arched her back. He pulled it off and bent to her. Lips to her jaw, he touched his tongue to it, trailing down the salty skin, smelling her hair, tasting her neck, down to her chest, down, his path defined.

"You know what I want, Emme," he said against her skin, and she did. He knew it when her fingers curled into the cup of her bra and pulled down.

Her breast was as gorgeous as the rest of her.

He closed his mouth over her nipple and drew in hard.

Her back arched, her soft hips grinding into his hard ones and she moaned a sexy-as-fuck moan he felt in his dick.

He drew her nipple in harder.

"Jacob," she breathed, fingers sliding into his hair.

"Other one," he ordered, then circled the tight bud with his tongue and he felt her resulting shiver.

Without delay, her other hand lifted to pull down the other cup of her bra and he switched sides.

She bucked underneath him.

Fuck, so goddamned hot, he needed to know what that was doing to her and he needed to know immediately.

So he set about finding out.

Rolling so she was on top, he knifed up, undid her bra and pulled it away, tossing it aside. He lay back, taking her with him. Rolling again, he got her under him, put his hands under her arms and jerked her all the way up the couch so her head was on the armrest, the sexy little gasp this caused he also felt in his dick.

Then he slid down, yanked down the zippers on her boots, tugged them off, then socks, jeans, panties, all cast aside.

"Spread," he growled.

On another sexy mew, Emme spread.

Deck bent forward and fed.

Christ. Hot. Drenched. Pure beauty. Absolute.

Hands in his hair, one leg over the back of the couch, she shifted the other over his shoulder, digging her heel in his back as she rolled herself up, offering her pussy, seeking his mouth, demanding he take everything she had.

He took it until her movements and noises got desperate.

Then he rolled off the couch.

Her head moved his way, those exotic fucking eyes of hers closed but she opened them to blink in surprise and he reached down and took hold of her arm. She cried out, the noise part turned-on gasp as she came up fast. He caught her bare, round ass in a hand, his other hand drove into her hair and tipped her mouth to his.

He felt his gut tighten when, even with the taste of her in his mouth, she let him take it as she wound her arms around his shoulders and her legs around his hips.

Kissing her, he walked her through the house to his bed.

Putting a knee to it at the foot, he walked her up, rested her on the pillows then slid away. He stood at the end of the bed, hands going to the buttons of his shirt as she looked down the bed at him. Eyes lazy. A blush in her cheeks.

She was gone.

Fuck him.

"Jacob," she whispered, starting to close her legs.

"Stay spread for me, baby."

Her teeth found her lip, her cheeks got pinker, she hesitated but let her legs settle open for him.

Christ.

Her hair all over his pillow, her sex glistening wet and gorgeous, the taste of it still on his tongue, her eyes half closed, her face flushed, his dick started to throb.

He wasted no time taking off the rest of his clothes and joining her. Reaching beyond her to the nightstand, he opened the drawer and left it open after he grabbed a condom.

Kneeling between her opened legs, he held her eyes as he rolled it on.

"You're beautiful, Emme," he whispered.

"Jacob—"

He fell forward and covered her, lips to her lips, he rolled his hips and positioned the tip of his cock inside.

"I'm big, honey," he murmured against her mouth.

"I noticed," she breathed, her arms rounding him.

He slid an inch deeper.

Tight.

Heaven.

Fuck, he wanted to bury himself inside.

"You can't take me, tell me, or you can't talk, bite my shoulder."

"More," she panted, lifting her hips.

Fuck yes.

He slid an inch deeper.

He closed his eyes and rested his forehead against hers.

Slick. Close.

Fucking heaven.

"More, honey," she begged.

He gave her more, slid out and partially back in.

"Jacob—"

"We go slow."

He gave her more, slid out and then partially back in.

She squirmed under him, tipping up her hips.

Beautiful.

Fuck. Killing him.

"Jacob—"

"Slow."

"God," she whimpered as he gave her more, slid back out and then in.

Her legs rounded him and her nails again scraped his back.

"Jacob—"

He opened his eyes. "Slow."

"But—"

He slid out and back in.

"I—" she began.

"Sl—" he started to repeat, but she tipped her chin, caught his lower lip between her teeth, locked her eyes with his, let his lip go and begged, "Please, honey, fuck me."

Her words, her actions broke his control and he couldn't hold back any longer. He thrust in savagely and buried himself to the root.

Her neck arched back, mouth open, moan silent, limbs convulsing, sex rippling, she took all of him and liked it.

Fuck.

"More," she breathed.

That was all Deck needed.

He pounded deep, watched and felt her reach for it, take hold and slide over the side, crying out, her neck arced, the elegant line of her jaw exposed, then her head shot forward and she buried her face in his neck.

He rode her hard, harder, then he planted himself, and Emme's fire dancing behind his eyes, Emme his entire universe, Deck exploded on a long, deep groan.

After it left him, he felt her pussy slick and tight around his cock, her body soft and yielding under his, her limbs wrapped around him tight and her face was still buried in his neck.

He turned his head so he could find her ear with his lips and when he did, he whispered, "Like I was sayin', Emme, you were *not* a mark."

Her body tensed under him, her limbs starting to release.

He pressed his hips into hers, she stilled and he growled, "That went a lot faster than I reckon you were ready to go, but doesn't matter. This is where we are now and this is the beginning. And don't piss me off by stayin' angry when you now know you got no call to be and tryin' to push me away by tellin' me that wasn't as hot and fuckin' great for you as it was for me because I won't believe you."

She said nothing.

So he went on.

"And, babe, you're pissed, you got a filthy mouth."

Again he felt a tensing of her body before she relaxed.

"You curse all the time," she whispered.

"I'm allowed. I'm a guy."

This time, her body jerked, her head snapped back and her eyes found his.

Hers were sated, surprised, confused and peeved.

It was a hot look. It also was a cute one.

He grinned at her.

The peeved left, soft came in and she whispered, "You're teasing."

"Yeah."

Her eyes moved over his face, around his head, then back to his before she asked, "Did we just do what we just did?"

His grin got bigger. "Oh yeah."

"I'm not sure I can face Buford again. He saw me naked."

Cute. Sweet.

Emme.

Fuck.

He was buried inside Emme.

Sweet.

"That's not good, babe, 'cause I'm not gonna lock him outta my room seein' as it's his room too so he's gonna see a lot of that."

Her expression shifted in a way he didn't like and she started, "Jacob—"

He had a feeling they were getting into the confused part of her earlier look, which could mean Emme's retreat. Something he was not about to let happen.

Not after the beauty she just let loose and gave him.

To stop it, he dropped his mouth to touch it to hers, lifted up and said, "I gotta get rid of this condom. Then I gotta put on my jeans and make a dozen calls to guys I got all over the county lookin' for you. Then I gotta pull your Bronco in the drive 'cause we're gettin' weather tonight and I got a three-car garage so I don't have to scrape the windshields of any vehicle. I'll get you a tee. You get your ass to the kitchen because I haven't eaten dinner seein' as I've been all over the fuckin' place lookin' for you. So as penance, you're gonna make me a sandwich. We'll talk while I'm eatin' it."

"You and a bunch of guys were looking for me?" she asked, her eyes bigger, her look stunned.

"Babe, you don't gotta be a genius to know something's up when you call me at the drop of a hat to connect and suddenly you're hangin' up on me after you get a visit from the sheriff about a ring you told me about. But, reminder, I *am* a genius so I figured it out. I got worried. You were pissed. Probably hurt. And not home so that meant both of those and in a car. So I sent men searching."

"I don't know whether to laugh because you're funny. Apologize that I put you to that trouble. Or be hurt and angry because you didn't tell me Dane was a serious bad guy and not only does he work for me, I was seeing him."

Fuck. It appeared he'd solved one problem giving her an orgasm, now he had a different one.

He slanted his head, brushed his lips up her jaw and, in her ear, whispered, "We'll talk over a sandwich."

She hesitated before she agreed, "Okay."

He slid out and liked the way her limbs tightened around him as he did. Then he slid his lips over her chest as he rolled them across the bed and finally pulled her out of it.

He put her on her feet, grabbed her hand and led her to his chest of drawers. He opened one and yanked out a tee but he didn't give it to her. He shook it out, bunched it up and pulled it over her head.

Emme pushed her arms through and the tee dropped down to her thighs.

He cupped her jaw with his hands and bent close.

"You want me to go get your panties?" he asked.

"I'll get them," she whispered.

He nodded, lifted up, kissed her forehead, let her go and moved to the bathroom.

He had his jeans on, pulled on a sweater and had his phone to his ear while he was making his way through the house to the garage when he saw Emme in his kitchen, her back to him. She was at the counter with bread, condiments and Ziplocs of deli supplies spread around her.

All that was Emmanuelle Holmes in his kitchen in his tee making him a sandwich after he'd fucked her and they'd both come hard.

That did *not* suck.

He grinned at his phone as he told one of his boys to go home.

Then he saw her jeans folded on the couch, made a correct guess and found her keys in a pocket. He went out and pulled in the Bronco. It hurt, even driving a few feet in a Bronco with a butterfly hanging from the rearview mirror, but he survived it.

He did this on the phone and by the time he got back to the kitchen, she had a sandwich on a plate with chips, pickles and an open beer on his bar and he was on his last call.

"Right. Thanks. Later," he said into his phone, his eyes on her where she was all the way across the kitchen, facing him, back to the counter, arms wrapped around her stomach, eyes on him.

He disconnected and put his cell to the bar.

Then he said gently, "Come here, Emme."

"I made roast beef and Swiss, seeing as you had them I figured you liked them. But I didn't know what condiments to use. If you were a beef and mayo man. A beef and mustard man. Or other," she informed him.

"Come here, Emme."

Uncertainty moved through her features and she whispered, "That never happened to me."

"We got chemistry. Personally, babe, I'm not surprised," he replied.

"Not that." She was still whispering.

He took a guess and went to her.

He was intense during sex. Their late-night conversation the other night exposed she had concerns about pleasing him, and he deduced this was because she wasn't exactly experienced.

This was not a surprise. But it was something he told himself to have a mind to. When she went wild on him, he'd forgotten that.

He stopped close to her, but not too close, curved his fingers around her hips and dipped his face to hers.

"Right, honey. That got outta hand and I saw your indecision when I told you to expose yourself to me. Just know, I know what I like in bed. I get it even if that means I give orders to get it. But I hope you get with what just happened, even though I control everything there, I'll always take care of you, and no matter what I ask or do, you're safe."

"Not that," she repeated. "The orgasm."

His chin jerked back.

"What?"

"I...um...no one's ever..." Her eyes went anywhere but to his. Then, pure Emme, she couldn't hold evasive for more than a few seconds, they came back to his. "I was concerned it was me," she finished quietly.

Deck stared.

"No shit?" he asked.

"Well..." she trailed off.

"No man's ever made you come?"

She tipped her head to the side and shrugged.

He couldn't believe this.

"Seriously, you light up like that and no man's ever taken that home?" he pressed.

"I don't, well...normally light up like that." She took in an unsteady breath and stated, "I don't know what came over me."

Deck fucking *loved* this.

He fought a grin as he suggested, "Maybe because it's never been me?"

Her head jerked, her eyes flashed and she replied, "You think a lot of yourself."

"Babe, you got your tits out for me. You spread yourself over my couch for me. You opened yourself for me in my bed. And you begged me to fuck you and you came hard and fast for me. Yeah. After that, I do."

Her peeved expression came back.

"I hardly need a blow-by-blow, Jacob. I was there," she snapped.

"Well, I don't want you to forget any of it seein' as I won't and we're gonna act out that scenario again. It was so hot, maybe repeatedly."

"Jacob—"

He rounded her with his arms and pulled her into his body, one hand sliding up her back into her hair.

He quit fucking with her and gentled his voice when he said, "Emmanuelle, that was good. Explain to me why you seem conflicted."

"Because I was really angry with you and then I was all over you. Then you were all over me and I liked it and I'm not sure angry sex is healthy sex."

Yeah. Definitely inexperienced. Angry sex arguably could be the best sex you could get.

Teasing but hoping she took his point and it eased her mind, he replied, "Then I'm fucked because, with you, angry sex is fuckin' great sex and I hope it happens a lot."

"I'm being serious," she whispered.

"So am I," he replied, and she blinked.

"You are?"

"Babe, you're here, in my tee, I think you get I didn't play you, so we worked it out." He gave her a squeeze. "In a good way. So I'm not complaining. We argue, that's the end of the argument, I won't complain then either."

Again, her eyes roamed to anything but his and he gave her another squeeze.

"Talk," he ordered.

Her eyes came back to his. "I don't have a lot of experience."

"I know. You did, I wouldn't have gotten that phone call late the night before last that was not about what Elsbeth said about me but about you worried you weren't gonna please me. I got it then. I got somethin' that pleased me fifteen minutes ago. Better yet, for the first time, you got somethin' that pleased you." He moved his face closer and finished, "Honey, it's all good."

"You need to eat your sandwich," she informed him, blatantly changing the subject.

Deck denied the subject change. "Not before you tell me you're good."

"I'm good...*ish*."

He fought back another grin then demanded to know, "Explain the ish part."

"Dane."

It was definitely time to get conversation about that moron over and done with. So Deck sighed, turned them, rested back against the counter and pulled her close so her body was resting on his. She allowed it and he spoke.

"I know you've heard this more than once but I can't talk about my work."

She opened her mouth. He shook his head.

"Give me a second, Emme."

She shut her mouth.

"Within a day, you'd decided to break up with him. You weren't broken up about it. You hadn't been seein' him long. You were more worried about workin' with him once it was over than hurtin' his feelings or nursing your own hurt. You weren't sure. You were right not to be sure. You were gonna end it. I was workin' on ending other things for him. So even if I could have talked, for you, there was nothin' I could say. If you were in deep with him, that would have been different. But straight up that first night you stated you weren't. Fifteen hours later, you were done with him. You did my job for me 'cause knowin' what I knew and not likin' the guy even if he wasn't a felon, I intended to make you done with him. Either way, it got done. In other words, baby, this point is moot."

She held his eyes then she looked to his sweater. Seconds later, she collapsed into him. Her weight pressing deep, her forehead to his chest, she pulled in a breath that hitched and his arms got tighter.

"Emme," he whispered.

"He was creepy because *he's creepy*," she told his chest, her head jerked back and she cried, "That boy shot himself because of stuff Dane's involved in! And I slept with him!"

Deck was having great difficulty dealing with talking about this guy, knowing McFarland had her and had her recently.

For Emme, he pulled it together to keep dealing and lifted a hand to her hair.

He slid his fingers through it and murmured, "You sensed it, you were gonna end it. Now it's all done, honey."

She shook her head even as it drifted to the side, stammering, "I...I..." She looked back to him. "That's gross, Jacob."

"He's a good-looking guy, Emme. Lots of women would go there. He's a dick. He's a criminal. He's a liar. And I learned tonight he's shit in bed. But none of that is on you. You felt it. You were making moves to end it."

"You don't think this reflects on me?" she asked.

"I don't think you should care what people think," he answered.

"I *don't* care what people think. I'm asking *you* because I care what *you* think."

That meant so much to him, his frame froze solid.

She was detached and had always been that way. Her cadre was small and tight and she didn't often let people in.

But even if she let you in, even though she was warm and affectionate, it was strange, but she still somehow managed to be distant. Therefore, not always, but sometimes with Emme, you had to search for clues that something you said or did meant something. And since he told her where he was going to take them, he'd been searching. She gave it to him, but he'd also had to look for it.

Except when she told him she missed him, wanted the change in their relationship and, just now, telling him she gave a shit about what he thought.

"So, do you think this reflects on me?" she pushed, feeling

the tenseness in his body, her eyes filling with concern she didn't hide.

He forced his body to relax.

"I think you traded up and that works for me," he answered and moved to conclude discussion about fucking McFarland by saying with finality, "That's what I think."

She studied him a moment before her body melted against his and she smiled, the dimple appearing.

Fucking finally.

"Now can I eat my sandwich?" he asked on a grin.

"I saw the kaleidoscope by your bed," she whispered.

"Yeah," he whispered back.

"Just now and when I spent the night before."

"Yeah," he repeated.

"I wasn't a mark."

Irritation flashed and he gave her a warning squeeze. "Emme, I told you—"

She cut him off, "Just my way of saying I'm sorry, honey. I should have thought about that before and known I was wrong. I just," she shrugged, "got bad news, reacted and by that I mean flew off the handle. I'm sorry I put you to trouble and lost it with you." Her head tipped and her eyes lit. "Though, maybe not so sorry, considering how that concluded."

He'd been worried for hours.

He'd just had his girl, gave her her first orgasm during sex and now they were cool.

So he was over it.

Before he could tell her this, Emme rolled up on her toes, touched her mouth to his, pulled back and asked, "Now, do you take mayo or what?"

Deck looked into her now just inquisitive eyes a second before he burst out laughing.

After he was done, he saw her smiling at him, gave her brief kiss getting a hint of the strawberry of her hair as he did it and liking it. He set her away from him and grabbed the mayo in answer to her question.

He went to the sandwich.

She went out of the open kitchen and he watched her walk to her clothes on the couch.

Then he watched her pick them up and start heading toward his room, Buford following her.

"Emme, where you goin'?"

She turned and looked at him. "Getting dressed then going home."

He stopped squirting mayo and felt his eyes narrow. "Babe, just put Cletus in the garage."

"Sorry, right, you probably didn't have to do that. And her name is Persephone."

Deck ignored that and stated, "You're spendin' the night here."

Her head tipped to the side. "Why? Dane's behind bars so I'm safe to go home."

Why?

"Emme, you're not spendin' the night here because I want you safe from McFarland. You're spending the night here because I want you in my bed."

Her body froze.

"Oh," she mouthed as he saw her lips form the word but he didn't hear it.

Cute.

Little experience and no man had even made her come.

It was up to him to get in there and teach her. Something he liked. Something he looked forward to.

Something he was starting now.

"Have you had dinner?" he asked.

"I was too angry to eat. I thought I would, well..." she threw out a hand, "get something when I got home."

"You're not goin' home so get something here."

She stood there unmoving before she said, "Okay," and moved.

Buford followed her.

He probably liked the smell of strawberries too.

She dumped her clothes on the couch, made a sandwich and slid on a stool beside him at the bar.

He swallowed his bite, looked at her and asked gently, "Is my girl good?"

She had her sandwich to her mouth. She took it away, looked at him and replied, "Your girl's good, honey."

"Good," he muttered, bent in, touched his mouth to hers before she took a bite and he went back to the remnants of his sandwich.

CHAPTER EIGHT

Girl Posse

I SLID UP and on the downward glide I knew it was coming.

And like last night, both before and after sandwiches, it took me by surprise.

But this time, I was riding Jacob so I didn't know what to do while riding a man and having an orgasm.

In the end, I couldn't do anything but what my body told me to do.

And that was slam down hard on his cock and feel it pulse through me, radiating everywhere, shaking me through and through so intensely I arched back and had to brace myself by curling a hand around his thick, hard thigh.

So totally better than self-induced it wasn't *funny*.

"Baby, do not fuckin' stop," Jacob growled, his hands on my hips coaxing but I was too far gone.

So far, I barely felt Jacob sit up but I did feel his thigh come up as he cocked his knees. Then I had an arm around my waist pulling me up and slamming me down.

My head tipped down and I lifted my eyelids as far as they would go, which was about a quarter of the way up.

"Honey," I breathed as he pulled me up and slammed me back down.

That felt good and a low sound escaped my throat, I lifted my hands to his shoulders, used them as leverage and took over.

"Thank fuck," he muttered but didn't release my waist.

"This is fun," I whispered, sounding slightly surprised, moving on him fast and hard.

"It'll be more fun you take me there, like, soon," he replied.

Wasn't I doing it right?

I bit my lip and grew uncertain.

Jacob's eyes narrowed on my lip.

A second later I was on my back in his bed, he was pounding deep and he had a hand between us, thumb pressed to my clit and one could just say he knew how to use his thumb.

"Jacob!" I gasped.

"Now this," he grunted as he thrust, "this, baby, is fun."

He could say that again.

He didn't.

He kissed me.

I came again a few seconds later.

Then he did the same a minute after that.

*　　　*　　　*

"We gotta go, honey. You have insulation to install and I have chips to pour into bowls," I said after Jacob got back from the bathroom, rejoined me in bed, settled on his back and cuddled me close to his side.

"We can eat them out of bags," he replied.

"Okay, then I have a fridge to check and make sure it's working, and if it's not, I have beer to shove in snow to make it cold."

His body shook with silent laughter before his arm got tight when I tried to pull away. "In a minute."

"Jacob—"

"I like this."

I did too.

And I liked it that he liked it. Jacob Decker, my friend reunited, now my lover (and a great one), wanting to cuddle in bed after sex with me.

But this being Jacob, all he was and all he was to me, that made it even better.

So I settled in.

The one good part about Dane was that he liked to spend the night with me. Sex with him had its moments, none culminating, but there were moments. But sleeping with him was always nice. He was also a cuddler and I liked that too.

My only lover before him, Jerry, cuddled a bit after but always went home to his own bed or expected me to go home to mine. I'd had him while Jacob was with Elsbeth but he never met anyone because he didn't last long and it never got serious.

Between Jerry and Dane, a long dry spell that was okay by me.

Jacob, too, was a cuddler, but with his long frame, it being so big, and his innate bossiness, it was different than Dane. Dane spooned but if I moved, he let me go my own way. Jacob slept and I slept with him however that came about. I moved, he moved me back or moved into me (mostly moved me back). If he moved, he took me with him.

It was weird and it didn't sound like it would be good.

But since he was Jacob, all he was and all he was to me, it was fantastic.

Thinking these thoughts led me to thinking that switching creepy, the-only-thing-good-about-him-was-cuddling-and-he-could-be-sweet, felonious Dane right away with everything-was-good-about-him-except-he-was-sometimes-bossy Jacob didn't suck.

This thought was so funny that me, *me*, Emmanuelle Holmes, thirty-four years old and only having two short-term boyfriends moved right from one guy, felonious or not, to another, *and* traded up to one who was hotter, nicer, funnier, smarter, richer and had the capacity to give orgasms every time (sometimes two!) made me start giggling.

"What?" Jacob asked.

"Nothing," I choked out through giggles.

Jacob's hand came to my chin and gently forced it up so he could catch my eyes.

His were smiling.

"What?" he repeated.

"I'm a slut," I announced, still giggling but harder now. It was full-blown laughter. "In the blink of an eye I go from a felon to a mysterious crimefighter or whatever you are." I started laughing so hard I hiccupped and pushed out, "Trading up."

My laughter only started to die down when I noticed Jacob's eyes were no longer smiling.

"What?" I asked when I got control of my hilarity.

"Been cool about that Emme, but heads up, that cool ends now. I may have found you again when you were with him but I didn't like him from the start. Ten minutes later I found out there was a lot not to like. And now the only good part about you bein' with him is that you were smart enough not to get too deep and he's gone. But I don't find it funny."

I sobered immediately and whispered, "Sorry."

"And you're not a slut," he stated. "A woman who's never had a man make her come, except one, the one she's currently in bed with, is, by definition, not a slut."

"Okay," I agreed quickly, mostly because of the look on his face and his tone.

Normally, I would have begged to differ, seeing as I had a nonexclusive boyfriend I had yet to officially break up with and I was currently naked in bed with Jacob which I thought, by definition, nonexclusive or not, was pretty slutty. But I was sensing (accurately) that now was not the time to debate that point.

Then again, the look on his face, it was more likely never would there be time to debate that point.

"We might have to talk about him seein' as you're a witness, him givin' you that ring. So, they don't confess, that shit goes to trial, this isn't done for you. But, if we're not talkin' about the case—not him, the case—he doesn't come up at all. You with me?"

I was with him. This annoyed him. So Jacob could be seriously bossy and bossily serious, the second one when discussing my criminal, very-soon-to-be official ex-boyfriend.

So I should likely avoid that.

"I can do that," I told him.

"Good," he muttered.

"You heat your pool," I blurted to change the subject, and his brows drew together.

"What?"

"You say I heat my mountain. You heat yours too," I informed him.

"Yeah. Difference is, I got the money to afford it."

Him having his big mostly mansion that had nothing to fix and was all perfect, I figured he was not wrong.

"It's environmentally unconscious," I pointed out.

He stared at me then pressed his head back into the pillows and looked at the headboard, muttering, "Here we go."

"It is," I pushed.

He looked back at me. "Babe, I don't give a fuck."

"Well, I do. You should turn off the heat when you're not using it."

"I turn off the heat, I want to use it, it takes hours to heat it, by that time I'm over wantin' to use it."

"Then you should put a cover on it," I went on.

"It doesn't look as good with a cover on it," he replied, and I felt my brows go up even as I pushed up and glared down at him.

"You're destroying the environment for cosmetic purposes?" I asked.

"Yeah," he answered indifferently.

"That's irresponsible."

"It's my money."

"You're a citizen of this earth just like me, Jacob Decker. It isn't about money. You're accountable to future generations."

He grinned. "That's a lot of folks, Emmanuelle. I hope I die before they incarcerate me for my pool heating irresponsibility and I have to stand trial in front of an angry environmental mob."

I hated it about as much as I loved it (the second part after it was over, of course), when Jacob started teasing when we were debating.

But while we were doing, it was all about hating it.

"Don't be flippant," I snapped.

"I'm not. I'm just waitin' for you to want to use the pool and then you won't be bitchin' about it bein' heated."

"A cover is a good compromise," I noted.

"Not if I don't like the way it looks."

I shut up and stared at him, knowing he was enjoying this. Therefore it could go on for hours as it had in the past, so I would get nowhere, which was where I got in the past.

Therefore, when I spoke again it was to say, "Let's not argue."

Suddenly, he rolled me so he was pressed into my side and also on me and his handsome, morning-stubbled face was close.

God, he was beautiful. His weight was heavy, his body strong, warm. And those eyelashes.

Amazing.

"No, baby," he murmured, lips tipped up. "Let's argue so we can make up."

This gave an interesting slant to our sometimes-heated debates that I suddenly had a hankering to try out.

His body started shaking but before I could see his laughter on his face, his head dipped and he ran his lips up my jaw to my ear.

"I gotta get my girl in the shower so I can get her home and install her insulation."

My breath was coming fast but I still managed to say, "Buford's riding with me."

His head came up. "You're riding with me and Buford's stayin' here. He gets out there and catches a scent of something in those woods around your house, we won't see him for a year."

My head cocked on the pillow. "Really?"

"He's a bloodhound, Emme. Yeah. Really."

"So does that mean he can never come over?"

"No, that means he can't come over when I'm installing insulation and can't pay attention to what he's doin' when he's out."

"Oh."

Jacob grinned. "Love it that you like my dog."

I looked to the side and saw Buford's paws stretched out on the floor by Jacob's side of the bed, the rest of him I couldn't see. He'd ceased his bed-hogging activities when Jacob woke me up to make love to me. Now he appeared to be taking a snooze.

I looked back at Jacob.

"He's likable."

He grinned, bent his head and kissed me. He didn't do it long but it tasted and felt fantastic. Kind of like the first time (and all the times besides) except without me losing my mind and my control and having the best sex of my life (by far).

When he lifted his head, I asked, "Why am I riding with you?"

"'Cause you're sleepin' here tonight and since you are, no reason for us to take two vehicles."

My heart tripped. He wanted me back. And soon. Which would mean more sex with Jacob. And soon. And just more time. And lots of it.

I liked that.

"I am?"

"Buford needs company and he can't come over so you're comin' back."

"Okay," I agreed.

"Tomorrow night, after we go out on a proper date, we still end up pickin' up my dog and goin' to your place or not pickin' him up and stayin' at mine."

A proper date. I liked that too. I hadn't had many of those and none with Jacob.

And more time.

I liked that better.

And hopefully, since one or the other of us was spending the night, more sex.

"Okay," I repeated.

He studied me before remarking, "You're docile in the morning when you're not talking about pools."

He was wrong. Usually I was somewhat grouchy in the morning.

But I was docile in the morning when I had back-to-back orgasms I didn't have to give myself. And, incidentally, I'd never had back-to-back orgasms at all and having had them, my guess would be they'd make anyone docile.

"Let's not talk about pools," I suggested and got another grin.

Then I got another kiss.

After that, I got pulled out of bed, across a room and into a shower.

*   *   *

Two hours later…

I was sitting in my family room surrounded by women with the addition of rollicking children.

This was because, up in my attic, nine men and one woman were laboring. Those men not Jacob were named Chace (I knew him at least), Max, Tate, Ty, Reece, Deke, Bubba and Wood. The woman there was named Twyla.

They were all brawny (Ty especially, that guy was *huge*; and, not in a mean way, but it must be said, Twyla was brawny too). They were all handsome (not as handsome as Jacob but they were definitely on the mouthwatering end of the good-looking spectrum, and even a masculine woman, Twyla, was not hard to look at either, if you didn't count her lady mullet). And there were a lot of them, thus it was likely my insulation under the roof of a sprawling mansion would take about an hour to install.

The thing was, they brought their women with them.

I did not know this was going to happen. And when trucks and SUVs started rolling into my vast circular drive (something I was lucky to have seeing as it fit all those trucks and SUVs), I noticed that Jacob, standing next to me with his arm flung around my shoulders, scowling, didn't know these men were bringing their women either.

And he didn't like it.

At first, I thought that was weird.

Then, I thought it was wonderful.

I thought that when Faye and Lauren jumped down from their respective husbands' SUVs (those being Chace Keaton and Tate Jackson), Jacob's lips found my ear and he said, "Say the word, I'll have a word and move the women out. I know you aren't big on socializin' and I got a bad feelin' about this 'cause got more men who have women comin'. You don't want company, I'll deal with it."

I loved it that he knew that about me and I loved it that he was willing to move to protect me.

But it wasn't that I wasn't big on socializing. It was that I wasn't very good at mingling. Small talk did nothing for me. Connecting in a vague way that was meaningless left me cold.

This was why, back when Jacob was with Elsbeth, he and I almost always ended up during a party or after dinner (or during dinner, even with people around us) holed up away from everyone else, or focused on each other, deep in a conversation or in the throes of a heated debate.

On that memory, it hit me in a way it didn't hit me when he brought it up that Jacob was kind of right. He was with Elsbeth but I'd never seen him deep in conversation with her and definitely not in the throes of a debate. Their relationship was close, affectionate and loving (a painful memory that wasn't less painful now, alas), but there were parts of it that weren't deep.

Those parts, Jacob had, as far as I could tell, only with me.

And I had the close, affectionate and loving bits too. Just not in some of the ways Elsbeth had them (until now).

This thought made me dread surprise-hostessing a bunch

of women I didn't know (though, I did want to meet Faye since Chace was a really good guy I always liked) a whole lot less.

I turned my head, caught his eyes and whispered, "Thank you, honey, but I'll be okay."

"Sure?"

God.

So nice!

"Yeah," I assured him.

His arm around my shoulders gave me a squeeze.

More trucks came up my drive.

So now men (and one woman) were up in my attic and I was sitting in my thankfully big family room with a bunch of women I did not know, though I also kind of did. Or, at least, some of them.

First there was Lexie Walker, the fabulous brunette married to Ty Walker. She worked at the spa I went to in Carnal to have my hair done. She did facials or something in the back room (I got my facials with my friend Erika in Denver). I hadn't met her but I had seen her around the spa and said hi. I also kind of knew her since she and Ty had made national news when it was exposed he was framed for a murder he didn't commit by the racist jerkface ex-now-dead chief of police in Carnal (Ty was half black).

The others included Lauren Jackson, a blonde married to Tate Jackson. Both Tate and Lauren were famous too, as they also made national news when she was abducted by a serial killer and her husband saved her.

We'll just say, the county having a gang of thieves hitting houses and using high school students to do it was unfortunately one in a long line of scary shit that had been happening. Thus, I figured, the reason they'd called in Jacob. I didn't know police did that, but, seeing as everyone had been arrested and Jacob wasn't on the job for very long, it was obviously a good plan.

Also in my living room, there was the redheaded Faye Keaton, Chace's very heavily pregnant wife, as in *very* pregnant.

And Nina Maxwell, Max's wife. She lived in Gnaw Bone. I knew Max as he owned a construction company and was a customer at the lumberyard. I'd even met his kids since he brought one, the other, or both on occasion when he was making or picking up an order. But that was business. I'd never met Nina. I'd seen her and Max a couple of times around town, but even though I'd smile and wave and he'd tip up his chin, I never approached mostly because they always were so into each other it seemed like it'd be an intrusion. Or they had their kids and thus their hands full.

Then there was Zara Reece, another blonde, Graham Reece's wife. She, too, was pregnant but not as far gone as Faye. She also just reopened her shop, Karma, a shop I'd visited frequently before she was forced to close it, and chatted with her impersonally when I did. So I kinda knew her too. Her shop, it must be said, I was glad she reopened because it was awesome.

And last, there was Krystal Briggs, a woman with a very large chest and very attractive hair I'd never guess would be attractive seeing as it was a mixture of flaming red with blonde streaks à la Ginger Spice in the heyday of the Spice Girls. But she worked it. She was married to a guy everyone called Bubba who was nearly as huge as Ty.

There were also four children, ranging from small child to toddler, wrestling on my rug. Two were Nina's. Two were Lexie's.

They told me Wood's wife, Maggie, couldn't make it.

For this, I hid being grateful.

They were enough.

It wasn't because they weren't friendly. They were.

It wasn't because they didn't quite hide their curiosity about me. I got that.

I got it because Chace and Jacob were tight, Faye was married to Chace, and these women were close. I knew women talked so I'd be an object of fascination, what with Jacob corralling their men to install insulation, which said it all about how a man felt about the woman whose insulation he was installing. The girls had shared early on in getting cups of coffee and settling in that all their men had helped find Faye during her ordeal, Jacob included in that, which, when something like that happened, was an unwanted but definite bonding ritual and these men had bonded through it.

The odd man out in that was Graham Reece, who wasn't around then. But he was a good friend of Max's so Max figured many hands made light work, especially if those hands are connected to brawny hot guys (though Max probably didn't think about the hot part) and he'd asked Reece to come along.

I was glad for the help, which cost me nothing but beer and chips and brownies (that I'd had just enough time and just enough luck the oven was working to make).

But I was overwhelmed because these women were tight.

I didn't fit in. They had history, a lot of it intense, and it was my experience that a latecomer to that might be welcome but she was never *in*.

And I'd decided long ago, in college actually, when I'd been bit by a couple of girls who were mean girls and were mean to me, that my time and energy in friendships should be saved for only those who deserved it. Seeing as I liked my own company and my life, filling it with people I genuinely cared about who genuinely cared about me worked.

So I didn't know how to do the girl posse. I didn't have a lot of experience with it, by design. And being in a chatty, close-knit one in my own house but still the outsider wasn't much fun.

I wouldn't tell Jacob this. He'd worry or maybe ask them to leave.

So I had to suck it up and deal.

I was thinking this when something weird happened.

And that weird something was, with Krystal leading the pack, all of them set about making me *not* the outsider, folding me in the posse, and doing it genuinely but also *honestly*.

Krystal started this by asking, "How you holdin' up with your uber-alpha?"

I blinked, stared because I thought her question was weird, then asked, "Pardon?"

"The mighty have fallen," Lexie noted, grinning at Lauren, "Only Deke left."

Deke, I forgot to mention, was a big guy with long blond hair in a ponytail. And he didn't bring a woman.

"So, Emme, how you holdin' up?" Krystal repeated.

"I, well..." I started but trailed off, unsure.

"Just so you know," Faye, who'd brought a couple bags of herbal tea and had a mug of it in her hand that luckily my stove was working in order to boil the kettle to make, was talking to me, "Chace is super-happy you and Deck reconnected. He said he's always liked you."

That felt nice since I'd always liked Chace.

Nice enough for me to reply, "Just so you know, Jacob is super-happy Chace found you."

She smiled at me.

"You call him Jacob?" Krystal asked then looked at Faye. "Does anyone call him Jacob?"

"Not that I know of," Faye answered.

Krystal looked at me. "What's with 'Jacob'?"

Until right then, I didn't understand I called him that because no one else did, except my mom and dad, but including Elsbeth. I called him that likely to be outside the pack. I called him that unwittingly creating something between us, an intimacy he shared with no one...but me.

And he never said a word.

This made me feel mushy.

"I like the name Jacob," I told her, and it wasn't a fib.

"It's a nice name," Faye murmured, grinning into her tea.

"Just so you know," I said to Faye. "Jacob is also super-honored you're naming your son after him."

Faye smiled at me again.

"Yes, that's sweet, Faye," Lauren put in.

"Okay, is it just me, or has anyone noticed Emme hasn't

answered Krys's question?" Lexie stated at this point, and my eyes went to her.

"That's because I don't know how, exactly," I admitted.

"Oh boy," Krystal sat back, looking at Lexie, "this is not good."

My gaze went to her. "Why?"

She leaned into me and warned, "Do not let that man walk all over you."

I blinked.

Jacob would never do that. I didn't even know why she'd think that. I'd said nothing that would lead her to that.

"I—" I began.

Faye got there before me. "Deck's an alpha but he'd never do that."

I was relieved she felt the same and verbalized it.

"Bullshit," Krystal said.

My head jerked.

"He wouldn't," Faye replied to Krystal.

"They all try," Lexie put in.

That wasn't good news.

"Is the sex good?" Krystal asked me, and my head jerked again.

"I, well...it...we just started—" I stammered, not even knowing why I was stammering instead of telling her that was none of her business.

"I hope it's good but not great," Krystal remarked. "Sex slave to an alpha. Bad news."

This time my head didn't jerk. I blinked again.

"I'm a sex slave to an alpha and I have no complaints," Lauren muttered, grinning at Zara.

"Me either," Zara replied, grinning back.

"I've had mine longer than all of you," Nina announced. "And I'm of a mind that there will never be a time I complain mostly because it's been years and Max has given me nothing to complain about."

"Don't tell me Tate Jackson isn't addicted to all that,"

Krystal said to Lauren, ignoring Nina and throwing her hand up in the air to indicate all that was Lauren, and there was a lot.

She had to be in her forties but she hit that age in a happy way, lots of hair, biker babe look that I thought was the bomb, a fabulous figure. Tate Jackson was extremely good-looking but he hit the jackpot with his wife, and unless he was stupid, which I didn't figure he was, he would know it.

"This is where things are interesting," Lexie declared. "I would have thought it'd be hard, especially out here without a huge pool to pick from, for Deck to meet his match but he has. I mean, it isn't like there are a bunch of skanks around, mountain girls have it going on, but not Jacob Decker caliber of have it going on." Her eyes pinned me. "That's good news for you, honey."

"Pardon?" I asked.

"You. Are. Hot," Krystal stated, answering my question to Lexie. "That sultry, don't-give-a-damn, I-don't-need-a-man, exotic kind of hot."

Another blink then, "I am?"

"Babe, totally. This is why I'm concerned. You lose that edge, you're screwed," Krystal answered.

It was then I found my mouth sharing (and I didn't know why), "I think last night I told him in the middle of a rant that I was lonely."

"Oh fuck," Krystal muttered.

"You're lonely?" Zara asked, her warm brown eyes holding a hint of concern.

"Well, I got sick a while ago, like really sick, hospitalized sick." I watched all the women get concerned looks so I went on quickly, "I'm okay. Totally fine. It's all good but it wasn't fun to do that alone."

"I'll bet," Lauren murmured.

"Being sick alone *is* awful," Nina declared and grinned. "Being sick around an alpha is a lot less awful."

I found this comment intriguing.

She and Max had been together a while so it was likely she'd at least gotten a cold or something, so she would know. But Max didn't strike me as a care-for-his-sick-wife-with-kindness-and-adoration kind of guy. He struck me as a she'll-get-over-it-I'm-going-to-go-chop-down-some-trees-for-firewood kind of guy.

"Glad you're better," Faye said quietly. "But sorry you were sick."

"Yeah, that sucks," Lexie agreed.

"I'm okay now," I assured them.

"We can see that, *anyone* can see that," Krystal said, eyes moving the length of me in my armchair then coming back to mine. "Does Deck know you were sick?"

I nodded.

"And does he know you didn't like to go that alone?" she asked.

I nodded again.

She sat back, muttering, "Not sure what to do with that."

It was at this point I was beginning to think this conversation was all kinds of weird.

"I couldn't exactly keep it from him. I was sick for a year and we're starting a relationship," I told her.

"A year?" Zara asked.

"Yeah," I answered.

"Bummer," Zara replied.

"It's all good now," I stated.

"Krys," Lauren called, and Krystal looked at her. "I don't get where you're going with this. It's not like you aren't sitting in a room full of women who are hooked to badasses who are doing a little bit of a whole lot of all right."

I was glad to know Lauren thought this was weird too.

"Yeah, I know," Krystal returned. "But, A, it took some head butting, a lot of bullshit and a fuckload of emotion to get you here. And B, no offense, Laurie, but Emme here," she flung a hand out to me, "is different."

"She is?" Lexie asked at the same time I asked, "I am?"

Krystal looked at me, her face was normally a hint hard but I saw her eyes were now soft.

She was very, very pretty.

With that look in her eyes, she was a knockout.

"Babe," she said quietly, "Deck is a good guy. I can't say I know him all that well, but I know he'd do anything for Chace and Faye and he's proved that. A man can be a good friend, the best kind of good friend there is, that means he's a good man. But you aren't like normal women and I've seen a lot of women and the kind I like best is your kind. You got a life. You got a mission, this house. You got your world and your way of doin' things. And a man like Deck can come into that life and make it all about him just by bein' Deck. He wouldn't do it intentionally. With the force of his personality, he'd just do it."

I didn't know how she figured that all out about me.

Maybe she had awesome mental powers like Jacob.

She leaned over the side of the couch she was sitting by and into me before she continued.

"He's into you and, just sayin', he's into you because of all that you got goin' on. Don't lose that because of who he is, how he is, or that he can give it to you like you like it. Don't lose it for you. And don't lose it because, you do, you might lose him."

Fear gripped my insides as my mind reeled back wondering if, even at this early juncture, that was already happening.

"Krys, you're freaking her out," Faye murmured.

She totally was.

"Good," Krystal stated as she sat back. "She'll have a mind to all this and not let it happen."

"You'll be fine. Deck will be fine. Krys is just a little cynical," Lauren told me. "Don't worry, Emme."

Too late. I *was* worried.

So worried, I was immensely relieved when I heard my cell phone ring in the kitchen and that meant I had an excuse to mumble my apologies and hurry out of the room.

Unfortunately, I was so intent on taking the call I took it even though the display said "Unidentified Number."

"Hello?"

"Em."

Oh no. It was Dane.

I said nothing.

"I...Em...do you know where I am?"

"I know where you are," I whispered.

"I figured you did. They said they have your ring."

My ring?

It wasn't *my* ring. I didn't even want it to be *my* ring when I didn't know it was a stolen ring. But it being a stolen ring, it was never *my* ring.

I again said nothing but I did start fuming.

He said something.

"This is my one call. I've been waiting to make it so I didn't wake you or something. I...things aren't good and I fucked up with that ring. I fucked up with a lot. I know you're probably freaked but I need to talk to you. Babe, please, can you come down to the station? I can have visitors."

He wanted me to come to the police station where he was incarcerated and have a chat?

Was he insane?

"Today, I was going to break up with you," I informed him.

"Shit," he whispered.

He knew it.

He didn't like it.

And, I guessed, if he wasn't currently residing in lockup, he would have tried to talk me out of it.

"So, no. I can't come down to the station because we *were* done and now we are so totally done, we've redefined the word done."

"Em, this is fucked up. They don't have it right. I mean they do, parts of it, but other parts—"

I interrupted him, "Please don't call me again, Dane."

"Emme, honey—"

"*Ever.*"

Then I hung up.

I stood there staring at my phone in my hand trying to figure out what I was feeling.

Outside of feeling totally stupid that I said yes to a date, continued to date and let that man in my bed, I realized I didn't feel much of anything else. Other than the fact I was relieved I didn't have to break up with him face-to-face and could do it over the phone during his one phone call after being arrested.

That was weird, insane and made me feel creepy.

But at least it was done.

"Emme?"

I turned my head and saw Faye standing there, watching me closely.

"Hey," I replied. "You need more tea?"

"Who was that?" she asked, still watching me closely.

"No one," I answered. "Tea?" I dipped my head to the mug she was still carrying.

She got closer. "Chace can't say much but I kinda know what's going on."

I didn't speak.

She continued, "That, well, we all, since the kitchen is right off the living room, we all heard it so I know that wasn't no one."

They all heard it because they were all listening. Not a surprise or annoying. I figured that was law for girl posses.

"It's okay," I told her. "It's over. I'm good."

She got even closer and her crystal blue eyes (that were seriously pretty) didn't leave mine.

"He's calling," she said quietly, maybe so the other girls wouldn't hear, maybe seeing to my state of mind. "You should tell Deck."

No way. Jacob got bossily serious about Dane and didn't want to discuss him anymore. I was just getting to know him as Jacob, the man who gave me orgasms during sex, but I knew enough to know he'd lose his mind if he knew Dane used his one phone call to call me.

Not to mention, Krystal was right. I was my own woman

who'd taken care of myself for a long time. This wasn't a big deal. I could deal with the little deal it was, and I didn't need to drag Jacob into an issue with my recently ex-boyfriend he didn't like to talk about.

"Really, Faye," I told her. "It's all good."

She got even closer, reached out and took my hand.

"Okay, this is going to seem weird. I don't know you, but those women in there, I know their stories and I have my own. I know that things happen. And some of them aren't good things. And I know the men attached to those women, what kind of men they are, having one myself. And last, I know Deck. I know the way I saw him holding you and looking at you when we walked up to your house. I know in the time I've known him I've never seen him look or hold another woman like that."

That felt really, really good. Like, blow my mind, make me want to run around singing and dancing, or better, finding Jacob and kissing him hard kind of good.

She kept talking.

"So I know two things. One, it's important *he* knows everything that might be going down around you just on the off chance it might turn bad so he can stop it from doing that before it starts. And two, a man calls his woman, it is not good to keep it from him, because that's sure to turn bad."

It was then I was seeing the wisdom of doing what I could to amass a girl posse who knew how to deal with "uber-alphas" because they could share *their* wisdom.

And because it felt nice she cared enough to take the time to advise me.

But bottom line, she wasn't wrong.

This county had seen serial killers, innocent men being framed for murders and women being buried alive.

Heck, the guy who owned the yard before Dad had murdered a bunch of people and successfully conspired to murder another guy. If town lore could be believed, Nina and Max were involved in this in a bad way, with Nina nearly being a victim and Max rescuing her seconds before that happened. Though, I'd never asked Max about it, seeing as, "So, is it true your ex-friend, the ex–lumberyard owner almost killed your wife?" wasn't idle chitchat.

Now a gang of thieves that were worse than your average everyday thieves had run amuck throughout the county. And I'd been dating one. One who called me from jail after getting arrested for running amuck.

Perhaps I should tell Jacob that Dane had called.

"I'll go tell Jacob," I decided.

"Good thinking," Faye replied on a smile and a hand squeeze.

I squeezed her hand back and realized this might be my shot at having genuine, real, true friends close to home (and a lot of them, shocker!). They'd given all the signs and even if I was the latecomer, they still were letting me in.

I liked that.

I let her hand go, put the phone down, walked through my house and up two flights of stairs to the opening that led to my attic.

There were stairs folded down. There were also two dozen huge rolls of insulation lining the hall. And at the end of the hall, a massive pile of old insulation that didn't look nice, fluffy, pink and clean like the new stuff.

I actually felt my heating bills decreasing, and the warmth wash through me that Jacob was doing that for me, as I called up the stairs, "Jacob? Honey?"

"Yeah?" he called back.

"Can I talk to you a sec?"

"Can it wait a minute, babe?"

"Well, not really!" I yelled.

Five seconds passed and I saw his head appear in the opening, leather-gloved fingers curling around the side.

It was then I noted, even just seeing his head and fingers encased in work gloves, or maybe *because* his fingers were encased in work gloves, Jacob Decker was all kinds of hot.

"You okay?" he asked.

"Can you come down?"

His eyes moved over my face.

Then his head disappeared but his whole body appeared as he climbed down the ladder.

There it was. Proof. Jacob Decker was all kinds of hot and it wasn't about the work gloves.

He had magnificent thighs. They were thick. Pure muscle.

This was a good thought to hold on to (and a good visual to have) while I waited and watched him reach the bottom and turn to me.

"What's up?" he asked.

"Dane used his one phone call to call me," I answered.

After I said that, I took a step back.

This was because his face turned to stone but his hazel eyes started glittering in a way that freaked me right out. It was a look I'd never seen. It was weirdly sexy. It was also totally scary.

Then he thundered, *"Chace!"*

"Honey—" I whispered but he didn't reply or even look at me.

His head was tipped to the opening to the attic.

Chace's head appeared there.

"Jesus, what's happening?" Chace asked upon one look at his friend.

Jacob was yanking off his gloves as he said, "Come down. We need to take a ride to the station. McFarland used his one call to phone Emme and I need him in a room where I can explain that Emme ceased to exist for him the minute his fuckin' fingers dipped in the print ink."

Chace said nothing but his head disappeared. I heard him talking to the guys as his body appeared and he moved down the ladder.

Just to say, he had nice thighs too.

I didn't think on that too hard. I moved to Jacob and put my hand on his chest.

His eyes tipped down to me.

Still glittering.

"Really, I made my point on the phone," I told him.

"And I'll make my point in person," he told me.

"Ja—"

His hand came up and cupped my jaw and his face filled my vision.

His voice was scary when he stated, "Emme. No. Get this and get it now. *No.* I know this guy. You dated him for four months and you don't know this guy. But *I know this guy.* And he needs to get my point *in person.* Yeah?"

My first thought after this pronouncement was, *What would Faye do?*

And I decided by his scary-glittery eyes, his stony face and his even scarier voice that Faye would advise I just nod and agree, "Yeah."

So that was what I did.

He nodded back, stepped back and dropped his hand from my jaw.

Chace broke into our exchange by saying (also in a hard, kind of scary voice), "Let's go."

There it was. I was right to stand down. Even Chace thought this was important enough to get this done and get it done now, whatever it was.

"Well, uh . . . good luck," I said, looking from Jacob to Chace.

Chace was scowling at me, but at my words, he smiled a smile that fortunately reached his eyes.

Jacob's hand came back to my jaw, his fingers dug in and I was compelled to roll up to my toes, which was good seeing as that meant his head had less distance to go when his mouth landed hard on mine. The kiss was closed mouthed, short, but undeniably angry.

Even so, it still felt good.

He lifted away and muttered, "Be back soon, babe."

I nodded.

He dropped his hand and moved away.

Chace moved in. "Boys'll keep working."

"Okay," I replied. "Thanks."

Chace jerked up his chin and moved away.

I sighed, tipped my head back and called, "Anyone need anything?"

"Beer!" was shouted back in a deep voice I didn't recognize. But then again, I'd only been briefly introduced before Jacob put them all to work.

"Fuck, Deke, it's barely eleven," another deep voice said.

So that was Deke.

"I sweat, anytime I sweat, I do it drinkin' beer," Deke returned.

"Beer it is!" I shouted, thinking that wasn't a bad way to go about life.

I hustled downstairs, got a bunch of beers and a bunch of bottled waters.

Then I went back to the girls and hoped that Jacob was not soon going to wipe the floor with Dane in an interrogation room at the Gnaw Bone police station and thus be fingerprinted just like Dane.

The girls knew this was my fear and further proved their genuineness when they had a mind to it and a mind to taking my mind off it.

So yeah.

Girl posse.

Maybe not so bad.

CHAPTER NINE

Harvey

Nine and a half hours later...

OH GOD, THIS was...

Oh God.

"Jacob," I whimpered, taking my hand from between my legs where I'd split my fingers to feel where I was taking his big, wide, rock-hard cock and darted it to lay my palm flat on the headboard to steady my jerking body that was on all fours, taking his thrusts.

This was extreme.

Too much.

But somehow, I wanted more.

"Hand back between your legs, Emme," Jacob, powering in behind me, grunted.

"I can't," I panted.

A second later, I felt him bend over me.

He wrapped an arm around my ribs and hauled me up, impaled on his cock.

Oh *God*. Fabulous.

His forearm stayed around my ribs but he lifted a hand up to cup a breast, his finger and thumb found my nipple and rolled just as his other hand plunged between my legs. His middle finger found me, pressed hard and circled.

My head fell back to his shoulder. I turned it, pressed my forehead into his neck and moaned.

"Fuck. Strawberries," Jacob murmured against my temple. His finger between my legs started twitching and his fingers at my nipple started pulling. My hips jerked, I felt my sex clench tight around his cock and he groaned, "Hurry, honey, need to move in that pussy."

Oh God.

Too much.

"This is . . . this isn't right . . ." I whispered.

"It is. Hurry, Emme."

Another pull, more twitching.

Oh God!

"Hurry, Emme."

"Jacob . . . I can't . . . this is . . . I'm gonna—"

I didn't finish when my hands flew to his as it ripped through me, huge, leaving me raw.

Jacob bent forward, pushing me down. I felt his hand between my shoulder blades so I was cheek to the pillow, both his hands went to my hips, hauling me back as he drove in and I took him, still coming, being devoured by a climax.

I opened my eyes, hands clutching his pillow at the sides of my head and felt his thrusts, the power of his body, the fullness of his invasion, and it came back.

I slid my hand out under the pillow, pressing it against the headboard, rearing back.

"Fuck. *Fuck*," Jacob growled and proved what I thought was impossible—his ability to fuck me harder than he already was, because he did it.

My head jerked back, my hips tipped up and I cried out as it tore through me yet again.

"Keep givin' me that," Jacob grunted, slamming in again and again. "Give me that, Emme."

"Honey," I breathed, still coming, then I listened as he grunted then groaned through thrusts that were no less powerful but no longer had rhythm. They were out of control—*he* was out of control—and it was fantastic.

He'd found it.

I'd given it to him at the same time he'd taken it.

I loved this. I loved that I gave that to Jacob.

I also loved knowing it wasn't me who didn't know what I was doing.

I'd just been with two guys who didn't know what they were doing.

I knew it was leaving him when he planted himself inside and stayed there, not moving, hands gripping my hips, pads of his fingers digging in and there was something about being connected to him like that, held by him like that, no movement, just that.

All that he had was his. My sex. My hips. My body on its knees before him. Just his.

I was Jacob's.

I shivered.

Jacob pulled out. I felt his lips trail across the small of my back as his fingertips drifted down the side of my thigh before he leaned over me.

"Now, baby, you curl up under the covers," he said gently in my ear. "But, want you to know, there'll come a time, later, when you're used to me, I'll leave you like this. You'll stay like this. So when I come back, I can get under you and eat that wet you give me."

That sounded decadent and thrilling and it kind of scared me, but I wanted to do it now.

"Drop and curl up for me, Emme."

I fell to my side and curled up.

Jacob yanked the covers out from under me and pulled them over me. He slid my hair off my neck, kissed my jaw and I felt the bed move as he exited it.

When he disappeared in his bathroom (that would be fabulous bathroom, massive sunken Jacuzzi tub, the room also decorated in creams and blacks with the rich addition of midnight blues), I tore my eyes from their avid contemplation of watching his muscles move while he walked and spied the kaleidoscope sitting on the carved wooden box on his nightstand.

Even as this sight warmed me, knowing and seeing the proof Jacob kept me close, I didn't want my mind to go where I felt right then it was taking me. I was sated. I'd come twice. Hard. And I was naked in Jacob Decker's bed, he was Jacob and he was also a man who could make me come while making love to me (twice).

But seeing the kaleidoscope I gave Jacob so close at hand, my mind went there.

I was happy to live my life disconnected.

Until that day I handed that kaleidoscope to Jacob.

I'd seen it in a shop and thought it was stunning.

I didn't know what drove me to go back and get it when I heard what happened with Jacob and Elsbeth. I just went, found out from a mutual acquaintance where he was staying and took it to him.

Once I knocked on that hotel room door, he didn't make me wait. I knew he saw me through the peephole and didn't have to think about it before opening it to me.

It hurt he didn't let me in but I understood. So I handed him the box, watched him open it, pull out the kaleidoscope and handle it with care, turning it in his big hands.

I also remember thinking, as I watched him handle that stained glass, it felt almost like he was touching me with that kind of care.

You think you lost beauty, Jacob, but you didn't. I'd said and I'd smiled what I was sure was a sad but stupid smile. *Just turn the dial.*

I'd wanted him to know she wasn't good enough for him. I'd wanted him to know I understood she made a bad mistake and he was worth taking any way he'd want to give himself. I'd wanted him to know he could, and should, find better.

I'd wanted to take his pain away.

I'd failed in that.

What I didn't see was what neither of us saw but what Elsbeth did. Right under her nose, he'd found better.

Me.

But when he kissed my cheek, said sweet words to me and closed the door, I walked away.

I didn't try to go back.

I wasn't happy living my life disconnected, especially not disconnected from Jacob. I just didn't realize it and went about my life like I'd been doing before, burying the fact that I'd found the man who was meant for me, and let him go.

Of course, he was my ex–best friend's boyfriend.

But then he wasn't.

And I let him go.

Just then, looking at that kaleidoscope, I knew why.

Harvey did that to me.

Jacob sauntered out of the bathroom, taking my attention again, giving me the opportunity to debate if his front was better than his back (front won because it included his face, which had a hank of hair that had fallen over his eye).

It also gave me a brief but happy moment to study all that was him.

My first viewing was that first night we made love, so turned on, I didn't know a person could get that turned on, watching him at the foot of the bed taking his clothes off, exposing the power that he hid underneath that I thought was only barely hidden.

But seeing it all, he was hiding a lot.

What seemed like miles of defined muscle, broad shoulders, ridged abs, thick thighs, expansive smooth chest, bulky arms and how he was endowed, the biggest I'd ever seen, and also the most beautiful.

Watching him expose it to me, I got even more turned on.

And even just coming twice, watching him walk that power to me right then, I again got turned on.

He joined me in bed, hauling me over him so I was lying on top, flat out.

His eyes came to mine, his head gave a short jerk and his fingers at my hips dug in.

"Emme," he whispered.

Clearly, I was wearing my thoughts on my face, and not the ones about his big, beautiful body.

"There's something you need to know about me," I announced.

His hands at my hips slid up and around so he was holding me lightly as his eyes held mine.

"Tell me," he encouraged, his words quiet, interested, coaxing but not demanding.

Such a nice guy.

"When I was twelve," I started swiftly so I wouldn't back down from saying it, "I was kidnapped."

He closed his eyes and his arms convulsed.

"He was a good man," I declared.

Jacob's eyes shot open.

"His name was Harvey," I shared.

"Em—"

I kept going, talking over him to get it out.

"He'd lost his daughter and wife in a car accident. I looked like his daughter. He went a little loopy, which is understandable, saw me, snatched me from recess at school and took me to his house. He had me three days. He did five years in prison for three days."

"Baby—"

"He asked me to wear his daughter's clothes. I did. I was too young to know that was weird. He fed me her favorite foods. That was okay because hers were mine. He didn't let me leave the house or get near windows. And he cried a lot."

One of his arms wrapped tighter around my lower back, one of his hands slid up my spine and into my hair as he said, "Emme, honey—"

I kept going.

"Outside of snatching me, which was scary, he didn't touch me. Nothing bad happened. He didn't even call me her name. He knew I wasn't her. He was just messed up. Sad and messed up."

"Baby, can I say—?" he started, but I kept talking.

"In the end, he knew he did wrong and took me to the police station himself. When Mom and Dad got to me, that's the only time I knew that something really bad had happened. I mean, I knew things weren't right, I missed them and I was worried about them, knowing they would be worried about me, but that's the kind of care Harvey took with me. Mom and Dad were beside themselves. Then Dad got really mad. If I wasn't so young, I would have talked to them. Told them not to press charges. Encouraged them to get him the help he needed. I was too young. Dad lost it. They threw the book at him. And Harvey took it because he thought he deserved it. He had a daughter. If someone did that to her, he would have done the same."

Jacob's eyes were intent on me when he asked, "How do you know that?"

I didn't answer his question.

Instead, I shared, "But he marked me."

Another arm convulsion but this one didn't loosen. "It would anybody."

"No, Jacob, not like you might think. See, seeing him and how much he loved his wife, his daughter, how much he missed them, I changed. I was careful about letting people in my life. People I could lose. People who, losing them, could hurt me. Even the ones I loved, I held myself remote from, so if I lost them, I didn't allow myself to feel that hurt. Not hurt like Harvey's that slipped over the edge of sanity. *Any* hurt."

My eyes slid to the kaleidoscope then back to him.

"Like losing you," I finished.

His eyes closed again, his arms tightened further and he rolled me so he was on me, weight held up by a forearm in the bed but his forehead was resting on mine.

Then he opened his eyes and they were all I could see.

Concern.

Warmth.

Beauty.

Have mercy.

Looking into his eyes in that moment, I realized I'd been in love with Jacob Decker for fourteen years.

Fourteen years.

And I let him shut the door on me.

"Yesterday," I started on a whisper, "I was angry and I said it was you that had to open the door because I would be a reminder of Elsbeth so that was up to you. I was wrong. I could have opened the door too."

"Emme, stop talking."

I closed my mouth.

"I knew all this. Elsbeth told me."

"Pardon?" I breathed.

His eyes held mine as he lifted his head. Then his hand came up and his eyes watched as he brushed my bangs across my forehead so the ends didn't spike in my eyes.

His gaze came back to me.

"Elsbeth shared that, baby," he said gently.

I felt my jaw tighten before I stated, "That wasn't hers to share."

"No. You're right. But she did."

Outside of her breaking up with Jacob, which, belatedly, was a very, very good thing, that was the first time I was mad at her.

Really mad.

Fucking angry.

"That wasn't fucking hers to fucking share, Jacob," I mostly repeated.

"Shit, you're cursing," he muttered.

"Damn right I am!" I snapped. "What the fuck?"

His hand came to my jaw. "Emme, what I'm saying is, I know this and I know why you were remote. So, knowing it, it *was* me who should have opened that door. I didn't. I took that kaleidoscope and closed the door in a way you couldn't misinterpret and I didn't open it, babe. It was you who came to me on the street and asked me to dinner. You got your shot, you took it and you opened that door."

This was true.

I relaxed under him and the anger ebbed out of me.

He felt it and continued.

"Now, some of the shit you shared makes me uneasy. You got it in you to go over it?"

I didn't have an answer to that because I couldn't fathom why he'd be uneasy.

"Why are you uneasy?"

"Because, at twelve, you were snatched from recess at your school by a man you didn't know who made you wear his dead daughter's clothes, eat the food she liked and kept you away from your family, and you don't seem much to mind."

On the face of it, that sounded crazy.

It just wasn't.

"He didn't hurt me," I reminded him.

"He scared you and marked you, babe, you said both."

"He was sweet," I whispered, and Jacob blinked. "He was sweet and sad and grieving, and," my arms around him got tight, "adults miss a lot of things, so involved in themselves, their lives, their stresses, their responsibilities. But kids don't miss much. I knew he'd never hurt me. I also figured he'd eventually let me go. I knew he was in pain. It was weird and it was wrong but he was kind to me, it didn't last long and then it was done."

He studied me and his voice was very gentle when he asked, "Can you take a moment to think on everything you've said and see why you saying it would trouble me?"

"You weren't there, honey."

"You didn't take a moment, Emme."

I didn't have to.

He didn't know, and with this reaction it was clear I had to find the right time to tell him, and the right words to explain it, that now Harvey was a part of my life. We exchanged emails. I visited him. I'd sought him out because I never forgot him, as I wouldn't, and he'd touched me in a way that might be twisted, but it didn't feel that way to me.

He didn't want me to be a part of his life, not because I hurt him, reminding him of his daughter and what he'd done. But because he was concerned for me.

I changed his mind.

So I'd gotten to know Harvey and why he did what he did. I'd also gotten to know the pain he suffered, the relief he felt at paying for his "crime," and his depth of feeling that I forgave him. And last, I'd gotten to know the beauty of having him in my life knowing he felt the same having me in his.

Not his daughter. He always knew I wasn't her.

Me.

No, I didn't think at this juncture Jacob would get that.

Still, I could remove myself and see why it troubled him.

He was just wrong.

I wasn't going to tell him that either.

"I get why it troubles you," I told him.

"Do we need to take you to see somebody?" he asked.

No way.

I'd already sorted most of it out (obviously not all). And I'd done that with Harvey.

"I'm coming to terms with some things on my own," I shared.

"Emme, a professional—"

I cut him off with, "Let me think about it," then I moved to change the subject, "Can we talk about what happened at the station now?"

We hadn't talked about that. That was because, when he and Chace got back, there were women to entertain and men working. Jacob and Chace joined the boys in the attic immediately.

And I wasn't wrong. It took longer than an hour for the guys to install my insulation, but by midafternoon the entire job was done.

Then Faye suggested we all go eat Mexican food at Rosalinda's in Chantelle and I decided that was a good idea so I could pay and thus repay the boys for their help.

We went.

Jacob decided he'd pay.

We had words.

Everyone (and that was everyone) thought this was hilarious by the looks they gave us, Bubba cracking up laughing and, last but not least, Deke looking at Jacob, grinning and proclaiming, "Dude, you are so fucked."

I quit arguing with Jacob at Deke's comment but commenced pulling a fast one. I said I needed to powder my nose, then caught the waitress and gave her my credit card.

Jacob lost his mind (mildly).

I ignored this and told him if it made him feel better, he could buy me another margarita.

Krystal nodded to me with approval.

Nina, Lauren, Lexie, Faye and Zara glanced at each other with concern.

Jacob paid for margaritas and beers all around (except Faye and Zara had juice).

I could tell Jacob was still irritated in the truck on the way home. So when we got to his house, I turned in the hall just inside from the garage, got up on my toes and gave him a kiss.

He took me right to bed.

He got over his irritation quickly.

Taking us to now.

"I'll give you that play," Jacob said, regaining my focus, referring to my change of subject away from Harvey, "'cause I'm tired, I just came hard, got two outta you, so I don't wanna go there, but more, I don't wanna take you there."

At least there was that.

Then he took it away.

"But we're not done talkin' about this," he warned.

I looked to his chin, knowing he wouldn't let me get off the hook about Harvey so easily, and murmured, "I figured."

"Emme, look at me."

I looked at him and he got even closer.

"What that guy did was not good, it was not right and not just because it was not legal. It was whacked. He paid, which *was* right. It concerns me you've twisted that in your head to make it seem okay. It wasn't. None of it was. You were too young to understand but you're not too young now. It's good and I'm glad you're takin' time to reflect and untwist things, see how that affected you. But, baby, you gotta see that through."

I agreed because I thought that was my best course of action at that juncture.

"Okay, Jacob."

"Okay," he replied.

"The station," I prompted, and Jacob just stared at me.

Then he said, "Fuck me."

"What?" I asked.

"Right, backtrackin' for a minute, I'm lyin' on top of you, both of us naked in my bed. I think you get that what we've just started is somethin' I want to build on, even if it took a long time to start and started a little whacked. Seein' as you're here, naked in my bed, I'm readin' you wanna build on that too. What I need from you is not to be with me and be remote. You're either with me or you aren't, and babe, I'm gonna make the effort to keep you with me."

I didn't understand what he meant.

"Jacob, I'm with you."

"You don't think I know you just agreed then changed the subject so I'll shut up about something you don't agree with me about?"

It was at that moment I was realizing that having a genius as a boyfriend might not be all fun and games.

Sure, he could measure the insulation I needed in my attic not using a tape measure but the power of his mind.

But other times, it was going to suck.

"Honey—"

He shook his head. "I'll give you that play too. Just doin' it lettin' you know that I know you're makin' a play."

I was going to get nowhere with this and I knew it.

So I murmured, "Oh, all right."

"And last thing I'm gonna say about this is, I also knew then and even more now that shit made you live remote, behind a veil, givin' but holdin' back. That shit starts to leak back in, I'm gonna put a stop to that too."

"You know, now you're annoying me," I shared.

"Good, bein' annoyed means you feel somethin' so I'll take that," he returned.

I glared.

He took my glare for a moment then grinned.

"Station!" I snapped.

His grin got bigger.

My gaze narrowed on it so they saw his lips start to move and returned to his eyes.

"McFarland gets me. He gets Chace. He also gets Mick Shaughnessy. Chace shared with your top man at the Gnaw Bone station that McFarland called you and before you knew any of this was happening, you'd made the decision to scrape him off. So he was with us when we shared our understanding that you are done with him so he'll also need to demonstrate he understands that. You hear from him again, like you did today, you tell me immediately. But, my guess, you won't hear from him again."

This was very good.

"What's going on with all that?" I asked, expecting he would shut it down, but hoping he didn't.

He didn't.

He told me.

"Regardless of the evidence, no confessions and no one is fingering the ringleader. The group is tight. There are some indications McFarland is the weak link, not least of which that moron gave you a stolen ring. Their attention is focused on him. They'll go up for bond hearings tomorrow and we can hope to Christ they'll be set high and they can break McFarland before that happens. We'll see."

For the Dane who could be sweet, I felt badly.

But I didn't feel much else.

I took a moment to reflect on this because I'd spent three years working with him and four months dating him, and outside of being creeped out I did the latter, I didn't feel much about him at all.

"Emme, what's in your head?" Jacob asked, and I focused on him.

"I don't care," I told him.

His brows drew together. "What?"

"About Dane. I'm still creeped out about..." I hesitated as a dark look started to enter his eyes so I chose the words, "You know. But mostly, I don't care and I'm trying to figure out if that's me being remote in order not to get hurt or feel other things, or if I just don't care."

"Baby, a lot I'd do for you 'cause you're my Emme, but lyin' naked in bed with you sortin' out your feelings for McFarland is not top of that list."

What he said made me laugh out loud, holding him tight as I did.

When I finished, he was grinning at me.

I liked that so I asked, "You know what I like about this?"

"This?"

"Us."

"The fact that I can make you come while I'm fuckin' you, sometimes repeatedly?" Jacob guessed.

I started giggling again but shook my head. "No. Though that's a bonus. It's because we're working things out, finding our way in a new way, but you always find a way to lead us back to who we were. Taking me to familiar. Making me know I won't lose that. And I loved that. I lost it once, so I don't ever want to lose it again. That's what I like."

He was not grinning when I was done talking.

He was looking at me in a way that made that pulse beat someplace awesome.

Then his head dropped and he was kissing me. Not hard and closed mouthed. Not slow and sweet.

Rough and hungry and claiming.

And after he kissed me rough and hungry and claiming, Jacob did other things to me that were rough and hungry and claiming.

And I came while he was doing them.

Repeatedly.

CHAPTER TEN

Sour in My Gut

DECK PUT THE bowl of food on the floor and Buford stuck his nose in it immediately.

He rose and turned to face the kitchen, seeing Emme, hair wet and pulled back in a wide band, his T-shirt on, no panties (he'd copped a feel after dressing and following her there and made this phenomenal discovery), makeup half on, shoveling oatmeal in her mouth and sipping coffee, doing all this in a hurry.

Deck moved to his own bowl of oatmeal that she'd made him as Emme slugged back some joe, looked down at Buford and addressed a dog with a fresh bowl of food thus a dog who forgot she existed in this world.

"You need to tamp down your instincts to hunt, puppy, so you can come to my house because the drive to work from my house is fifteen minutes and the drive from here is twenty-five and I don't like getting up early so I'm not a big fan of getting up *earlier*."

"Emme, it's ten minutes," Deck pointed out.

Her eyes sliced to him, her head tipped and her brows went up. "Morning sex?"

He grinned. "Okay, forty-five minutes."

"Right," she muttered tetchily as the phone in her purse on the counter opposite him rang.

She glared at it and walked there.

Deck's grin turned into a smile.

Apparently, the orgasms he gave her half an hour ago wore off.

She put down her mug, pulled out her phone, looked at the display and Deck's gut clenched when her face lit up.

Fuck, she was gorgeous.

She put the phone to her ear and chirped, "Hi, Dad!"

His gut clenched again, but a different way.

This time it was just plain *fuck*.

Her face grew confused so this time he verbalized in a mutter his, "Fuck."

She didn't hear him. She was listening to her dad.

He knew what she was hearing.

He forgot, when he was putting the finishing touches on the case, and McFarland was definitely going down, he'd called Emme's dad, Barry Holmes. This was before he knew Kenton Douglas had gone to Emme to question her and get back the ring.

He meant to tell her.

In all that happened, he did not.

Her eyes cut to him and they narrowed.

He repeated, "Fuck."

"Yeah, Dad, I know but—"

She was obviously cut off. Two seconds later, her jaw got tight.

Deck sighed.

He knew Barry. He'd spent time with him at some of Emme's dinner parties. He and Elsbeth had also been invited to their home for their annual Christmas party four years running and they never missed it. Now he knew he never missed it because it was a chance to see Emme. Then he just thought it was because he liked and admired Barry Holmes.

The man came from money, was given it and still, he worked for it. He was funny, shrewd, hardworking, honest, and he loved his family.

He made a mint but when his kids went to college, Barry

paid room and board but his kids were responsible for tuition no matter how they had to go about that. Getting jobs, working for scholarships, applying for grants. It wasn't heartless or miserly. He gave them their tuition back in full as a graduation present. He just made sure they worked for their education so it meant something to them.

They all did.

Elsbeth thought Barry was too hard on his kids.

Deck never agreed.

This was because he reckoned he'd do the same with his kids if one day he had the money but didn't want them to grow up feeling entitled to it, like Elsbeth often demonstrated she felt.

But also because, with his kids, there was nothing hard about Barry Holmes. He might want to teach them life lessons and they might not be easy, but he often told them he loved them, shared wide and in their presence he was proud of them, and the family was close.

And last, even though he could afford country clubs and sprawling estates, his home was nice, large, well decorated, but it was warm and welcoming and not much more than a family of six needed. Just a solid, attractive, family home for him, his wife, two boys and two girls, a brood where Emme was the youngest.

Talking to Barry days ago, he'd called up the fact that losing Elsbeth had meant losing Emme and that had meant losing Barry, his wife, Maeve, and Emme's loving but far-flung siblings (a sister in India, a brother in New Zealand and her other brother lived in Boston). All who, however far-flung, often came home to visit.

It hadn't sucked as much as losing Emmanuelle. But it sucked.

"No, I'm not there because I'm, um…um…" Emme's words brought his attention back to her. "Staying with Jacob." Her eyes were big, pained, totally pissed and still on him. "Yes. Jacob Decker." Pause then, "He's…well, sure. He's right here. We're eating oatmeal."

She made her eyes even bigger at him and if looks could kill, he'd be fucked.

Then again, he was in danger of choking on the laughter he was swallowing.

"Sure, right, he's eating," she said as she made her way to him. "But he can talk." She stopped two feet away. "Yeah." Pause. "Okay." Pause, then softer, "Love you too, Dad."

The soft went out of her face when she took the phone from her ear and extended it to him.

"He wants to talk to you. And after you're done, I'll want to talk to you too."

He reckoned so.

He fought back a grin but felt his lips twitch. They twitched more when her eyes narrowed on them.

He took the phone and put it to his ear.

"Mr. Holmes?"

"Barry. Barry. Son, for years, been telling you to call me Barry."

Emme was pissed.

Barry Holmes sounded like he just won the lottery.

"Right. Barry," he felt Emme's eyes sharp on him at his familiarity with her father which was obviously invited, "what can I do for you?"

"Just to say, going into the office to get things started. I'll be staying today, just in case. When's that bond hearing you were talking about?"

He had explained to Barry what was happening, had been relatively forthcoming and asked him to come up to deal with McFarland should he be bonded out and head to work or even call in.

He did this because Deck needed that man far away from Emme. And that included him getting him suspended from work.

Barry had explained he had all employees sign contracts and he also had extensive employee handbooks. Barry then shared that an employee could be suspended pending investigation or fired outright should they engage in criminal acts, either on or off the job.

So McFarland was fucked.

But Barry was going to handle that particular fucking.

Emme was having nothing to do with it.

"Ten o'clock," he answered.

"Good, good," Barry replied. "I'll have a natter with the boys, look around, visit with my baby girl and wait for your call."

"Sounds like a plan," Deck agreed.

"Now, before you go, I'm standin' outside this money pit my girl bought and lookin' at a big pile of insulation tied under a tarp at the side of her house. Did my Emme get that sorted, do you know?" he asked a question he was not asking.

He wanted to know if Deck, suddenly very in Emme's life, sorted that for his girl.

"Me and some of my boys saw to that yesterday, Barry."

Mental spears pierced his skin. He looked to Emme then quickly looked back to his feet in an effort to hide his smile.

Definitely *pissed*.

"Son, I cannot tell you, she bought this place, so excited, 'Dad, Dad! You gotta come up and see!' I came up and saw. Nearly had a heart attack."

Deck kept smiling at his feet.

Barry kept talking.

"Her mother and I bought that boiler for her, scared as shit the one she had would blow sky high. Tried to pay for the electrical work, she refused it, cleaned out her accounts to do it. I told her insulation was next. She renovated the master bath. I told her insulation was next. She renovated the master. You've been here. You see where I'm going with this. Offered to have it put in, she says, 'Dad, it's *my* house. I'll see to it.' Told her she might as well build a fire in one of her five thousand fireplaces and throw her money in it, not having insulation. Two months ago, she calls me and asks, 'Dad, can you come up and help me get the chandelier in the front room down?' Chandeliers!" he yelled. "She's cleaning chandeliers before putting in insulation? I gave up. I'm glad you got her to see the light. Now we just gotta work on her getting these windows fixed."

"She's getting bids for those, Barry."

"Hallelujah!" Barry shouted.

Deck bit his lip to stop from laughing.

"I'm glad you think this is funny," he heard Emme hiss.

His eyes came up from his feet, his hand covered the phone and he whispered, "Baby."

She stomped out.

He went back to the phone because Barry was speaking but he did it with his eyes on the backs of Emme's legs exposed under his tee from mid-thigh down.

"Now, Jacob, I'm seeing you can make my girl see sense. You get those bids, you talk her into letting her mother and me pay for those windows. She balks, get her to accept half. She balks at that, she's getting a big bonus for doing a good job at the yard, seeing as she actually does a good job at that yard just like I thought she would, but that bonus is gonna be whatever you tell me those bids say. You hear?"

The only people in his life who called him Jacob were his mother, Barry, Maeve and Emmanuelle Holmes, the last three because he allowed it and liked it. The first one because he had no choice but he still liked it.

He was Deck.

Everyone called him Deck.

This was because his father nicknamed him Deck when he was a kid, starting so young, Deck never knew anything but, and his dad, then others, never called him anything else.

He liked the nickname.

But he loved his dad.

Therefore the only time he got sharp with Elsbeth was when she once called him Jacob. He shut that shit down the minute it started. It hurt, she showed it, and she gave him that look every time she heard him allow Emme to use his given name.

But he didn't care.

Fuck, he had a 150 IQ and he still was a dumb fuck.

"Barry, I'm thinkin' that Emme likes to do things on her own. I'm also thinkin', since a lot of shit has gone down the last coupla days and I forgot to tell her I phoned you, I got an angry woman on my hands. So, we'll talk about the window bids later. Yeah?" he asked.

There was silence then, "Son, you best get on that. Emme's her own girl, always has been. So when she gets irked, things can get iffy. Then again, she's always had a soft spot for you so you'll be all right."

The call to Barry days ago had included Barry being surprised as well as delighted not only to hear from Deck but also to know Deck had reconnected with his daughter. Though, he hadn't been delighted at what Deck had told him and Deck hadn't shared how he, at the time and accomplishing this since, intended to connect with his daughter.

"I hope you're right but I best get on that," Deck replied.

"Right. I'll let you do that, just one more thing," Barry said.

"Yeah?" Deck prompted when he didn't give Deck that one more thing.

"I know this question might seem strange but I'm a father, far's I know you're not, but if or when you are, you'll understand me. She's there first thing in the morning. I'm here with the insulation you pulled out of her house. Does this mean good things?"

Deck knew what he was asking.

"By good things do you mean am I seeing your daughter?" Deck got to the point.

"That's exactly what I mean," Barry answered.

It wasn't strange but it was nosy.

He shouldn't answer, but a man whose daughter was kidnapped when she was a child and now what was swirling around her, he felt should have his mind put at ease.

"I don't find that strange and in normal circumstances that should come from Emme. Since you asked and with what's goin' on, you should know she's covered, as in safe, as in I intend to keep her that way. And I intend to do that 'cause she's Emme and I've always had a soft spot for her but also because I'm seein' your daughter."

"Hallelujah," he breathed.

At least he had Barry Holmes's approval.

He still had a pissed Emme on his hands.

"Means a lot, Barry, that's your response. No joke," Deck told him. "But I really gotta go."

"Right. Right. See you in a bit."

"You will. Later, Barry."

"Later, Jacob."

He disconnected and put Emme's phone by her purse. In an effort to give her time to burn at least a little of it out, he picked up his oatmeal but his eyes went to his dog who was sitting on his ass, having wolfed down his food, and he was staring up at Deck.

"Go in and butter her up for me, will you, pal?" he asked between bites of oatmeal.

His dog ambled out, headed in the direction of the master. Deck wanted to believe his hound was smart enough to understand him, but it was more likely he was on the trail of strawberries.

Deck finished his breakfast, ran water in the bowl but left it in the sink, got a cup of coffee and belatedly followed Buford.

He heard a hair dryer, saw his dog on the bed, eyes aimed to the door of the bathroom and he found his girl in the bathroom wearing nothing but jeans and bra, torso bent over, ass his way, drying the back of her hair.

Deck settled in with a shoulder to the jamb of the door, sipped his coffee and enjoyed the view.

The view turned more spectacular when she flipped her hair back. It got even better when he saw the sexy, lacy white bra she was wearing.

Her eyes caught his in the mirror and flashed.

He pressed his lips together.

She aimed her angry eyes at herself in the mirror and kept drying her hair.

Deck didn't move.

He'd discovered, you pay attention and a goodly amount of it, every day you could learn something. You watched how birds flew, expressions on faces, traffic flow.

And how women got ready and went out to face the day.

Emme now had on full makeup and it looked good on her. Fucking good.

It wasn't like back when he knew her before that she didn't wear it. She just wore enough she had a mask on to go out. Emme was all about the mask, and makeup was just part of it. But it was clearly something she did as habit. Not something she enjoyed.

As with a lot of things about her, that changed. Her makeup wasn't heavier, as such, though there was more of it. But it was far more expertly applied, like she gave shit, not like she had to do it and get it done with.

Same with her hair, which was not only a fuck of a lot longer and had highlights, but had a healthy sheen it didn't have before.

She also now didn't wear a perfume that was a floral scent that was nice enough, though a little overwhelming, like she used to wear. Her old perfume was a perfume for women to like. Not one that would lure a man. The smell and the amount she used was likely another unconscious indication she wanted people to stay back.

Now her perfume was far more understated. You had to get close to smell it. It was still floral but more mellow and musky.

It was a perfume a woman might like but a man definitely would.

Until he saw her on the street just days ago, he didn't give one fuck what it said about him that he liked his women to take care of themselves. Unshaved legs, visible roots, unkempt eyebrows and a thrown-together outfit was a massive turnoff.

The truth of the matter was, the more high maintenance, the better.

It wasn't about perfectly toned bodies. It was a demonstration they gave a shit, not just for him, for them. They had the confidence and energy to trick themselves out and make an impression, even if it only made them feel good. No, especially if it seemed they did it for themselves, because they liked it, because they got off on it, and it wasn't about attracting a man.

He thought that was sexy as hell.

The last few days, he'd struggled with the fact that it was not lost on him that Emme not doing this years ago meant he didn't see deeper what she had to offer nor did he feel how they'd connected. He'd lost time, they both had, because he was young and shallow, blinded by Elsbeth having that without having what was more important.

That said, he sure as fuck wasn't complaining that Emme now had it all.

The dryer went off and she immediately yanked out the plug, turned and dumped it into her overnight bag that was sitting on the floor behind her.

"Babe—" he started, and she whipped around, her hair flying with her and again it was a spectacular show.

"You know, I've had two guys before you. Just two," she announced.

Her eyes on him were flashing fire. Her words making him war between elation that that number was so low and meant even at their ages he had a shot at giving her a lot of good shit she'd not yet had, and distress that all that was Emme was wasted so long and his girl had spent so much time alone.

She went on.

"And neither of them lasted long so I really don't know how to do this relationship stuff. I don't have a lot of practice since obviously neither of those went the distance or, really, *any* distance."

"Emme—" he tried again, but she talked over him.

"But I still know you calling my father about a work issue, *my* work, is *not* okay."

"This isn't a work issue, this is a guy issue," he corrected.

"Oh yes?" she asked, putting one hand on her hip and tipping her head the other way, not a stance any man wanted to see, ever, even if his woman was wearing only jeans and a bra doing it. "So, you didn't phone my father to come up and deal with Dane's suspension and/or termination should he show at work after his bond hearing? And you didn't do that without telling me?"

"I did that because it's not safe for you to be near this guy and I intended to tell you but you got pissed and disappeared, I searched for you, only found you because you were at my house, things got heated then other shit took it off my mind."

"So you did," she stated. "You did phone my father to deal with a work issue."

He pushed away from the jamb, her eyes fired and she took a step back so he settled in where he was, putting his mug on the counter and crossing his arms on his chest.

"I keep tellin' you, I know that guy and I don't want you anywhere near that guy," he said.

"Well, luckily, I haven't gone temporarily and spontaneously deaf every time you've mentioned that so I actually *heard* you say that. But this isn't the same."

"He's that guy and you dealin' with him in person or on the phone is just not gonna happen."

"When it comes to my work, Jacob, you don't get to make that call," she declared.

"When it comes to my girl bein' at work and dealin' with this guy, I do," he shot back.

"So, say, you're out crimefighting or whatever you do and I feel it necessary to make sure you're fed properly because I feel it's my job to see to you, it's okay I infiltrate your secret lair without your knowledge or permission to bring you chicken noodle soup and crackers?" she asked sarcastically.

He was finding it unfortunate she was in that bra that made

him want to trail the lace at her tits with this tongue, those jeans that rode low on her hips that made him want to peel them off, she was cute, funny, and smarter than any woman he'd ever met, which meant she could go head to head with him and sometimes win. And he was finding this unfortunate because he didn't know whether to laugh, grab her and kiss her, or growl.

"I meant to tell you about the call to your dad," he reiterated.

"How about this for an alternate scenario?" she suggested, still sarcastic. "*You* talk to *me* about such things, including and especially if it involves speaking to my dad who's my dad but he's also my boss. Then I decide, or if necessary, we discuss how said speaking to my dad will happen."

"He was happy to know, Emme," Deck informed her.

"Yeah, Jacob," she leaned toward him, "*I know*. He is right now lamenting the fact that I didn't run into you on the street months ago so he could invite you to our annual family trip to Breckenridge and he is currently out buying you your own personal snowmobile. Which FYI, me, all my siblings and brother and sisters-in-law all have at Dad's place in Breck. In other words, not only is he coming up to take care of business that he pays me to do, he's either figured out we're together or is praying to God at the same time doing a voodoo love dance, hoping we'll get together because he's always liked you like I always liked you. A lot."

"He knows we're together," Deck told her.

"What? Did you tell him that too?"

Deck said nothing.

She stared.

The stare turned into a glare.

Then she hissed, "I cannot *believe* you."

"Babe—"

"Don't *babe* me, Jacob!" she snapped, her voice rising and her hands flying out to her sides before she clamped them both on her hips. "I can't believe you told Dad we're together!"

"Is it a secret?" he asked.

"No! But you haven't seen him in nine years. I have, like, *regularly*, and I'm also his daughter, the fruit of his loins, so I think I should get to share with him who I'm dating, don't you?"

The fruit of his loins.

Fuck, he wasn't going to be able to stop his smile.

She caught it, the vibe in the bathroom turned heavy and her voice got low. "This isn't funny, Jacob."

"Emme, you don't want me to laugh, don't rant at me saying shit like 'fruit of his loins' lookin' cute and sexy in jeans and a bra."

He knew that was the wrong thing to say when she closed her eyes, looked away, then turned back and opened her eyes again.

"You are very intelligent," she said quietly. "But because of that, you do not know all and get to do whatever the fuck you want to do. We're talking about my job and my father. Discussing those how we're discussing them and why is not amusing. I don't care if I'm wearing a clown suit."

Yeah. It was the wrong thing to say.

But something struck him about her reaction and this entire scenario.

She was pissed but this was something important that they could work out, even if the dialogue was heated.

So she wasn't cursing like a sailor. She wasn't shouting. She hadn't lost her mind.

She was holding it together, sharing what was on her mind and calling up patience in an effort to get it through to him.

And fuck, he liked that.

He uncrossed his arms from his chest, planted his hands on his hips and spoke quietly in return.

"You're right. You're cute, sexy and funny, even when we're arguing, but you're right. And, just so you know, he knows about McFarland's issues with the law but he doesn't know about your relationship with McFarland."

Relief flashed in her face and Deck kept talking.

"But I don't seem to be able to impress on you I got concerns about this guy, I don't want you to have fuck-all to do with him no matter how that comes about, and I think the fact that I'd go to your dad to deal with him should say just how fundamental those concerns are."

"Okay, Jacob, I hear you, but you need to understand, things that are important to me, my family, my job, my house, you don't make unilateral decisions, act on them and inform me later...or not. You talk to me."

"Point taken," he conceded and she blinked.

"Pardon?" she asked.

"You're right, baby. I acted out of concern but fucked up. It won't happen again."

"You...I..." she blinked again, this time she did it twice and fast, "just like that?"

"Just like what?"

"You're agreeing with me?"

"Yeah, Emme. You're right. I fucked up. I'm admitting it. Shit happens like this again, which I hope to Christ it won't, I'll discuss it with you before I carry a decision forward if that decision affects you."

"I..." she hesitated, "don't know what to say."

"Nothin' to say. We don't have time for makeup sex, seein' as your dad's lookin' forward to seein' you, I gotta drop you at work then I gotta get to the courthouse for the bond hearings. So you need to get dressed and we need to go."

"Can I at least kiss you?" she asked, and Deck grinned.

She was indicating the fight was over and now he could appreciate her being cute and sexy again, up close.

"Yeah," he agreed.

She started toward him, stopped and her brows drew together.

"Why are you dropping me at work? Persephone is here. I can drive to Gnaw Bone and you can go to the courthouse."

"Cletus is stayin' in the garage since you're spending the night."

Her face softened, she liked that idea but she said, "Dad's in town."

Fuck.

"Your dad, your call to make, Emme. But whatever bed you're in tonight, want you to know, my preference is that I'm in it with you."

"I renovated the guest room so Mom and Dad would have a nice place to sleep when they came up."

"Then it's your place."

She held his eyes. "Dad will love Buford."

He grinned again. "And me in your bed."

"Yeah," she whispered, and he knew she liked that idea.

Seeing her room during and before his tour, not to mention seeing her sleeping naked in her bed, he did too.

"You gonna kiss me and get your ass in gear or stand there staring at me?" he asked.

She moved forward, rolled up on her toes, rounded his shoulders with her arms and she kissed him.

Deck bent into her and kissed her back.

*   *   *

Three and a half hours later…

"Hey, honey."

That was the greeting Deck got from Emme on his phone as he was walking out of the courtroom after the hearings.

"How's everything going?" he asked.

"Dad's communing with the men, cracking jokes and generally being his normal awesome. He's happy we're in the black and how in the black we are. He's ecstatic I have new insulation. He's disappointed you didn't drop me at work so he could see you. And he's decreed I'm not cooking tonight, we're going to dinner in town. And just so you know, when that happens, he pays and don't even try to fight him. A couple of my sister's boyfriends tried to do that and it got ugly. So, unfortunately, our date night is screwed but on the bright side, I get to spend time with my dad *and* you, which far from sucks."

He was glad she was having quality time with her father even if the reason it came about was fucked.

But no one paid for his dinner and now no one paid for his girl's. She pulled that shit last night and then distracted him before he could have it out with her.

And he didn't give a shit if it got ugly. Barry would have to deal. And the kind of man Barry was, Deck reckoned he'd get it. But if he didn't, they'd split the check.

"Sounds like you're havin' a good morning," Deck noted as he moved to his truck.

"Yeah," she replied. "How's yours?"

He got close to his vehicle, bleeped his locks and answered, "Judge set bail. After that, shit can go fast, honey. And McFarland had a nice condo and a nice truck. I found a storage unit with a shitload of stolen property in it they hadn't got 'round to fencing but Chace phoned this morning and said the inventory the boys were doin' shows that a lot of shit that was reported stolen was not in that unit. Which means it's already been fenced, he probably got his cut so he could have the collateral to make bond in the form of cash. And that cash won't be in a bank account they can freeze. So you need to go talk to your dad. He's up."

"Okay," she said on a sigh.

"No phones, Emme," he warned. "Your cell only if you know who's callin'. But other than that, your dad or someone else mans the phones. You good with that?"

"Don't you think Dane has enough problems, imminently losing his job being another one, that he won't be thinking about bothering me?"

She just wouldn't get this. Then again, she'd twisted in her head that the whackjob who snatched her from a playground at school was a good, kind guy.

But he saw the photos of her with McFarland. She was affectionate and enjoyed affection. He was over the top. He gave her a stolen ring to press his suit. He'd used his one phone call to phone her, not an attorney, not a relative, not anyone who could do something for him, but Emme to talk about whatever the fuck he wanted to discuss with her, being incarcerated and knowing she knew she gave her a stolen ring.

This guy was bad news. Deck felt it in his gut. He was not the ringleader of that crazy shit. But he was stupid enough to get pulled in. And stupid enough to do something for a woman he was gagging for that would bring them all down.

The rest of that crew, they found out about the ring, if they didn't already know, were going to be pretty fucking angry.

He needed McFarland's focus off Emme and he needed to be certain no other focus turned to her.

Shit like this went warped in a blink of an eye, and people like Emme got caught up in it in ways no one would imagine if someone didn't pay attention.

He stopped at his door of his truck, hand on the handle but turned his sole attention on her.

"I get you don't want to think bad things about anybody, about bad shit that may be comin' your way or about a guy you spent time with, baby," he said quietly. "But I'm asking you if we can end this go-round we got goin' about this guy, and to do that, I'm askin' you to trust me. Be safe and be safe by lettin' me keep you safe however I gotta do that. Now, do you trust me?"

There was a moment's hesitation before she said, "I'm sorry, honey. I'm being obstinate about this and I don't know why. Maybe denial."

"How about you don't think about it, let me think about it, and you just go about your day. Yeah?"

"It's…it's…this is really cool of you, Jacob," she said, her voice now soft. "We just started. We should be about fun stuff, not you having Dane always in your face. This is a pain and—"

"Babe, just starting or not, this isn't a pain. You're in my life, when it comes to you, this is my job. You get a good man, he'll think of it that way. And he won't give a fuck it's a pain."

To that he got nothing.

So he called, "Emme?"

"I really like you," she whispered, and he closed his eyes as her words made his blood heat.

He opened them and yanked open his door.

"I really like you too," he replied.

"I'm glad." She was still whispering.

"Go talk to your dad," he ordered.

"Okay, honey. When are you coming 'round and are you bringing Buford or going back for him after dinner?"

"Your dad know I'm spending the night?"

"Yes, and please don't worry about that. I'm thirty-four. He's not stupid. He's got three other kids older than me and has been through this before prior to them being seriously dressed up in a church. Not to mention, he thinks you can draw up the plans in your mind for a spaceship that can get us to Mars in four hours not four years and at the same time go three rounds with Mike Tyson and best him. He's not got a problem with you spending the night."

As she was speaking, he'd angled in his truck and closed the door.

Well before she was done, he was smiling at his steering wheel.

"Good to know," he murmured then said, "Don't want Buford ambling around your house alone first time he's there. Also don't want him to sit in a cold truck while we're eatin'. I'll swing back by my house after dinner and get him."

"All right."

"Gonna let you go."

"Okay, honey. Talk to you later."

"I'll be at your house around four thirty."

"Works for me."

"Good, baby. See you then."

"Okay, Jacob. 'Bye."

"Later, honey."

He disconnected with a smile still on his lips and he was about to toss his cell on the seat beside him when it rang.

The display said "Lee Nightingale calling."

He put the phone to his ear. "Lee."

"Yo, Deck. You got time to talk?" Lee replied.

"Yeah," Deck answered, settling back, eyes scanning the area outside his windshield, attention on the phone.

"Did what you asked, set Hector on it, got a verbal report this morning," Lee told him.

"Give it to me," Deck invited.

"Harvey Feldman. Sixty-one years of age. Did a nickel for kidnapping, refused to be considered for parole. Did the whole run, his decision. Got out, did his stint in a halfway house. Got a job. Got a house. House paid in full now. Car paid in full. Bills paid on time. Taxes filed on time. Goes to work on time. No sick days. Stellar performance evaluations. Well liked at work. Not a loner. Goes out for drinks with the boys. Looks after his neighbor's cat when she's on vacation. Mows his other neighbor's yard 'cause she's eighty-nine and refuses to go into a nursing home. Described as kind of quiet, but friendly, and kind. Although not a loner, never remarried. No one's ever seen him even datin'. Puts money in a 401K that'll mean his retirement will be comfortable but he won't be in the lap of luxury."

Deck didn't have a good feeling about this.

Too perfect.

And it fit something Emme said in a way he didn't like.

"There more?" he asked when Lee stopped talking.

"Yeah. Hector said Harvey Feldman is the most boring assignment I've given him and he says you now owe him too."

Deck didn't smile.

Instead, he noted, "Squeaky clean. Hector get eyes on this guy?"

"Yeah," Lee answered.

"What's the vibe? He report that?"

"Outside of the job being boring, no. And if Hector got a

vibe, he'd report it. Regular Joe outside of out of the blue once kidnapping a twelve-year-old-girl. Got no priors to that, no problems after. Not even a parking ticket."

"I don't like this," Deck muttered, unable to put his finger on why he didn't.

"You wanna clue me in on who Emmanuelle Holmes is to you?" Lee fished.

"She's in my bed," Deck gave it to him.

"This guy make an approach to her?" Lee asked, his tone, usually alert, was now more so.

Then again, Lee was married, he loved his wife, didn't mind people knowing it, so he'd get a man looking into the kidnapper of the woman in his bed.

"Not that I know of."

Her words came to him.

And Harvey took it because he thought he deserved it. He had a daughter. If someone did that to her, he would have done the same.

She called him Harvey like she knew him.

He'd asked how she knew that about the man, she hadn't answered. Something was not right, and it wasn't just how Emme had twisted all that to okay in her head.

She'd laid it out, surprisingly honestly.

But this evasiveness was why he didn't ask her straight up if she had some current connection with Harvey.

She was figuring things out, untwisting what she had twisted in her head, emerging from behind the veil, letting him in. He didn't want to trip a trigger when she was working on all that, a trigger that might drive her away.

Especially if there wasn't something to worry about.

But he had a sick pit in his gut telling him there was something to worry about and, until he knew what it was, to avoid tripping that trigger and in order to form a plan on how to deal with it before he approached her about it, he couldn't broach it with Emme.

"I'm goin' to Denver, tomorrow or next day. I'm settin' up

eyes on his house," Deck told Lee. "You got another marker, you let me send those feeds to your control room and your boys keep an eye on that house."

"No marker, men in that room 24/7, Deck. We can do that, not a problem. I just gotta know what you're lookin' for."

"I also want ears on his phone. Don't give a fuck about anything he does, says or who he talks to, except Emme phonin' him or goin' for a visit."

"She's visiting him?" Lee asked.

"Don't know. Got sour in my gut, though, so I just gotta go with it until I can work it out."

Lee Nightingale understood that sour in your gut.

This was why he said, "Let us know when you're in Denver. I'll ask Vance to go out and help you with the feeds."

"Obliged."

"In the meantime, we'll get into his phones."

"Thanks, Lee."

"Again, not a problem. Later, Deck."

"Later."

They disconnected but Deck didn't turn on the ignition or throw his phone aside.

He tapped it on the steering wheel and looked straight ahead, unseeing.

It was coming to her, what that whackjob wrought when he took her, how she'd slipped behind that particular veil, breathing but not living, not connecting. Twenty-two years later, it was coming to her.

But she seemed entirely calm and unaffected when she talked about the kidnapping, only concerned that what she was learning it did to her cost her time with him.

She showed no fear whatsoever when it came to Harvey Feldman.

Deck had taken two contracts where he'd tracked, and rescued, kidnapped kids.

He'd also worked a situation with Chace that led to two kidnapped kids.

They were not calm and unaffected in the slightest.

That sour feeling in his gut, he pulled his thoughts out of that shit, tossed his cell aside, turned on his truck and guided it into traffic.

He drove three blocks.

Then he positioned.

* * *

Forty-five minutes later...

Deck stood, ass and shoulders to his truck, feet out in front of him, ankles crossed, arms crossed, shades on, eyes to the door.

The crew came out one by one.

McFarland was the fourth one out.

Deck had no interest in the rest but McFarland felt his gaze from twenty yards away and looked immediately to him.

Deck didn't move. Not his shades. Not a muscle.

McFarland looked to the ground, jaw tight, pissed off and hustled to a black SUV that was idling outside the jail.

He got in and took off.

Deck watched him go.

Only then did he get back in his truck and drive away.

* * *

Late that night...

Deck's eyes opened.

Emme was sprawled half on him, dead weight, where he'd put her when he was done with her and where she'd stayed.

The guest room was at the other end of the hall. Still, when he did her, he had to do it with his mouth on hers nearly the whole time, stifling her mews, moans, whimpers and, finally, cries.

Not to mention using her mouth to smother his groans.

The moonlight was coming in through her sheers, something he liked even though it was possible heat was escaping her windows, heat the curtains would trap. Still, the house was warmer and it was likely the boiler didn't have to work as hard to make it that way.

She still needed new windows.

She was naked, something he asked for and got. Taking back that memory of McFarland leaving her that way, making that his.

He was awake because he didn't sleep much. Usually when this happened, he got up, worked out, went for a run in the dark, worked or read. The last couple of nights with Emme, he lay with her cuddled close and let his mind wander. This was not an issue, he'd done that plenty in his years of short sleeps. It was just better with Emme's strawberry in his nostrils, her soft body tucked close.

Now he lay with her but he was unsettled.

This was because, even with the nonverbal warning Deck gave him by standing outside the jail, McFarland had gone right home to his truck then right to the lumberyard.

He was met by Barry Holmes, and according to both Barry and Emmanuelle, Emme didn't even see him.

Barry suspended him without pay pending the outcome of the investigation of the charges filed against him. He'd be terminated officially when he went down, but the deed was done. He was gone.

Barry also told him he would be officially terminated if he got anywhere near lumberyard property or anything associated with it, including vehicles, clients or employees.

McFarland took this and went away.

But it didn't say good things he ignored Deck's multiple warnings as well as Shaughnessy's.

It was partly about keeping his job.

But Deck reckoned it was mostly about Emme.

Knowing he wouldn't sleep and his mind too cluttered to enjoy lying there with his girl, he carefully slid out from under her. She curled around a pillow as he angled out of bed.

"Stay," he murmured when Buford's head came up.

Emme had a king-size bed. He had a California king but Emme's bed was far from small. Even so, looking at the bed, Deck and Emme had been taking a quarter of it. His hound had claimed the other three.

Buford put his head back down on a groan. Deck reached out over Emme and ran a hand down his dog's side. That got him a quieter groan.

He went to his bag, yanked out a pair of pajama bottoms and a thermal, tugged them on then rooted around for his book. Nabbing it, he moved back through the room, a room he still found it hard to believe Emme refinished by herself.

The floors had been sanded and restored, now gleaming. The same with the woodwork and mantel. Beamed wood ceilings, the wood cleaned and polished. Reskimmed walls, painted a soothing light green.

The furniture in there was not modern or antique. It was welcoming and comfortable with a bent to feminine. Two overstuffed easy chairs angled in a corner with ottomans and a table close at hand with a silver-based lamp. Heavy glass-based lamps on the nightstands by the bed. Soft cream sheets with green stitching. Downy, green-colored comforter cover. Warm woods all around, but with carving and scrollwork that gave it femininity and personality. Thick woven large area rugs on the floors, delicate patterns in them reflecting the room's colors.

Nothing in your face. It was subtle. Attractive. Inviting. It wasn't a room you slept in. It was a room you spent time in.

All created and chosen by Emme.

It was so remarkable she did this all on her own, it was almost humbling.

He liked that.

He also liked her room.

Maybe when they were deeper in their relationship and she was used to him and his sleeping patterns, he'd leave her in bed, go to one of those chairs, turn on that lamp and read with her close.

Maybe, if she could sleep through the light, he wouldn't leave her at all, turn on the lamp by the bed and read with her curled into him.

He'd have to explain his sleep and ask.

He hoped she was up for the latter.

But now was not that time.

Instead, he headed to the family room to read but changed paths when he saw a light coming from the kitchen.

He wasn't surprised to see Barry sitting at the kitchen table with a mug of coffee in front of him, robe on, slippers on his feet.

And he was again reminded that even as smart as he was, he could be dumb.

Barry, not a young man, was still a handsome one. Dark hair now densely silvered with gray. Dark brown eyes. Fit body. Not brawny. Not lean either. Tall.

His wife, as displayed in pictures in their house, had been stunning and given her eyes to both her daughters. When Deck met her, she could still turn heads.

And all their kids were the same, save Emme way back when, who was, she just didn't show it.

Nor did Deck look for it.

Seeing Barry up late, drinking coffee and appearing reflective, Deck knew why.

Deck had not only shared that McFarland was an employee run amuck. He'd also carefully shared that he might have an unhealthy fixation on Emme. He had not, however, shared that Emme was seeing McFarland. Making that decision, which had turned out to be a mistake, was hers to share with her father and her boss.

When he came in, Barry's eyes came to him and Deck asked, "Can't sleep?"

"Father's intuition," was Barry's reply.

Deck nodded and joined him at the table.

"Get you a cup?" Barry asked, tipping his head to his.

"I'm good," Deck declined.

Barry nodded, put his eyes to his cup and lifted it to his lips.

Only when he put it down did his eyes go back to Deck and he noted, "I'm feeling I'm missing something in all this."

His father's intuition was on the mark.

"Emme was not pleased I didn't give her the opportunity to share direct with you something like this was happening with one of your employees," Deck told him. "If something's missing, this morning I promised to let her share that or discuss it with her before it's shared."

"So I'm missing something," he surmised.

"Askin' you not to put me in this spot, Barry," Deck replied softly. "Ask your daughter."

Barry nodded and looked to the dark window over the kitchen sink. He couldn't see anything out that window, but Deck knew he wasn't really looking.

"Why are you up, son?" he asked the window.

"Sleep four hours a night. Use the extra time to do shit I don't have time to do during the day." Barry looked back at him and Deck tapped the book he'd put on the table. "Thought I'd read awhile."

"Don't have to keep me company if you don't like," Barry told him.

"Don't have to keep you company if you don't want me to," Deck replied, and Barry shook his head.

"Liked you the minute I met you, Jacob. Liked you and liked how you were with my girl. Never quite understood why Elsbeth ended things with you. Maeve said she was plum stupid. I agreed. It appears things work out the way they're meant to be, or at least that's my hope. Bottom line, nice to spend time with you again seeing as I enjoyed having that opportunity occasionally back in the day."

"Sentiments returned, Barry."

"But if you break my daughter's heart, I'll break you."

Deck's head jerked at this swift turn in their conversation.

"Know how sharp you are," Barry continued. "Don't know

what you do for a living but I suspect it's interesting. But money goes a long way, I got a lot of that, and you hurt my girl, I'll use everything I got to hurt you back."

"Barry, this isn't—" Deck started to assure him.

"She's different," Barry whispered, and Deck shut his mouth at the pain and worry stark in Barry's eyes.

Old pain and worry. Etched there. Hidden by strength of will. Exposed now for a purpose.

"I know what happened to her," Deck told him quietly, hoping to ease the burden and not make him say those words out loud.

But he'd find with what Barry said next there was no way to ease this burden.

"Man lives three days not knowing where his daughter is," Barry replied. "Three days not knowing if she's eating. Not knowing if someone's touching her. Not knowing if she's dead in a ditch. Torture, Jacob. Utter torture made worse by looking at my wife, my boys, my other little girl, knowing they have the same thoughts eating away their brains. We got her back, we went on but we never recovered. You don't. You don't forget that feeling. You wake up tasting it in your mouth and you go to bed and send your thanks to God you got through the day and she's somewhere you know where she is, sleeping safe."

"I can't imagine, Barry, and I don't want to," Deck said truthfully, holding his eyes.

"No. You don't. But what I'm saying is, not one thing is going to harm my baby girl. Not again. I like you, Jacob. I respect you. I got the feeling you're a good man, and I'm rarely wrong about that. And she likes you too, a great deal, years ago, but now, it's a whole lot more. So if you hurt her, I will break you."

"Again, I know what happened to her. You don't know me well but I'll tell you straight. I would not be at this table with you coming from where I just came from, knowing what I know Emme endured, knowing the woman your daughter is, how I feel about her, taking us where we are and leading us where I want us to be if I wasn't very serious about being on that path."

Barry's gaze didn't waver from Deck's for long moments before he nodded.

"You'll take no offense," Barry stated, ending it.

"Absolutely," Deck agreed.

He should have expected it just because Barry was the man he was. And that was a man who loved his daughter and took care of her no matter what her age. In other words, he argued about the bill that night and only backed down when he took a good look at Deck's expression and the bulk of his frame. But when he backed down, he did it only slightly.

He was a man like Deck. No one paid for his meal. No one paid for his girl.

They split the bill.

Barry kept talking.

"As her father, I got to let her be free to live her life, make her decisions and make her mistakes. As her boss, the same. As both, I got to give her the freedom to share about her decisions or her mistakes if she feels she needs to do that. Emme's her own girl, and I reckon you had an interesting conversation this morning but tonight you both made it clear there are no hard feelings. I appreciate the respect you're giving her by making a promise and keeping it. But as just her father sitting at three thirty in the morning at her kitchen table with the man who's making my baby girl his, I got to know how worried I need to be about what I don't know."

"I'm not a father. I can't answer that. But I reckon whatever I say is not going to make you worry any more or less than you already are. The only thing I can tell you is I've shared my concerns with the right people, including Emmanuelle, and she's got a lot of eyes on her, including mine. That's all I have to give now, Barry, and I hope you can accept that."

Barry sighed before he stated, "I'm getting the impression this is new for you two, so I hope in return you don't mind me cramping your style because I'll be taking more frequent trips to Gnaw Bone, Jacob. Not because I don't trust you. But when it comes to Emme, it's just what I got to do."

"Understandable."

"I'll give you space but I'll be around."

"We'll work with that."

"And, you need me to, you two go on a date or something, I'll watch your dog because he's a cute, droopy bugger."

Deck smiled. "Might take you up on that."

Barry nodded. Then he patted a hand palm flat on the table before he got up and walked his cup to the sink.

He turned around and declared, "Maeve tells me she has nightmares about this kitchen."

"I don't doubt it," Deck replied, still smiling.

Barry smiled back. "I'm gonna hit it and try again to sleep. See you in the morning, son."

"Good night, Barry."

"'Night, Jacob."

Barry walked out. Deck picked up his book, turned out the lights and went to the family room to settle in.

He opened his book making the decision to speak with Emme, tell her what happened with her dad and encourage her to lay it out so Barry had the information he needed to focus his attention and his worry.

Then he put his eyes to his book and read.

When the time was right, he stopped reading, switched out the lights, walked upstairs and slid back into bed with Emme, woke her gently then proceeded to do things to her where he had to use his mouth to stifle the noise.

CHAPTER ELEVEN

Give-and-Take

DECK HEARD HIS garage door go up and he grinned at his stove.

And he was grinning because he gave Emme a remote.

He heard claws on the floor then he heard a door open.

After that, he heard Emme's voice, crying, "Hey, puppy!" and his grin turned into a smile.

At hearing that, it was not lost on Deck that he could hear that same thing every night, Monday through Friday, heralding Emme was home. Her smile and eyes over dinner. Later, her body in his bed.

This would absolutely not suck.

On this thought, his smile got bigger.

There were long moments where he suspected there was a rubdown and tail wags before he heard claws on floor, this time coming back, and he twisted to look over his shoulder. Therefore he saw Emme rounding the wall that led to the open-space great room that included dining room and kitchen.

Her eyes came to him, they lit with warmth but she dumped her purse on the bar, slumped her shoulder so her overnight bag fell to the floor then she shrugged both shoulders to take off her jacket and throw it on a barstool.

She then put her hands to the bar and announced, "My dad the father was not pleased his daughter chose a felon to date.

My dad the boss was not pleased the manager of his lumber-yard dated an employee. He chewed me *out*."

He'd told her about his conversation the night before with Barry and advised her to come clean. She told him she would.

She obviously did.

The look on her face told him she might have been chewed out but everything was okay.

Plans that night were that Emme had her talk with Barry then Barry was giving them space, staying at her place while they spent the night at his. He wasn't leaving until after the weekend. Maeve was coming up on Thursday. She was doing this likely because she was worried about her daughter. She was also doing it likely because she was curious about Deck being her daughter's new man.

"Come here, Emme," Deck ordered.

She didn't come there. Her eyes went to the stove and they lit with a different light.

"What's that I smell?"

"Murgh makhani. Pilau rice. And naan bread that's going to become cheese naan soon but it's gonna suck because I don't have a tandoor." He told her and finished with, "But we'll make do."

Her eye drifted from the stove to him. "What's murgh makhani?"

"Indian butter chicken."

Her face got close to the look it got when he slid his cock inside her.

He was about to order her to come to him again when she went on.

"What's a tandoor?"

"A traditional Indian clay oven."

"I'm getting you one of those for Christmas," she declared.

Deck burst out laughing.

When he stopped, she was smiling at him.

"Come here, Emme."

Finally, she hauled her ass to him.

He pulled her into his arms for a quick kiss and when he lifted his head, she stated, "I'm not joking about Christmas. My sister lives in India. I'm going to ask her to send me one."

"It'll probably cost a mint to send it here but, just sayin', it will not go unused."

Her eyes slid to the stove then back to his. "I hope not. That smells awesome."

He kept an arm around her, turned her to tuck her into his side and went back to the stove after kissing her temple.

"I brought my bathing suit," she informed him.

"Won't need it," he informed her.

Her arms, both around his middle, gave him a squeeze and a slight shake.

"Jacob, honey, I want to go swimming because I want to go swimming and because I feel it's my environmental duty to use that pool as often as I can seeing as you're wasting so much energy to heat it."

He looked down at her. "I didn't say we weren't going swimming. I said you won't need your suit."

Her face changed, her eyes drifting half closed and he felt her body shiver.

"And I also didn't tell you, murgh makhani comes with my personal label ale and leads into turtle sundaes," he continued.

At that, her body melted into his side.

"Awesome food, homemade beer and skinny-dipping," she whispered. "Have I told you I like you today?"

"No. You told me you *really* like me," he contradicted, and she did, that morning, about thirty seconds after she watched him come, which was after he made her come.

She melted deeper into him, tipping her head back. "You're right. That's what I said because that's what I meant."

Her body, the invitation of her mouth, her words, he didn't let it slide.

But when he bent his neck to take her mouth that time, it wasn't quick.

*   *   *

Three hours later...

"Fuck, Emme."

He was close but she was closer, losing concentration while riding him, his ass to one of the steps of his pool, water up to his neck, Emme holding on tight, moving through the water, her sex convulsing as she took his cock, something he knew meant she was near the edge.

Something he knew she'd let fly.

He liked that, loved giving it to her, but he was as close as she was and watching her come without taking that pussy was pure torture, and when she lost concentration, he might have her pussy but he wasn't taking it.

So he put his hands to her waist and pulled her off his cock. She cried out as he surged out of the water, taking her with him by bending at the same time, wrapping her around his neck.

She cried out again but this time it was, "Jacob!" as the slap of cold air hit them, her hands grabbing on to him as best she could.

He went to the French doors, threw one open, got them in the warmth and pushed it closed. Then he stalked to the couch.

"Jacob!" she yelled again. "We're all wet."

He bent his back and neck, tossing her wet and naked on his couch. "Don't fuckin' care."

"We're gonna ruin your—"

"Spread, baby. Now. One leg over the back of the couch. One foot to the floor."

She shut up, her eyes locked to his, her face flushed, hair wet, tangled and all over his couch. She opened her legs, throwing one over the back of the couch, putting one foot to the floor.

Fuck him.

Gorgeous.

He covered her, took her mouth and thrust deep.

Her arms rounded him and her whimper raced down his throat.

Soon, her pussy convulsed as she took his cock and her whimpers turned to heated mews.

But he was close too.

And he brought them home together, bodies and mouths connected, her cry mingled with groan.

Magnificent.

*   *   *

Two days later...

It was four o'clock in the morning and Deck was in Emme's library, at her desk, computer on, file spread out at its side, working.

He'd decided that, once they sorted the outside and the kitchen, he'd talk her into focusing on this room because he liked it.

She'd cleaned it, polished the copious wood of the shelves and carved paneled inlays and it was furnished. But there were holes left from the rewiring and parts of the wall that were not wood but plaster had been papered circa 1968 and whoever chose the wallpaper had not chosen something that would become retro chic. There wasn't much of it, but it was so bad, the little of it there was was an eyesore.

"Honey, is everything okay?"

He turned and saw his girl, barefoot, hair tousled and in his shirt, only a few buttons done up, walking his way.

Seeing her in his shirt, he mentally calculated the distance to the guest room, inventoried the library's furniture and decided on the couch and uninhibited noise. No way their sounds would carry up to the guest room, even if her mom and dad were awake.

Still, they'd close the door.

"Things are fine," he answered as she stopped at his side.

Her eyes slid over the desk and computer and he turned in her chair, a big baronial one she said she inherited from her father when he redecorated his office in Denver.

"Come here," Deck murmured. She looked to him, down to his lap, around the chair, hesitated a second then climbed on, knees in the seat beside him, ass to his thighs.

He put hands to her ass, pushing up his shirt and finding no panties.

He started to get hard.

Fuck, he'd had his share of women, but none had made him react like Emme did.

He knew it wasn't all about her beauty, that hair, those eyes.

It was about her going wild.

And it was that her face still registered surprise sometimes when he was giving it to her, she knew she was going to get it, it wasn't going to slip away, and he liked that. It was cute. It was hot. But it was something only he gave her, which was well beyond cute or hot.

It was also, he reckoned due to what they had before, that she trusted him so she felt free to explore, opened herself to him and let him take what he wanted, was comfortable and relaxed so he could guide her there. Enough to wander around without panties. Enough to sleep naked when he asked. Enough to come hard, never be guarded, occasionally expose uncertainty and let him take over and guide her out of that too.

It was just Emme.

"Why can't you sleep?" she asked, and he stopped concentrating on the feel of her ass in his hands and focused on her.

"Told you I only sleep four hours a night," he reminded her and he had, over murgh makhani and turtle sundaes, before the pool, two nights ago.

Her eyes held his as her hands slid up his chest to his neck.

"Is this healthy?" she asked softly.

"Been like this my whole life, baby. Never had any issues with fatigue." He glided his hands up her back, pulling her closer and she didn't fight it. "It's just me. Looked into it, it's not unusual. Other people are the same."

"Are those other people exceptionally bright, like you?" she asked.

"Don't know," he answered, liking also the way she teased him about his intelligence, brought it up often. It was something she understood, something she was not in awe of but that didn't mean she didn't admire it. She did. She made that plain, just in a playful way that meant she wasn't intimidated by it as many people, men and women, were.

"So, are you working?" she asked.

"Yeah," he answered.

Her eyes wandered to the desk then back to him.

"You said you'd never talk to me about your work," she remarked in a leading way.

Deck didn't like this turn of conversation.

Close to her ending things, Elsbeth bitched about this. Mostly the fact that, in establishing his business and reputation, he didn't make near the money he did now. But Elsbeth was not the only woman Deck had in his life, nor was she the only one who bitched that what he did was confidential, he couldn't share, but also, sometimes what he did was dangerous and he wouldn't share in order not to cause concern that was unfounded.

Because Deck never took an uncalculated risk.

And Deck was very good at calculation.

He took one hand from her ass to brush her bangs out of her eyes as he suggested, "Maybe we shouldn't discuss this at four o'clock in the morning."

To that, she strangely asked, "Do you mind talking about Elsbeth?"

He didn't know where she was going with this new conversational turn, but he answered, "No."

"She never told me about your work," Emme shared.

"That's because she also didn't know."

She nodded, pressed closer and continued, "Though, she did say that you didn't make much money doing it."

"Back then, I didn't," Deck confirmed.

"That's obviously changed now, what with your minimansion and environmentally unconscious pool-heating waste."

He grinned, wrapped his arms around her and again

confirmed, "Yeah, Emme, that's changed now. I established a reputation, jobs more frequent, I can charge more."

She held his gaze steady, nodded and asked, "Do you like what you do?"

"Yeah, baby."

"Does it challenge you? Mentally, I mean."

"Yeah."

"Did you know, back then with Elsbeth, that you'd eventually be this successful?"

His chin jerked back but he held her stare.

He never took an uncalculated risk.

He knew.

Elsbeth dumped him because his carefully crafted plan was not reaping the rewards she wanted by the time she expected.

He, on the other hand, did expect it to take time and he'd told her it would.

She'd lost patience with their two-bedroom apartment and not trading up their cars every year like her father had been doing since she was sixteen. Something, even though she also had a job, she expected him to bear the brunt of, like her father had been doing since she was sixteen.

She'd also held off accepting the engagement ring Deck had given her three years in, not wearing it, not making it official, not planning a wedding, waiting.

Then giving up.

And he'd let her. It wasn't like they hadn't had words when she told him it was over.

It was just that he didn't do too much to change her mind.

Fuck.

"I knew. I also told her," Deck shared.

"She just didn't wait," Emme guessed.

"No, she didn't," Deck told her something she knew.

"More fool her," she murmured then the dimple appeared, "but lucky me."

His hands started roaming and he grinned back. "Thinkin' that too," he replied. "Just about me."

At his words, her eyes warmed, she pressed closer and whispered, "Mom likes you."

Maeve had shown that day. Maeve had also cooked dinner for them that night and done it the entire time complaining about the stove, the flooring, the state of the countertops and how she'd probably wake screaming from her nightmares about Emme's kitchen.

In other words, Maeve Holmes was funny, like her daughter. But she did not make Shake 'n Bake.

"I like your mom," Deck whispered back, hands still roaming.

"Can I ask one question about your work?"

Sneak attack.

"Emmanuelle—"

She lifted a hand to his jaw, gliding her thumb along his lower lip and interrupting, "Just one, Jacob."

"You can ask it, baby, but in askin', I'm askin' you, please do not be pissed I can't answer it."

She again held his gaze steady and nodded.

"I don't know what you do, not really. And I may not *want* to know what you do, considering it might be scary."

Again, pure Emme. Not fucking stupid.

She went on, "I probably should have issues with that but I really don't, if you like it and it challenges you. Except one. You're not going to talk about it, you've made that clear. So that means you're never going to be able to share about it, and by that I mean the stresses, the frustrations, things people usually can let go of during a mind dump with someone they care about. Which means you'll likely hide those things from me as well. Therefore, what I'm going to ask is, will you pay attention to how it's going, how it's affecting you and stop doing it if it makes you unhappy?"

Staring in her eyes, hearing her words, Deck's blood heated, his chest got tight and his gut clenched.

But his mouth said, "We haven't had the conversation, but I seriously hope you're okay I fuck you without a condom."

Her head jerked even as she blinked and asked, "Pardon?"

He slid his ass down in the chair, his hands down her back to her ass, pulling her over his lap and saying, "Need to fuck you right now, don't have one, so I hope you're good with that."

Her hips jerked in his hands, her lips parted and he took one hand and moved it between them, finding her wet. At his touch, her eyes lowered slowly, her teeth sunk into her lip, and when her eyes opened again, she didn't open them all the way.

Fucking gorgeous.

"Is that a yes?" he asked, his fingers toying between her legs.

She let her lip go, her hips undulating with his fingers and her eyes attempting to focus. "I'm..." her eyes slowly closed and again opened halfway, "on the Pill."

"Saw your pills, Emme, baby, is that your yes?"

Another slow blink.

Fuck.

Gorgeous.

"Have you always used protection?" she asked.

"Always," he answered.

"Positive?" she pressed.

She was getting wetter and her face was getting hotter.

He needed in there.

"Positive."

"I have too," she replied. Her hips moved, her eyes tried and failed to focus on him, and she whispered, "You didn't answer my question, honey."

He knew exactly what she was talking about and answered immediately so he could move this shit on.

"I'll stop doing it if it makes me unhappy. Now, you good with no protection?"

"Yes," she breathed, more than likely because he slid two fingers inside as she said that one word.

He slid his fingers out, freed himself, positioned and slammed her down on his cock, filling her.

Her head flew back, hair flying with it, then it fell forward. She pressed her face in his neck, and she started riding him.

"What if Mom or Dad comes in?" she asked his neck.

"They won't," he grunted, helping her move, his fingers digging deep, pulling her up and driving her down.

"What if they do?" she pressed.

"They won't."

"Ja—"

"Baby, favor, you're takin' my cock, we don't talk about your folks."

She lifted her head, still moving on him and showed him the uncertainty.

He grinned, took one hand, slid it in her hair, pulled her to him and stopped grinning when he took her mouth.

Five minutes later, he lifted her, still connected, walked her to the couch and finished taking them both there.

Five minutes after he brought them home, hands trailing, lips drifting, hers found his ear.

"What brought that on?" she asked.

"Need a reason to fuck you?" he asked in return.

"No, but—"

He turned his head, caught her languid, beautiful eyes and she stopped talking.

"Means a lot you give me my head to do my job, something I enjoy doing, something that challenges me, something I can't discuss with you and something I know I can now do without you eventually bitching, nagging, wheedling or manipulating."

"Oh," she whispered.

Deck held her eyes.

"Means a fuck of a lot, Emme."

"Oh," she repeated on a whisper.

Deck lifted a hand, trailed the backs of his fingers along her cheek, the corner of her mouth and down her neck before he rounded her with both arms.

"You wanna snooze here while I work?"

She nodded. "I'll go get cleaned up and come back."

He dipped his head, kissed her and pulled them both to their feet. Emme disappeared for five minutes, came back with a thick throw from the family room and stopped at Deck to touch her mouth to his. Then she went to the couch and curled up.

She was asleep within minutes.

Deck worked for half an hour and only stopped to watch Buford amble in, look at Deck, look at Emme on the couch, take half a second to make a decision, then move to Emme and settle with a groan on the rug in front of her.

Grinning, Deck went back to work and did it until it was time to wake Emme so she could get ready to go to the yard.

*   *   *

Six days later…

Deck watched as Emme slid down his chest, her lips moving across it, no tongue, just lips, featherlight, the barest whisper, echoed by her hair which was drifting everywhere.

She moved down and ran her mouth across the ridges of his abs.

Those abs contracted.

Her exotic eyes lifted to his. There was fire in them but not all that fire was about what she was doing.

Seeing it, knowing what it said, his abs contracted again as his chest got tight.

"Have I told you I liked you today?" she whispered.

"No," he whispered back.

"Well, I like you." She kept whispering.

"I like you too, baby."

He watched her face get soft as she smiled, gifting him with the dimple.

"Come here, Emme," he ordered.

She slid back up his body.

When her face get close, he drove a hand in her hair, wrapped an arm around her back and pulled her mouth down to his.

She gave it instantly.

Keeping their mouths connected, Deck rolled her onto her back.

Then he gave as good as he got.

And better.

* * *

Four days later...

"I don't believe you," Emme snapped, the fire in her eyes flashing.

Deck swallowed a laugh and said, "Babe."

She planted her hands on her hips. "Babe? Babe? That's your response? Babe?"

"How's this for a response? Babe, you're just plain wrong," he told her.

"I can't be wrong about an opinion," she told him.

"You can when you don't know what you're talking about," he fired back.

She threw her arms out, narrowly missing slamming one into her avocado fridge.

Buford, lying on the faded linoleum of Emme's kitchen, lifted his head from his paws, gave her a look at her agitated movements then dropped his head back to his paws, getting used to this because this was Emme.

And Emme, being Emme, kept going.

"Gun control laws are too lax."

"You own a gun?" he asked.

"I don't need to to know that's true," she said by way of answer.

"I own seven."

Her eyes got huge.

Cute.

He powered through her cute and kept talking.

"Because of a bunch of assholes, you cannot take away someone's right to own a gun. Or seven of them."

"That's insane," she breathed.

"Why?" he asked.

"Who needs seven guns?"

"I do."

"Why?" This was pitched high.

"Work, and I like shootin' 'em."

"Can't you shoot just one?" she asked.

"Not if I don't have to or I don't want to and luckily, with the laws the way they are, I don't have to so I get what I want."

"Bad people get their hands on guns, Jacob," she pointed out.

"And they would even if they were illegal, Emme. People get their hands on drugs, have no problem doing it, some of them they even order on-line, and they're illegal."

"And therein lies the problem. Guns should be illegal but drugs should be legal."

Deck stared at her in astonishment at this proclamation before he dropped his head and looked to his boots.

"Alcohol is legal," she informed his bent head. "I don't understand why drugs aren't. And think of all the money we'd have for socialized medicine if we could tax the sale on narcotics *and* stop spending huge amounts of tax dollars on fighting the war on drugs."

He lifted his head and begged, "Please, can we not talk about socialized medical care? I like you now and I wanna fuck you later. I don't mind fuckin' a woman I don't like, especially if she looks like you, but it's more fun fuckin' one I do."

She wasn't listening and he knew this because she didn't fire back but also because her eyes were narrowed on the stove.

"Shouldn't that burner be red?" she asked, and Deck looked to her rickety, ugly, avocado stove.

Then he moved to it.

He carefully touched the side of the pot that should be water getting warm to boil new potatoes.

Ice cold.

He then put his hand to the door of the oven where a still very raw beef tenderloin was sitting.

"Fuck," he clipped, and felt Emme come close to his side.

"Have we lost her?" she asked, and he looked down at his girl.

"I think she gave up the ghost, honey."

Emme rested a hand on the edge of the stove and murmured, "She had a fine run, what with allowing Alice to cook all those meals for Greg, Marcia, Jan, Peter, Bobby and Cindy."

Through his chuckle, Deck replied, "Yeah, she did. Though I wish she didn't kick it when I put a forty-dollar piece of meat in her belly."

Her head jerked up. "That roast cost forty dollars?"

"Yep."

Her mouth dropped open.

Deck dropped his to it and brushed his lips against it, and seeing as it was open, he took that opportunity to stroke her tongue with his own.

He lifted his head and asked, "Do you think your phone will work long enough to order a pizza?"

The wonder swept out of her face as pique entered it. "There's nothing wrong with my phone, Jacob. Or my cell phone. Or yours for that matter."

"Good, then get your ass to one of them and order pizza. A large one. I don't care what's on it, just not pineapple. And boneless wings, at least twenty. Yeah?"

She moved away, mumbling, "I'll go get my credit card."

He quickly caught her, wrapping his arm around her neck and hauling her against his body so they were front to front.

He dipped his head to hers. "You get your credit card, I tan your ass."

Her head jerked and she pointed out, "Jacob, you bought the roast. We'll eat that tomorrow at your place. I'll get pizza."

"Babe—"

She cut him off. "The bids for the windows were insane, all four of them, and I just lost my stove, but Dad says I'm getting a bonus this quarter so I can afford pizza *and* windows."

He ignored the comment about her father giving her a

bonus that would just happen to be very close to the amount of
the cost of new windows that came in on a bid from a man he
trusted, namely Holden "Max" Maxwell. Max was also going
to be the man who was going to install Emme's windows even
if his bid wasn't the lowest.

Instead, he repeated, "You get your credit card, I tan your ass."

"Jacob, really."

His arm tightened, he curled his other arm around her and
dipped his face closer.

"I'm not joking, Emme. You pulled that shit over Mexican coupla weeks ago, I didn't like it. There's things a man
like me has gotta do and you gotta let me do them. You don't
pay. No reflection on you and your ability to take care of yourself. It just means something to me. You push this now, I will
turn you over my knee and spank that sweet, round ass of
yours. You do it in the future, you'll get the same thing until
you get it. You with me?"

"Are you serious?" she whispered, neck pulling slightly at
his arm which stayed firm.

"Deadly," he answered.

"You'd hit me?" Her eyes were big and she quit pulling at
his arm.

"Spank you."

"That's hitting me, Jacob," she said softly.

"That's spanking you, baby, and when I do it, your ass will be
bare and it'll end in an orgasm but it'll also end with a red ass that
hopefully will teach you the lesson not to test a man like me."

Her lips parted but her body melted slightly into his.

Fuck him.

He'd half been bullshitting to get his point across, half test-
ing the waters.

Her reaction indicated the waters were warm.

He felt his dick start getting hard.

"You like that idea?" he whispered.

"I'm not sure...I'm not..." she stammered, swallowed and
asked, "Is that supposed to make me do what you want me to do?"

This meant she wouldn't do what he wanted her to do in order to get her spanking.

She liked that idea.

"Rewards can get sweeter, you're good," he told her.

"Have mercy," she breathed, and he smiled.

"You're kind of already getting those, baby, but you want an adventure, we'll take it up a notch."

Her body melted deeper and she repeated, "Have mercy."

Fucking cute.

So cute, he had to bend his neck and take her mouth.

She melted completely in his arms, wrapped hers around his neck to hold on and let him.

He lifted his head and watched her eyes slowly open.

When his face was three inches away, she stated, "Krystal Briggs said I shouldn't become your sex slave."

"Krystal Briggs is not gonna come as hard or as often as I'm gonna make you come tonight, honey, you get your phone and my credit card."

Her head tipped to the side and she asked curiously but hesitantly, "So this kind of thing is about making me mind you?"

"No, this kind of thing is about giving you good stuff you're really gonna fuckin' like. The credit card thing is about me tellin' you it's important to me to do that and you givin' me that. It's not asking much."

"You paid for my insulation too," she reminded him.

"Explained that then, keepin' you warm and liquid."

Her body tightened slightly and she started, "Jacob, this makes me a little—"

"It's important to me, Emme," he interrupted. "It's also important to me you have a new kitchen but you aren't seein' me rip out this old one to give it to you against your wishes because I know I shot my wad with the insulation. I pushed that, you relented, but it's your house and I gotta be smart enough to know when to stop pushing. Insulation was a priority. You've got no stove, but you've got a man who does so that isn't as big of a deal right now as it normally would be. This is give-and-take, you and me. You gotta learn to let me give so that means you gotta learn to take."

"And when do I give and you take?"

"Every day, sometimes more than once, when you tell me you really like me when you mean somethin' else and I know my future includes hearin' you comin' home sayin' 'hey, puppy' to Buford."

That got him a soft look and her eyes fired in that way he liked a whole fuck of a lot but he wasn't done.

"Because of that, for the first time in a long time, that future looks bright. You're not the only one's been lonely, Emme, hoping the right one will come along so you don't go home to an empty house and climb into an empty bed. So you give every fuckin' day, and what you give, I like takin'."

Her body melted into his again and she asked, "You've been lonely?"

"Watched my boy fall in love with a good woman, watched her give that to him in return. It's a beautiful thing, honey. You don't know what you're missing until you have it or see someone have what you want. When Chace got that, I knew what I was missing."

She held his eyes then dropped her forehead to his chest but almost instantly tipped her head back.

"Pizza, restaurant bills, bar tabs, they're yours," she announced. "Big stuff, we discuss, but I'll have a mind to you being a protective uber-alpha just as long as you have a mind to me having taken care of myself for a while and being used to it." She paused, then quieter, "And spanking and taking it up a notch, just so you know, I'm willing to explore."

Yes. Fuck yes.

Emmanuelle Holmes had it all.

His arms tightened around her and he murmured, "Deal."

She rolled up and touched her lips to his.

When she rolled back, she asked, "Will you sort the stuff on the stove while I call in pizza?"

"Yeah."

She gave him a grin and a squeeze. He returned both and let her go.

She lifted her hand between them and said, "Credit card."

He got it out, gave it to her, hooked her around the neck and pulled her to him for a quick, hard kiss.

When he let her go, he got her dimple.

Then he got to watch her ass in her tight jeans as she walked away.

*　　*　　*

Three hours later…

Emme was collapsed on top of him, her face in his neck, her knees in the bed on either side of him, straddling him, her chest pressed to his, near on dead weight.

He ran his hands down the heated, soft skin of her bare ass and whispered, "Tender, baby?"

She mumbled, "Mm…" and fell asleep in the middle of mumbling it.

Totally out.

Deck smiled at the ceiling and wrapped his arms around her.

Suffice it to say, Emme got off on taking it up a notch.

In a big way.

Yes.

Absolutely.

His girl had it all.

*　　*　　*

Five days later…

Emme's arm tightened around his stomach.

"Mm…no, honey, read here. I can sleep with the light."

Her words were muffled since her face was mostly smushed in his chest. She'd just felt him make a move to leave the bed.

She liked him to stay close.

He liked to give her the option.

"Sure?" he asked.

She didn't answer. She was gone.

He carefully shifted, turned on the light on her nightstand and looked back down at her.

She didn't even twitch.

He grabbed his book from the nightstand, shifted up the headboard and took her with him.

She didn't move or make a sound.

One-handed, his other arm around her curled into his side, Deck opened his book.

Buford got up, circled the bed then collapsed on it lengthwise, four legs spread out, his groan sounding only after he was settled in.

Deck watched this and smiled.

His eyes went back to his book, and he smelled strawberries so they tipped down to Emme's hair all over his chest. Her body warm, legs tangled with his, arm still draped over his stomach.

He looked to his dog taking most of her bed then to his girl.

Even as the blood in his veins heated, something warm settled deep in his gut.

This time, he was not going to miss it.

This time, he knew exactly what it was.

This was because he knew he didn't have it totally right.

His girl had it all.

And now he did too.

CHAPTER TWELVE

Bottom of My Soul

Two days later...

"ONLY YOU WOULD grill chops in a fuckin' snowstorm."

Deck looked from the built-in grill on his back patio to Chace. They were outside. They were wearing jackets. They were drinking beer and Deck was grilling chops. It was, in fact, snowing. However, they were covered by the patio's overhang.

"Look at these chops," Deck ordered. Chace looked to the thick pork chops on the grill then at Deck and he grinned. Deck grinned back and finished, "Now, quit your bitchin'."

Chace kept grinning then his eyes wandered to the huge windows and he kept his grin but it changed.

Deck looked that way too and saw Emme and Faye sitting on one of his couches. Emme, unsurprisingly, was talking. Faye was smiling.

Deck had to admit Faye was all kinds of pretty. The mountain girl next door. Even prettier now, heavy with Chace's baby, glowing, happy, expectant.

But Emme—in a form-fitting, stylish sweater, tight jeans and bare feet with her toes painted wine red, her hair gleaming, bangs falling into her eyes, face animated—was stunning.

He looked back to Chace. "Surprised you're here, man. What is she now? Two days past due?"

Chace tore his eyes from his wife and looked to his friend. "Yeah. Two. But she got to talkin' to Emme, Emme mentioned she wanted us over so you could cook food that makes The Rooster seem like Taco Bell, and they could bond. Faye said no time like the present. My girl," he shook his head, "nothin' fazes her. She says Jake'll come when he comes, and she figures our kid wouldn't want her hanging around doin' nothin' while she waits for that to happen. So she's not gonna do that."

That sounded like Faye.

And Deck loved that Chace was naming his firstborn after him. Loved it so much he was going to return the favor. It might make things confusing, kids running around with their names, but he didn't give a fuck.

It said a lot.

It meant a lot.

So he was going to do it.

"I gave in," Chace went on, and Deck focused on him, "mostly because your house is closer to the hospital." Another grin before, "Her bag's in the car."

Deck smiled. "Good thinking. Give her what she wants but have what you need."

"Yep," Chace replied, taking a sip from his beer. When he was finished, he asked, "Things cool with Emme?"

Deck looked back down to the chops but he knew his lips were curved up. "Yeah."

"She okay with your folks comin' to town?"

This was the most recent news.

Deck's mom and dad were coming for a visit.

Deck was born and raised in Colorado, just outside Aspen.

Years ago, when Deck was in college, Deck's dad had declared he was done with snow and took a job in San Diego. After retiring two years ago, they stayed. They didn't visit often, Deck normally went to them, and they never came in winter or spring.

But his mom had called and Deck had told her about Emme. Then his dad got on the phone.

Deck remembered they'd met her once, one of the many times Emme popped by Deck and Elsbeth's place. He remembered but they didn't. That said, Richard Decker heard how Deck was talking about her and decided they were due for a visit. In March. When they avoided Colorado until June, earliest.

Though he was worried she wouldn't, Emme took this news in stride. She seemed completely unaffected by it. But Deck was keeping a close watch on her in case she was hiding nerves.

To all appearances, she wasn't.

"Seems to be," Deck answered Chace.

"Outside the norm, Rich and Karla comin' out when snow's on the ground," Chace remarked.

Deck finished flipping chops and looked at his friend. "Didn't say it, where I am with Emmanuelle, but you know Dad. He heard it. Then he laid it out. He's thinkin' Emme and me bein' together less than a month and this bein' where it's at is too soon. So he's settin' up to check things out and offer a father's wisdom."

"If it's right, it's right," Chace stated quietly, and he would know.

After his life turned to shit, when it made the turn back, he'd connected with Faye, gave her no space whatsoever from the start and from the first night he had her in his bed, he'd never slept another one without her at his side.

"Dad's Dad, Chace. You know him," Deck replied. "He sticks his nose in anything he can when it has to do with his boys. Or, for that matter, fuckin' anything."

"I know, Deck, but you're not twenty-three and thinkin' with your eyes and dick."

Now he was talking about Elsbeth, and Deck took no offense. They both knew that was the God's honest truth with what went down with her, and they both had a bent toward stating it plain.

"Elsbeth was sweet, when she wasn't being a grasping

bitch, but Emme, pure you," Chace continued, his eyes drifted to the windows and he muttered, "Fuck, like she was made for you."

Deck looked to the windows and watched his girl smile, her dimple appearing as Faye burst out laughing. He saw Buford, flat out on his side by the one foot she had on the floor. Her other leg was tucked under her. She was leaned into Faye, hands up, still gesturing even as Faye laughed.

Watching her, he couldn't say he wasn't thinking with his eyes and his dick. It was just that, this time, they weren't disengaged from his brain.

"Right," Chace stated, and Deck's eyes went back to him. "Freezin' my ass off and salivating just watchin' those chops cook, might as well take this time to fill you in without the women around."

He was talking about the case that the task force was still working to put the finishing touches on for the DA.

"Give it to me," Deck invited.

"That crew we brought down, bein' good. Not associatin' with each other. Checkin' in with their bondsmen. Keepin' their noses clean. Dane McFarland, though, is also keepin' his head down. Way down. He's got a brother and sister tied up in that mess, but far's we can tell, they've cut ties."

"Glad you're keepin' an eye on him, but like I said, he's a fuckwad creep, Chace, but he's not the ringleader. His best friend, that dealer, Danny, called the shots," Deck told him.

Chace nodded but replied, "I get why you'd think that. But the man McFarland had a meet with that night you searched Emme's place the night before you were deputized by Kenton was not found for questioning. Nor was he implicated by anything you turned up. Plate I ran from his truck puts him in Carnal. Been by his house a dozen times since then. He's not at home, boss says he's on extended leave, family emergency, unknown when he's comin' back. That's fishy, Deck."

It was.

It was also a dead end Deck ran into weeks ago.

"Nothing led to another party being involved," Deck reminded him.

"Seems odd this mysterious guy who's since disappeared is takin' a late-night meet with McFarland, don't you think?" Chace asked.

"I do. But I also turned over a lot of stones. I don't know who that guy was, just found nothin' to tie him with that crew. Also found nothin' hot on him, no record, no known associations. And last, I *did* find that he has a family emergency. Mom's got multiple sclerosis and she isn't doin' too good. Maybe he was buyin' fenced property, somethin' you'd do during a clandestine meeting, and fencing that shit is likely all the mental capacity McFarland had to give that crew. Buying stolen property isn't legal, but as it stands, you got no call to get a warrant to search this mysterious guy's place. He's a dead end, Chace."

"I'm not feelin' Danny, the dealer, as ringleader," Chace replied, and Deck felt a moment of unease mostly because he wasn't certain that was true either.

McFarland's best friend, "Danny, the dealer" was a far sight smarter than McFarland. Danny had a jacket that was more than a few pages long but nothing on him the last three years since it took him time to learn how to be smart.

Danny was also good-looking in that dangerous way that might compel high school boys, who they expected were that crew's chosen tools, to turn to the dark side.

But there was something off about him in a way that even high school boys would likely read and therefore not follow it. Danny had danger and danger could be intoxicating. He just had no charisma.

"You get anything on any kids?" Deck asked.

"Got three who are possibles, one in Carnal, two in Gnaw Bone. Other teachers say they had unusual bonds with the teacher McFarlands, Dane's brother and sister. Also said the kids were often in their rooms when class was out, before school or after. Sat down and had chats with those kids at the school with the principals and their parents. They gave us nothing but they did it cagey so I figure they got something. Hopin' the parents will feel the same and turn at least one to doin' right. But days are passing, we've applied mild pressure, and nothing."

"You still got enough to take that crew down," Deck pointed out. "Direct links to the storage unit where they kept the stolen property. Fingerprints on that property. DNA in the stolen cars that were seen at the houses hit at the times the crimes were committed. Eyewitness reports of either the suspects or their cars in the vicinity of the houses when none of them lives anywhere near, indicating they were casing them prior to hit. This gets closer to trial, Chace, you know the drill. They'll start pointing fingers and making deals."

"Still not feelin' good that whatever that crew did to induce high school kids to commit felonies is in the wind," Chace replied.

"That shit feeds from a source, Chace. You cut off that source, it starves and dies."

"Those kids still committed felonies, Deck," Chace returned.

"Eyewitnesses saw shadowy figures who they reckoned were young. In other words, we don't even know any kids beyond the one who got intimate with his dad's gun was involved."

Chace held Deck's eyes. "I get you. I also got a feeling."

Deck knew that feeling. He'd had it. Hell, he had it now with this case.

"You want me to keep diggin'?" Deck asked.

"You ever finish an assignment knowin' in your gut it's not done?" Chace asked as reply.

He hadn't. Never.

Fuck.

Deck drew in a deep breath.

Chace kept talking but did it quietly.

"Makes me all kinds of happy you found her, man. She's it for you, written all over her but also stated clear every time her eyes turn to you. Glad you got a woman like that, looks at you, you light her world."

Fuck, Deck liked that.

Chace wasn't done.

"I get why you'd focus on her. But this shit is not done, man. You know it. You feel it like me. You just got good things in your life right now, so you don't have the time to focus on it. You put a stop to that mess as it stood, but there's more out there that has not come to light. It's buried deep. So deep, *you* didn't even find it. And where there's deep, there's dark. Our work is not done."

"Got other jobs that pay as I charge, Chace, and shit I need to see to with Emme," Deck told him, and Chace's brows drew together.

"She okay?" he asked.

"Seems so," Deck answered. "Just too okay. Too adjusted. Too together for a woman who disconnected from life for years. That shit went down with McFarland, she's cool with it. She fell in with me..." He shook his head. "She hasn't had a lot of men, Chace, but she's let me in, and deep. Time spent together is good. She's funny. She's sweet. She pisses me off in a way that I like it. The sex is fuckin' great. It's like we've been together for years and she's had practically zero practice with this shit. We talked about what happened to her when she was a kid, she's totally okay with it."

Chace cut in, his tone disbelieving. "Totally okay with it?"

Deck nodded once. "Completely. Forgives the guy. Even defends him. She came back into my life, I called a friend in Denver to look into things, just checkin' up. The man who snatched her, clean. Lives a good life and does it honest. Still, got a bad feelin' in my gut about that too, so he's still on him."

"What's your bad feelin' about this guy?"

"It isn't so much about him. It's about Emme. Things she's said, I think she's connected with him since he got out of prison."

Chace's chin jerked back. "No fuckin' shit?"

"Had eyes on him and ears on his phone for weeks. Nothin'. Just a feelin'. But I get those, they're rarely wrong."

"She's doin' that, that would not be good, man," Chace noted.

"You're tellin' me somethin' I know," Deck replied.

"Victims of shit like that, especially kids, things can get twisted."

This did not make him feel any better.

"Again, you're tellin' me somethin' I know," Deck said.

"You've spent time with her parents, you ask them?"

"Barry brought it up, what happened. He's not over it. Not even close. I reckon Maeve's got dark memories too. So unless it's more than a gut feeling, I don't want to bring that back or make them worry."

Chace nodded. "So, what you're sayin' is, lookin' into somethin' that important, you don't have the focus for an ongoing investigation."

"What I'm sayin' is, funds put aside to contract with me were not enough in the first place. It sucks, what was goin' on. Even so, man, that kid hadn't taken his own life, wouldn't have even considered that job. Emme involved, that capped it. But on the face of it, job's done, contract's done. Far's the task force is concerned, they got their man, in this case, four men and one woman. I do this, it's my dime, my time and you know it. Neither the county nor the town have it in their budget to keep me on so I can dig deeper."

He drew in another breath, knowing there was something off, that puzzle was not solved and equally knowing, no matter how much he needed to focus on Emme, he'd still never be able to live with that.

So he made a split-second decision and finished, "But you're right. I know in my gut we're missin' something. So I'll do it."

Chace smiled and murmured, "Freebie."

Deck shook his head but it wasn't in the negative. He had

no choice. Chace was concerned and Deck knew that puzzle wasn't solved. Deck didn't like unsolved puzzles, the money wasn't there, so it was a freebie.

Then he said, "Need those kids' names, man."

"You got it," Chace replied.

Emme's voice came from behind them and they both turned to see just her upper body swung out the open French door, bare feet still firmly planted inside.

"Well, second priority, calling a cleaning service to clean your couch." Her eyes moved to Chace, she smiled a sweet smile and her voice got soft. "First priority, getting Faye to the hospital since her water just broke."

Deck's eyes flew to Faye on the couch. She looked like she was deep breathing and she had an arm wrapped around her belly.

She caught their eyes, lifted a hand and waved.

Chace was on the move and Deck watched Emme, still grinning at Chace, jump out of the way as he ran into the house.

Emme looked at Deck.

At the same time, they both smiled.

*   *   *

Five hours later…

"Jesus, does it take this long?" Deck growled.

"You're a genius, honey, you know it does," Emme replied.

Deck stopped pacing and looked down at his girl. She was sitting, looking up at him from her phone on which she was playing some game.

His eyes moved to Sondra Goodknight, Faye's mother, who was sitting across the hospital waiting room, reading. Her daughter Liza, head back, eyes closed, headphones in, foot tapping, was sitting next to her.

Sondra'd had three kids. Liza two.

Then he looked at Silas Goodknight, Faye's father, who was, like Deck, pacing.

"Sit down next to me," Emme invited, bringing his attention back to her to see she was patting the seat beside her.

Was she insane?

"I can't sit," he told her.

"Pacing is not going to make the baby come faster," she pointed out.

He knew that but his boy was in there. Chace. A man who went through hell and came out the other end walking straight into heaven. This baby solidified the destination of that journey. All Chace Keaton ever wanted he was about to get. A good woman in his bed. A job he was proud of doing. And a family.

But Chace's luck had not been the greatest—case in point, to get his happily ever after, he'd had to endure his woman being buried alive.

"Jacob, honey, please sit," Emme whispered.

He focused on her then moved close, crouching down in front of her.

"They've had some bad times," he shared quietly.

She leaned close. "Those bad times, tonight, are officially over."

"Shit goes south for Chace."

Her eyes warmed, she leaned closer and lifted a hand to rest light on his cheek. "It's going to be okay."

"She's past due."

"That happens."

"She was buried alive, baby."

"Almost two years ago, honey."

Deck fell silent.

Emme moved closer, touched her mouth to his and pulled back an inch before she teased, "I find it fascinating, and indescribably hot, that the most intelligent, most logical man I know totally loses perspective when his best friend's wife is having a baby."

He felt his lips twitch before he replied, "This does not bode well for you, Emme, we find a time when we're in the same room and you're pushin' out my kid."

Her eyes flashed, her head jerking and it wasn't the usual flash of fire he got.

It was something different.

Before he could ask, they heard announced, "Faye's fine. Jacob's fine. Everything's good."

At hearing Chace's voice, Deck straightened, feeling Emme come up beside him.

Chace was smiling huge, relief and joy plain on his face.

Deck held back, Emme sticking close, while Silas, Sondra and Liza rushed him for handshakes, hugs and happy tears. They received murmured encouragement from Chace to go to Faye's room and in unison took off like a shot.

Only then did Deck approach his friend, Emme coming with but this time not sticking close. She was giving the men space.

Deck did not go for the handshake. He lifted his hand and wrapped his fingers in a firm grip around the side of Chace's neck.

They locked eyes.

"Happy for you, man," he whispered.

Chace lifted his hand and reciprocated Deck's gesture. "Yeah."

"Fuckin' beside myself, Chace," Deck went on.

Chace nodded.

"Bottom of my soul," Chace stated, voice thick.

"Same," Deck replied.

They held each other's eyes until Deck rocked Chace back, let go and stepped away. Emme moved in for a hug but she let him go quickly so he could get back to his wife.

Chace didn't delay.

"I'm going to go get coffees," Emme told him. He felt her fingers curl around his and looked down at her. "Do you want to come with, give them some time and crash the party later?"

He didn't answer. He pulled his hand from hers, caught her on either side of her neck and yanked her to him, moving her head at the last second so she hit his chest cheek first.

Her arms instantly slid around him.

Holding her cheek to his heart with one hand, Deck curled his other arm around her.

Both of them held tight.

*   *   *

One hour later...

It was Deck's turn and he was hogging the action.

He just didn't give a shit.

"You wanna let my wife hold her new baby?" Chace called from his place stretched out beside a tired but grinning Faye in her hospital bed.

But something made him turn his head.

When he did, he saw Emme, shoulders to the wall, removed from the folks in the room, likely because she didn't know most of them and those she did she didn't know well. But she had a grin playing at her mouth and her eyes on him.

No. Her eyes—warm, sweet, the look in them she gave him when she told him she really liked him but slightly unfocused as if her thoughts were a million miles away—were on Deck holding little Jacob in his arms.

His blood started running hot.

"Deck, my son?" Chace prompted, his voice vibrating with humor.

Such was her concentration, Deck watched Emme's body jump with surprise and her head swung toward the hospital bed.

Deck looked there too.

"My namesake," he reminded Chace.

"Yeah. We gave him your name but that doesn't mean you get to keep him," Chace replied.

Faye giggled.

Deck smiled and started walking toward the bed.

He was waylaid with a hand on his arm and he looked down to see Emme suddenly close.

She was looking at Chace and Faye.

"Two seconds," she said softly. "I just want a snuggle. Do you mind?"

"Of course not," Faye replied.

Her head tipped back to Deck and she held out her arms.

Carefully, he transferred little Jacob into them.

She curled him close, dropped her head to peer at the bundle she carried and murmured, "Hey, little man."

When she did, Deck's blood already hot, he felt his heart start pumping hard, his gut clench, his chest get tight and his throat closed.

But somehow, none of this felt bad. Instead, it all felt really fucking *good*.

Fuck, was that what she felt when she was watching him?

He didn't get near as long to watch even though she didn't take two seconds. She took more like twenty but then she moved toward the bed, bent in and gave Faye her son. But she touched little Jacob's cheek before she moved away.

"Right," Sondra started. "My daughter needs a rest. Visiting hours are over."

"The matriarch has spoken," Liza muttered, giving her sister big eyes and a bigger smile.

Chace slid off the bed for more hugs and handshakes as all said good night.

As Deck walked Emme down the corridor toward the elevators, arm around her shoulders, feeling hers tight around his waist, she remarked, "I have a feeling those chops you spent seven thousand dollars on aren't gonna taste that great when we get home."

Her feeling would be right seeing as he did nothing but turn off the grill, load his girl in his truck and follow his friends to the hospital.

He stopped them at the elevators, turned Emme into his front and she tipped her head back to catch his eyes.

She was smiling.

He was laughing.

Then he bent his neck and they were kissing.

*   *   *

One and a half hours later…

"Say it," Deck ordered gruffly, moving inside her, doing it slowly, taking his time, feeling her snug and wet around his cock, her limbs wound tight around him, holding on, one hand in his hair.

Gorgeous.

"Say what, honey?" she asked, her voice breathy, eyes languid.

"You haven't told me today," he replied.

She tipped her hips up, bit her lip and her limbs got tighter.

She was getting close.

"Told you what?" she asked.

He kept moving, slow, sweet, building it, loving it.

But he wasn't going to give it until he got what he needed.

He dipped his mouth to hers, brushed her lips and whispered, "How you feel about me."

Her pussy clenched around his cock and her voice was breathier when she said, "Right now, I really, *really* like you."

And right now, he *seriously* liked her.

Then again, he always had.

He slid in deep, stayed there and encouraged, "Say it like it is, baby."

Her body squirmed under his. "I just did."

"Say what you really mean."

"Okay, I really, really, *really* like you," she breathed. "Now will you go back to moving?"

He grinned down into her gorgeous face but slid out to the tip and stayed there.

Her eyes opened further, not full, but he had her attention.

"Say what you really mean," he repeated.

"Jacob," she whispered.

"Say it, Emme."

She squirmed more, her limbs tightening further, her hips seeking his cock, her hand fisting in his hair. "I need you back."

"You got me," he informed her. "Tell me what that means to you."

"Jacob, seriously, I was close."

He was getting there too. And now it was torture but he slid in then pulled out to the tip and again stayed there.

"Honey," she begged, her voice and limbs now trembling.

"Say it, Emme."

"Please."

His hand cradling one side of her face shifted so he could rub his thumb over her lips as he whispered, "I know you feel it, baby. Say it."

She lifted her head, sliding her cheek along his until her face was in his neck.

"Please give me you," she whispered against his skin.

So sweet.

Torture.

He turned so his lips were at her ear. "You got me, baby. You know you've got me. Tell me what that means."

"I mean I want you to give me a specific *part* of you."

He grinned even as his body pulsed to be buried inside her but he held on to his control, though just barely.

"Give me what I want," he demanded.

"Honey."

"Give it to me, Emme."

She shoved her face further into his neck then turned her head, her fist in his hair loosening as she slid it to the back of his neck and said so quietly, even as close as she was, he barely heard her, "I love you, Jacob."

Fuck.

Yes.

Deck drove in deep and she gasped into his ear, her hand sliding back up to clench in his hair.

"You love me?" he asked.

"Yes," she panted.

He pulled out and drove in again.

Exquisite.

"Look at me and say it, baby."

Her cheek slid back until her lips were against his, eyes open and so fucking close, that fire in them that said what her lips were about to utter was shining right there. So bright, so heated, he thought it would scorch him.

"I love you, honey."

He took her mouth, took her cunt and took both until he took them both home.

After, planted deep inside his Emme, Deck ran his nose along her jaw and when his mouth found her ear, he murmured, "Love you too, baby."

Her limbs, still tight around him, clamped.

She liked that.

She wanted it.

So much she was holding on to it with all she had.

And this was it.

This was "hey, puppy" for the rest of his life. This was knowing he had in his bed a woman who wanted medicine socialized and not giving a fuck. This was good family, hers and his, mingling to make it better. This was working until he never saw that surprised look on her face just before she came. This was having something warm snuggle into him while he read because he didn't sleep.

This was a kaleidoscope of beauty, the dials spinning, ever changing, but never anything short of spectacular.

Deck lifted his head and looked down at her.

Tears were pooling in her beautiful eyes and her lower lip was quivering.

He'd never seen anything as beautiful.

And the kaleidoscope spun.

"Wanna build a life with you, Emmanuelle," he whispered.

"Jacob," she whispered back.

"And Buford needs a momma," he declared as a tear slid out the side of her eye and a trembling smile touched her lips.

Deck caught her tear with his thumb, swept it across her cheek and rubbed the wetness against her lips.

Then he dipped his head and kissed her like he made love to her. Slow and sweet and for a very long time.

When he lifted his mouth from hers, she said quietly, "Now that you've rocked my world and blown my mind on top of us having minor roles in the miracle of birth tonight, all of which, I'll note, I endured without dinner, I need to clean up and get some sleep, honey. You may be able to exist on a genius's ration of shuteye, but I'm not that lucky and I've gotta go to work tomorrow."

He chuckled, liking the look the movement this caused put on Emme's face since he did it on her and in her. Then he dipped his head, kissed her jaw and gently slid out and off.

She rolled with him so she could touch her lips to his chest before she slid out of bed.

Deck watched her ass and legs as she walked to the bathroom.

Buford jumped up to claim his lion's share of the bed before Emme got back.

After Emme climbed over him and Deck pulled up the covers, she settled into his side and claimed the lion's share of Deck.

"'Night, honey," she murmured sleepily into his chest, giving his stomach a squeeze as she did.

"'Night, baby," he replied, pulling her closer, smelling strawberries.

She was dead weight within minutes.

Deck stared at the ceiling, the vision of Emme holding little Jacob seared in his brain.

So when his eyes closed, he fell asleep with his lips tipped up.

*   *   *

Emme

Thirty minutes later…

Forcing my body to stay relaxed just in case Jacob woke to find me awake, I stared unseeing at Jacob's chest.

And I was unseeing not just because it was dark.

All I could see was him holding Chace and Faye's baby, cuddling him close to his big man's body with his mighty arms, his head tipped down, his handsome face holding happiness and awe.

So beautiful.

Extraordinary.

Even profound.

Love you too, baby.

There the words came as they had again and again the last half an hour. His deep voice saying those words sounding in my head.

And then, *Wanna build a life with you, Emmanuelle.*

I clenched my teeth.

And I clenched my teeth because seeing Jacob holding his namesake in my mind's eye, hearing his words ringing in my ears, I felt nothing.

Nothing but sheer terror.

CHAPTER THIRTEEN

Puzzles

Two weeks six days later...

I WAS PULLING the utility knife through drywall when I heard my phone ring in the kitchen.

I dropped the knife, dashed from the makeshift workstation I'd set up in the dining room and snatched it up just in time, seeing the display said "Jacob calling."

I put it to my ear. "Hey, honey."

"Where are you?"

He didn't sound happy.

I felt my brows draw together and answered, "At home, cutting drywall to patch over the electrical work." I paused before I went on with a smile, "Having Buford around, I'm now determined to become a puppy momma. And that would be to an actual puppy, as in one who's just been weaned. Not a dog who's still a puppy to me, he's just old enough to know he should no longer chew everything. So I need to do something with this exposed wiring."

"You're cutting drywall," he stated, still sounding unhappy, and I still didn't get it.

I was cutting drywall, not boiling bunnies.

"Yeah," I confirmed.

"Aren't you supposed to be somewhere else doing something else?"

I blinked, cast my mind out, remembered and couldn't believe I forgot.

But I did. Totally. It didn't even enter my head from waking up until now. All my thoughts were on drywall and puppies. I'd even woken up to Jacob kissing me before he took off to do whatever Jacob Things he'd been taking off to do recently in the early morning and then I went back to sleep.

He hadn't said "see you later" but then he probably didn't think he had to.

How could that be?

My eyes flew to the clock on the microwave, my heart sank and feeling the unhappy vibes beating at me over the phone, I whispered, "Oh no."

"Yeah," Jacob bit off.

"I got caught up. I'm so sorry. I need to shower," I told him. "But I'll be quick then I'll be over."

"That'd be good," he replied, still angry.

"Are they there yet?"

"Just called. They're ten, fifteen minutes out."

Oh no!

"I'll hurry," I promised.

"Right," he clipped. "Later."

Then he was gone.

He never ended a call like that.

Totally angry.

But there was a reason he was angry. His parents arrived in Denver three hours ago. And I was supposed to be at Jacob's half an hour ago in order to be there when they got there so we could start bonding without delay.

Now, with shower, meet-the-parents prep and travel time, I'd be way late. In other words, there was no time to waste since there was no time *at all*.

So I did what I promised.

I raced upstairs and hurried.

*   *   *

I opened Jacob's back door thinking inanely, from the SUV I saw in his driveway, his parents didn't mess around with rentals. The minute I got the door open, I saw Buford who, as always, came to greet me.

"Hey, puppy," I murmured, bending and giving him a rubdown, which, out of necessity, had to be a quick rubdown since I had to get my behind into the house to meet Jacob's parents.

I gave him an extra ear scratch to make up for it, straightened and saw Jacob moving down the hall.

This did not bode well. Jacob never met me in the back hall.

I smiled at him hesitantly. "Hey, honey. Sorry. I hurried as best I could. Did they have an okay trip?"

He stopped, did a top to toe with his eyes, didn't answer my question and asked his own, "Where's your bag?"

"My what?" I asked.

"Bag, Emme. Your overnight bag. Did you leave it in Cletus?"

"Persephone," I corrected automatically, but didn't get the usual grin that came fast and easy whenever we were talking about my Bronco.

Instead, his mouth got tight.

It was a scary look and indicated he was still angry.

I didn't know what to do with this. I didn't think Jacob had ever been angry with me. Not real angry, as in we weren't fighting about gun control, which he didn't really care what I thought about, he just liked fighting about it. But instead, he was actually upset with me.

It did not feel very good to have him upset with me, not at all. More so because he had reason.

And further, I didn't understand why he was asking about my bag.

"I, well…didn't bring a bag," I admitted.

His mouth got tighter.

Then he muttered as he reached out and grabbed my hand, "Doesn't matter. You got enough shit in the bathroom here to work with and you can sleep in one of my tees."

I did have enough "shit" in his bathroom. That was, if he was referring to shampoo and moisturizer and stuff. I'd doubled up on a few things so I didn't have to lug so much around all the time.

But sleep in one of his tees?

I wasn't spending the night with his parents there. I may have forgotten about meeting them but I didn't forget about us making plans for me to spend the night. I would have remembered that, as in discussed it and declined the option.

It was okay for Jacob to spend the night at my house when Mom and Dad were around. They knew him.

His parents didn't know me.

They might think I was a floozy. The last impression a girl wanted to give the parents of the man she loved on first meeting them was that she was a floozy.

I wanted to tug my hand to stop his advance in order to explain this to him as he was now dragging me down the hall, but I didn't figure that would better his mood. So I let him drag me down the hall.

We moved through the opening to the great room and I saw Jacob's dad sitting at a stool at the bar and his mom standing behind it. Both of them were sipping coffee.

Even though I met them only once and spent maybe ten minutes with them, I remembered them vividly. This was because Jacob meant a lot to me so meeting his parents would too.

This was also because they were a surprise.

He got his coloring from his mother. Same hair, same eyes, same olive skin tone.

She was, however, relatively petite. She couldn't be over five foot five. And she was rounded. It was in a pleasant way that she obviously liked because she didn't try to hide it. She also didn't hold herself like she wasn't comfortable with it.

His dad, however, was the big surprise.

Although there was a hint of his strong, handsome features in Jacob's face, Richard Decker was fair. His blond hair had still been mostly blond when I met him over a decade ago.

Now it was a silvery white. He also had blue eyes. He was tall and built, now slightly soft, and that would be slightly soft in a way he clearly liked his beer because he had a relatively large beer belly. He was way taller than his wife but he was nowhere near as tall as Jacob. Maybe six foot.

I knew Jacob had a brother named Shane who I'd never met. But I'd always wondered if Shane looked like his dad or mom or if he was like Jacob, a best of both but even better kind of offspring.

"Hi," I greeted, pinning a smile to my face.

Returning my greeting, I saw Karla Decker eyeing me closely but her expression was friendly and welcoming.

Not returning my greeting, Rich Decker was also studying me, doing it closely, but there was speculation in the back of his eyes. It wasn't that he didn't look friendly. It was just that, with one look, I knew I was under review and needed to pass inspection.

In order to do that, I pulled my hand from Jacob's and moved to his father first since he was the closest. I lifted my hand and made my smile bigger.

"I'm really sorry I'm late. I have a project I'm in the middle of that's so far lasted three years," I tried to joke. Rich didn't crack a smile. This made me nervous, so I kept going. "Sometimes when I'm in the throes of it, I lose track of, well . . . pretty much everything," I told him, still smiling.

Rich took my hand, his grip firm, his eyes never leaving mine. "Deck's told us about your house, Emme. But good you could finally make it to his."

That wording wasn't the greatest.

And he still hadn't said hi or anything close.

Even with that not-so-good start, I persevered when he let me go. I pulled my purse off my shoulder, dropped it on the bar and moved around to Karla, hand up.

"Hi. So nice to meet you. And again, I'm so sorry," I murmured.

"That's okay, honey," she murmured back, her eyes also

never leaving mine and her grip was warmer. "That's a pretty sweater," she remarked when she let my hand go.

Well, that was better.

"Thanks," I mumbled, stepping back and running into Jacob.

I instantly got an arm around my chest at the same time I felt a wet nose on my hand. Jacob and his dog, both claiming me.

Instantly, I pulled away from Jacob to bend to Buford, explaining, "Poor puppy. He didn't get his usual rubdown when I got here. Best see to that."

If his tail wagging was anything to go by, Buford approved of my choice.

If the look I caught when I glanced over my shoulder at Jacob as I straightened away from his dog was anything to go by, I'd made a big mistake.

I bit my lip and Jacob's arm again came around me, this time at my belly, whereupon it clamped tight so my back was snug to his front, so I decided my best bet was to go with it.

I looked between his parents.

"How was your trip?" I asked.

"Over," Rich answered, his eyes on Jacob's arm around my waist.

Then they came up to my face.

I gave him another smile but it was shaky.

He did not smile back.

"I'm just glad we had good weather," Karla noted, and I looked to her.

She didn't look speculative or angry. She was calmly sipping coffee.

"I am too," I agreed.

She stopped sipping coffee and gave me a genuine smile then said, "Let's just pray we keep that good fortune and don't have snow while we're here. Not real fond of the white stuff."

"Forecast is good for that," I shared.

She smiled again then took another sip of coffee.

Everyone fell silent.

It was not comfortable. What it was was surprising. This

was because it was the kind of thing Jacob would normally forge into in order to make everyone comfortable, including, and maybe especially, me.

I hadn't been nervous about meeting the Deckers.

Now, because I'd been an idiot, I was.

Stupidly, I decided to break the silence.

"Have you all had lunch?"

"We've been waitin' for you," Rich informed me then his eyes lifted to his son. "Starved, boy."

At his words, I quickly jumped away from Jacob, headed to the fridge and announced, "Right. Lunch is my domain. I'm killer with cold cuts and Jacob's always stocked up. He'll have everything. I'll take orders."

"Lunch is your domain?" Rich asked.

I stopped with hand on the handle of the fridge and looked at him. "Jacob is a master with things that require pots, pans and broiling, so he gets dinner. I've got a mean hand with a spreader so I get cold cuts."

"Can't you cook?" Rich asked.

"Dad," Jacob murmured.

"Uh...yes, I can. It's just that Jacob is better at it," I told him.

Although I thought this was a compliment to his son, it was clear by the look on Rich's face this was not the right answer, seeing as his jaw got hard and his eyes went to his coffee mug on the counter.

"Actually, if we're just having sandwiches," Karla waded in, moving toward me, "I can take care of that." She caught my eyes. "Since you've been working on your house all morning, and all. I wouldn't know but my guess is, that's exhausting."

"And you've spent your morning journeying from southern California," I reminded her. "I'm fine, Karla, I can make lunch."

"How 'bout someone slaps some meat between some bread so we can all eat?" Rich suggested, giving the impression sandwiches was not his chosen lunch but at this point he'd take what he could get.

"Dad," Jacob repeated but this wasn't a murmur. It was a growl.

One could say things were not going smoothly.

Karla got close and said softly, "We'll work together. Get these men fed."

I gave her a relieved smile and replied, "Good idea."

I pulled out the stuff from the fridge. Karla pulled out chips from the cupboards. And when I was at the counter, I chanced a look at Jacob.

He was studying me but he seemed lost in thought. When he felt my eyes on him, he focused and I gave him a nervous smile.

Then I mouthed, *I'm so sorry.*

He watched my mouth then looked into my eyes.

Finally, I watched the skin around his eyes go soft and his lips tip up. Better, he moved to me, leaned in and touched his mouth to mine.

When he pulled back an inch, he murmured, "It's all cool, baby. Yeah?"

I nodded.

He lifted a hand to my neck, swept his thumb along my jaw and moved away.

I took in a breath, let it out and caught sight of Rich when I was looking to the packs of deli meats on the counter.

His eyes were on me and they were still speculative. The good news was, now they didn't seem annoyed. Just thoughtful.

I tried another smile.

It took him a second, but he smiled back.

The problem was it didn't quite reach his eyes.

*   *   *

Eight hours later...

Sitting next to Jacob and opposite his parents on Jacob's couches in the great room, Jacob tried to curl me into him with an arm around my shoulders.

He failed because I stiffened.

Therefore Jacob stiffened.

Suffice it to say, the day had not gone great.

Lunch seemed to appease his father and we hit a happy spell that made me somewhat relax.

Things degenerated when we sat down at Jacob's table for a game of euchre, boys against girls. This was when I discovered that Rich was highly competitive even though neither Jacob, Karla nor I were.

Competitive people always rubbed me the wrong way and I usually extricated myself from those situations.

This one, I had no hope of extricating myself from, so I did my best to ignore it.

It was difficult when Rich questioned nearly every card I threw even though I wasn't his partner, finishing the fifth game they won (and thankfully the last game we played) by saying, "Thank Christ we didn't switch it up, boy girl, boy girl."

His meaning was not lost on me.

It was also not lost on Jacob.

The good news was, at that, if Jacob was still upset with me for being late, he no longer was.

The bad news was, he no longer was upset with me because he was all kinds of pissed at his dad.

I knew this when he said, "Dad, got something to show you out back," in a way that meant his father was going to go with him or Jacob was going to haul him there.

Rich gave a look to his wife who was also looking at him like he was not her favorite person. Then he followed his son.

When they got back, we slid into a somewhat comfortable spell, which was broken when we went to Rosalinda's for dinner and conversation turned to our current president.

Like his son, Rich and I didn't see eye to eye in regard to the man who held that office.

Unlike his son, it wasn't fun debating it with him. This led to me getting more and more uncomfortable, Rich pushing more and more to force me to explain my clearly idiotic opinion (according to him) and me trying harder and harder to extricate myself from the discussion.

Jacob was my wingman in that one. He didn't agree with my opinion, but he did try in a polite way to move the conversation to a lighter tone.

His father was having none of it.

Therefore, Jacob started to get pissed. I saw it, felt it, and at one point, when a low, short rumble slid from his throat, heard it.

I wasn't pissed.

I was freaked.

The day was an utter disaster (partially due to me) and Jacob's father totally hated me.

It was Karla who cut into that by catching her husband's eyes, stating quietly but firmly, "Enough, Richard," then looking at me and just as firmly changing the subject.

We had not recovered from that and were back at Jacob's, his dad, Jacob and me enjoying a glass of Jacob's beer, his mom finishing the night with a glass of wine.

This was the only thing anyone enjoyed. Conversation was stilted and I was a nervous wreck.

I caught Rich's eyes narrowed on me stiffening away from his son, but fortunately, right after, he stood and announced, "Time for some shuteye."

I couldn't tamp down a relieved sigh.

I'd not finished sighing before I heard Jacob make an irritated noise low in his throat which told me he heard my exhalation, knew it was relieved and didn't like it all that much.

In order to cover, I popped up and pinned the three thousandth fake bright smile I'd affected on my face that day and lied, "Today has been great." I didn't lie when I went on to say, "I hope you sleep well."

"We will, honey," Karla murmured, giving me a warm look, giving her husband a cold one, doing all this while getting up from the couch.

Good nights were exchanged. Jacob got a hug from his

mom. I got a cheek touch. Jacob got a slap on the arm from his dad. I got a distracted chin lift he threw my way when he was almost in the mouth to the hall.

They disappeared.

I closed my eyes.

"Babe."

At Jacob's call, I opened my eyes and announced in a quiet voice, "Time for me to be getting home."

It was then Jacob's eyes narrowed.

Not a good sign.

Apparently, my bad day was not yet over.

"What?" he asked.

"I should get home. Like, now." Then I added for effect, "I'm super tired."

"You're sleepin' here," he stated, and I shook my head.

"I think maybe your folks will want to have an Emme-Free Zone when they get up in the morning."

He got closer and dipped his chin to hold my eyes. "Emme, you're sleepin' here."

I lifted my hand and put it on his chest, leaning into him.

"It's also important to me that they don't think I'm a floozy."

Jacob's head jerked even as he did a slow blink.

Then he informed me, "They came into the twenty-first century right along with us, Emme. And I haven't discussed it with either of them, hope to God I never will, but I still reckon they know I'm not a virgin."

That was funny so I smiled up at him, leaning in further.

"Today hasn't been good, honey," I pointed out quietly. "My fault, but also, I think maybe they need some quality time with their son."

"They'll get it and get it with their son's woman."

"Ja—"

He interrupted me to declare, "Haven't slept apart since that first night we got together. Not startin' now."

I liked that that meant something to him and wanted to keep our roll going, just as much as it kind of freaked me out.

But no way I was staying.

"Okay, let me rephrase," I began. "Today hasn't been good *for me*. Your dad isn't my biggest fan and—"

He cut me off. "He'll come around."

I felt my eyes get big and I leaned closer. "Jacob, he was totally pissed I was late. He didn't get over it all day and let me know it."

I said that but what I didn't say was that, even though it was rude to be late, it wasn't like I breezed in having forgotten them because I was at home inserting razor blades into Easter candy I'd pass out at church to all Gnaw Bone's children.

I'd screwed up and people did that.

I also apologized.

Which meant his dad didn't like me but I also was not a big fan of his dad.

"Last woman I got serious about was Elsbeth," he remarked.

I shut my mouth and leaned a bit away.

Jacob lifted a hand to curl around the side of my neck and he brought me back, dipping his face even closer.

"You know how that ended. So do they," he finished.

"It's been nine years and I'm not Elsbeth," I replied.

"I been hung up on her for nine years and you're not Elsbeth but you knew her. You know she was notoriously late for every-fuckin'-thing. He probably got a flashback and if you wouldn't pull away or act like my touch burns every time I get close, he'd get over it."

"I didn't pull away or act like your touch burns," I returned.

"Babe," he stated and said not another word but his mouth got tight after he was finished uttering it.

Then again, for once, "babe" said it all. Jittery and freaking out, I did just that and we both knew it. Therefore I couldn't argue that point.

"Okay, how about this?" I asked. "*I* want to go home because *I* need a break. I need to regroup and maybe you can bring them around tomorrow for a tour of my house and I'll try again."

"How about this?" Jacob responded immediately. "You sleep where you belong, beside me, and we all go over there tomorrow so you can give them a tour after lunch."

"Honey, can't you understand where I'm coming from?" I pleaded.

"Baby, I could if you hadn't fuckin' forgotten my fuckin' *parents* were comin' to town. Somethin' you've known for weeks. Somethin' we made concrete plans about days ago. Somethin' you gotta know means somethin' to all involved. Then you show and act not you, which, since we're havin' this conversation, I'll point out, you been actin' not you for a while."

I blinked at his words, not to mention his sneak attack, and pulled at his hand at my neck.

It tightened so I stopped pulling and asked, "What?"

"Since Faye had the baby, you've been off."

"I have not," I replied. "I've been me. And, by the way, I acted not me today because Rich put me on edge."

He ignored my second statement and returned to his earlier theme.

"You miss my calls, when you never missed my calls. You call back hours later, but only if I leave a message. You never call me, which you used to do just because. And you're comin' to my place later and later, or textin' me to ask me to show at yours later and later 'cause you supposedly have shit to do."

"I'm one man down at the yard and in the middle of hiring a temporary replacement who actually won't be a temporary replacement once Dane goes down, so he has to be the right guy for the job," I reminded him.

"You shiftin' lumber?" he asked.

"No," I answered.

"Then you gotta put an ad in the paper and sift through applications, Emme. It isn't like you're out in the yard workin' shoulder to shoulder with your boys."

I felt my back get straight and my eyes get squinty. "You don't know all the ins and outs of my job, honey."

"I know hirin' one guy doesn't take five extra hours of your day, babe."

"I didn't say it *was* taking five extra hours," I shot back.

"Then why are you suddenly unavailable pretty much all fuckin' day?" he asked. "Unavailable when before I always got you."

"We're settling in, Jacob. Before, what we have was just starting. Fresh. New. Now it's a part of life."

"Emmanuelle, we been seein' each other not even two months. It's *still* just starting. And, babe, just sayin', that just starting feeling is the best one to have so maybe we might want to hold on to that for as long as we can."

"I have a life, Jacob. I have to live it *and* fit us in it."

This was the wrong thing to say.

I knew it when he pulled away, dropping his hand from my neck, and said, "Sorry, babe. Had no idea it would be tough for you to fit me in. Fit in gettin' to know my folks. Put a little effort into makin' my dad like you. Shoulda had a mind to that."

He was taking this too far.

"That's not what I meant," I snapped.

"It's what you said," he fired back.

I pulled in a ragged, annoyed breath.

Then I said, "Maybe we should finish this after your folks go home, or at least when they're not just down the hall."

He shook his head and stated bizarrely, "Told you, it started happening, Emme, I'd put a stop to it."

I felt my brows draw together and asked, "Stop what?"

"You disconnecting."

Another sneak attack, one I responded to physically.

I took a half step back and whispered, "I'm not disconnecting."

"You totally fuckin' are." His eyes on me grew intense and he went on, "Just don't get what tripped it. But whatever tripped it, I'm putting a stop to it."

"Jacob—"

"And I'm doin' it by sayin' you're spending the night. You don't, we got problems. And tomorrow, you're gonna suck it up and give it another go with my dad. He knows you, my Emme, the Emme you give me when you aren't pullin' away, he'll love you. Then, when they leave, we're gonna sit down and talk about a variety of shit."

I wasn't doing *any* of that and therefore informed him, "I'm not down with that plan, Jacob."

"I don't give a fuck, Emmanuelle."

It was definitely time to lay it out but what I had to lay out could not be overheard.

So I got close and whispered, "Okay, I was late. That was bad. I forgot. That was worse. I shouldn't have done either, but I apologized. I know you love him and you're close but it was your dad who was uncool with me, Jacob. All day. And if you're so close with him and can't see it, hark back to how your mom reacted to it. She was not pleased because she knows, like I know, it was uncool."

"He wants his son to be happy and a woman who doesn't give a shit enough about a meet with his parents to remember it and then acts like she'd rather be anywhere else, say, nailed to a cross, is not gonna be the kind of woman who might make his son happy."

It kind of sucked that he could be funny when we were arguing.

I powered through Jacob being funny.

"Uh...pointing out, I *did* want to be somewhere else seeing as your dad wasn't being cool with me. And now I want to be somewhere else seeing as *you* aren't being cool with me."

Jacob held my eyes a moment, looked to his boots then he looked back at me and instigated yet *another* sneak attack.

"I love you," he whispered.

I felt those words like a body blow and lost my breath.

Like the first time he said them.

Which was the only time he said them.

"Love you, Emme. Said it once, haven't said it again. You

said it, haven't heard it again. So I'm gonna make it clear. I love you, baby, and I feel you disconnecting from me. You love me and I hope me tellin' you that's what I'm feelin' means something, enough of something for you to listen and help me put stop to it."

My voice was gentler when I said, "I'm not disconnecting, honey."

"Feel it, Emme."

I didn't want that. I never wanted that. Not ever.

To stop it, I whispered, "I love you too, Jacob."

His eyes closed, relief sweeping through his handsome face.

Such relief, it rocked me.

Such relief it made me ask myself, was I disconnecting?

Before my mind could answer that question, he moved fast. Lifting both hands, he put them to my neck, sliding them up in my hair and he got close. But he brought his face closer.

"You're right. All day, my dad was a dick. You forgot, you were late, that was disappointing. I didn't get it, but you apologized. I talked to him, didn't help for long. Tomorrow, he pulls that shit again, I'll take your back. But Emme," his voice now held a warning, "we had our chat, he didn't hear me. So tomorrow, if he makes me do it again, I'm not gonna take him outside to say what I gotta say. To make my point, I'm just gonna let fly. Today, I had a mind to you bein' not yourself. Tomorrow, I'll do what I gotta do. You need to be prepared for that."

That didn't sound like fun.

Therefore, I suggested, "Maybe you should give him a safe place and talk to him in the morning with me not being around."

"And maybe *we* should make the statement that you're here, this is *your* safe place, my home or anything that has to do with me, and he has to have a mind to that."

His suggestion was better.

And his words were amazing.

In this entire messy discussion, I knew a few things for

certain. If it wasn't important, Jacob wouldn't have mentioned it. If he said he was feeling something from me, he was feeling it. And if he was feeling something, maybe there was something to feel.

Which turned my mind to the fact that, bottom line, I forgot about meeting his parents. That was crazy. He was right. I'd known for weeks they were coming and we'd made plans I should never have forgotten. I'd never met a boyfriend's parents, but that didn't mean I didn't know it was important.

I wasn't flighty. I wasn't forgetful.

I didn't know how it happened. I just knew it did.

And it shouldn't have.

Therefore, it was time to backtrack.

I lifted my hands to his chest, leaned in and admitted, "I screwed up. I don't know what I was thinking. How I got caught up in what I was doing and forgot. I don't even know why I started doing what I got caught up in doing. What I do know is, screwing up so bad, I got nervous and that's why I was funny with you today." My voice dropped. "And the more your dad came at me, the more nervous I got, the worse *it* got. But it wasn't your dad. It started with me, and for that, I'm truly sorry, honey."

Jacob's eyes held mine a moment, they did this intensely, and it wasn't comfortable mostly because it felt like he was trying to see through my eyes to read the words written on my soul.

Fortunately, it was just a moment before he moved in for a lip touch, which felt really sweet since that was Jacob's way of accepting my apology.

He pulled back and one of his hands stayed in my hair. The other one slid down my spine and he wrapped his arm around me.

"Over and done," he murmured but his gaze never left mine as he asked, "Were you nervous about meeting them?"

I didn't think I was. People liked me. I didn't think I was the awesomest person on the planet but I wasn't a bitch.

But maybe that was it. Maybe it was latent nerves, I woke up that morning, and because of that, blocked it and acted like an idiot. And maybe that was why I'd been being weird lately, giving Jacob the vibe I was pulling away.

Hopefully that was it.

"I didn't think so but maybe I was," I answered honestly.

He nodded then shared, "Seriously, babe, they're usually very cool. Dad especially."

I pressed my body to his, slid my arms around him, but I did this straightening my spine with resolve before I declared, "Tomorrow I'll win him over."

I declared it. I was going to try it. I just hoped I could do it.

Jacob finally smiled and it was then, relief swept through me.

"I know you will," he said softly.

Then he came in for another lip touch.

I leaned into it, squeezing him with my arms, and it became a short, sweet kiss after which he lifted his head and suggested, "Let's go to bed."

Messy discussion over. Bad day over.

Done.

Good stuff to come.

So it was then, I smiled.

*   *   *

Five and a half hours later…

I opened my eyes to dark and felt the bed empty (save Buford).

Jacob was up but not reading.

He did this, not often but he did it, and told me when I got up he'd either worked out, gone for a run or did some work. So when it happened and I woke up during it, I usually went back to sleep.

But this time, I didn't go back to sleep because this time, after a very bad day, I worried he left me for other reasons.

I love you, baby, and I feel you disconnecting from me.

I didn't think I was doing that but with what he said, he

wasn't wrong. I let the phone go, even when it was ringing right beside me and I saw his name on the display. I did this telling myself I was busy and I'd get back to him when before, I'd snatch it up before it rang twice.

I also used to call for whatever reason—your place or mine, what's for dinner, this annoying thing just happened and I have to get it off my chest—and he always picked up right away. But now, even when I had something to say, I told myself he was too busy to get a call from me.

Even though it seemed he worked a lot, lately even more, he'd never been too busy to get a call from me. Hell, he'd even told me straight out he was *never* too busy to take a call from me.

"What's happening with me?" I whispered to the pillowcase.

No answers swept through my brain. Not liking it, it feeling weird, not having enough experience to know, just knowing I couldn't let it go on, I got out of bed, leaving a slightly snoring Buford behind and wandering into the dark hall.

I found Jacob in his office, his back to me, facing the computer.

So he was up and working.

"Hey," I called when I hit the doorway and he swiveled his chair to face me.

His eyes immediately warmed.

That was a good sign.

"Hey," he replied. "Why you up?"

I moved to him and when I stopped close, I answered, "Bed was empty."

His eyes got warmer and he curved an arm around my hips, pulling me to the side of the chair and tipping his head way back. I bent at his invitation and touched my mouth to his.

I pulled away, not intending to go very far but not getting there anyway because his other hand lifted and curled around my neck.

I settled in and asked, "Working?"

"Yeah. Case not adding up. Something's wrong. I can't get a lock on it."

That was a good sign too. He left me not because of our messy discussion or unease with what was happening between us driving him away. He left because he had something else on his mind he had to work out.

At this news, I grinned at him and teased, "You, the Mighty Jacob?"

He grinned back and replied, "Yeah. Me."

I slid a hand up his chest and whispered, "You'll sort it."

"Yeah," he whispered back.

"You've got a puzzle you can't solve, I get you wanting to get on it," I told him then said, "But I like waking up with you."

His eyes got even warmer. "I'll give this a couple hours, come back and read."

"Thanks, honey."

"Anytime, baby."

I slid my hand up further, stopping to curve it around the dark stubble at his jaw and I bent in again for a lip touch.

This time when I pulled back, I stopped, held his gaze and whispered, "Love you, Jacob."

Heat in his eyes, soft in his face, lips tipping up, so beautiful, all for me, he whispered back, "Love you too, Emme."

I glided my hand down, drifted my thumb along the corded ridge of his throat, memorized the look on his face and gave him a grin.

I pulled away and Jacob let me go. I turned to the door and stopped dead.

This was because Richard Decker was standing at the door in pajamas, arms crossed, shoulder to the jamb, watching.

"Fuck. Seriously?" Jacob growled.

He'd seen his father too.

I heard his chair roll, felt it moving away, then felt him standing beside me.

I also felt he was angry.

That was when I felt my body grow tight.

Okay, officially it was the next day, so this did not bode well it would be a better one.

"Now that," his father announced, "*that's* what I like to see."

I relaxed slightly but only because this confused me.

It didn't confuse Jacob.

I knew this when he bit out, "Dad. Not. Fuckin'. Cool."

Rich completely ignored him and looked at me. "Today, Emme, I was an ass. I apologize. You were nervous, it was obvious. I kept bein' an ass. I apologize for that too. I'll make it up to you by making you my world-famous pancakes tomorrow morning."

Maybe I was wrong. This sounded like indication that today would be a better one.

"Dad, your pancakes suck," Jacob replied.

My eyes got big and my head shot back to see him scowling at his father.

He was screwing up a potential good day!

To get him to stop doing that, I elbowed him in the ribs. He acted like he didn't feel it and kept scowling at his father.

"Forgot. It's Shane who likes my pancakes," Rich mumbled.

"They aren't pancakes. They're crêpes. And crêpes suck," Jacob returned.

Totally screwing it up!

"Jacob!" I snapped.

He wasn't done, unfortunately.

"Unless they have that hazelnut chocolate spread in them, something I don't have."

"You have a grocery store," Rich shot back.

"I'm not haulin' my ass to the grocery store on a Sunday morning for hazelnut spread," Jacob retorted.

"Then quit bitchin' about it," Rich ordered.

"I'm not bitchin'. I'm sayin', I bought Mom buttermilk for her pancakes, which I actually like. Which is what we're gonna have. And, incidentally, you hear words as me bitchin' when instead I'm pissed you're lurkin' around spyin' on Emme and me," Jacob stated.

I closed my eyes.

"I wasn't spyin'," Rich replied.

My eyes shot open because that was a bald-faced lie.

He was leaning in the door watching us!

"You stand in my door without me or Emme knowin' it and listen in?" Jacob called him on his lie.

"Yeah, but that isn't spyin'. You hide when you spy. I wasn't hiding. I was listening."

Jacob looked to the ceiling.

Truth be told, he had a point. A funny one. So I burst out laughing.

I swallowed it when Jacob stopped looking at the ceiling so he could turn his scowl to me.

"It's not funny," he declared. "He's a nosy bastard. Always was. It wasn't okay when I was a teenager coppin' a feel from my girlfriend watchin' TV in our basement. It's *definitely* not okay when I'm a thirty-seven-year-old man havin' a moment with my girl in my own fuckin' house."

All I could think to that statement was that I was glad Jacob eschewed the norm and didn't cop a feel when his dad was watching.

All I could say was, "You shouldn't call your dad a bastard."

"Emme, it was *our* moment, not his," Jacob stated.

"This is true but we weren't exactly hatching plans for our world takeover so now that he knows, we have to kill him," I pointed out.

It was at that, Rich burst out laughing.

I looked to him and felt something inside me loosen. It might have had to do with the fact that Rich laughing was the only time he looked a lot like his son, in other words, extremely handsome rather than just plain handsome. It mostly had to do with the fact that he was doing it at all and it was me who made him do it.

I didn't want to be a brown nose but I felt it important to press the advantage, so when he quit laughing, I told him, "I'll eat your crêpes in the morning, Rich."

Still grinning, he replied, "They're pancakes, Emme."

"Okay," I whispered.

"Can you two do me a favor and bond when it's not three thirty in the morning?" Jacob asked.

There it was again, screwing things up.

I tipped my head back and glared at him.

He caught my glare, the scowl left his face and he grinned at me.

Then he bent and brushed his lips on mine, pulled back and said, "Buford's lonely."

I had no chance to reply because Rich offered, "I'll walk you to your room, Emme."

Jacob and I looked to his dad.

"It's down the hall, Dad," Jacob pointed out. "I think she can make it there unaided."

"Yeah. I know. She's still gettin' there with me," he returned.

I wasn't sure if that was good or bad.

"She gets there, she gets there good to go back to sleep," Jacob warned.

Clearly, Jacob was thinking it was bad.

"Already told you I'm done bein' an ass," Rich replied.

"See that's true so my girl can sleep easy," Jacob ordered.

I wasn't breathing easy then. Father and son were in a stare down. I didn't exactly know why since it seemed everything had worked out so I didn't exactly know what to do.

What I did know was that Jacob wasn't wasting any time "taking my back" with his dad.

Which made me feel all mushy.

But me, being me, also didn't let it go on for the time it appeared it was going to (that was, eternity), so I waded in.

"I started my day with sawhorses, utility knives and sheets of drywall. So I should probably rest up so I'll have the energy to eat pancakes tomorrow in whatever form they come to me."

This worked. The stare down ended. Jacob wrapped an arm around my waist, gave me a squeeze and bent to give me a kiss on the side of my head before he let me go.

I moved to his dad, doing it looking over my shoulder and saying, "'Night, honey."

"'Night, Emme," Jacob murmured then his eyes went to his father. "Dad."

"Deck," Rich replied, his lips twitching.

I made it to the door. He moved out of my way and we both moved down the hall. It wasn't a long distance but we did it in silence so it felt like a football field.

I stopped at Jacob's door and heard Buford's quiet snoring.

I got a handsome, tall, strong, affectionate man who was a genius and didn't snore.

Total score.

But he came with a dog who hogged the bed and did snore, even though it was quietly.

This was a tie. It forced me to cuddle with Jacob, seeing as I had no room to move, but then again, I had no room to move. And snoring—dog, man, Martian—was no fun. Still, Buford was droopy cute and liked me so I shouldn't complain.

I pushed these thoughts aside and turned to Rich.

"Well, thanks for walking me," I said lamely.

We were in shadows but I still saw the white flash of his teeth before he replied, "'Night, Emme."

"'Night, Rich," I mumbled, moved into the room, put my hand on the door and was about to close it when I stopped, seeing Rich was still standing there.

This indicated to me we weren't done.

I braced and it was a good idea.

"That other one, she did a number on him," he told me quietly.

"I know," I said the same way.

"I was worried."

That was sweet.

I pulled in a breath, forced what I hoped was my last fake smile for the next year and said, "I'm sorry. And I'm sorrier I did something stupid to make you worry."

He accepted that with a nod but noted, "You two are goin' fast."

"I know."

"He's in deep."

He's in deep.

I said nothing but I felt everything. Too much of it. Too much to breathe.

"Deck, he doesn't like simple," Rich continued. "Never did. Doesn't have the patience for it. He likes complicated. The more complicated the better. But, see, Emme darlin', some puzzles, they don't have solutions. He's lucky, he's never found one he couldn't solve. Doesn't mean he won't find one. And my son, the way he is, the way his mind works, if he encounters that, he'll keep searchin' for the solution until it drives him crazy."

I didn't know what he was driving at so I took a wild guess. "I... do you think I'm a puzzle, Rich?"

"I think there's a reason my boy's in deep. I think that's because you're complicated. That doesn't mean he won't be happy when he finds the solution. I'm just hopin' whatever it is can be solved."

I shook my head. "I'm not a puzzle."

"Three girls I met today, Emme. One didn't care enough to remember to meet her man's parents. One was stiff and nervous. One was soft and sweet. That's all I know. I don't know about a puzzle. I just know that's complicated."

I didn't want to go over that day, *again*. I also didn't want to remind him he had a part in it going bad.

So instead, I warned him carefully, "I'm not sure this discussion will give me sweet dreams."

At that he leaned in so suddenly it stunned me.

"Be that girl," he whispered fiercely. "Be that girl who just gave my boy sweet. Please be that girl, Emme."

Startled, I whispered back, "I *am* that girl, Rich."

"Deck, that other woman, he was in so damned deep. Like his dad, he finds what he wants, he gives it his all. She wasn't worth it. Be the girl that makes it worth it."

It wasn't his business just as it was, unfortunately, and we were suddenly having an intense conversation about important things, also unfortunately, so I shared, "I'm in love with him."

"So was the other one," he replied.

My hand tensed on the door. His comment beyond annoying and not a little out of line, I was unable to think of what to say.

Then I thought of what to say. "I'm not Elsbeth. Not even a little bit."

He leaned back, I heard him pull in a deep breath and his voice was less severe when he stated, "I'm his father. I'm going to want the best for him."

"And I'm the woman who loves him. I'm obviously going to want the same. But, no offense, what I don't want is his dad intimating that is not me. I understand you love him and want to protect him. But I made a mistake. It annoyed Jacob. It upset you. You were both entitled to those reactions because it was a big mistake. But now it's over. Can I ask that tomorrow, when we wake up, we start over?"

He studied me through the dark a long moment before he agreed, "I can do that, Emme."

"I'd be grateful, Rich."

"Now, just to say, I just came on strong and Deck's right, I'm nosy, especially when what I'm nosin' around matters. But we just made a deal. I don't go back on what I say, so even though we had these words, tomorrow, as I said, we're startin' over. So I want you to sleep easy."

Like that would happen.

"Buford's good at keeping me company," I assured him on a fib. He was, just not when he was sleeping. "I'll be fine. But thank you for saying that anyway."

He held my eyes, nodded and murmured, "'Night, darlin'. Tomorrow will be a better day."

"Thanks, Rich, I'm sure it will. And good night."

He hesitated before he moved away.

I shut the door and moved to the bed.

As I settled in bed, Buford woke up long enough to roll to his other side, stretch out and start snoring again.

Back to the door, eyes open, I went over the day. And again. And repeat.

It made me all kinds of uneasy.

There were obvious reasons why.

And there were some that were not obvious.

Therefore, I stayed awake for a long time, turning it over in my head, trying to relieve the unease.

But I fell asleep before I could.

Luckily, I did it before Jacob joined me.

CHAPTER FOURTEEN

Game Changer

One week later...

I SAT IN the salon chair, hair in foils, celebrity gossip magazine forgotten in my hand, eyes on my face in the mirror.

This is a game changer, Emme.

Jacob's words from last night assaulted my brain and I closed my eyes.

A game changer, Emme.

I opened my eyes and jumped when I felt a light touch on my shoulder.

I tipped my head back and looked at Dominic, stylist to practically anyone who lived in the county who had the money and good taste to go to him. He owned Carnal Spa. It wasn't too far from Gnaw Bone but even if it was five hours, every six weeks I'd make the trip in order to have him give me a cut and highlight. He was that good.

"You okay, girlie?" he asked, his gaze moving over my face.

"Fine, Dom," I assured on a complete and utter lie. "Just have a lot to do this weekend and prioritizing it in my head." This was another lie.

Dom knew it, I could tell. But Dominic was a gay man who spent his days around women and their problems, so with one look at my face he knew better than to push it.

He smiled, lifted his hands to my hair, checked a foil and murmured, "Five more minutes, darling."

Then he wandered away.

I looked to the back of the spa where Dom had a couple of rooms where they did massages and facials and stuff. I knew Lexie was back there with a client. I'd seen her earlier. She'd also seen me. We'd gabbed for a bit between her clients then she'd disappeared.

I wished she'd had a free half hour. At a time like this, a girl needed a member of her girl posse. I'd never had that kind of time and I still knew this was that kind of time.

Definitely.

A game changer, Emme.

As his words filled my head, his face filled my vision. Surprise there, also disappointment, wariness and maybe even pain.

I never wanted to give Jacob pain.

I looked back to myself in the mirror, my hair out to there with silver sticking out all over. I looked ridiculous. But I knew it was worth it because the results would be astounding.

Why, when for years I didn't give a crap about my hair, did I care about the results being astounding?

What was going on with me?

Having pushed it down all night and all morning, suddenly unable to fight it, I let it wash over me.

The last week had been good. Jacob and I had our messy discussion and got back on track.

It started on Sunday with his dad proving what he promised. To him, a deal was a deal. He did not act like an ass. He was friendly. He was funny. It was awesome.

However, Jacob was right, his pancakes sucked.

That said, things had turned so far to the light side, at Rich's request, when I hesitantly shared this honest opinion, Rich laughed out loud for a long time.

Things got even better when we went to my house.

Karla wandered around with us during my tour trying to

hide looking slightly aghast. Her wide eyes, hand lingering at her throat and hesitancy to touch anything meant she failed spectacularly at hiding it.

Rich had the exact opposite reaction. He loved my house and didn't mind sharing. The tour, which usually took a while seeing as it was a big house, took three times as long because he was interested in everything I'd done, was doing and intended to do. He gave suggestions. He gave instructions. And as a retired electrician, he inspected the wiring I'd had laid and gave it his stamp of approval.

Better, by the end of the tour, I knew that stamp extended to me. Rich was a little surprised I'd taken on that kind of a project and it being so big, but it was clear he thought it was admirable.

And with me more relaxed and not stiff around them or Jacob, our natural affection with each other was something else Rich liked.

And he showed it.

So that was all good and a huge relief. The day was great. Jacob was right, both his parents were cool and the rest of the visit went well. I'd had to leave them to work on Monday and Tuesday but we'd had dinner together, I'd spent the night each night at Jacob's and we'd had a fantastic time.

They'd left on Wednesday, and Jacob and I settled back into the good that had been us before I went wonky. I called him whenever. I picked up immediately when he phoned. And when I did, I couldn't believe I stopped doing it. I liked connecting with him, even if it was just to discuss whether we'd go out for a meal or if we'd make something at one of our houses.

And there were no more coming home later and laters.

It didn't escape me after Jacob pointed it out that I was creating busy work to keep me from him.

This concerned me, and the only reason I could come up with as to why I would do that was because I'd never met a boyfriend's parents much less the parents of the man I loved and wanted to spend the rest of my life with. I'd obviously been denying my anxiety of their impending visit and doing stupid stuff because of it.

Whatever it was, it was gone. It was back to good.

No. As with everything with Jacob, it was back to beauty.

Until last night.

A game changer, Emme.

I jumped again when Dom came back and put his hand on the back of my chair.

He smiled at me in the mirror and stated, "Time to wash you out."

I smiled back, we chatted on the way to the sinks and we kept chatting until Dom started the head massage he always gave when he was letting the conditioner do its work.

Usually, this reduced me to jelly. Dom had strong hands. I'd only had one other head massage in my life—the one given to me by the stylist in Denver Erika took me to to give me my new look. But Dom's were *way* better.

But that time, when I closed my eyes and tried to relax, it rushed me.

You don't want kids?

No, honey.

Seriously?

Hesitation. *Seriously.*

Then that look. That look on his face, so close, us naked, Jacob lying on top of me.

That look of shock.

Disappointment.

Pain.

That look that shattered me because I knew what I'd said had shattered him.

We'd just made love. We were snuggling, touching, whispering, planning. Planning our lives and how they would come in the now. How neither Jacob nor I were happy he had to go to Denver for work and would be gone for the weekend, not back until Tuesday, which meant we'd be separated for the first time since we got together. How, after Jacob sorted this case that was troubling him, we were going to plan a vacation to somewhere exciting. Paris. London. Prague.

Then we moved on to planning our lives how they would come in the later.

And that was when Jacob asked me how many kids I wanted.

And my response was unexpected.

And unwelcome.

Not even one?

Honey.

I felt my eyes sting as Dom rinsed the conditioner out of my hair.

This is a game changer, Emme.

Dom wrapped my hair in a towel and announced, "You're done, darling. Sit up. Let's get you back to my station and unleash that beauty."

I looked over my shoulder at him, smiled and chatted as we walked to his station.

It wasn't until he was blow drying my hair and we couldn't chitchat anymore before it came back to me.

That morning.

I saw Jacob standing in front of me. He'd pressed me into the side of my Bronco in his garage.

I was going to Dom's. He was heading to Denver.

He kissed me, hard, long, amazing but also there was a hint of something else.

Longing.

Bleakness and longing.

It hurt.

Yes, a kiss hurt. But I felt it and when he lifted his head, I knew he felt it too.

"I'll call," he whispered, his hand at my neck, his thumb stroking my jaw. "But we'll talk when I get home."

I knew my eyes were wet because the vision of him was swimming as I said, "Okay, honey."

"We'll figure it out, Emme," he promised.

I wanted to believe him. I really, really wanted to believe him.

But I didn't believe him.

"Love you, Jacob," I whispered and he smiled.

That was bleak too.

"Love you too, Emme."

He gave me another kiss then waited until I climbed into Persephone so he could swing my door shut for me. I smiled at him through the windshield, another fake one, as he thumped his hand palm flat on my hood and moved away from the truck.

I pulled out of his garage and did it with my eyes glued to him. He stood in his garage, tall, strong, pure male beauty, arms crossed on his chest, long, long legs planted.

Mine.

All mine.

Not even one?

Honey.

Just one, Emme.

I've never wanted kids, Jacob. That might be weird but it's true. I just...that's just not me. It's never been me.

Long, painful pause then, *This is a game changer, Emme.*

"Voilà!"

I focused on myself in the mirror and forced yet another fucking smile.

"As usual, Dom, you've created a masterpiece," I told him.

"For every artiste, to do such a thing, he must have the best material at his disposal," he told me.

Dominic. He was such a cool guy. And right then he was cool because his compliment was genuine and his eyes were kind but concerned. The former made me smile sincerely. The latter just felt nice because he cared.

I paid and tipped huge.

Before I left, I gave Dom a hug at the same time I got a message whispered in my ear, "You ever need to talk, the line between stylist and client is a vague one, darling. Just call the salon and I'll call you back as soon as I can."

He totally knew I wasn't all right.

"Thanks, Dom," I whispered back, knowing I'd never, not in a million years, do that.

And wondering again what was wrong with me that I wouldn't.

He gave me a squeeze.

I gave him a smile as I left and got in Persephone.

Game changer, Emme.

I shut my eyes tight. Then I forced them open and looked to my purse. My phone was in my purse. Jacob would be in Denver by now. So if I called he wouldn't be talking while driving.

I reached to the phone but stopped.

The truth was, I didn't want kids.

I wanted a puppy.

I also, later, wanted a cat.

I wanted my house to be fixed up and I didn't mind the fact that once it was, I'd be rambling around in it all alone. There'd always be a change of scenery. There'd always be something to do in the garden or somewhere on the property.

I'd never thought on it much, not before I was sick and truly, not even after. But when I did, I knew I wanted a man. A partner. Someone to share my time with. But only because it hit me unexpectedly just how alone I was.

But I'd never thought about kids.

I didn't lie to Jacob. That just wasn't me. I was thirty-four years old, had done my own thing and been responsible only to me for a very long time. Fitting a man in my life worked, that man being Jacob, it worked spectacularly. We were good together. We slid into that easily.

You didn't fit a kid in your life.

A kid became your life.

And kids, plural, consumed it.

But Jacob wanted kids.

And that was just not me.

My eyes again stinging, I lifted my head and looked down the Main Street of Carnal. I'd spent time there more than once since moving to the mountains. They had an awesome coffee shop called La-La Land that not only had great coffees but amazing cakes and treats. They had a cute gift shop with great pottery.

And they had Bubba's bar.

And Bubba's was owned by Krystal Briggs and Tate Jackson. So, by extension, it was also owned by Lauren Jackson.

Two members of my girl posse.

Outside of Faye, who I talked to and visited with regularly now that Jacob's namesake had entered this world and Jacob seemed intent on being little Jake's first living memory, I had not spent much time with my new girl posse.

I had fielded calls. I'd even made calls. On a lunch hour, I'd popped in for a gab with Zara and to do some shopping at Karma. Jacob and I had run into Max and Nina at The Mark when we went there for dinner and we'd stood at their table and shot the breeze for ten full minutes. And I'd run into Lexie and Ty when they were visiting Chace and Faye after the baby was born at a time when Jacob and I showed to do the same.

All of this was welcome, to me and to them.

But I had not connected in any real way. With the phone calls, the invitation was there.

I just didn't take them up on it. Too busy.

Always too busy.

What does that say, Emme?

The question hit my brain like a shot and I just as quickly ignored it.

But even ignoring it, I threw open my door, hopped down from Persephone and hoofed it down Main Street.

Destination: Bubba's.

I walked in and saw that both Krystal and Lauren were there. So was Bubba.

Bubba was at one end of the bar, shooting the shit with a couple of patrons. Lauren was at the other end, talking to an old guy wearing a baseball cap. Krystal was in the middle.

All their eyes came to me.

With smiles and waves to Lauren and Bubba, I made my way to Krystal.

I hiked my ass up on a stool and looked at her. "Hey."

She looked at me.

Then she declared, "Houston, we have a problem."

Fantastic.

"Is it that easy to read?" I asked.

"Babe, you look like you just stepped into the street and noticed, too late, a Mack truck heading your way."

Yes, it was that easy to read because that was precisely how I felt.

"I..." I hesitated then shared, "Have an issue."

"No shit?" she asked.

In what seemed to be pure Krystal style, that didn't sound like it welcomed heartfelt sharing at the same time it demanded it.

I wondered how she did that but didn't ask. There were other things more pressing on my mind.

I looked to the taps beside her then back to her. "Can I have a beer?"

"No."

I blinked. "No?"

"I been behind this bar a long time, so trust me on this. Your face doesn't say beer," she informed me. "Your face says vodka, tequila or bourbon. Your pick. On the house."

I was a beer drinker. If I was somewhere fancy that required me drinking something out of a glass, I'd have a martini.

Therefore, I requested, "Vodka."

"On it," she muttered, and moved to the glasses at the back of the bar.

Lauren moved in when she did. "Hey, Emme."

"Hi, Lauren."

Her head tipped to the side, her gaze never leaving me. "You okay?"

So totally easy to read.

"She has an issue," Krystal reported, putting the shot glass to the bar and grabbing a bottle of vodka.

She poured. She slid the glass my way. I picked it up and threw it back.

Then I remembered why I drank beer. Not as sharp. Far more mellow. Vodka packed a punch. Beer was cool and refreshing.

And Jacob's homemade ale was the best beer I'd ever tasted.

I closed my eyes tight.

"Emme, honey, talk to us," Lauren encouraged gently.

I opened my eyes and she was leaned into her forearms on the bar toward me. Krystal was close to her side, not leaned in, but I had her attention.

"I don't want kids," I announced.

Krystal and Lauren looked at each other then back at me.

"Okay," Lauren prompted.

"Jacob does," I went on.

"Oh fuck," Krystal murmured.

"Yeah," I agreed.

She grabbed the vodka bottle and poured another shot.

I grabbed the shot glass and threw it back.

When I was done, Lauren asked carefully, "You sure you don't want kids?"

I nodded. "Absolutely. Don't have that urge," I told her. "And if I was going to get it, Jacob asking me how many I wanted after we'd made love would be the time that would happen. And Jacob telling me me not wanting them was a game changer would *definitely* do it."

"A game changer?" Lauren whispered in a horrified tone.

"Oh fuck," Krystal murmured.

"Yeah," I agreed.

"So you had this conversation when?" Lauren asked.

"Last night," I answered. "Unfortunate timing. Jacob's in Denver for four days, seeing to some business." I drew in a breath then continued, "It's the first time we've been separated since we got together."

"Yep. That's unfortunate timing," Krystal confirmed.

I bit my lip.

"Is he...was he...did he..." Lauren was having trouble getting it out then she powered through, "How did he seem when he left?"

"He said we'd figure it out," I told her.

"Well, that's good," Krystal put in.

"But he kissed me before I took off this morning and it... well," I closed my eyes, opened them, leaned in and whispered, *"Hurt."*

Krystal leaned in too. "He kiss you hard?"

"A lot of the time he kisses me hard. I like it like that. He likes it like that. But it wasn't like that. It was...sad." I shook my head, threw out my hands and carried on, "I know it sounds weird, a kiss being sad." I felt my lip quiver, and to stop it I kept going. "But it was a sad kiss."

"The good-bye before the good-bye," Krystal said quietly.

"Krys," Lauren said warningly.

Krystal shut her mouth.

But she was right and I knew it.

I put my elbow to the bar and my forehead in my hand.

"Emme," Lauren called.

I kept my head in my hand but lifted my eyes to her. "I love him."

"Oh, baby," she whispered.

"I...he was...we've known each other for years and it's always been him for me," I shared.

Krystal leaned into her forearms on the bar and said, "If that's so, girl, then maybe you should rethink this kid thing."

I kept close but dropped my hand to the bar. "That's not me."

"For him can you make it you?" Lauren asked.

"Kids consume your life," I told them.

"They don't," Lauren replied. "Even as they do. It's just that it happens in a way you like."

I didn't agree.

Lauren went on, "I've never carried a child but Tate's got a son. If you've been around these parts awhile, you probably know that his mother was killed, so Jonas is with us all the time. We're a family. I got him when he was older but I treasure the day he came into my life and every day he's been in it since."

"That's cool. You're cool," I stated. "You're that kind of lady. But I promise, after that discussion, that kiss, I've been rolling it over and over in my head and I think about it. I think of giving in. And I just…" I swallowed. "Don't want that to be my life. I never thought about it. Thinking about it, bottom line, it's just not me."

Lauren looked at Krystal but Krystal was looking at me.

"You two, you'd make beautiful babies," she declared, and something about that hit me like a punch right in the middle of my chest, winding me.

"Been 'round Faye and Chace's a lot the last coupla weeks. Faye says Deck's been around a lot too. Sometimes with you, sometimes durin' the day just to check in," she informed me.

I knew this. Again, Jacob was determined to make a lasting impression on Chace and Faye's baby and when he was determined, he did something about it even if the thing he was determined about couldn't cogitate.

More, he and Chace were very close. Jacob was super happy that Chace was happy. And he was the kind of man who enjoyed sharing that kind of thing with someone he cared about.

That thought also hit me in the chest.

"Faye says that kid's the apple of his eye," Krystal kept talking. "Says it's cute, how he is with little Jake. Now, we all know, nothin' about Deck is cute, but I figure that'd be all kinds of cute, that big man bonding with a little baby. He has that with his best friend's kid, what's he gonna give your family?"

It was then, the vision of Jacob holding the newborn Jake, completely consumed by the child he held so gently in his strapping arms, hit me, which delivered another blow to the sternum and I was again finding it hard to breathe.

It'd been beautiful. The most beautiful thing I'd ever seen.

Until later that night when he'd lifted his head, looked in my eyes and told me he wanted to build a life with me.

"My advice," Krystal cut into my thoughts. "Do not make any decisions about ending things. Do not make any declarations about anything. He's gone four days. You take four days to think on the man you got in your bed. How he looks at you. How he treats you. How, honest to God, there are not many good men out there. How he is with little Jake. How you got that rambling wreck of a house and how it'd come alive, filled with babies. And you reconsider."

"Krys," Lauren again said warningly, and Krystal's eyes shot to her.

"Am I wrong?"

Lauren held her gaze then she looked at me. "She's not, you know."

"I—" I started, but Lauren darted her hand out and took hold of mine.

"Like Krys says, no decisions, no declarations. Four days and you take that time to think. If it really isn't you, okay. If it's something else, explore that. If you have some issue with carrying a baby, then consider adoption or surrogacy. If it's something deeper and you can't talk with Deck about it, you call me, Krystal, Faye, whoever, and chat. We won't say anything to anybody. And we'll listen."

She gave my hand a squeeze and looked deep in my eyes, hers searching, and she kept going but this time softly.

"But Krys is only mostly right. My experience, but that's only been lately, is that there are good men out there and that number is not limited. But that doesn't mean they're easy to find, easy to get or easy to keep." Another hand squeeze then, "That also doesn't mean you have to give up bits of yourself to get them. Give in to something you don't want that will change the course of your life to keep them. But it does mean you need to think very hard about any decision that will affect your future with them."

Like Jacob that morning, my vision of her was swimming when she was done talking and I whispered, "Girl posses are awesome."

The blurry vision of Lauren smiled.

"They're about to get awesomer because we're bringin' in sandwiches, we're gettin' some of Shambles's cakes from La-La Land and you're drinkin' yourself stinkin' drunk with your girls," Krystal declared.

I blinked my tears away, looked to her, gave her a wobbly smile and she went on.

"You're trashed, Bubba'll drive your car while Laurie or me drive you home. So you're covered. Food. Booze. Company. And a safe way home. Now settle in, girl, we're about to perform the initiation ceremony."

My wobbly smile got stronger.

She didn't smile at me.

She poured more vodka in my shot glass.

When it was full, I took it and threw it back.

*　　　*　　　*

Five hours later…

When I got home I went straight to my computer in the library.

I dumped my bag and turned my computer on.

I wasn't exactly drunk, seeing as I'd switched to beer and sipping, and sandwiches turned into pizza later. Still, I was in no state to drive, so Krystal brought me home with Bubba driving Persephone (and complaining, with a hint of teasing but more grumpiness, about my "Free to Fly" butterfly on my rearview mirror, proving Jacob right about the whole Bronco thing).

As the computer came on, my eyes wandered to the wall-paper and my mind wandered to the fact that I really needed to do something about it. There wasn't much of it but it was seriously ugly. The walls would look better stripped, even if it would likely take a year and a half to cover them with something better.

On this thought, my phone in my purse rang.

I pulled it out and saw it said "Jacob calling."

That punch in the chest came back.

I took the call and put the phone to my ear.

"Hey, honey," I said quietly.

"Hey, baby," he replied in the same tone. "You have an okay day?"

"Well, my hair looks fabulous so it's a shame you're missing it. But having it done in the proximity of Bubba's meant I didn't come home and waste it on fitting drywall patches over exposed wire. Instead, I shared it with Krystal, Lauren, Bubba, a really nice guy named Jim-Billy and the clientele of a biker bar."

There was a smile in his voice when he replied, "It's good you didn't let that go to waste."

I liked the sound of that smile and I loved him.

I loved him.

I again closed my eyes tight, opened them and stated conversationally, "I had a good gab with Krystal and Lauren."

He knew what I was saying.

I knew this when he hesitated before replying, "That's good, Emme."

"We'll talk when you get home," I whispered.

Another hesitation, this one heavy before he came back to me, his deep voice holding a hint of relief, and God, *God*, I might have even heard hope when he said, "Okay, honey."

"Okay," I replied, sat up straighter, cleared my throat and asked, "Your day okay?"

"It just got better."

Yet again, I closed my eyes.

His voice came back to me and I opened them.

"Do my best to get this shit done early so I can get back to my girl."

"That'd be good."

"Hang on," he said, suddenly distracted. I hung on and half a minute later, he told me, "Gotta go, babe. Sorry. In the middle of something. Thought I had time. I don't."

"Okay, honey."

"I'll call tomorrow."

"Right."

"Have a good night, sleep well, baby."

"You too, Jacob. Later."

"Later, babe."

He disconnected.

I put my phone on the desk, stared at it and lost sight of it when the image of Jacob holding little Jake filled my head.

I shook my head to clear it and looked at the computer. I logged in and pulled up Outlook.

Then I sent a message to Harvey.

It had been a while since we had a visit, and with Jacob gone, it was a golden opportunity.

But more, Harvey had lived a tough life. He'd made mistakes. He'd paid for them. He knew me. And he was wise.

So I wanted to talk to him about Jacob, about where we were, get his thoughts, see if they matched Krystal and Lauren's. Then I was going to do what the girls advised I do.

Think very hard about a decision that would affect my future with Jacob.

My email to Harvey included me asking if he was free for a visit the next day. After it was sent, I wandered around doing normal things. Setting up the coffeemaker to make coffee for the morning. Putting away the clean dishes in my dishwasher. Going back to the computer to sort through emails that had come in.

While I was doing that, Harvey emailed back.

Always have time for you, Emme. How about noon? I'll give you lunch. Drive safely.

I replied that I'd bring dessert, finished with my other emails and shut down my machine.

*   *   *

Fifteen hours later…

I parked on Broadway in Denver.

I was early.

I was early because I hadn't slept great, thus was wide awake and ready to face the day at a God-awful hour. With nothing to occupy my mind except things I didn't want occupying it, I decided to hit the road.

Harvey was expecting me at noon, which meant I had time to stop at Fortnum's Used Books to get a coffee. When I lived in Denver, I went there all the time because the coffee was sublime. But also because it was just a cool place where you just wanted to hang. And the staff were hilarious.

I jumped down from the Bronco, cleared the door, my hand to it to slam it shut, my eyes moving the quarter of a block to the door to Fortnum's that opened at a diagonal to the street corner.

I stopped dead.

And I stopped breathing.

But my heart started bleeding.

This was because Jacob was coming out of Fortnum's, white paper coffee cup in his hand.

And with him was Elsbeth.

My hand clutched the edge of my door so hard it bit into my flesh as I stared, shocked, disbelieving, eviscerated, as they stopped on the corner.

Jacob looked down at her and gave her a small grin.

Already shredded, more pieces of me were torn away.

Elsbeth looked up at Jacob and returned his grin with a radiant smile.

Ragged and bleeding, more of me was stripped away.

Then Elsbeth moved into Jacob, rounded him with her arms and gave him a hug.

At that, standing there, seeing, breathing, feeling, still there was nothing left of me.

I could take no more.

I got in my truck, not looking, not doing anything but concentrating on getting the fuck out of there. I turned the ignition on Persephone, guided her into traffic, kept my eyes from Fortnum's and drove right past.

Luckily, just blocks down Broadway, there was an interchange to I-25.

I took it and headed home.

Harvey was going to worry.

I'd explain it to him later.

*   *   *

Three hours later...

I zipped up the bag on Jacob's bed that held all my stuff.

I swallowed.

I looked down at Buford.

His tail wagged.

The vision of him started swimming.

I blinked and moved to grab my bag.

I stopped when I saw the kaleidoscope on Jacob's nightstand.

I was wrong earlier. There was something left to me.

I knew this because seeing that kaleidoscope sliced away the final part of me.

I went to it, picked it up, held it carefully, studied it.

It really was a thing of beauty.

Suddenly, my hand fisted around it and I whirled, my arm flying out.

Buford got up to his feet and backed away.

But my grip refused to let it go. So when my motions were done, I was cradling it to my chest.

"Why?" I asked Buford.

Buford stared up at me, tongue lolling.

"Why was he with her? He said he hated her. He said he never wanted to see her again."

Buford said nothing.

I shook my head, lifted the kaleidoscope and put it to my eye.

I turned the dials.

I didn't see beauty. What I saw just made me dizzy.

I put it on the nightstand, grabbed my bag, bent to Buford and gave him ear scratches.

"I'll miss you, puppy," I whispered.

He turned his head and licked my wrist.

I walked out of Jacob's house, so in a state, I totally forgot to engage the alarm.

I also ignored it when I heard Buford start barking. He didn't bark much so if I wasn't in such a state, I would have paid attention.

I didn't.

I had other things on my mind.

But before I drove away, I went next door and asked the woman there if she'd see to Buford.

With a curious look at me, she agreed.

*   *   *

Dane

"Shut it," Dane said to the damned dog, kicked him back and shut the door to the bedroom, keeping the dog out.

Dane had been following Emme and when she arrived at this place, he'd slipped into the big, fancy-assed house behind her.

And he'd watched.

And he fucking hated what he saw.

His eyes moved to the kaleidoscope, then he walked there.

He picked it up but all he could see was Emme holding that fucking thing to her chest like it was her baby.

And that thing was *Deck's*. It was in *Deck's house*. And it was something that meant something to that guy, with his big house and heated pool who thought his dick was big enough he could stand outside the courtroom and stare *Dane* down like Dane was scared of his ass. Like Dane wouldn't give a shit that *Deck* had moved in on his woman practically the minute they met on the street.

And he'd met Emme on the street when Dane was right fucking there.

Right *fucking* there.

That kaleidoscope was something that meant something to Emme too. It meant something to Emme *and* that fucking guy. Enough for her to cradle it. Enough for him to keep it on his nightstand.

So fuck him.

And fuck Emme.

Dane kept hold of the kaleidoscope and grabbed the box that obviously came with it and he moved to the window. He removed the screen, stole out, closed the window and put the screen back. He couldn't lock it in place from outside but he didn't give a fuck. If it fell out, it fell out.

Standing outside that fucking guy's fancy-assed house in the cold, Dane made his decision of what he was going to do with that fucking kaleidoscope.

Then he did it.

* * *

Emme

Two hours later…

My phone rang.

Again.

I ignored it and ripped off more paper.

It stopped ringing.

I held the steamer to the wall of the library.

"No," I whispered, pulling the steamer away and ripping

off more paper. "No," I repeated, putting the steamer back to the wall.

My eyes went fuzzy.

My cheeks got wet.

"No," I whimpered. "All I need is me. Just me. That's all I need."

I ripped off more paper.

*   *   *

The next morning...

I sat at my desk in my office at the yard.

My cell on the desk rang.

I ignored it.

CHAPTER FIFTEEN

Always

That evening...

THE FIRST THING I noticed while driving up to my house was Jacob's truck.

Strike that, it was Jacob leaning against the tail of his truck, arms crossed, ankles crossed, looking very angry.

He was home early.

To take my mind off that, the second thing I noticed was that Max and his crew had gotten a number of windows in.

Dad had given me my bonus. I'd given Max the go-ahead. He'd been working on my windows for a week. This was the start of week two.

At the front, there were now no boards on any windows as Max, per Jacob's orders, saw to those first.

So now, outside of the fresh wood needing painting on the windows, my house looked like that. A house. A beautiful one.

Not a dilapidated wreck.

This should have made me happy.

It didn't.

Because it was not lost on me that my bonus coincidentally coincided almost to the penny to Max's bid.

I knew Jacob and Dad were conspiring.

I said nothing.

This was because, two weeks ago, I thought this was sweet. Sweet and protective and maybe even a little funny.

Now I absolutely did not.

I parked opposite the front door to Jacob's truck and swung out of my Bronco. As I rounded the hood, I noticed Jacob had moved. He was now standing at the foot of my front steps.

I looked right in his eyes.

He didn't look away and he didn't hesitate.

"Donna called. Said not to worry. She'd look after Buford."

"Good she handled that," I replied, walking right by him to my front door.

I inserted the key then exerted some effort to push it open and I walked in.

Unsurprisingly, Jacob followed me.

I heard the door close then I heard, "What the fuck, Emme?"

I turned, and standing on the magnificent starburst in what, by God even if it killed me, would one day be a magnificent, opulent front entry, I locked eyes with Jacob Decker and I didn't hesitate either.

"On a wild hair, Sunday, I went to Denver to do some shopping."

This was a lie, of course, but I didn't give a fuck. What I did with my time was no longer his business.

"You were in Denver and you didn't call me?" he asked.

I found this a strange question for two reasons. One, I hadn't even thought of calling him, even to ask if he had enough time to grab some lunch together. Two, that he'd suggest he wanted to see me when he was seeing Elsbeth.

I decided it was best to ignore this and carry on as if he hadn't said a word.

"And I popped by Fortnum's to get a cup of coffee," I shared, and watched with grim fascination as his entire body jerked and his face flinched. "Yeah, honey," I whispered. "You and Elsbeth looked good together. Then again, you always did."

"Emme—"

Oh no. I was not going to listen to his shit.

"Save it," I snapped. "I don't want to hear it. I don't fucking care."

"There's an explanation."

I threw out a hand and replied, "I bet." Then I pulled my purse from my arm, walked to the table I had in the entry and dumped it while finishing, "I just don't give a shit what it is."

"It isn't what you think," he told me.

I turned to him. "What I think is you told me you hated her. You told me you never wanted to see her again. And yet, there you were, giving her a grin and a hug."

"She ran into Erika," he stated.

"Whoop-di-do," I shot back. "That shit happens. Denver is a big city but it's still a small town. That happens all the time. Hell, when I lived there, I couldn't go anywhere without seeing someone I knew. Though, I must admit, I do find it odd that Elsbeth had the itch to share with you over coffee that she ran into Erika. What's odder is that you'd meet her so she could share that with you."

He ignored that and informed me, "Erika told her about you and me."

"This isn't a surprise," I returned instantly. "I haven't had a long girlie chat with Erika recently, what with spending the last couple of months getting fucked over by you. Oh! And the months before that getting fucked over by Dane," I added, and his face got hard but I did not fucking care. "But she has called, and silly me, I was happy so I shared we'd hooked up. She was happy for me. She never really got on with Elsbeth so I bet she was double happy sharing it with her."

Jacob again ignored all I said and kept on with his story.

"When I got to town, babe, Elsbeth gave me a call outta the blue and asked to meet. Just a coincidence I was in Denver."

"Clearly, you jumped right on that."

His voice suddenly went low. "Baby, please, hear me out."

"Why?" I hissed.

"Because this is not what you fuckin' think and I need to straighten it out."

"You know," I started chattily, "part of me wants to hear you out just to see what bullshit you've got to say. The other part of me does not give one shit and would rather not waste another second on you."

"Fuck, Emme," he growled.

Something snapped, I lost it, leaned into him and yelled, "You met with *Elsbeth*! You smiled at her! You held her! Both of those aren't hers, Jacob. Both of those are *mine*!"

"I didn't hold her," he returned.

"I saw her hug you," I retorted.

"Yeah, she hugged me, babe, but I didn't hug her back."

My head jerked because that might be true. I saw Elsbeth go in for the hug but I never saw Jacob put his arms around her. I'd looked away the minute she touched him.

"She's happy we're together," he declared.

I snapped my mouth shut and my torso swung back.

"Yeah. Shocked the shit outta me too," he continued. "She said it on the phone when she called me. I reckoned she said it so I wouldn't hang up on her ass. She kept talkin', I was sure she was playin' me. But I couldn't shake that she sounded like she used to sound. Like she used to be."

"So you thought, Elsbeth swinging back, now you're rich and successful and she'd probably not blink at the opportunity to push out an entire Decker football team for you, you'd check out the lay of the land," I guessed acidly.

"Fuck no," he clipped, beginning to sound angry. "I only met with her because she told me she wanted to patch things up with you. And I reckoned if I didn't meet with her, she'd go straight to you and I wanted to say face-to-face I was not down with that."

Again, I clamped my mouth shut.

"She misses you, Emme," he told me.

"Right," I said sarcastically. "Suddenly, after nine years, I'm with her ex, she misses me and contacts *her ex* to talk about patching things up."

"She didn't think you'd be receptive."

"She was right. The weird thing is, after what you told me happened last summer, she should have thought *you* would be *less* receptive."

"Emmanuelle, you close down, nothin' gettin' in unless it shoves its way in and you know that's no lie. But, just sayin', she had a few things she had to say to me too."

The first part he said was indeed no lie so I had no response. The second part I didn't want to know. So I said nothing.

Jacob did.

"Babe, you two were tight."

"We're not anymore."

"Emme, *fuck*."

He took a step to me but stopped when I took a step back.

Then he kept talking.

"She said she always knew it would happen between us. She said she even knew it was happening back then. We both know this. She's now admitted it. She's divorcing her husband. She's not happy but she's not with another guy and not looking to hook up. She's trying to figure out where she went wrong and get her life back on track. But she's doin' that without a guy. And one of the places where she went wrong was settin' up a life where she got what she wanted but not what she needed and lost a whole load of shit in the process. And yeah, part of that was me. But the part she's concerned about is you."

"Do you honestly think I'll believe this crap?" I asked.

"Yeah, I honestly do because it's the truth."

"So, breaking this down," I began, crossing my arms on my chest. "You got a call from your ex, my ex–best friend, about her burning desire to mend fences. You didn't tell me about it, thought it was a good idea to have a heartfelt, soul-exposing chat over coffee and fill me in later. Do I have that right?"

"If I said she called. If I told you what she wanted. If I said I thought it might be good you explore that, what you lost with her, what might be good to have back. Or if that wasn't the way it swung, still give you the opportunity to put a line under it and move on, for you, for her, for me. If I suggested that maybe it might be a good idea to talk with her and think about why you scraped her off in the first place. If I gave you all that, Emme, what would you do?"

"I don't know," I replied. "And now I never will since I wasn't given that shot."

"Emme, you got shit you're workin' out which is big shit you need to concentrate on and I need to keep you on that path. I also need to make certain nothing veers you off that path and I *definitely* need to be certain to protect you from something that'll *shove* you off it. Say me havin' a meet with my ex."

My head cocked with confusion and I asked, "What the fuck are you talking about?"

Then he said something totally bizarre.

" 'I won't lie there and think how fucked-up shitty it is to be so goddamned alone and so fucking lonely. Scared I'll die, no one will care. No man. No kids.' "

My brows shot together because he was making no sense whatsoever.

"Jacob, what the fuck?" I mostly repeated.

"That's what you said to me."

"What?"

"When you lost it when you thought I was playing you."

I probably said that, just like that. Jacob remembered everything.

I still didn't get it.

"So?" I asked.

"No man," he stated then finished with emphasis. *"No kids."*

Hearing his words, *my words*, my entire body locked.

Jacob kept going.

"You said that. You said straight up you thought about kids. You said it, giving me indication, since you were open-ing yourself up to finding a man, that man bein' me, you also want kids. Then, you take hold of Chace and Faye's son and the world melts. It's just you and him. You were so into little Jake, there was nothin' else but you and him. Weeks later, we're there, we're in love, we're movin' down that path, I ask you how many kids you want, suddenly you don't want any. Suddenly, you've never thought about kids. Suddenly, that's *not you*."

"I—"

"Disconnecting. Again."

"Jacob—"

He interrupted me again. "See, babe, for some reason I cannot get a lock on, you're clueless. One minute, you're sweet, so fuckin' sweet, swear to Christ, Emme, don't know what I did in my life to deserve that kind of sweet. Perfect for me, top to toe, brain and body, free and easy givin' me not just everything I want but everything I *need*."

I sucked in a sharp breath as his words hit me hard in my sternum.

Jacob must not have noticed my reaction because he kept speaking.

"The next minute, you're sharin' your past with me, workin' it out in your head, tellin' me how you understand that guy who snatched you scarred you. Then the next minute, back to clueless, and out of the blue you're slippin' away. You don't see it happen, feel it happen, even know you're doin' it. But *I* feel it. I don't get how you don't get it when you fuckin' told me you got it. And last, I don't know how to fix it, and when it happens, it kills. So I gotta be on the lookout for everything," he leaned in, "every-fucking-thing you could use to tear yourself away from me. So yeah, Elsbeth called, she seemed to be pulling her shit together, I took the meet and I didn't tell you about it precisely because of this. Because you'd use it to tear yourself away from me."

Again, I had no response. This time because everything he said was right and I was freaked because I didn't know why I was so clueless, how I didn't get it and I also didn't know how to fix it.

Jacob didn't seem to mind I had no response. He kept sharing.

"And by the way, Emme, she also wanted to apologize about pulling that shit on me last summer. And that was genuine too, so it was another reason I took the meet. It obviously seems fucked to you, since you're in your head and can't pull yourself out, but I'm glad I did. Months I spent wonderin' what the fuck was wrong with me I fell and did it deep for a total fuckin' cunt. It was good to know she wasn't. It was good to know she was messed up and doin' stupid shit at the same time tryin' to sort herself out. It was good to know I fell in love with a decent woman who made stupid choices."

That all made sense too, which sucked.

But he wasn't done. He'd saved the best for last.

"And it might make me a dick but it was good to be drinkin' coffee with a woman fucked up because she fucked me over knowin' in the end it worked out for me. Because I was not with a woman who was not right for me. I was with the woman who was made for me."

"I'm glad you got that, Jacob," I replied, and I kind of was.

But I was also more than kind of reeling, scared, freaked and still angry. Since I couldn't deal with the scared and freaked, I held on to the angry.

Thus I continued, "But it doesn't erase the fact that you purposefully didn't tell me."

"And I explained the reasons."

"Was it so important to you that you'd risk this," I threw a hand out, "just to know you didn't make a jacked choice that affected you for a decade?"

"Jesus, Emme, *yeah*," he clipped then went on, "But actually, I didn't expect you to be in Denver. So I didn't expect you to know at all until I told you."

"You have a habit of telling me stuff after the fact," I pointed out, and he lifted a hand and raked it through his hair.

"Christ, Emmanuelle, the last time that shit happened I was workin' a confidential case."

"Okay, how about my windows, Jacob?" I shot back. "Were you ever going to tell me you and Dad were in cahoots to get me something you both wanted me to have but I wanted to get my own damned self so you both played me?"

His chin jerked back and his eyebrows shot together before he asked, "Are you fuckin' shitting me?"

"No. I absolutely am not. You stood in my kitchen and told me you'd have a mind to me, how I do things, how I'm used to doing things myself. But I guess that mind you're gonna have is operating behind my back to do things your own way."

"So we're moving from you wedging Elsbeth between us to you using this?" he asked incredulously.

"Jacob, you *lied*," I snapped. "And you dragged my dad along with you."

"Baby, do you really fuckin' care that your man and your dad are lookin' out for you, you're so goddamned stubborn we gotta make a play so we do, and I'll repeat, we do it lookin' out for you?"

"It's the principle of the thing," I hissed.

"It's bullshit and you know it," he fired back, and I leaned back, throwing both arms out this time.

"Oh," I drew that word out derisively. "It doesn't mean shit to you but it means a lot to me and it's bullshit?"

"Fucking hell, Emme, listen to yourself," he ordered.

"I don't have the concentration, Jacob, since I'm using it all to listen to you," I returned.

"Okay, babe, then concentrate on this," he bit out. "Fourteen years ago, you showed at Elsbeth and my place. Elsbeth wasn't there. You said you'd leave, I asked you to stay. We got drunk on the balcony and laughed our asses off. We were at it for hours. Got you a taxi home. But not once in that entire time with just you and me, your girl not even there, did we miss her. She didn't exist. We had no problems conversing, connecting, enjoyin' the shit outta each other's company. When I had Elsbeth and you, I had *you*, Emme. All of you. And you know why I had you so fuckin' totally?"

I said nothing.

Jacob didn't need me to.

"Because you were safe in the knowledge you couldn't have me."

Suddenly I started breathing heavily.

"I thought you were just a loner," he went on. "You're not. You're just determined to be alone."

"I'm not a puzzle to figure out, Jacob," I told him, my voice quieter.

"You are, Emme, the most frustrating one I ever found and the one it's most important to solve."

"I'm just me."

"No, baby," he said gently. "You're not just you anymore. Now you're mine. That means you're part of an *us*."

At that, I just quit breathing.

"You're damaged," he declared.

"I'm not," I forced out.

But I was thinking I was.

"Broken," he went on.

"I'm not," I repeated on a wheeze even though I was thinking I was that too.

"And I'm going to piece the parts back together, Emme."

I shook my head but said nothing.

"For you and for me."

"We don't work," I replied, pushing it and I didn't know why.

"We've always worked, Emme. *Always*."

I loved that. That was beautiful.

Beautiful.

I shook my head again but this time did it hard, suddenly so panicked, it was near paralyzing.

Shoving down the panic, I held on to the angry with everything I had in me.

Doing so, I remembered seeing him with Elsbeth, how that destroyed me and I thought...no way. I wasn't spending another hour of my life now or in the future feeling like I felt the last two days.

He wasn't the man for me. I thought he was. He just wasn't.

He wasn't.

I was better off alone so hurt like this couldn't touch me.

I had to end this now.

"You collude with my father. You keep important things from me. You're an uber-alpha and I'm an independent woman. You want kids and I don't. And... and... you're a Republican."

It was a lame finish but it was all I had.

Jacob knew it was lame and he smiled.

God, he was handsome when he smiled.

He started walking toward me.

I started backing up.

Unfortunately, this time he didn't stop but he did start moving fast when I hit wall and made to change directions and dart through the doorway to the hall.

He cut me off and fenced me in.

I tipped my head back and caught his eyes.

"You're scary liberal," he whispered.

"Jacob—"

"And I don't give that first fuck."

"You—"

"You want kids, you just won't admit it. Or, alternately and more likely, you won't allow yourself to have them."

"Please—"

"You love me but won't let yourself have me."

"I—"

"And, baby," he lifted his hand to my jaw and dropped his face closer to mine, "I'm gonna figure out why. Fix what's broke in you. Then turn my attention to givin' you the best life I can for the rest of the time you're on this earth breathin'."

Too much. Too beautiful. Too everything.

So much, it terrified me.

As in full-blown-panic, heart-beating-so-hard-I-thought-it-would-burst, *-have-to-get-out-of-here!*, terrified-me-in-a-way-I-couldn't-hold-it-in-check kind of panic.

"Please move back," I whispered.

"I will. I'll also give you space. A strategic decision that might bite me in the ass but you need time to think. Seein' as you're goin' to Krys and Lauren when you got time to think, you might get yourself to good women who can give you advice. So that tactic, I reckon, is gonna work for me. What I won't do is give up. And when I walk away in a second, baby, that's the only thing you gotta take from this. I'm walkin' away but I'm not givin' up. Not on you. Not on us. And straight up, it's selfish, because I'm doin' all this shit for me."

"Why?" I asked, and I genuinely wanted to know.

And I wanted to know because I was scared, freaked, angry, panicked, wondering what the hell was wrong with me but I also was clearly a pain in the ass.

"'Cause you piss me off. You make me laugh. You make me think. You're absolutely fine with me bein' nothin' but me. You're fuckin' gorgeous. You're a great lay. And you like my dog."

I stared in his eyes, still terrified, still feeling too much of everything but I said nothing.

This time, Jacob didn't either.

Not until he bent his head, touched his mouth to mine and I felt that soft touch spread through every part of me.

Only when he lifted his head did he say, "Later, baby. And, heads up, there will be a later, Emme. And it'll be soon."

He shifted two inches away, lifted a hand to sweep the bangs out of my eyes, slid his finger down my temple, over the corner of my lip and along my jaw.

That touch spread through every part of me too.

Then his hand dropped away and I watched him walk to the door.

But he stopped in it and turned to me.

"Pisses me off you took it. Pisses me off I gotta live without you for a while at the same time live without it for the first time in a decade. But for now, I'll let you have it. When I come back, though, Emme, I'll want my kaleidoscope back."

I blinked in surprise.

Before I could tell him I didn't have the kaleidoscope, Jacob disappeared.

CHAPTER SIXTEEN

Confirm It's Her

Three days later...

WHAT WAS I doing?

I heard the door to the café open, I lifted my head to look toward it and saw her.

Elsbeth.

God, she was still beautiful.

"What am I doing?" I muttered to myself.

I'd asked for and received her email from a still-mutual friend. I'd emailed her. I'd asked her to meet me for lunch. She'd said yes. So I'd taken a day off work and drove to Denver.

Now I was about to have lunch with my ex–best friend, my maybe-still boyfriend's ex-girlfriend.

And I had no idea why.

Except for the fact that evidence was suggesting it was a good possibility I was totally fucking psycho.

She stopped by the table.

"Emme, wow, you look ... you look *amazing*."

She did too. But she always had. Lots of blonde hair. Warm green eyes. Fabulous figure. Fantastic outfit.

"Hello, Elsbeth," I said.

"Uh ... hi," she replied.

I tipped my head to the seat opposite me. "Do you wanna sit down?"

She looked at the seat then at me, both uncertain.

She made her decision and I didn't know if it was the right or wrong one when she sat. From the expression on her face, she felt the same.

She pulled off her jacket, hooked her purse on the back of her chair and looked at me.

"Deck told you we talked," she guessed.

"That he did," I confirmed.

"I, um...he told me that you know..." she trailed off.

"I know everything," I verified what she didn't exactly say.

"He was always straight up about stuff," she murmured.

She would, of course, living with him for years, having him for longer than I had (in certain ways), know that.

And I didn't need the reminder that she did.

Again, what was I doing here?

The waitress came. I already had a Diet Coke. Elsbeth ordered a sparkling water.

No, Elsbeth hadn't changed. Beauty. Class. Even ordering a sparkling water made her seem sophisticated and cool.

The waitress left and Elsbeth's gaze came back to me. "I'm glad you emailed."

"So it's true what Jacob said," I told her. "Mending fences."

She nodded, her eyes on me not like she was looking at me but like she was watching me.

"I know, it seems weird that I'd...well, find out about you two and that would..." She shook her head and didn't finish the thought. Instead she said, "I just did. But then, that's always been the way between us three."

That was an interesting statement.

"What's been the way?"

"We just work together."

I stared at her.

Maybe *she* was psycho.

"Doesn't seem that way to me," I pointed out.

I watched her straighten her shoulders before she said, "It's weird but it has."

"Do you want to explain that?" I requested.

She didn't answer immediately. She kept looking at me like she was watching me.

After she did his for a while, she said, "Okay, Emme, I don't want this to be ugly, and right now in my life, honestly, I can't take that. So you should know, if it turns that way, I'm leaving. But you should also know, I was happy you emailed and I'd hoped this would lead to good things, however those came about. I knew, what with the way things are, that it might be difficult or upsetting, but I'd hoped we'd work past that because this means that much to me. And, in the end, I'd hoped that even if it's weird, our history, things with Deck, maybe we'd reconnect."

"According to Jacob, I don't connect very well," I shared.

"Deck's always right," she replied immediately, and I blinked. "What?"

"You're the best friend I ever had," she announced.

At that, I again stared.

Elsbeth went on.

"You're smart. You're funny. You're loyal. You're thoughtful. You knew I was messed up, young, stupid, immature, but you were sensitive enough not to lay that out for me. You knew I had an idiotic idea about the life I was meant to lead and you tried to guide me out of that. I still messed up. But I didn't lose you because you were angry I broke things off with Deck. I lost you because you were getting too close to me. We were BFFs. You were over all the time and not just because of Deck. So you found your reasons to scrape me off and move on. Then you found your reasons to pretty much scrape everyone else off and move to some crazy mountain town hours away where you knew absolutely nobody. Coming back to Denver for quick hit visits with friends that mean nothing. Then off you go to your mountain town where you could be what you need to be. With just Emme."

I hated to admit it but what she said made sense and that sucked.

I looked down at the table.

"Emme," she called.

I swallowed and looked at her.

"I missed you," she whispered.

My throat closed.

Her eyes got bright but they didn't move from me.

"I knew. I knew back then that he was into you. But he couldn't be *into* you because he'd convinced himself he was in love with me. And I knew, in the way you would allow yourself to be, you were into him too. I don't know why I didn't love you both enough to step aside. Maybe because I was twenty-five and selfish. Maybe because Deck was everything to me, I just didn't see it nor did I see I wasn't and would never be everything to him. But I've been living with a jackass for eight years so I could have a maid and a Mercedes and when a woman makes a choice like that, losing everything that was worth anything, if she's smart, she learns not to make any more choices like that."

"I can't...I..." I stammered, pulled myself together and got on with it. "Honestly, Elsbeth, I'm really happy you've made these realizations. I think that's good. Jacob says you're spending time with you and I hope as you do you find out what I knew many moons ago. That you're worth spending time with."

She smiled. It was small but it was sweet.

I kept talking.

"And I didn't know why I asked you to meet me for lunch but now I'm glad I did."

"I am too."

I nodded. Then admitted, "But I think it's because I'm trying to work some things out. Come to my own realizations."

"And I think *that's* good," she said softly.

"I broke up with Jacob," I blurted suddenly.

She blinked.

Then she asked, "What?"

"He didn't exactly accept that," I shared.

It was her turn to stare at me.

Then she burst out laughing.

"It's not what I would consider amusing," I said into her laughter.

She swallowed it down and focused on me.

"You know," she started. "I'd always get so jealous when I heard you call him Jacob and he let you. He didn't let anyone call him that, except his mom and you. Not even me. And I hated it when he'd say, 'Babe, call Emme, ask her around for dinner,' and I knew he wanted to spend time with you. And I hated when we'd go to your place and you two would eat and argue and laugh and it felt like I wasn't even there."

We did that to her. Not even knowing it, we did it.

Being in my end of that triangle, I didn't see it. Jacob didn't either.

But Jacob was right. Elsbeth did.

"Elsbeth," I whispered.

"Yeah," she grinned, "my boyfriend was totally cheating on me with my BFF and neither of them knew it. But I did."

"Oh my God," I breathed.

I breathed it because my lungs had caught fire and they'd caught fire because we'd done that too.

"Lots of ways to cheat," she told me, her smile fading. "Last summer I did my last stupid act on earth, swear to God, Emme, and I'm sure you know what it was. Totally messed up. But that was where my head was at. I needed proof that I'd made a mistake, I had to rectify it, namely making the decision to leave my husband, and to do that, I retraced my steps to find where I went wrong. Unfortunately for Deck, he gave me that opening by calling me."

"That wasn't cool," I told her quietly.

"It totally wasn't," she agreed. "It was selfish and stupid and hurtful. But it was the old me. It was the last thing I vowed to myself I'd do as the old me. And doing it made me see I had to get rid of the old me and find a new me."

"I wish you'd left Jacob out of it."

She pulled in a breath and replied, "I wish I did too. But I can't change history. I can just make sure it doesn't repeat."

I was not really fired up about where our talk was leading, so I noted, "This is a very weird conversation."

"Yeah," she said softly.

"I don't much like it," I told her. "This part, that is."

She pulled in another breath before she said, "I understand that, Emme. Years ago I messed up, hurt Deck, lost him and lost you. I messed up again, again hurt Deck and by extension you. I'd hoped I could make amends, explain, apologize, I don't know, whatever I needed to do not to have either of those things happen, losing Deck or you. But I understand if they do."

I studied her.

Then I stated, "I'm glad you understand because I can't go there right now. I'm dealing with some stuff I have to straighten out. And what you did wasn't cool, back when you broke up with him or last summer. I appreciate you having the courage to call Jacob, explain and apologize and also come and meet me. But I can't see where we would go, you and me, or you, me and Jacob. Not right now. Maybe someday."

I took a breath, gentled my voice and finished.

"But the way our conversation turned indicates that's always going to be between us three. And I don't want to hurt you, but, truthfully, I think the water's under the bridge. We're both safe on our opposite sides. Maybe we should stay that way."

Her eyes still watching me, I could tell she didn't like it but she still said, "Okay, Emme."

Her sparkling water came.

She poured it, watching her glass fill, saying, "Maybe it's best that we don't, uh . . . have lunch. I'll leave you be." She put the bottle down and looked at me, "But can I say one thing?"

I didn't know if I wanted her to. This was strange. There were ways it was a good strange. There were ways it was a bad strange. But the whole thing was just strange.

The only reason I could think for why I was doing what I was doing that day was that, using intuition, I was amassing whatever it was I needed to figure out what was up with me. Then I could sort through the good and bad and find out what was inside me that was apparently making me stop myself from being happy.

I mean, boiling it down, I broke up with Jacob (unsuccessfully) mostly because he was a Republican.

And that didn't hint at psycho.

That just was.

Because of all this, I answered Elsbeth's question with a, "Sure."

"Do not let him go."

I drew in breath through my nose.

"He thinks the world of you, Emme. Way back when and the way he spoke about you last weekend. You need that. Every girl does. If you let everything else in your life slip through your fingers as you move on to whatever it is you're searching for, keep hold of him."

I couldn't tell her the thought of that terrified me. And it wasn't that I couldn't tell her because I couldn't explain why, even though this was true. It was just not hers to have.

Instead, I said, "I'll keep that in mind, Elsbeth."

She nodded and took a drink.

I lifted my Diet Coke and did the same.

Then she grabbed her purse, put money on the table, pulled on her coat and stood.

I kept my seat but looked up at her.

"Be happy, honey," she said quietly.

"You too, Elsbeth."

She smiled a small smile.

Then she turned and walked away.

*   *   *

Two hours later...

"So, that's what's been happening," I finished.

Harvey, sitting with me at his kitchen table, stared at me.

"Harvey?" I prompted when he said nothing and this lasted awhile.

"Give me a sec, Emme."

I shut up.

Harvey looked at his lap. He did this a long time.

Then he looked back at me.

"Okay, so, you're sick for a while, don't know what it is. You get better, pull yourself together and start dating a man who you don't know is a felon. You haven't officially broken up with him, you're gonna do this not because he's a felon but because he creeps you out, and immediately take up with another man you've known for years. A man who has always shown interest in you. A man who has always shown he cares about you. A man who wastes no time and is very clear after you bumped into each other again that he wants more. Then he spends months treating you the same way, with care and interest, doing so by telling you he loves you and wants to build a life with you. And now you've broken up with him because, though I kinda lost it at this part, he and your dad got you new windows. But you haven't really broken up with him because he refuses to accept that."

"That about sums it up," I told him then clarified, "Except the new windows part."

He stared at me again.

"So what do you think?" I asked when he again said nothing.

"What do I think?" he asked back.

"Yes," I answered.

"About what?" he asked.

"Anything," I replied. "Everything."

Harvey took in a deep breath.

Then he said, "What I think is, it's way too soon, just a few months, for you to share vows of love and start talking about building a future with any man. My daughter told me she'd found a man and was doing that, I'd be all kinds of worried."

"Okay," I said slowly when he stopped talking but I knew there was more.

"I also think that no man like the man you described takes a kaleidoscope made of glass everywhere he goes and sleeps with it on his nightstand."

I pulled in a sharp breath.

This time, Harvey kept talking.

"Further, I think that a girl like you should in no way be living her life in a crumbling mansion up on some mountain all by herself."

"Harvey—"

"And last, Emme, and most important, I think it's time you stopped existing and started living."

I sat back and it was my turn to stare.

Harvey never laid it out. He was gentle in every way, including verbally.

"Now what do *you* think about what I think?" he asked.

"I think I'm in love with him," I whispered.

"I believe that. You say his name, your eyes get funny. Sad. Like you've lost him somehow but, honey, all you gotta do to get him back is make a phone call."

I closed my eyes.

"Emme," he called.

I opened them.

"I thought I could make a phone call to get my wife back, my finger would be bleeding, dialing that number over and over again."

This time, when the tears hit my eyes, it was Harvey who was swimming.

"You get me, honey?" he asked gently.

I could tell him. I could tell Harvey. I didn't know why I couldn't say it to anyone else.

I just knew I could say it to him.

"He terrifies me," I whispered.

He leaned in and grasped my hand, holding it tight. "This man does not terrify you, my beautiful Emme, something else does. Now, please pay attention to what God granted you. He did not offer you a weak man who could not see whatever this is through. He offered you a strong man who can help you keep those fears at bay as you deal with whatever this is."

"But he's what I fear," I semi-repeated.

"Why?" Harvey asked.

"I don't know," I answered, voice trembling.

"He's told you he wants to lead you to answers. Let him," Harvey replied.

"What if he's—?"

I stopped speaking when Harvey jerked my hand and leaned close.

"Let him, Emme."

I didn't know where it came from but it came from somewhere because my lips were saying it. "There's something wrong with me."

"Stop going it alone, lean on a strong man who loves you and find out what that is. Then let him help you fix it."

"I'm scared of it."

Harvey held my eyes and mine were watery, but if I wasn't mistaken, his were watery too.

"I'm scared too," he replied.

That confused me.

"Why?"

"I'm scared for you, honey."

That made sense.

"Go home, go to him," he urged.

"You sure?"

"No way on this earth would I ever tell you something like that if I wasn't absolutely certain it was the right thing to tell you."

I gave his hand a squeeze.

"I love you, Harvey."

His hand spasmed in mine, something sharp and wounded passed swiftly through his face before he hid it and whispered, "I love you too, my beautiful Emme. Now get out of this old guy's kitchen and find your man."

The word was again trembling when I agreed, "Okay."

He stood, and with his hand in mine, brought me up with him.

It was me, it was always me, who went in for the hug.

But always upon always, Harvey hugged me back. Firm, sweet and for a long time.

This time, he did it for longer.

Then he waited until I grabbed my jacket and purse and he walked me out to Persephone.

I waved as I drove away.

Harvey waved back.

* * *

Two minutes earlier, in the control room of Nightingale Investigations...

"Confirm it's her," Luke Stark, Lee Nightingale's right-hand man, demanded over the phone to Jack, the man who most frequently worked the control room.

And the vast amount of time Jack spent in that room, he did it eyes to the large bank of monitors.

"Confirmed. Caught her goin' in, didn't get a clear visual. Caught her goin' out and saw her full face. Got the photo Deck gave us. It's her. She was there an hour. Lee's off-line, but orders are, Deck knows the minute we see her there."

"I'll call Deck. Out," Luke said.

Jack heard the disconnect.

Then his eyes went back to the monitors.

CHAPTER SEVENTEEN

Lost You

Three hours later…

I DROVE BACK to the mountains and went straight to Jacob's.

I was terrified, I didn't know why, but I was. I'd admitted that.

And he'd told me he was intent on helping me figure it out.

And I loved him.

My finger would be bleeding, dialing that number over and over again.

Throughout the journey, I heard Harvey's words repeating in my head.

And that was what did it for me.

I loved Jacob in a way that I knew life without him would be no life at all.

Like Harvey's life was without the ones he loved.

And I'd known that for years. Even when I didn't have Jacob, I'd known it.

Now I had him and something was wrong with me. But he wasn't running for the hills, knowing it the same as me, and not wanting anything to do with it.

No.

He was with me.

With me.

Wanting to fix me.

Wanting a future.

Wanting babies.

Wanting *me*.

It was me holding back. Holding back for no reason that I understood.

But the most intelligent person I knew was Jacob Decker. So if someone could help me understand, it was him.

Having made my decision, I went to Jacob's but he wasn't there. I sat in his driveway, pulled out my phone and was about to call him when I decided against it.

I'd call him when I was home. For this, whatever it was going to be, I decided I needed to be home. And Jacob, being Jacob, he'd come to me.

He'd come right to me.

Any girl in her right mind who knew that down to her bones would squeal with pure joy.

It petrified me.

Yep. Something was *not* right with me.

Luckily, it petrified me in a figurative way, not a literal one, so I could drive home.

When I did, I found that, just like when Jacob was looking for me and I'd been at his place fuming, when I was looking for him, he was at mine, hopefully not fuming.

He'd given me space like he said he would. Three days.

I guessed he was done doing that.

This was good because I was too.

It didn't mean I wasn't still terrified.

It was dark but I'd left the outside lights on and I saw his truck. He was in the shadows but I still saw him at the tail in the exact same position he'd been in three days earlier.

I parked where I'd parked three days ago. But this time, I didn't open my door, jump out of my truck and round the hood to find Jacob at the steps waiting for me.

I opened my door and jumped out of my truck to find Jacob standing in my door.

"Honey, I'm glad—" I started.

"Get in the house, Emme," he clipped, and my head jerked at his tone.

Okay. Apparently he was fuming.

"I—"

He leaned into me so suddenly and so deeply, I had to lean back into the cab of the Bronco.

"Get in the goddamned, motherfucking *house*, Emme."

I felt my eyes round.

He'd never spoken that way to me. In fact, I'd never heard him speak that way to anybody.

I stared at his face.

He was angry.

No. That wasn't right.

He was enraged.

"What's happening?" I asked carefully.

"Get in. The goddamned. *House*," Jacob repeated.

What was going on?

Although I wanted to know (or perhaps I didn't), I didn't think it was my best play to ask him right then.

So I said softly, "I will, honey, if you'll get out of my way."

He immediately moved out of my way.

I immediately moved to the front door, nervous, freaked, confused and still very scared, but now for a different reason.

I let us in. Jacob slammed the heavy door and the way it thudded in its frame seemed to rock the house.

Have mercy.

"Library," Jacob ordered.

I turned to look at him. "Can we—?"

His voice dipped to a sinister whisper. "Ass to the library, Emme."

I didn't get this. I didn't like this. I wanted to tell him that but I also didn't think that was my best play at the moment. So I swallowed, nodded and moved to the library.

Jacob followed.

When we got there, he didn't delay.

"You're seein' him," he announced bizarrely the instant I turned to face him.

My head jerked. "I . . . what?"

"You're seein' him," he repeated.

Okay, now I was really confused.

Did he think I'd been out with another man?

"Seeing who?" I asked and that was when he lost it.

Leaning in, he roared, *"Harvey!"*

Oh no.

He knew.

How did he know?

I looked at his face and didn't ask. Instead, I took a step back.

Jacob kept speaking.

"Have you lost your mind?"

I lifted a hand his way. "Let me explain."

"He snatched you from a playground."

"I know it sounds weird, but please, let me explain."

"Your father and mother didn't know where you were for three days."

Reflexively, my head shook and it did it hard, my hair flying with it, like this action could deflect his words and my ears wouldn't absorb them. A defensive response I didn't get and Jacob didn't catch.

He started stalking toward me.

"Not knowin' if you were eating."

I retreated.

"Not knowin' if you were bein' touched."

Another shake of my head, both my hands up now.

Not imploring.

Protecting.

"Not knowin' if you were dead in a ditch."

"Stop talking," I whispered.

"No way they know you're seein' him. Your dad talked to me about what happened to you. How he's not over it. How he wakes up every day with the taste of bein' out of his goddamned mind worried about you in his mouth and it's been fuckin' twenty-two fuckin' years."

I couldn't hear this. I didn't want to know this.

I had to stop it.

"Stop talking," I repeated.

"And you're seein' him."

"Please stop talking."

"Why are you seeing him, Emme?"

I shook my head.

"Why, in God's name, would you be seein' that... fuckin'...*man*?"

You scream, you'll never see your mother and father again.

The words violated my brain. Words I refused to remember for twenty-two years.

I tripped over something, righted myself and kept moving backward.

You scream...

"No," I whispered.

You'll never...

I shook my head hard, hit wall and slid across it.

"Emme?"

See your mother and father again.

"No," I begged.

Strong hands on my arms.

"Emme!"

Emme!

My head turned and instead of a bookshelf, I saw them there.

Emme!

Their faces.

I couldn't bear the faces.

I closed my eyes.

The hands left my arms, slid up and curled around my neck. "Baby, what's happening?"

Emme!

I saw their faces behind my closed eyelids. Burned there. Burned there for eternity.

You scream, you'll never see your mother and father again.

"Please, Emme, baby, talk to me."

"No," I forced out on a tortured whisper.

"Where are you, honey?" The hands at my neck gave me careful squeeze. "Jesus, Emme, come back to me."

Emme!

Those faces.

"No," I pleaded.

Emme!

"*No!*" I shrieked.

Yanking my neck from the hands, I tried to escape.

Arms caught me.

I fought, vicious, kicking, snarling, scratching, bucking.

Remembering.

I was standing behind the kissing tree at recess waiting for my kind-of boyfriend to meet me there.

The tree was in the corner of the far end of the playground. Perfect spot to hide from the teachers and try out kissing. It was also where the chain-link fence had been pried away from the post so the bad kids could go out and smoke cigarettes, or whatever they did.

I had my back to the fence, my hands to the rough bark, my body tipped to the side so I could look around the tree to see if my boyfriend was coming.

Suddenly, a hand came over my mouth.

I froze.

I jerked.

A mouth came to my ear.

"You scream, you'll never see your mother and father again."

In the library in my home, I screamed.

Back then, I didn't scream.

I didn't…fucking…*scream.*

"It's me, baby, fuck, shit. Fuckin' hell, Emme. It's me."

My back arched, the hold didn't let go, and I collapsed.

"Emme!"

I was sitting in the police station. I heard my father's voice and turned my head.

Mom and Dad were there, rushing to me, bumping into each other at the same time they held on to each other and raced my way, their eyes glued to me.

They hit me and took me off my feet.

But I didn't fall. Dad's arms had closed around me.

Then Mom's arms closed around me.

Both so hard I couldn't breathe.

But I heard Mom sobbing. I felt the wet of her tears in my hair.

"We thought we'd lost you. Oh, my precious baby girl, we thought we'd lost you."

Dad's voice in my ear. Agonized. Pain so bad, it cut right through me then burrowed in, never to leave.

Never to leave.

"We thought we'd lost you."

Lost you.

Lost you.

"Baby, you don't say something, I'm calling an ambulance."

I looked at Jacob.

We were on the couch. I was in his lap. His arms were tight around me.

"I can't lose you," I whispered.

His chin jerked back. "What?"

"I can't have babies."

"Emme—"

"I can't lose them."

His eyes went from alarmed to wary and his mouth closed.

"I can't do it," I told him. "I can still see their faces."

Gently, Jacob asked, "Whose faces, baby?"

"Dad and Mom at the police station."

Understanding sparked in his eyes. His head dropped. His eyes closed. Then they opened and he pulled me closer.

"Harvey knows," I told him.

"What does he know?" he asked on a whisper.

"What losing someone means."

Jacob pulled me even closer.

"You don't identify with him, honey."

"I know loss," I contradicted.

"You were lost. You don't *know* loss," he corrected.

"I know loss. For three days, that's all I saw. And I saw it in Harvey."

His arms tightened around me as the alarm came back to mix with the wary in his eyes.

"I need to call someone to see to you. It kills me but I don't know how to give you what you need right now, baby."

I ignored what he said and announced, "You scare me."

"Emme—"

"No, you terrify me."

"Baby—"

I lifted a hand and cupped his jaw. "I can't lose you."

"Fuck, Emme." His words were anguished.

"If you gave me babies, I couldn't lose them."

"Honey, let me—"

It was pouring out of me. Truth. Undiluted. I didn't hold it back. I couldn't anymore.

I'd been holding on to it for too long.

I could see their faces.

"I've loved you since Elsbeth first introduced me to you," I declared, and Jacob's mouth closed. "You smiled at me, shook my hand and said something to make me laugh. You were so beautiful. You were so nice. I took one look at you and it felt like I'd been asleep for decades and seeing you, feeling your big strong hand wrap around mine, woke me up."

He pulled my hand from his jaw, pressed it tight over his heart and didn't say anything.

Not with his mouth.

His eyes were speaking though.

And what they were saying was amazing.

"I was the fairy-tale princess waiting for her prince to wake her from a deep sleep. And there you were."

He curled his fingers around mine and he did it tight.

"But I couldn't have you," I went on. "If I had something as glorious as you and lost it, I'd be Harvey. Crazy. Alone. Buried under despair. Unable to go on."

"You aren't Harvey, Emmanuelle."

I closed my eyes tight, bent my neck, pressed my forehead against his lips and only moved back when I felt him kiss me there.

And when I moved back, I looked direct in Jacob's eyes.

"I know I'm not Harvey, honey. But that's what he taught me. He showed me that despair and he gave it to my parents and then they showed it to me. That's what he taught me. That's what he left me. That's what's been buried in me for..." I leaned closer, *"forever."*

His hand gave mine a squeeze as he murmured a hoarse, "Baby."

I took in a stuttering breath and continued.

"I understood it. Logically, it came to me and I told you about it. But I didn't *understand* it. I didn't panic about it until I knew I loved you and you told me you loved me. I didn't put it together that I saw how Harvey lost everything, everything he loved, and what that did to him. I didn't put it together that, even as I was reaching for it because I wanted it so badly, I wasn't going to allow myself to build any of that because he'd taught me to be terrified of losing it. Then I saw you with little Jake and you two were so beautiful." I pressed closer to him and my voice dropped lower. "So, so beautiful, honey."

He closed his eyes but opened them again when I kept talking.

"I wanted that. I wanted you to give me that, giving it to me by holding the baby we made in your arms. I wanted it more than anything else I've ever wanted in this world, except you. But Harvey lost his daughter and for three days my parents lost me and I couldn't hack it. So I did what was safe. What was familiar. What you knew I was doing. But I couldn't help it because I didn't even know I was doing it. I felt the terror of possibly losing you, losing a child I'd made with you, and did what I'd trained myself to do since he took me. I retreated to protect myself from the possibility of that ever happening to me."

"Baby, I love it that you're seeing this. That you get this. But we've been here before and you still pulled away from me. What happened five minutes ago, it's clear you aren't dealing, and like your dad, you haven't been dealing for twenty-two years. To do that and do it right, you have to talk with somebody," Jacob said gently.

"I know."

I watched him blink right before relief, sweet and pure, suffused his features.

"They're burned on the backs of my eyelids, honey," I told him.

"Who?" he asked.

"Mom and Dad at the station. But I trained myself not to see."

He nodded. More understanding.

God. Jacob Decker.

So fucking amazing.

"Are you good with letting someone help you erase that?" he asked carefully.

I didn't answer. Instead I stated what I knew. What I'd been denying. What, if I allowed myself to understand it, I knew would kill me.

"Dad sees it, like me. I know he does sometimes in the way he looks at me."

"He loves you, baby."

Yeah. Oh yeah. My dad so, *so* loved me.

Tears filled my eyes. "Yeah."

"You can't see Harvey anymore."

Poor Harvey.

Poor me.

I should never have gone to him. It probably wounded him every time.

But I needed him.

Now I didn't.

But I'd miss him.

Tears slid down my cheeks. "Yeah."

"And I'm gonna see to you."

I knew it. I knew he would.

Jacob loved me.

Jacob had always loved me.

My breath hitched and I repeated, "Yeah."

Then I dissolved.

Jacob pulled me closer, tucking my face in his neck.

And as I leaked everywhere, finally let it out after holding it for so long inside me, Jacob didn't allow me to fall apart.

In his lap, on my couch, his big strong arms around me, he held me together so maybe…maybe…

I could finally find me.

And then be happy.

*   *   *

Deck

Twenty hours later…

Deck pulled up to the curb, shut down his truck and swung out.

Before he was halfway up the walk, the door opened.

He stopped at the bottom of the two-step stoop and took in Harvey Feldman.

Not surprisingly, the man looked old and beaten.

Surprisingly, he also looked kind.

"Emmanuelle will not be coming to see you again but if you attempt any form of contact, you'll be seein' me," he stated.

Harvey Feldman closed his eyes and whispered, "Thank God."

Deck stared.

The man opened his eyes and Deck spoke.

"I see you're down with that."

"No, sir. I am not down with that. I get the impression you know what it would be like to lose Emme. What I am is relieved to know that Emme finally has someone looking after her."

The last part was a surprise.

The first part he did not like.

"I suggest you get down with it," Deck warned.

His eyes grew intent and he asked, "I assume you're Jacob Decker?"

This also wasn't surprising. In the last day, when she wasn't sleeping, Emme had shared everything including the fact she'd told Feldman everything.

So Deck didn't answer. Instead, he jerked up his chin.

Feldman nodded. "Then, Mr. Decker, I'll tell you that the first time Emme came to see me, I knew I had not yet endured my penance. No prison can accomplish that. Being locked away with men like the men I shared time with was not fun. But it is no penance. No." He shook his head. "My penance was different. My penance was doing what I did because I lost all that I had lost and then God giving me the opportunity to get to know Emme knowing someday I'd lose her too."

Christ.

He cared about her.

Genuinely.

Not expecting that, Deck had no response to it.

"I'll ask one favor," Feldman said, and Deck had a response to that.

"You'll get no favors."

"I have a feeling you'll give this one to me."

Deck held his eyes and ordered, "Spit it out."

"I'll need your contact details so I can get in touch with you should she attempt to contact me."

"She won't do that," Deck returned firmly.

Feldman shook his head, a ghost of a smile on his lips. But it was no ghost, the pain lurking in his eyes.

"She hasn't given herself completely to you. When she does, you'll see."

"Man, I'm not in the mood to play word games," Deck bit out, not liking any of this shit and wanting it to be done so he could be on the road to get back to Emme.

"Sweet to the core, that's Emme. She'll worry about me, Mr. Decker, and eventually she'll try to contact me."

"I see you've seen the error of your ways and know what this is, so it gives me no pleasure to tell you, when she had her breakthrough, it was not pretty. She is currently under mild sedation in her bed at her home with her mother and father watching over her. It took a lot of talkin' to stop her father from comin' with me or comin' on his own. You lucked out this visit is from me. Emme's already spoken to a counselor and she's committed to doin' that until what's twisted in her head gets straightened out. When that happens, she'll know not to contact you."

"She will."

"She absolutely will not."

"Do you know, Mr. Decker, the only thing that can hold back goodness and light?"

What was up with this fucking guy?

"Again, in no mood," Deck clipped.

"Darkness," Feldman answered his own question. "And, since Emme shared you're highly intelligent, I know I don't have to tell you that darkness drowns out light. But when that light is freed, when so much has been stored for so long, nothing can dim that beam." He paused to suck in a breath before he finished, "That beam is Emme. When she was twelve, I did something that drowned that beam. If I'm assuming correctly, seeing as you're visiting me, that beam has been freed. And because Emme is Emme and she carries that light, she'll contact me."

Already creeped way the fuck out by this guy, he was concerned about his girl. Now he was more concerned because she spent time with his whackjob. Not to mention, not wanting to be there at all, what the man said made Deck more of all of that.

So he moved to shut it down by asking, "Are we done?"

"Make her happy."

That meant they were done, thank Christ.

"Already planned on doin' that," Deck muttered, turned, walked two steps then turned back. "I'll get you my email address. She contacts you, you don't open your door, answer the phone or reply to an email. You email me."

Feldman nodded.

Deck walked to his truck.

Then he wasted no time getting home to Emme.

*   *   *

One day later...

"Okay, so, nervous breakdown...check," Emme said, and Deck's eyes went from his book to her at the opposite end of the couch.

She was slouched down, feet in his lap, head to the armrest. But her hand was up, palm facing herself like she was holding a notepad, other hand holding an imaginary pen and her eyes were on him.

"So, now that I've done that, what do you suggest I add to my bucket list?" she asked.

"You ever fucked on a beach?" he asked back.

Her eyes fired but her lips said, "Uh...no."

"Add that."

She turned her eyes to her palm and faked scribbling on it, mumbling, "That sounds a lot more fun than a nervous breakdown."

Deck smiled, tossed his book on the coffee table, leaned into her and hauled her to him. Stretching out full on the couch under her, Emme instantly settled full out on him.

Buford, lying on the floor beside the couch, lifted his head.

He inspected their new position, approved and settled back down on a groan.

"Um...honey," Emme called, and he looked from his

dog to her. "As you know, my parents are in town on the supposed errand of picking up a bucket of chicken. As the nearest chicken joint is in Chantelle, this will take a while. But as they're multi-tasking and using this," she arched her back so she could lift her hands off of his chest to do air quotation marks, "errand to make clandestine phone calls to my siblings in order to give them status reports on the state of my sanity, that said sanity being in question, they'll be back soon. So, to sum up, you can't make love to me on my couch."

This was a shame.

It was also true. All of it.

And last, it made it even more clear something he'd been noticing since Emme and the doctor agreed she could go off the sedative.

Harvey Feldman was right.

He'd drowned out Emme's light.

Now it was beaming so bright, he was blinded.

"You're right," he replied. "So we'll just make out."

"Making out with you tends to lead to other things."

He grinned and asked, "How do you know? We've never made out."

"This is how I know, honey. Because it's always led to other things."

Deck burst out laughing.

In the middle of it, he felt Emme's mouth touch his so it faded to a chuckle.

When he caught her eyes, they were shining.

He stopped chuckling and his blood began to burn.

"I've always wanted to do that while you were laughing," she whispered. "Always."

Fuck. He wanted to make love to her.

He hadn't had her in over a week.

He needed her now.

"You need to stop bein' sweet or I'm barring the door against your parents. They can have chicken. I'll be havin' you."

He watched her eyes fire again as her body melted on his and her hand slid up his chest to his neck.

"I think Dad would break down the door. He's a little..." she paused, "in my space right now, and I need to give him that."

That was the damned truth.

"Yeah," Deck reluctantly agreed.

"But, even though I've slept more in the last two days than any healthy body needs, I'm suddenly feeling really tired so I figure I'll have to go to bed early. And I don't think they'll mind if you didn't keep them company."

"This sounds like a plan," he murmured.

"I love you, Jacob," she declared suddenly, and his arms around her gave a squeeze.

"I know you do, baby."

"Thank you for not giving up on me."

Fuck, but Feldman was right. That beam was blinding.

He rolled so he was on top and her arms adjusted so they circled him. He lifted his hand and brushed the bangs off her forehead.

Then he caught her eyes. "You up for talkin' about something?"

"Considering I'm entering intense psychotherapy tomorrow, I hope so," she teased.

"Baby, I'm serious."

The light of humor faded from her eyes. He missed it but he'd work at getting it back. But now they had shit to go over.

"I'm up for talking about anything, honey," she told him.

"Right," he said quietly. "When shit went down, what got us there was me comin' down on you."

"Jacob—"

"Let me finish, Emmanuelle."

She closed her mouth.

He kept going.

"I was pissed. Out of my mind with worry. I got the call you'd visited him and I had to wait for you to get back. That didn't make me in a better mood. I lost it and the results were fuckin' great but the path to those results was a little shaky."

He'd told her, due to his concerns, he'd had Feldman's house watched and his phones monitored. He had not, however, had his emails checked, which was how they always communicated.

Emme had not been angry. Then again, when Deck had shared this, she'd been mostly sedated.

However, she didn't get angry at the reminder now either.

Instead, she replied, "Things happen for a reason."

"And those things would have happened without me losin' my mind on you. No excuse, but you deserve an explanation."

After he said that, she said nothing so he kept going.

"I had no idea where your head was at. You kept disconnecting and I also had no idea how to stop you from doin' that. I had six days of not bein' with you except for maybe twenty minutes, that whole twenty minutes we were up in each other's shit. I knew something was wrong. I knew it was dark. I knew it had to have something to do with what happened to you when you were a kid. But I had no clue how to guide you where you could share, and I knew when you did, I was powerless to right what was wrong with you. I didn't have those skills. I didn't like that. Any of it. So I lost it."

"Jacob, honey, stop it."

"Emme, baby, that shit was not right."

"You know," she started, cocking her head on the seat of the couch, "when all that went down, I was coming home from Harvey, ready to face you, ready to try to work it out, whatever was wrong with me. And you know something else? It so totally was going to fail."

He felt his brows draw together. "What?"

"I was so deep, so beyond reach, my parents after years didn't reach me. My brothers. My sister. Friends. And even you, the first time I met you. The only thing that could break through was something *breaking through*. And that something had to be powerful enough to accomplish that. And that something powerful was your anger." She gave him a squeeze. "You were angry at me but you were angry for a reason. I was doing something crazy. And you tried other ways but you weren't getting through to me. It's understandable you lost it, and bottom line, things happen for a reason."

"I'm glad you think that way, baby, but—"

She cut him off. "And I was kidnapped for a reason."

Fuck.

"Babe," he said low.

"No. It's true. If I wasn't, I would never understand in the way I do now how much I love you. How important your love is to me. How precious. How I don't ever want to lose it. And, belatedly, how I should work not to do that."

That he'd accept because he fucking loved it.

And he did that by dropping his forehead to hers and murmuring, "Honey."

"Same with Mom and Dad. Same with everybody. It took me a while to learn the lesson. But one could say I've learned it." He watched her eyes smile. "Definitely."

"It is not okay what he did to you," Deck said gently.

"No. It absolutely isn't. But it's also not okay for me to live through that and not learn. He did wrong. He hurt me, my parents, you, anyone who loved me. Life has a lot of lessons, some of which I was too scared for too long to learn. Now what I have to learn is not to let that happen anymore."

When she was done speaking, she tipped up her chin to touch her mouth to his.

When she settled back he lifted his head and she spoke.

"Please don't be upset you got that angry with me. I can see why you would be but what I want *you* to see is why I *needed* you to be."

All right. It was safe to say he was done.

"You're bein' sweet," he warned, and she grinned.

Then her grin faded and remorse filled her eyes.

"So are you, honey. But then, you always were to me." She took in a ragged breath and finished, *"Always."*

Deck suddenly didn't give a fuck about her parents maybe coming home soon so he dropped his head and took her mouth.

He got one sweet stroke of her tongue, her strawberry scent all around, when they heard Barry shout, "We got chicken!"

He felt Emme giggle against his tongue.

It sucked that he couldn't do what he wanted to do.

But that didn't mean the taste of her laughter on his tongue wasn't all kinds of sweet.

CHAPTER EIGHTEEN

More Bedrooms

Three weeks later…

DECK, WORKING AT his computer at home, stared at his monitor.

He was close to something on the robbery case. He just couldn't put his finger on what it was.

Their mystery man who met with McFarland months ago, a man named Jon Prosky, had not come back from seeing to his mom who was sick with MS. Now he'd lost his job because of it, but he was current with all payments on mortgage, credit cards and utilities.

The red flag was that he was paying from accounts in his mother's name. Accounts that held hefty amounts, made that way by cash deposits made relatively recently.

If that cash could be connected to robberies in the county, they'd nail him. But when local cops in Denver paid him a visit, he'd provided a trail from "friends and family" who gave cash gifts to help out with his mother's care.

Dead end.

And there was another red flag. When asked by the Denver police, Prosky stated he had no recollection of meeting with McFarland that night. When shown the surveillance photos Chace took that were dark but clearly showed his truck was there, even if the photos of him were indistinct, he'd said he'd loaned his truck to a guy from work.

That had been followed up, the man who supposedly borrowed the truck said this was untrue but he had no one to corroborate that he hadn't met with McFarland. Possibly substantiating Prosky's story, his coworker was getting rides to work at the time because his ride was in the shop.

One man's word against another.

Another dead end.

Deck further could not find any connections, outside of Prosky's now-alleged meet with McFarland. He had not worked with any of the crew who'd been tagged. He didn't go to school with any of them. He had no record so he didn't share a cell with the dealer. He had not been seen anywhere in the company of any of them. And he had no phone records that connected him with any of that crew. He also had no wife or relative who were associated with any of them.

Another dead end.

But Deck had gone to Denver on a variety of business, and some of that business was to spend time watching him.

McFarland was no boss. The dealer they hooked to that crew was a maybe.

This guy had what it took.

In photos, you wouldn't see anything but he was a decent-looking guy, tall and relatively well built.

In person, he was compelling. An easy smile he flashed often. An open manner that hid something someone not paying close attention, or a high school student not experienced enough to know, would miss.

This was that his manner and smile were surface. His smile didn't reach his eyes, his manner didn't expose openly that every movement he made made him seem like he was protecting something.

He was also pathologically social, like a con man on the lookout for his next mark. In the time Deck followed him, he watched Prosky befriend everyone he came into contact with from a gas station attendant, to the waitress at a café, to hooking up in record time with a woman in a bar so far out of his league, that score was downright chilling.

But with nothing to link to him, Deck had nowhere to take his investigation.

So he was looking into every known associate of this mystery man. Boss, coworkers, relatives, friends and especially those friends who "donated" to his mother's care.

The problem was, Deck's gut was telling him the key to breaking this was the kids. However, they had nothing at all on the kids and couldn't question them or follow them.

Clicking through credit reports, Facebook pages and any other thread he could pick up for the last two hours, he was relieved when his cell on the desk rang.

The display said "Emmanuelle calling."

He took the call.

"You need a ride?" he asked, knowing this call meant his purgatory in computer hell was ending, which in turn meant Deck's lips curved up.

"Yeah, honey," she answered.

"Am I bringing Buford?"

"Yeah," she repeated.

"Be there, twenty, twenty-five."

"Okay, Jacob."

"Later, babe."

"'Bye, honey."

He hung up and turned his attention to shutting down his computer.

Emme was at The Dog, a bar in Gnaw Bone. Girls' Night Out with Nina, Krys, Lauren, Lexie, Faye and Zara.

This was the third time they'd gone out since her breakthrough. Deck was her ride home though she was probably not inebriated. Emme didn't lose control like that, he'd noticed. Not back when, not now. But she would be tipsy.

Girls' Nights Out were happening because Deck had talked to Chace. Chace had then talked to Faye. Faye had done her thing with the girls and the girls jumped right on it. Then Deck had talked to Emme.

Connecting. Girls' Night Out, once a week. Form bonds. Build a life. Establish a crew to provide an ear, advice, support, but mostly fun.

Settle.

Find happiness.

Emme had agreed and even done it enthusiastically.

So now she was out tossing them back with some of the finest women he'd ever met.

All good.

Tonight, The Dog was on the rotation. Seeing as Krys and Lauren owned Bubba's bar in Carnal and Zara's man Reece managed The Dog in Gnaw Bone, there was friction about where the women would meet.

Zara had some legal case finish up that now made her a millionaire. But Reece was not the type of man who didn't work for his living. And Zara was the kind of woman, sudden millionaire or not, she looked after her man. Apparently, he got a bonus if he sold a shitload of booze, so Zara pushed for The Dog.

Krys and Laurie were not millionaires so they pushed for Bubba's.

Nina, Lexie and Faye stepped in and suggested the rotation.

So tonight it was The Dog.

Emme wanting Deck to bring Buford meant they were headed to her house. As both Bubba's and The Dog were a haul from his place in Chantelle, that meant she wanted to be home—and in bed with him—soon.

Emme, in bed, naked and tipsy.

Time to go.

After his computer shut down, Deck muttered to Buford, who was lying on the floor by his side. "Let's go, pal."

He did this smiling.

And he smiled all the way to his truck.

*　　　*　　　*

One and a half hours later...

Emme was lying full on top of him, knees bent, straddling his hips.

She'd cleaned up after they were done, wandered back while pulling on some panties and a camisole, hit the bed, which meant hit Deck, then settled in just like that.

A new thing for Emme.

They usually fell asleep with Emme tucked to his side, parts of her draped over him.

But after her breakthrough, she didn't claim the lion's share of Deck.

She just claimed Deck.

He was not complaining. After she fell asleep, he would slide her to his side. But while she was falling, he stroked her back and hair, enjoying the fact his girl's demonstration said she was done disconnecting. Now she wanted to stay as connected as she could get, as often as she could get it, for as long as she could have it.

So he gave it to her.

Trailing the fingertips of his hand along her spine, gliding the fingers of his other hand through her hair, he felt her body relax into his and knew she was close to sleep.

That meant Buford was going to have to adjust. He was flat out on his side, his back pressed to Deck and Emme.

This was also the new norm and when this happened, Buford protested with halfhearted groan when Deck slid Emme into his space.

But he adjusted.

Then again, Deck's dog had bonded with his girl and she'd done the same with his dog.

Another connection.

Deck grinned at the dark ceiling.

"I didn't scream."

Deck blinked as his hands stilled when her soft words hit the room.

"What, baby?"

"I didn't scream," she repeated, her voice sleepy and quiet.

He fought against his body tightening.

There was something else new happening with Emme.

She went to see a therapist twice a week, and after her sessions, she would be quiet, reflective and sometimes distant. This would not last long, and she'd quickly come back to Emme.

But she'd also have moments that had nothing to do with her therapy schedule where she'd wince or appear in pain, both for what seemed no reason. These moments didn't happen when they were talking, instead while they were watching TV, eating or lounging around reading.

But when this happened, she didn't share.

Deck also didn't push.

When she went into therapy, Deck had thoroughly researched post-traumatic stress disorder, and none of these symptoms was unusual.

As for how a loved one dealt: patience, understanding and listening were key. However, after her first few appointments and interviewing Barry and Maeve, Emme's therapist had suggested family therapy. The primary goal for that was to guide all of them to a better place as apparently Emme held some guilt for the fact her parents were still dealing with the trauma.

Barry and Maeve agreed. They were starting next week.

But now it was clearly time for her to share whatever was on her mind, something she hadn't done in any real way in three weeks. And Deck needed to be patient, understanding and listen.

The problem was, he didn't know what else he needed to be. And if it was time for her to share, he needed to be what she needed him to be.

"You didn't scream," he prompted softly when she said no more.

"When Harvey took me," she stated and stopped talking.

Deck closed his eyes.

Then he opened them and replied encouragingly, "Okay."

They lay there in the dark, his girl as close as she could be, her cheek planted in the middle of his chest, her face aimed to the windows.

She didn't move or speak.

Then he felt her heave a heavy sigh and she said, "If I had screamed, fought and screamed, a teacher would have heard. Or someone would have seen. Someone would have done something and it never would have happened. I could have stopped it if I just screamed."

It took a lot for Deck not to interrupt, to let her verbalize her feelings and not try to shut down her guilt.

He accomplished this and when she went silent, he remarked, "You know he was on the edge."

Another sigh then, "I know."

"Sometimes," he started carefully, "in certain situations, it's good not to fight and scream. It could be worse if you did."

"Harvey would never hurt me."

He clenched his teeth to bite back his retort, forced his jaw to relax, and when he had it together, pointed out again, "Baby, he was on the edge. Men driven to the edge are unpredictable."

At that, she lifted her head, put her hands to his chest and he looked at her face in the moonlight.

"Really," she said quietly. "I know he's not your favorite person, but Harvey would never hurt me."

Deck lifted a hand, brushed her bangs from her eyes and tucked her hair behind her ear, leaving his hand curled around her neck. "I know that's the man you grew to know. And that man you grew to know is Harvey Feldman. But the man who snatched you was not the man you know. The man who took you was a man driven to extreme behavior due to his grief. You can't know how that man would react if you didn't do what you were told."

Emme said nothing, but even in the shadows, he could see her face working as she thought this through.

Then she whispered, "He said, 'You scream, you'll never see your mother and father again.'"

Fuck, how could she spend time with that fucking guy? It may have been grief he couldn't control guiding his actions, but he still fucked up a young girl.

And that fuck-up started with those words.

In that moment, Deck would give up everything he'd worked for to have the ability to erase those words from her memory.

But he didn't have that ability.

The only thing he could do was whisper in reply, "You made the right choice, Emme."

"That was... what I'm saying is, that was not him. To say that. To threaten me like that. I think in some deep part of him he knew that he was going to return me to Mom and Dad. But he said it and he said it in a way that I knew he meant it."

"So you made the right choice," Deck stated.

"I have... I was..." She shook her head slightly then he heard her draw breath in through her nose. "I wish I'd screamed."

He lifted his other hand to curl around her neck. "Everyone, every person on this earth with enough age to have lived a life, has regrets. They look back and wish they'd done something differently. You aren't alone in that, honey."

"But what I wished I'd done differently would have saved Mom and Dad three days of terror, decades of fear and a man from spending five years in prison."

Oh yeah, she was holding guilt.

Fuck.

His fingers reflexively flexed into her neck, he forced them to relax and noted, "You were twelve, taken from a playground. This was not your choice. Your choices were taken away. You hold no guilt for what happened in the aftermath for everyone involved in dealing with one man's choice."

"I understand that logically, Jacob. But it's hard to piece that together in my head. Now that the floodgates have opened, it keeps coming at me."

"How do I help you get to piecing that together?" he asked instantly and watched her eyes close.

Then she dropped her head so her forehead was resting on his mouth.

This was another thing Emme now did. In ways that were unusual and sweet, she sought his affection and she did it when she needed him to balm some hurt she was feeling. After he'd see her wince for no reason, she'd come to him, wrap her arms around him, get up on her toes and press her face in his neck. They'd be lazing around watching TV, her face would hold pain, she'd turn her head and press her forehead to his lips.

And all he had to do was hold her or kiss her, she'd move slightly away but not pull away, look at him and the pain would be gone.

It was a gift she gave him, allowing him to take away her pain.

So that was exactly what he did. He moved to take away her pain and kissed her forehead.

But this time was different.

This time, she didn't pull away immediately.

Instead, she whispered, "You know, I really, *really* like you."

He smiled against her skin and muttered, "Yeah. I know."

She moved away and caught his eyes.

Another change, because this time, even in the moonlight, he could see the pain was gone but her eyes were still conflicted.

"I have to tell you something," she murmured so quietly, he barely heard her.

"What, baby?" he asked and she held his eyes.

Then she announced in a weighty voice that made Deck brace, "I lied."

"About what?" he asked carefully.

"Way back when, the first time I was telling you about what happened with Harvey. I lied," she told him.

"How did you lie?"

She drew in a long breath and let it out, saying, "I was terrified. The whole time I was with him. Totally terrified. From the moment he threatened me to the moment he took me to the police station and I saw my parents."

Deck said nothing. This was another breakthrough. Quieter and not terrifying to witness, but vitally important and he needed to let her sort it out in her head without intervening.

When he said nothing, she continued.

"I think…looking back, I think when I was with Harvey back when he took me, I shut down. He was acting so strangely, it totally freaked me out. And I think…I think…"

She trailed off, again appearing reflective before she came back to him and said in a whisper that sounded like a confession, "I think I sought him out after, when I was an adult, because I had to believe he was a good guy doing bad things. I had to find a way to erase that fear I held with me for three days, worried what he'd do to me, about how he was acting. Worried if I would see my family again. How I knew Mom and Dad were probably wild with terror. I knew it was all wrong and very, *very* bad, but I had no power and I was scared out of my mind. I sought him out later because of *why* he did what he did and that he took me to the police station. I had twisted it my head that he was a good guy and I needed to make that real, I think, in an effort to erase that fear. Maybe to get some of my power back. But also to give myself the ability to build a wall around those memories so they would stop tearing me apart."

Deck wanted to howl with elation that she'd finally untwisted that in her head.

But he didn't.

He simply gave her a smile and murmured, "I think you're right, baby."

"It just turned out he actually was a good guy," she went on.

"Yeah," he replied.

"I shouldn't have gone to him," she admitted softly.

"Don't hold that guilt," Deck warned quickly but gently. "I told you, he's good with this. He wants you to heal."

She held his eyes and nodded.

She again drifted away, her face working before she came back to him and focused.

"They told me," she declared.

They were going somewhere else now, he knew it. He just didn't know where she was taking them.

"Who told you what, baby?"

"Nina," she stated.

He felt his brows draw together. Then Emme, always challenging him in ways he liked, and some lately that weren't much fun, did it again. But in a way he didn't much like.

She did this by saying, "They know what happened to me and they were careful when they shared. But I asked, so they shared. They told me about Nina getting kidnapped and nearly shot."

At her words, he had a feeling he knew where she was taking them, his body got tight and he couldn't control it. But she didn't seem to feel it and went on.

"About Lauren getting kidnapped, stabbed and running for her life. About Lexie being kidnapped and nearly shot. And about Faye getting kidnapped and buried alive."

She stopped talking, and not knowing precisely where this was leading so not wanting to make assumptions, Deck said gently, "All right, honey."

"I thought I'd ask them because I knew some of that, and because, in a way, they're like me."

Deck thought this was good and began to relax.

She was right. They were like her in a way, though all that happened when they were adults. But, from the stories he heard, all those women took a minimal amount of time to adjust and move on.

They might be able to help guide Emme.

"I don't know what you do to make a living," she continued, blindsiding him. "But I figure it might have danger and you might have enemies."

Fuck.

Now he knew where her head was at.

Fuck.

"Baby—"

Her voice changed completely, it was trembling when she declared, "I can't go through it again, Jacob."

Fuck.

"Emme—"

"I don't want...I don't think..." she stammered, and Deck turned her.

Rolling her to her back with Deck pinning her down one side, Buford adjusted out of their way with a groan and a sniff.

But Deck only had eyes for Emme.

"Don't use this to pull away from me," he whispered.

She flattened her hands on his chest and admitted, "I'm trying not to pull away but I got to thinking and I got scared."

This was also new, brand new, and it was the good kind of new.

"Good," he replied. "Not that you're scared but that you started thinking and shared that with me."

"Jacob, if...I..." She shook her head on the pillow. "What happened to Faye had to do with something that involved Chace and—"

"Tomorrow, I start putting in a security system," he announced, and she shut her mouth. "And, babe, we're not arguing about who's paying. It's gonna be top of the line and it's gonna cost a whack. So I'm paying and installing."

Her voice was again trembling when she asked, "Does that mean I might be in danger?'

He ignored that and stated, "Also, I'm putting in outside lighting, front, back and sides of the house. Bright lights, long range with motion sensors. You can pick the fixtures so you have the look you want but I'm also paying for that."

"Ja—"

"And that outbuilding you have that looks like it's supposed to be a garage but is mostly a wreck, it gets new windows, new doors, new locks and a new garage door with remote. I want you parking in there because I want your vehicle secure so I need that building secure. When I move in, we'll scrape it and build a bigger garage."

He watched her blink, felt her body jerk slightly under his and she asked, "When you move in?"

"Yeah, when I move in. So this means I'm investing in what's eventually gonna be my own home so you can't find shit wrong with that."

"I...you...you're moving in with me?'

"Not tomorrow. Not in a week. Though, tomorrow, you're movin' in with me. I got an attached garage, security system, motion sensors on the outside lights and a dog. And, just sayin', we're focusing inside work on the wires so we can get a puppy. A German shepherd or a Rottie."

"We're getting a puppy?" she asked then went on before he could answer. "I'm moving in with you?"

"Until work is done here. We'll start lookin' for dogs now, though. Buford's got a helluva bark but his look could make someone underestimate him. Only a plain moron would underestimate a shepherd or a Rottie."

"Okay, I, uh...well, I'm not sure how we got here," she shared.

"We got here because, straight up, baby, every loved one of someone who does something like I do, shit like Chace does, if it gets extreme, they can be vulnerable."

He heard her sharp intake of breath, had no clue if what he was doing was the right thing to do, but he powered on doing it, hoping to God it was.

"But, just pointin' out, crazy shit has happened in this county. Too much of it. So much it's surreal. But Nina, Lexie, they didn't have a man or someone in their life that had a job that put them in that place. That shit can happen to anyone, baby. You didn't live here, you lived in Denver County when it happened to you. You also didn't have a dad who was a cop or did something that put you in jeopardy. But you have concerns. They're valid concerns. That means we alleviate the vulnerabilities."

He paused to make sure that was sinking in in the way he'd hoped. She nodded slowly, so Deck took that as a good sign and carried on.

"Best thing you can do to protect a home is have a dog. Next up, security system. Next up, good lights. People who do bad shit do not like dogs or lights, and most idiots who are fucked up enough to do bad shit aren't smart enough to bypass a security system."

"Oh," she mumbled. It was noncommittal but he could still tell he was getting in there. Her body was loosening under his and her face was getting soft in the moonlight.

So he kept going.

"We also step this up so you can feel good up here," he stated, lifting a hand and tapping her gently on her forehead. "Self-defense classes. You won't need them but they'll make you feel that you might know better how to handle a situation. Even if it is highly unlikely that situation will occur."

"That's actually a good idea," she whispered, and he grinned.

Then his grin faded, he dipped his face closer and he shared, "As much as it shits me, I cannot protect you from the bad things in life, baby. What both of us *can* do is be smart, be aware and be prepared. 'Cause, I know this. You can twist this in your head as another reason to disconnect from me, but even not being with me, that doesn't mean you can assure you'll be safe. What I know for definite is, you being with me, I will bust my ass and break the bank to do everything I can to keep you that way. So, in reality, being with me does not make you more vulnerable. It makes you safer."

Emme had no response.

Then, two seconds later, she did.

And this was to lift her hand to cup his jaw and whisper, "Seriously, Jacob. I really, *really* like you."

It was whacked but he almost liked hearing her say that more than hearing her tell him she loved him.

Almost.

Then again, coming from his Emme, it meant the same thing.

He let out a breath and with it went the tightness he felt in his gut. After, he dropped his mouth to hers and gave her a brief kiss.

When he lifted his head, she asked, "You're moving in with me?

His head tilted at the repeat in subject, and her baffled tone, and he replied, "Yeah, babe. Told you that. Not tomorrow or—"

She interrupted him. "What about your house?"

"We get to that time, I'll sell it."

This time, her head tilted. "You'll sell your house?"

He felt his brows draw together. "Yeah."

"But, don't you like your house? I mean, it's an awesome house."

"Yeah, Emme, I love my house. I worked my ass off for that house. But do I love that house more than you love this heap?"

He felt her body still under his.

"No," he answered when she didn't. "So, when we're at that place to make the change, I move here."

She was silent.

Utterly.

Then she wasn't. But she said something that made little sense.

"I have more bedrooms than you."

"Yeah, you do," he agreed unnecessarily.

"So our kids can have their own rooms, even if we have a bunch of them. Like, four. But, just saying, we'll need to keep a guest room for when Mom and Dad or Rich and Karla visit."

That was when Deck stilled.

"Though, I don't want four kids, just to say," Emme continued.

Deck had no reply.

This was because his blood felt like it was boiling, his heart pumping so hard in his chest, she had to feel it.

And Emme kept talking.

"Actually, I was thinking two. Girls."

Deck replied to that.

"One has to be a boy so I can name him after Chace."

"Chace?" she asked, then declared. "If we have a boy, we're naming him after Dad."

Had she lost her mind?

"I am not namin' a kid Barnard," he declared.

"We have to name him after Dad."

"That isn't happening, Emme."

"Okay, I get you. It isn't exactly a name in vogue right now so maybe we can use it as a middle name," she compromised.

"Babe, no," he refused her compromise.

Her voice was pitched higher, which meant more annoyed, when she asked, "Not even as a middle name?"

And it was then he realized they were there.

She'd been scared. She had logical reasons to be scared. She'd shared. They'd talked.

Now they were arguing about what to name their future son.

He wasn't pulling her back as she was pushing away.

They were talking about what to name *their future son*.

So Deck didn't even try to control it when he lifted his hands to frame her face and dipped his head so close to his girl, all he could smell was strawberries.

"You get the house we raise our kids in. I get to name our son Chace Richard," he whispered, his voice thick.

Her voice husky in return, her hands gliding down his chest then around to link at his back, she replied, "That actually has a nice ring to it."

He dropped closer and against her lips whispered, "Decided."

"Yeah," she whispered back.

"Love you, Emme."

"Love you too, Jacob."

When he got that, he took her mouth.

Then he gave back.

It took another two hours before Emme settled on top of him again.

And her voice stated plain she was almost gone when she sleepily said, "Your kaleidoscope will look awesome in this room. Maybe on the mantel."

She was not wrong. It would look good in this room.

But it wasn't going on the mantel.

"You feel the urge, baby, you can put it on my nightstand tomorrow."

"I would if I had it," she replied, her voice fading with each word then her body weight pressed into him as she fell asleep.

But Deck's entire frame strung tight.

Due to what was happening, he hadn't thought much about his missing kaleidoscope, which had gone missing during the time he was in Denver. Something that told him Emme, in a snit, had taken it.

And when he did think about it, he hadn't brought it up in an effort not to argue because he loved her and he got she was in a rough place and had been for years, but it pissed him off she took it.

He also hadn't seen it anywhere in her house.

Further, he remembered she'd looked confused when they'd been fighting and he told her he wanted it back.

Now she said she didn't have it and she had no reason to lie.

And he had not moved it.

So where the fuck was it?

CHAPTER NINETEEN

Everything to Me

A week and a half later...

DECK HEARD EMME'S whimper as he moved his mouth from between her legs to her belly.

Slowly, he slid his tongue up her body from navel, between her breasts, to dip it in the indent of her collarbone before he buried his face in her neck.

She circled him with her arms, wrapped a leg around his thigh and lifted the other knee high, pressing it tight to his side.

An invitation.

He nipped her earlobe with his teeth.

He felt her lips press against his neck and her soft breaths there.

"Do you love me, Emme?" he whispered.

"Yes," she breathed, writhing underneath him.

"Say it," he ordered gruffly.

"Love you, Jacob."

When he got the words, he slid in slowly, listening to her breaths become pants and feeling her limbs tighten around him.

She loved having him inside. All of him.

Fuck, every bit of her, sweet.

"Want you to kiss me, honey," she murmured as he moved, sliding out slow, sliding in slower.

He lifted his head to look at her. "Taste of you, baby," he reminded her.

"I don't care," she replied then lost patience. She bent her neck and took his mouth.

He let her taste him, and herself, then he took over, still moving inside and taking his time.

He kissed her as her hands moved on him.

He kept kissing her as he moved his hands on her.

It was when she broke her mouth from his, unable to take more of his tongue, that he knew she was close.

"Faster," she gasped.

He gave her what she wanted, his fingers at her breast honing in, rolling her nipple.

"Oh God," she whimpered, her hips jerking. "Faster, honey."

He gave her more and started pounding deep, watching her face. Then he drove in faster just looking at it coming over her.

He saw no surprise. She was used to him giving it to her now.

Fuck, seeing that, it felt like he'd conquered a world.

He went faster.

All her limbs convulsed and she breathed, "Jacob."

Close himself and quickly getting closer, he demanded, "Give that to me, baby."

"Jacob!" It came out as a cry.

She was nearly there.

He put his mouth to hers. "Give it to me, Emme," he growled, and tugged hard on her nipple.

She inhaled sharply then moaned, giving it to him.

Deck invaded her mouth with his tongue, liking the taste of her orgasm, and then he could take no more. He broke the connection of their mouths, shoved his face in her neck and thrust harder.

Faster.

Pumping inside her, her pussy spasming around his cock—fucking ecstasy.

He felt her hands at either side of his head. He knew what she wanted and he lifted up to give it to her just in time to plant his hips between hers, burying his cock to the root. His head jerked back and he groaned as he poured himself inside his Emme.

As it left him, Deck dropped his forehead to her shoulder, staying deep, and felt her hands move on him but her legs stayed tight, anchoring him to her.

That was Emme, now and since they began.

During sex, she liked to be connected. After sex, she liked to stay that way.

He slid his lips up her neck and murmured in her ear, "Love you, baby."

Her hands stopped moving so her arms could wrap around and hold tight.

"Thank you," she whispered into his neck, and he lifted his head to grin down at her.

"Babe, you don't have to thank me for an orgasm," he teased but the grin froze on his face as his body froze on hers when he saw the tears in her eyes. "Emme," he whispered.

"The orgasm..." she started but stopped when she hiccupped to swallow down a sob, the origin of which he had no fucking clue. He dipped his face closer, lifting a hand to cup her jaw and she went on, "It was great, honey. But I'm thanking you for bringing me back to... well, *me*."

Fuck yeah.

Every bit of her, sweet.

He dropped his head to hers on a groaned, "Emme."

"I..." her body jerked under his as she tried to control her sob and her voice was croaky when she continued, "don't know where I'd be right now without you."

He slid his thumb to her lips and whispered, "Stop."

"I can't," she whispered back, a tear sliding out of her eye. "I have to say it. You have to know. You have to know that I'd be alone, lost and alone forever, if I didn't have you."

He pressed his thumb against her lips and begged, "Stop it, baby."

She wrapped her fingers around his wrist, pulling his hand

away, tears streaming out the sides of her eyes, and declared, "You gave me my life back."

Fuck.

So sweet.

"Emme—"

"You didn't give up on me."

"Honey—"

Her fingers tensed on his wrist. "You're everything to me, Jacob."

He held her bright eyes then slid his cheek down hers to warn in her ear, "Can't take more of this sweet, Emmanuelle."

She fell silent.

"You're everything to me too, baby," he told her, and felt her shake her head.

"No. You have a house and a dog and a job that challenges you. You're close with your family. You have friends, good friends, so good they name their children after you. You have everything, including me. I have good stuff too. Now more than before, but only because of you. Because you led me to that. Stuff I held myself away from. Stuff I'd never have if I hadn't found you. Stuff I know I'd lose if I didn't have you."

"You wouldn't lose it, Emme."

"If I lost you, I'd lose everything, Jacob. I'd fade away, alone, denying all along I was lonely."

Jesus.

He lifted his head, locked eyes with her and told her gruffly, "You gotta believe, babe, you're everything to me too."

She shook her head again, opened her mouth but he cupped her cheek, thumb back to her lips, and dipped his face close.

"You're gonna build on what *you* started. We're gettin' a puppy. You're building a crew. You're workin' through shit with family. You're gonna have everything I have, Emme. But when you get all that, that won't mean I won't be everything to you and that holds true for me."

"I—" she pushed out from around his thumb, but he again pressed it to her lips.

"You're going to give me children."

Her eyes and mouth closed.

"You're gonna share my bed, my home, my life, and build a family with me, Emmanuelle," he told her, and her eyes opened, brighter now, tears again streaming. "That's everything, baby."

She pressed her lips together under his thumb and nodded so he slid his thumb away.

"You're right." She gave him a smile, it was trembling but it lit her eyes and pressed that dimple in her cheek. "That's everything."

He pushed his hips into hers, put his lips to hers and whispered, "Love you, Emme."

She curled her arms around him and whispered back, "I love you too, honey."

He slanted his head and took her mouth in a deep, searing kiss that demonstrated the words they'd just uttered.

And Emme gave back as good as she got.

                    *   *   *

Forty-five minutes later...

"Hi-yah!"

Emme attacked.

Buford barked.

Deck, walking out of the bathroom in nothing but a towel, getting attacked from behind, threw his hands behind his head. He grabbed Emme under her arms, hefted her up his back and took four strides to the bed. She squealed and Buford barked again when he bent at the waist and flipped her over on the bed. He leaned in, grasped her hips, twisted her around and dropped on top of her.

She huffed out a breath of air and blinked up at him.

Then she noted, "My instructor didn't teach that when we were going over scenarios of what to do when being attacked from behind."

Deck burst out laughing.

Emme had liked the idea of self-defense classes and wasted no time finding one and enrolling in it. It was held in the Community Center in Chantelle and she'd been to the first two of six weekly classes. They also did an advanced course, which she'd already signed up to take.

On the other hand, Deck had wasted no time installing her security system. Her windows were done and now Max was pulling together a bid to see to her garage. And while Deck worked on the system, Emme worked beside him, patching the walls around her wiring.

That evening, they were heading out to a ranch outside Gnaw Bone to have a look at Rottweiler puppies.

They had a plan, but better, they were wasting no time moving ahead on it together. And Deck wasn't dragging Emme along with him.

She was beside him all the way.

This meant his laughter was heartfelt in more ways than one.

"Usually you say 'hi-yah' right before you break boards with a karate chop," he informed her after he quit laughing.

"I also say 'hi-yah' to give my man advance warning I'm about to attack, something he apparently doesn't need."

He felt his brows rise. "Apparently?"

She grinned at him and stated, "Don't think I'll ever be able to flip someone ass over head over *my* head. So, first, that was awesome you doing it. Second, heads up, I'm so totally attacking and doing it repeatedly so you'll do it again. And last, even in defeat, I'm taking this opportunity to brag that at least I took my instructor down last night on try three. Though not by flipping him over my head as he's six one and may weigh twice as much as me."

"Well done, Emme," he muttered distractedly, not really listening as he was suddenly remembering he was only wearing a towel, noting she only had on his shirt, and as she always played it that way, it was doubtful she had on any panties.

"Jacob," she called, and his eyes that had drifted to her lips, drifted up just as his hand drifted down her side.

"Yeah, baby?"

"Your oatmeal is on the kitchen counter," she told him.

He dropped his lips to her collarbone and slid his hand up the shirt at her hip then in over her belly. "It's too hot to eat now."

"Honey, we just finished," she reminded him.

"An hour ago," he murmured against her throat.

"I have to go to work."

"You can be late."

"I can't."

"Your dad's the boss," he told her jaw.

"Precisely why I can't be late. He depends on me."

Deck lifted his head, looked down at her and at something she saw in his face, hers changed.

And Deck liked that change.

So he grinned and murmured, "Quick."

"Quick," she whispered, already lifting her mouth to his.

He didn't make her go far.

*   *   *

One hour later...

Deck and Buford stood in his garage watching Emme pull out.

But she stopped in the driveway, rolled down her window and stuck her head out.

"Persephone!" she yelled.

Deck smiled huge and tipped his chin up at her.

Before she left, after he'd kissed her and she climbed up in her Bronco, they'd had words about her truck's name, now with her word being the last.

Her head disappeared but he saw she was smiling through the windshield. She waved after she turned out of his drive and before she rode away.

Yeah. Emme's light was beaming, unrestricted.

And blinding.

Deck looked down to his dog. "How you likin' this Emme, pal?"

Buford's tongue lolled and his tail started wagging.

He liked her before so the point was moot.

Deck bent, gave Buford a rubdown, and as he was straightening, his phone rang.

He pulled it out of his back pocket and saw the display said "Chace calling."

"Yo, man," he greeted, at the same time moving toward the button that would close the garage door.

He was facing computer work that day. That afternoon, with no other options open to him as nothing was leading to anything with Prosky, staking out the high school. Then off to look at dogs.

Not a fun day, until the end.

"Where are you?" Chace asked, and his voice made Deck stop thinking about his shit day that at least would end well, and he stopped dead.

"At home. Why?" he answered.

There was nothing from Chace for a long moment before he asked, "Those prints you gave me to run, where'd you get those again?"

Deck's blood turned cold right before it ran hot.

Not hot the way Emme made him feel.

Hot the way he felt that night Chace had told him Faye was buried alive.

"Why?" he asked back.

"Just tell me, Deck."

"My nightstand," Deck answered tersely and again got silence. He moved to the garage door button, hit it, the door started sliding down and he and Buford moved into the house as he pressed, "Chace. Talk to me."

"I'm gonna preface this by sayin', we're on this. I'm callin' it in to Mick and—"

"Stop fuckin' with me. Say it," Deck growled.

He heard a sigh then, "Three prints you lifted and gave me

to run. Yours. Those belonging to Emme, probably in the system because they were put there sometime after she was kidnapped. And Dane McFarland's."

Deck instantly turned on his boot and started back toward his garage.

"Deck, listen to me—" Chace began.

"Jerkoff's been in my house," Deck bit out.

"Man, seriously. Listen."

He kept Buford back with a foot, entered the garage, closed the door and hit the button again for the door to go up.

"Emme was pissed, went off on one, took her shit, left," Deck shared. "He was following her, Chace. She asked Donna to look after Buford. Donna told me the security system had not been engaged the first time she came in after Emme. He got in," Deck told him.

He yanked the door of his truck open and swung in.

"Do not lose your cool," Chace warned.

"There is no cool in this, Chace. That asshole has been in my house. He took my fuckin' kaleidoscope."

Chace sounded confused when he asked, "Your what?"

"My kaleidoscope. That box I kept on the mantel?" Deck asked, shoving his key in the ignition.

"Sorry, Deck, I don't—"

"There's a kaleidoscope in it. Emme gave it to me."

Just turn the dial.

Deck closed his eyes.

McFarland had a piece of his Emme.

That fucking asshole.

He clenched his jaw and opened his eyes.

"How would McFarland know that?" Chace asked.

"How the fuck do I know?" Deck shot back.

Truck running, he threw it in reverse, looked over his shoulder and started backing out.

"Let Mick handle this," Chace stated.

"I will. Then I'll handle it," Deck returned.

"Deck—"

He hit the brakes before his truck hit the street and he focused on his steering wheel but his mind was focused somewhere else.

"He's followin' her."

"You don't know that," Chace replied. "He could have followed you there. Stewed on it, got a wild hair, thought to fuck with you, came back, found the security system disengaged and didn't waste an opportunity. Then he took something that looked like it meant something to you."

"Either way is uncool," Deck noted.

"It is, but stand down and let Mick deal with it."

"He gets him first. I get him after."

"Is anything else missing?" Chace asked.

"Nothin'. Looked, that's it," Deck answered shortly.

"Fuckin' with you," Chace stated.

"So I fuck back," Deck returned.

"Deck, we got a case against this asshole, do not fuck it up for a kaleidoscope."

Just turn the dial.

He didn't turn the fucking dial.

Not for a long time.

Then he did. He'd turned the dial.

You're everything to me.

And found beauty.

"I won't fuck up the case," Deck assured Chace, hitting the garage door remote, he reversed into the street.

"You're pissed and even you pissed, your judgment can be impaired."

"I won't fuck up the case," Deck repeated, disconnected, tossed his phone on the seat beside him and hit the gas.

*   *   *

Five and a half hours later...

Sitting in the middle of the couch, Deck heard the door open.

He didn't move.

Seconds later, he watched him round the corner from the entry hall into the living space of the condo.

Deck knew he'd been picked up and interviewed while the Gnaw Bone PD searched his house for a kaleidoscope they did not find. During his interview, he likely gave bullshit excuses, and with no material evidence, he was set loose.

Now he was Deck's.

Rounding the corner, impossible to miss, Dane McFarland saw him.

"Jesus, what the fuck?" McFarland hissed.

"Your life right now is shit," Deck started. "Your sentence will be a nickel, you'll do two years."

"You can't be in my house," McFarland declared, taking two steps toward Deck.

Deck straightened from the couch, McFarland's head tipped back as he did, and he stopped moving toward Deck.

"You give me back what you took from me, we'll leave it at that," Deck stated. "You play games with me, that time when you get out and set about puttin' your life back together will be the time when you really begin to feel the pain."

"I don't know what you're talkin' about," McFarland snapped.

"You know exactly what I'm talkin' about and you got three seconds to produce it," Deck returned.

McFarland leaned toward him. "You can't break into my house and threaten me."

"I can. I did. You don't give me what's mine, I'll do more. You do not want to know what more I can do but I'll give you a teaser. You will never get another job. You will never have another credit card. You'll never own another car. You'll never lay another woman. You'll never find another house. You'll never have another friend. You will be alone, broke and broken and you'll wish like all fuck you handed over right now what you took from me."

"Jesus, you're whacked," McFarland whispered, staring up at Deck.

"I'm a man who does not like his house violated and his things stolen. Now you got three."

"You can't do all that shit," McFarland retorted.

"Your ass landed in jail 'cause I got deputized and put you there. Task force investigating for six months, I had you there within days. So you're wrong. I *can* do all that shit. And trust me, you don't want to test that. Now, that's one."

McFarland's eyes got big and he murmured, "That's impossible."

"County records will show the sheriff had a subcontract. That subcontract was me. Now, that's two."

"Sheriff departments don't subcontract," he spat.

"They did with me, and, just sayin', I nailed you and I also got Prosky. Your boss is going down." He leaned forward. "Now that's three."

He was bluffing about Prosky, trying to rattle McFarland.

It was a good bluff.

Not surprisingly, considering he was a fucking moron, McFarland gave it away. His Adam's apple bobbed and his eyes widened before going shifty.

They still had nothing on him, but now Deck knew the boss of that crew was Prosky.

"Give it to me, I'll make certain no one knows you ratted out Prosky," Deck told him.

"I didn't rat out Jon!" McFarland cried and there it was, panic and proof.

Prosky was the leader.

"He'll think you did, you don't give it to me," Deck said.

McFarland shook his head. "You can't do that, man."

Deck's brows went up. "You took something that means something to me, broke into my house and took it, and you think I can't fuck with you?"

"It's just a fuckin' kaleidoscope." McFarland was now jittery.

There it was.

Motherfucker.

"Emme gave it to me and I want it back," Deck returned

and McFarland's body stilled, his lip curled and his eyes narrowed on Deck.

"I know. Followed her to your place, she didn't lock the door, got in behind her, wanted to know why she was all fired up to jump straight to you after she got shot of me." His sneer deepened before he finished, "Nice pool, man."

Deck stared at him, wondering where Buford was during this scenario.

But he knew.

Buford was on the scent of strawberries.

"Saw her clutchin' it to her chest like it was her baby," McFarland went on. "So, yeah. I know it meant something to Emme. An Emme you fuckin' stole from me."

Deck said nothing. Deck was dealing with this man following his woman, entering his home when Emme was there, and the knowledge that Emme, feeling betrayed by him, held the piece of art she gave him to her chest when she packed her shit and left his house.

But McFarland was still jittery.

"Dude, you cannot tell Jon I ratted him out. You can't tell any of them that shit. They're totally pissed about the ring—"

"You need to stop talking," Deck rumbled.

McFarland took a good look at his face and snapped his mouth shut.

Deck took a breath in through his nose.

Then he ordered, "Right now, get me what you took from me."

He immediately started looking even more jittery.

Fuck.

"I can't," McFarland whispered, and Deck had a feeling he knew why.

Pain seared through his chest.

His voice was low and dangerous when he asked, "Why?"

McFarland took a cautious step back before he answered, "I buried it at the bottom of your trash."

Deck sucked in another breath, this one sharper, and McFarland took another step back.

That bin had been wheeled out five times since the kaleidoscope went missing.

It was gone.

Just turn the dial.

His eyes focused sharply on McFarland.

"Every day," Deck whispered, "for the rest of your life, you will remember putting that kaleidoscope in the trash."

McFarland carefully threw his hands out to the sides. "I didn't know it was that big of a deal. It's just a bunch of glass."

"You knew," Deck replied.

"I—"

"Shut up, now, or I'll give you something else to remember."

McFarland snapped his mouth shut.

Deck stared at him and he did this a long time, utilizing everything he had to stop himself from pounding the shit out of that...*fucking*...*asshole*.

Just turn the dial.

"You're lucky I have her," Deck stated. "Now you are gonna call Mick Shaughnessy and tell him every fuckin' thing you know about Jon Prosky, those robberies and anything you got involving high school kids. When you do, you are not gonna use it to bargain for a plea. You're gonna do it simply out of civic duty."

McFarland's voice rose when he asked, "Why would I do shit like that?"

Deck leaned toward him and he took another step back. This one was quick.

"Because," Deck started, "you *wanna* be inside. You *wanna* be where I cannot fuck with you and you wanna be there for as long as you can be there. 'Cause when you get out, your years inside are gonna be your last happy memory."

"Jesus. It was a just kaleidoscope, man," McFarland said uneasily.

"It was her tellin' me she needed me and me not hearin' that shit. It was just *her*," Deck gritted. "It was all I had of her for nine years, starin' me in the face, tellin' me she needed me.

And I didn't fuckin' listen, asshole. So I wanted that piece of beauty she gave me always to be a reminder to look after my Emme. And I wanted to give it to our daughter's husband so I could use it to educate him about lookin' after my baby. And you took all that when you took it away from me."

"I was … I was just pissed that you—"

"Shut … the fuck … *up*," Deck growled. "Get on the fuckin' phone *now* and call fuckin' Mick … *Shaughnessy*."

"Prosky will fuck me up worse," McFarland informed him, but Deck shook his head.

"Oh no he won't."

"He will. That guy seems like a nice guy but he's got a mission, man, and he's focused. And anyone would think that mission is whacked, but you knew, you'd know it's a good one and he's committed to it," McFarland shot back, now way beyond jittery.

"He might fuck you up. But," Deck took a long quick stride forward, lifted a hand and shoved his index finger hard in McFarland's forehead, pushing off, and McFarland went back on a foot, "I'll fuck with your head. I will not stop until you have nothing and I'll keep going until you lose the last thing you got, not that it's worth much, your fuckin' mind. Now, motherfucker, do not try me further." He bent in, McFarland leaned back, Deck lost it and roared, *"Call Shaughnessy!"*

On the last syllable, they both turned to the door that they heard thrown open.

Not a second later, a scruffy, pimple-faced kid who couldn't be older than seventeen and looked freaked right the fuck out rushed in.

"He took a girl!" he shrieked, and Deck's heart stopped beating.

"Wade, what the fuck are you doing here?" McFarland shouted, eyes going back and forth between the kid and Deck.

"No, dude, no, no, no…" the kid chanted, rushing up to McFarland and grabbing his arm. "Jon's back, dude, and it's bad. He's pissed. He's pissed at *everybody*. And dude, he's totally pissed *at you*. He's off the freakin' reservation. He totally has this girl! Emmitt and Bryan are totally freaked!"

"A high school girl?" Deck asked.

The kid shook his head even as he looked to Deck and asked back, "Who are you?"

Deck didn't answer.

He clipped, "Did he take a high school kid?"

The kid looked him from top to toe and wisely decided to answer.

"No, she's an older lady. Like, your age."

"Her name?" Deck pushed.

"No clue," the kid answered. "Too freaked to pay attention. I just wanted to get out of there."

"What does she look like?" Deck asked.

"I don't know. She was like, normal. Pretty."

And dude, he's totally pissed at you.

Fuck, please God, tell him, because McFarland was gagging for her, Prosky wouldn't take Emme.

"What does she look like?" Deck repeated.

"I told you. Normal. Pretty."

"What does she look like?" Deck barked, and both Wade and McFarland jumped.

"Brown hair, like... long. Some, like, streaks in it. She's tall. Weird eyes—" the kid started to say fast.

Fuck. *Fuck!*

He had fucking Emme.

"Where is she?" Deck bit out.

"She's... she was at Jon's place but he was movin' her." Wade looked to McFarland. "That's how I got away. I slipped out when they were movin' her. You gotta do somethin', Dane. That's whacked. You gotta talk to him. When he got intense, you were the only one who could talk to him."

"Where are they movin' her?" Deck asked, the kid looked at him and shrugged.

"I dunno. I got outta there."

Deck looked at McFarland. "Where would he take her?"

"How would I know?" McFarland asked.

Deck moved and McFarland was on his back on the floor with Deck's knee in his chest and his hand fisted in his collar.

"Where would he fuckin' take her?" Deck snarled.

"I don't—" McFarland began.

"It's fuckin' Emme. He's pissed at you and he's got fuckin' Emme," Deck clipped.

"Oh fuck," McFarland breathed as it belatedly dawned on him, the fucking moron.

Deck took his knee out of McFarland's chest, lifted McFarland a foot up then slammed him back into the floor.

"Talk!" he ordered.

"Probably . . . we've got . . . well, this place. Off the access road a mile up Navajo in Carnal, into the hills, goin' toward the hiking trails."

Deck knew it so he wasted no time straightening, yanking McFarland up with him and pushing him off.

"You," Deck pointed at McFarland. "Call Shaughnessy, report this, *all* of this shit, fuckin' *everything*. You," Deck pointed at Wade then at the couch. "Sit your ass down."

"Shaughnessy!" Wade squealed. "Like, the cop?"

"Man, I cannot call Shaughnessy," McFarland said at the same time.

Deck pulled his gun out of the holster at his hip and both McFarland and Wade's eyes went to the gun and grew huge.

He pointed it at McFarland. "You, Shaughnessy." He pointed it to Wade. "Ass. On. Couch."

McFarland fished his phone out of his pocket.

Wade ran to the couch and planted his ass on it.

Deck breathed deep as his blood ran so fucking hot, it was a wonder he didn't burn inside out.

Prosky had Emme.

Just turn the dial.

Prosky had his girl.

You're everything to me.

Emme had been taken.

I can't go through it again, Jacob.

Deck heard McFarland's voice saying, "Yes, this is Dane McFarland. I need to speak with Captain Shaughnessy."

Deck holstered his gun then pointed his finger between the two of them. "You leave, he leaves before the cops get here, neither of you leave the hospital without a limp and you'll also be leavin' behind your balls 'cause I'm gonna cut them off and shove them down your throat. You get me?"

McFarland, phone to his ear, instantly nodded.

Wade swallowed and asked, "Seriously?"

"Confirm you get me!" Deck thundered.

"Yeah, yeah...totally," the kid said, lifting his hands into a don't-shoot position and shrinking into the couch.

Deck wasted not another second. He turned on his boot and left.

Sprinting down the stairs to the parking lot, his phone to his ear, Chace answered, "I don't clean up messes. Please God, tell me you do—"

Deck cut him off tersely, "Jon Prosky has Emme."

You're everything to me.

Fuck!

"Where are you?" Chace asked with urgency.

"In my truck," Deck answered, angling in. "McFarland's turning over. He's in his condo with a high school kid named Wade. They'll be here when the cops get here. Now where are you?"

Just as he suspected, there was no hesitation before Chace replied.

"Wherever you need me to be."

*   *   *

Emme

An hour later...

I was staring at the payroll reports when it hit me.

I needed a burrito. Badly.

I heard boots quickly coming up the wooden stairs outside my office as I reached for my cell.

Whoever it was could wait for the two minutes I needed to call Jacob and tell him Rosalinda's was up after we picked out our Rottie. The puppy could stay in Persephone while we got takeout.

My thumb was hovering over Jacob's name on my screen when my door smashed open.

My head flew to it and I saw Jacob standing there wearing an expression I'd seen before on two faces I loved.

My heart stopped beating.

At the look on his face, it took effort but I pushed out of my chair, opening my mouth to speak, but I got nothing out.

This was because Jacob rushed me. I got myself together to take a step back but it wasn't fast enough. Jacob was on me and I was crushed in his arms so tight I couldn't breathe.

I'd felt that before too.

"What's happening?" I wheezed.

Jacob heard my wheeze, pulled back but clamped a hand on either side of my head, bending deep so his face was in mine, his eyes scanning my features.

That look in his eyes. That look I knew.

I swallowed.

"What's happening?" I whispered.

"You been here all day, baby?" he whispered back, his voice gruff with emotion.

"Yeah, except I went to lunch at the café with Zara like I told you I was gonna do," I answered.

His eyes closed slowly.

Then one of his hands slid to the back of my head and he yanked my face into his chest. He held me there as his other hand went to his back pocket and he pulled out his phone.

"Jacob, is everything okay?" I asked, my voice trembling.

"Yeah, baby, it's okay." Jacob's voice was still gruff. "It's all good." Then he wasn't talking to me when he said, "Chace. Not Emme. She's at her office. Don't know who he's got but it's not Emme."

I felt my body go solid.

What was he talking about?

Jacob kept talking.

"Yeah, I probably should have given her a call," Jacob said, his voice weird. This weirdness being that it seemed he was admitting to doing something stupid, something he never did, so the tone was unpracticed and didn't sound right in his voice. "Gotta go, man. Emme heard that. Gotta explain then I'll be back on the hunt."

The hunt?

"Right. Later," Jacob finished.

I planted my hands in his chest and pulled away as he shoved the phone back in his pocket.

I looked up at him. "Please tell me what's happening."

Both his hands settled on my neck and he bent again so our faces were close.

"For some reason, the ringleader of McFarland's crew came back to town and lost his shit. Seein' as McFarland's hung up on you, when I got word that he took a woman, I made assumptions and thought it was you." His fingers squeezed my neck. "It wasn't you, baby, so I gotta get out there and help them find out who it is."

I nodded, not knowing how to feel about the dire news of yet *another* woman being kidnapped in the county. I just knew the phantom of fear that he still held in his eyes I didn't like all that much.

"I'm fine," I whispered the obvious in an effort to get that look out of his eyes. "Go find whatever girl he's got."

He nodded but didn't move.

"Don't leave here until I come get you," he ordered.

It was then I nodded. Someone was out there kidnapping people. I was totally down with that.

"Okay, honey," I also agreed verbally.

"It gets later, you keep a man here with you until I can get to you or I'll call Max or Ty to come get you."

"Okay."

He held my eyes.

"I'm fine," I repeated softly.

"Scared as fuckin' shit they had you," he replied.

This man was such a good man.

And he was *my* man.

On this thought, I gave him a reassuring smile and pressed my hands into his chest for good measure.

"They didn't."

His eyes continued to hold mine.

Then he asked, "You okay with this shit?"

Weirdly, I was. Then again, obviously, I wasn't.

"I'm safe. I have you," I explained the former. "But I'd really like it if you went out and helped them find whoever the bad man has."

Again, he held my eyes.

Then he nodded, pulled me in, kissed my forehead, pushed me back, gave me a small grin and strode to the door.

After he opened it, he stopped and turned back.

"Last hour proved what I told you today was true," he stated.

"What?" I asked.

"You're everything to me, Emme."

As tears hit the backs of my eyes, I swallowed as I saw in his eyes that phantom was gone but the words he just spoke were true.

Unable to say more, I said, "Right back at you, honey. Now, please go save the day."

He jerked up his chin then said, "Love you."

I smiled at him. "Love you too."

I caught Jacob's return smile before the door closed behind him and I heard quick footfalls on the wooden stairs.

I pulled in a breath and scanned my emotions, searching for fear or the urge to retreat.

All I found was hope that Jacob and the men out looking for her found the girl who was missing so she would no longer be missing and therefore feeling the things I knew she was feeling.

And also that he did it in time for us to get our puppy and pick up burritos.

EPILOGUE

Doing It for Free

Seven and a half hours later...

"BABE, SERIOUSLY," JACOB said, and I looked at him.

"She's just a puppy," I told him something he knew.

"Yeah, but she's just a *Rottweiler* puppy," he returned. "You don't let puppies chew your fingers. Rotties, you don't give *any* indication at *any* time it's okay to sink their teeth in flesh."

He had a point.

I extracted my fingers from Josephine's jaws and gave her head a rub.

She looked at me, went for the fingers I'd pulled away, gave up quickly, bounced up Jacob's chest and attacked his jaw.

It was after puppy adoption, burrito pickup and consumption, and a weird day that started great, went wonky and ended fabulously.

We were lying on the couch in Jacob's great room. Jacob was on his back, me tucked to his side, Buford on the floor by the couch, our new rambunctious puppy frolicking on Jacob's massive chest.

Once his jaw was attacked, Jacob moved. Josephine and I were forced to move with him, Josephine mostly because he picked her up and put her on the floor.

Undeterred, she attacked Buford's floppy ear.

Buford turned beleaguered eyes to Jacob, eyes that turned beleaguered about a nanosecond after Josephine was introduced and had stayed that way.

I fought back a grin.

Jacob gently pushed Josephine off his hound. Demonstrating she might have puppy ADHD, she instantly lost interest in Buford and attacked the rug.

I started giggling.

Jacob lay back on a sigh and curled me into him.

"So, okay," I began, and Jacob stopped watching our new puppy growling and attempting to find purchase with her teeth on the edge of his rug and looked at me. "Sock it to me," I invited.

Needless to say, since we got a puppy and I got my burritos, the girl had been saved and the bad guys were behind bars. But I had yet to get the full story.

"Fuckin' nuts, but now knowin' the whole story, it isn't that interesting," Jacob told me.

"For mysterious crimefighters, maybe not," I replied, "For average citizens like me, I'm thinking it'll be all kinds of interesting."

Jacob grinned, curled me closer, pulling me partially over his chest and his hand dipped under my sweater to make lazy circles on my skin.

That felt really nice.

He started talking. "Jon Prosky's mom has chronic progressive MS."

I stopped thinking how nice his fingers felt at my back and whispered, "Oh my God, that sucks."

"Yeah," he agreed. "Sucks more, she doesn't have any insurance or a husband. When she started gettin' bad, he couldn't deal. He took off a couple of years ago. What she did have was a son who loved her way too fuckin' much."

"Uh-oh," I mumbled, guessing what would come next.

"Yeah," Jacob again agreed. "He loved her, a lot of people loved her, but only he got desperate. But then, with the dad gone and no siblings, he was up. He's also, if you can believe this shit, a seemingly nice guy who did desperate shit that was also illegal shit and convinced himself along the way it was for a cause that was just. Made matters worse he convinced a pack of high school kids the same thing."

I knew something about nice people being moved by extreme circumstances to do extreme things but I wisely kept my mouth shut on that score and asked, "How did he do that?"

Jacob rolled to his side, wrapped his other arm around me and tangled his legs with mine.

That felt nice too.

"Bills started piling up," he explained. "Avenues for payin' them started dryin' up, and Prosky knew two things. One, he needed money. And two, he needed to be free to take care of his mom as things progressed."

I nodded when he paused and he continued.

"So he needed to recruit a crew to do the dirty work. He did that and took pains to be certain he was not connected with any of them. Finding the drug dealer wasn't hard. Convincing him to commit felonious acts was even less hard, seein' as the guy would get his cut."

"How did high school kids get involved?" I asked.

"The brainstorm came when he found out the dealer was dating a teacher," Jacob answered. "Prosky, being nice and having a mission, unfortunately also has natural charisma, and there's no denyin' he loves his mom. He conceived this plan, the drug dealer, his girlfriend, a teacher, her brother, another teacher and *their* brother, McFarland were recruited on greed alone. The kids were recruited to keep all their hands clean. He convinced the kids they were doing something worthwhile, saving a life. The teachers pinpointed the kids to approach and made preliminary connections. The dealer was the trainer, since he'd had some B&E's in his past, and enforcer in case they got out of hand or balked. McFarland was the good guy to the dealer's bad guy, keeping the kids from freaking. He also did most of the fencing. Prosky was the spiritual leader, keeping them on target."

"So did the kid who committed suicide think the dealer was going to hurt him?" I asked, and Jacob shook his head.

"No clue. He didn't leave a note. But his buds were all brought in when McFarland and Wade started spilling and they talked. They said it was more likely he was devastated that he might have disappointed Prosky and his mom. Part of the recruitment process was to meet her, see what that disease was doing to her, how money could help and he thought he fucked it all up. Kids that age get overemotional about a lot of shit. Prosky manipulated that, got them all worked up, feelin' they were doin' good deeds and screwin' that pooch would fuck with their head. It fucked with that kid's head. Then again, for any of these kids to be willin' to do his shit, they were all borderline anyway, something the teachers knew. They went over the edge just committing robberies. It wouldn't take more to tip shit further."

That made sense. It was whacked, sad sense but it was sense.

But one thing didn't make sense.

"What was with the girl today?" I queried.

"The girl was McFarland's brother's girlfriend. The deal was no one outside the team knew shit about anything. After he got arrested, so he wouldn't lose her, this guy talked to his woman to explain their mission, giving her the line they were doing bad things for good reasons. She didn't give a shit about some woman she didn't know in Denver who unfortunately has MS. She gave a shit that her man was going to spend the next at least two years honing his skills to become an ex-con, one who couldn't get out and get a job that had shit to do with his degree. She was making rumblings of talking to the cops about a deal so her man's sentence would be reduced, or even, since according to her his hands weren't that dirty, get immunity and not do time at all."

I didn't like the idea of a bad teacher getting off that lightly, but I could understand her concerns.

Jacob kept talking.

"Prosky didn't give a shit about all of them going down.

They got arrested, he hauled his ass to Denver, didn't look back and was already setting up another crew. What he couldn't have was him going down. There would be no one not only to pay for his mother's care but also no one to care for her as that disease took its course."

"So he took this woman to scare her? Shut her up?" I asked, and Jacob nodded.

"Desperate act. Then again, it all was, the disease wasn't going to quit, which means the acts would get more desperate so he was going to screw up eventually."

"How did he use the money to pay for stuff and not have it traced back to the robberies?" I went on.

"Like I said, he's likable. His mother, though, is beloved. Apparently an amazing woman, lots of friends. As the disease progressed, they did what they could but only so much folks can do. They had fundraising events and people ran races for her, shit like that. But her care ate all that up, and kept going. People have their own lives and they can give selflessly but they can't do it for eternity. So, given the opportunity to do more without it coming from their pockets or sweat, they did it. It didn't take much for Prosky to talk them into saying they gave a gift for her care, and as it was cash, it couldn't be traced. That said, when DPD officers went out to have chats after we got Prosky this afternoon, several of them 'fessed up. But they did it expressing concern for Prosky and his mom."

All this was sad, lives destroyed, a young man was dead and a woman would now face a bitter battle with a disease with no one at her side.

Part of me got why Prosky did what he did. That didn't mean I condoned it. Too much was lost, even if what he was trying to gain was honorable.

The rest of me just hoped myself or no one I knew faced the same kind of tragedy.

Jacob's words took me out of my thoughts.

"You okay with all this, honey?"

I focused on him as my body melted into his.

He was *such* a good guy.

And he so totally loved me.

"I'm okay," I assured.

"Brings up bad shit for you," he reminded me, scanning my face, looking for indications I'd inadvertently taught him to search for when it came to me. Hiding fear. Burying things. Preparing to retreat.

"I'm not happy someone got kidnapped," I shared, and his arms around me got tight. "But I'm here, with you, Buford and Josephine. I'm full of good burritos. And I'm learning how to count my blessings instead of fear they'll be swept away from me. So I'm good, outside of not being real happy you spent time today thinking I wouldn't be."

I got another squeeze on his, "I'm fine, Emme."

It was my turn to search his features to make sure he was what he said.

And he looked okay to me. Well, not okay. Handsome, intent and sweet, but that was his norm so that was okay.

It was time to move us on.

Not to bury it.

Just to move past it.

In order to do that, I asked, "You know what all this means?"

"I know what all this means to me, that this guy was completely fucked in the head," Jacob answered, and I grinned but shook my head.

"What all this means is that it lays testimony to the blatant fact we need socialized medical care," I announced.

Jacob stared at me.

Then he moved his eyes to the ceiling and stared at it.

"Admit it, I'm not wrong," I pushed.

At that, Jacob angled up, taking me with him. The move was so sudden, I cried out and latched on. We were front to front with my hands clutching his shoulders and my legs wrapped around his hips when he started walking.

Toward the French doors.

"What are you doing?" I asked.

Jacob didn't answer. He kept walking then dipped down to open the door.

Out we went with me crying, "Jacob! What are you—?"

I didn't get it all out. He made it to the edge of the pool, pulled me from his body even as I tried to keep hold and easily tossed me right into the water.

Fully clothed.

I came up spluttering, pulling my hair from my face and shouting, *"Are you insane?"*

Standing at the side of the pool, hands on hips, smiling, Jacob declared, "Just sayin', anytime you mention socializing medical care, you get tossed in the drink."

"You *are* insane!" I yelled, swiping an arm across the water in hopes of splashing him but I was too far away and thus failed.

He kept smiling.

Then he yanked his shirt over his head and I watched with some awe as he bent his knees and took off. His long straight body knifing through the air, it sliced into the water as he executed a perfect dive.

God. He could even dive perfectly.

In jeans.

Or maybe it was perfect because it was hot he was doing it in jeans.

Or maybe it was just hot because he was joining me.

I treaded water as he swam under it and came up in front of me, wrapping an arm around my waist and pulling me to him as he did.

I again grabbed his shoulders and wrapped my legs around his hips.

"I'm glad we're moving to my house," I announced. "I don't have a pool so when you don't want to concede a valid, and I'll just note, *accurate* point, you can't toss me into it."

"Emme," he said.

"What?" I snapped.

"Take off your sweater," he ordered.

I watched his face in the tranquil, revolving colors of the pool lights and noticed my man was not in the mood to discuss political ideology.

Suddenly, I wasn't either.

So I pulled off my sweater.

* * *

An hour later...

Jacob powering inside me, my back to the wall of the pool, my face in his neck, our soggy clothes strewn around the pool deck, my legs wrapped around his hips, he stated, "This summer, we're puttin' a pool in at your place, south side."

"Okay," I breathed instantly.

"And we're not namin' our puppy Josephine."

He kept powering up as I pulled my face out of his neck in order to look at him.

"What?"

He rammed in, I whimpered, he stopped so I whimpered again.

"We're namin' her Daisy Mae."

I felt my eyes get wide as my legs quivered and I repeated my question from earlier, "Are you insane?"

"Nope."

"A Rottie," he stroked, I stopped talking, he did it again and stayed planted so I kept going, "is," he pulled out then drove up again, I bit my lip then powered on, "a noble breed. We can't name a noble dog Daisy Mae."

He ground up and that felt so good my hand slid into his wet hair and fisted.

"Josephine doesn't go with Buford," he told me.

"So?" I asked.

Keeping one arm around me, his other hand slid over my belly, down and in.

Then his thumb hit me.

My head fell back and my entire body quivered.

"She's Daisy Mae," Jacob declared.

"Please move," I whispered.

"I will, you agree she's Daisy Mae."

He was. He was totally insane.

Or he was intent on driving me that way.

I righted my head. "That's not fair."

His thumb twitched and I moaned.

"Daisy Mae," he repeated.

"Ja—"

His thumb slid away and my eyes went wide as my arms and legs tensed around him.

"Jacob!"

"What's our dog's name?"

"Please move," I begged. "And I want your thumb back. We'll talk about this later."

His lips came to mine, they were curved up and his eyes were dancing. There was something about having Jacob buried deep inside me, the warm waters of a pool lapping around our naked bodies, and his eyes dancing with humor that was completely and totally amazing. A moment to remember. Forever.

Have mercy.

"Say it. Daisy Mae," he ordered.

"Right. Okay. Whatever. We can insult her by calling her Daisy Mae."

His smiling mouth took mine, his tongue sliding inside, as his thumb honed in and he surged out then up, again planting himself deep but this time doing it without stopping.

I forgot about Daisy Mae.

I forgot about everything.

And it would be fifteen glorious minutes before rational thought came back and it occurred to me I didn't really care our puppy was called Daisy Mae. That was actually kind of cute.

And more, I was super happy we were putting in a pool at my place.

But I was never going to tell Jacob that I hoped it was heated.

*　　*　　*

Thirteen months later...

The door opened and I saw my dad stick his head in.

He jerked his chin up.

I grinned at him then looked across the room to see Faye, as planned, had my mother's undivided attention.

Mom would freak if she knew what I was doing.

When my sister got married, she'd done the same thing.

Mom and Dad let their kids live their lives but when it came to their weddings, they stepped in, or I should say Mom stepped in, and demanded tradition. A church. A white or, if necessary (as I deemed it was), ivory gown. A reception line. Formal photographs. Proper speeches. And Jacob had been told in no uncertain terms that if he shoved his piece of wedding cake all over my mouth, Mom was confiscating his snowmobile.

Last, and most important, the groom didn't see the bride before the wedding.

Therefore, I'd spent the night at Jacob and my house, Jacob spent his at Chace and Faye's since he sold his place when he'd moved into mine six months ago.

But I had something I needed to do.

And I was going to do it.

Lifting my skirt in my hand, I hustled to the door.

Dad and Krys were outside when I got through.

Krystal was carrying a wooden box I'd dropped by Bubba's a few days earlier. She was also smiling.

Dad was deep breathing.

"My baby girl," he whispered.

I looked up to him, saw the bright mixed with admiration in his eyes and grinned.

"Do I look okay?" I asked, throwing out an arm.

He nodded, his throat visibly convulsing.

My grin became a smile. I wrapped my arms around him and got up on my toes to kiss his cheek.

He gave me a hug and let me go, whereupon he gave me a shaky smile so I leaned in to give him another kiss on the cheek.

After the kiss, I whispered, "Love you, Daddy."

"Love you too, my precious baby," he whispered back. "Also love that today I'm givin' you to a good man who'll see to you."

I drew in breath.

"Or maybe I don't love it," Dad went on. "But at least I can live with it."

At his words, I gave him a squeeze and another smile.

Then I turned to Krys.

She handed me the box.

I wasted no more time since I didn't have any and ducked out the side door. Carefully, on my fabulous and fabulously expensive ivory heels, I dashed around the back of the church and went in the door on the other side.

Chace and Rich were waiting for me.

"Is he alone?" I asked Chace.

"Yeah, Emme," he answered, looking me up and down then his gaze came to mine. Without further ado and absolutely no warning (except the intense look in his eyes), he proceeded to blow me away. He did this by whispering, "Love this, honey. I couldn't build a better you for my boy."

At his words, my heart skipped a beat and I had to let go of my skirt and put a hand to the wall to stay standing.

"That means a lot," I whispered, and it did. From Chace, it definitely did.

"I know," he replied.

I pulled in breath, and if I kept doing that, I was likely to pass out.

"Darlin', you gotta hurry," Rich said, and I looked to him. "You're both at the church on time but it's also kinda important for you to be in the sanctuary on time."

"Right," I mumbled, and he smiled at me.

Then he bent in to give me a peck on the cheek.

When he was done, I looked between the men, giving them a grin.

Then I went to the door they were guarding to keep visitors at bay. I lifted a hand and knocked.

"Yo!" I heard Jacob call, and that set my lips to again curving.

I turned the knob, put my hands behind my back to hide the box, and walked in. Closing the door with my foot, I saw Jacob standing in front of a mirror tying a dove gray tie.

Dark suit that fit perfectly. Dove gray tie. Charcoal gray vest. Ivory rose in his lapel.

God, he was beautiful.

Suddenly, I understood why a bride didn't see her groom before the wedding. Because if she saw him in all his splendor, she might not be able to fight back the urge to jump him and consummate the marriage precipitously, forcing everyone to wait to get to the buffet.

Luckily, Jacob and I had done that, repeatedly, and we didn't have time to do it again, so I was able to fight that urge.

Barely.

His eyes in the mirror came to me and his hands stopped moving.

"Hey," I greeted.

Slowly, he turned. As he did, his gaze was moving all over me but he said nothing.

Then he said something.

"Didn't know you could get more beautiful."

Tears hit my throat and so I wouldn't dissolve in a puddle of goo, or alternately messy sobs that would destroy my makeup, I quipped, "I aim to please."

"You excel at that, baby."

God, he wasn't making this easy.

He was making it beautiful, but he wasn't making it easy.

To get past that, I had to suck in a breath through my nose.

"You wanna make out before we get hitched, kinda hard to do with you across the room," Jacob remarked, and finally I grinned.

"You can't tell Mom I'm here," I told him as I started his way.

"I'm more likely to share government secrets with terrorists than tell your mother that," he told me, and I giggled as I stopped two feet in front of him.

Suffice it to say, Jacob wasn't a big fan of tradition when it came with being forced to sleep in a whole different town than me, pre-wedding or not. But Mom put her foot down in a way neither Jacob nor I could deny.

That still didn't mean he was happy about it.

"Hopefully, it won't come to that," I replied, and Jacob's focus intensified on me.

Or, more accurately, the fact that I stopped two feet away.

"Emme, baby, I'm supposed to step in a church in five minutes and I don't think you're supposed to be on my arm when I do that. You wanna clue me in why you're here?"

I pulled the box from around my back and lifted it up between us.

His eyes dropped to it and his body went completely still.

He'd told me about what Dane had done with his kaleidoscope.

It creeped me way the hell out that Dane was following me, so I decided to discuss that with my therapist and find a way to let it go. And I did that.

It hurt way too much to think of Jacob's kaleidoscope dumped out with the trash.

I didn't discuss that with my therapist, though.

I did something about it.

"I went back to the store where I bought it, but it's now a dry cleaners," I shared. Jacob's eyes didn't leave the box but I kept going. "So I asked Chace if he could help. Chace knows some woman in Denver who's good at finding stuff out and she got the number of the old owners of the shop. She called them and found out who made the kaleidoscopes."

Slowly, Jacob's eyes came to me and what I saw in them made my throat close and my nose sting with tears.

I swallowed and my voice was husky when I went on.

"She called that guy and he agreed to meet me. He's eighty-three and quit making them a few years ago. But when I told him our story," I moved the box toward him and finished, "he made this for you and me."

Jacob didn't move. Not for a long time.

I knew why and it was sweet. Very sweet.

But we were imminently getting married. I needed to move this along.

So I called, "Honey?"

He finally moved. His eyes and hands going to the box, he took it, flipped it open, and I heard his indrawn breath when he saw what was inside.

The old guy outdid himself. The last kaleidoscope was a thing of beauty.

This one could easily be declared a miracle.

I watched, deep breathing, as Jacob pulled it out, set the box aside and turned it around in his hands like it was the world's most precious entity.

And this time, unlike the last, I knew.

I'd had glorious months and months of knowing that those hands moving on me made me feel l just as precious.

"Do you like it?" I whispered, and his eyes shot to mine.

He said nothing.

He didn't have to.

Staring into his eyes, they said it all.

My breath hitched.

"You best go back to your mother, honey," he murmured.

"Yeah," I agreed softly.

Neither of us moved.

"Go, Emme, or the wedding's gonna be delayed an indefinite amount of time and your hair is not gonna look like that when you stand up in the sanctuary," he stated.

My hair was in an elegant updo à la Dominic (another Mom decree). It took two hours to achieve.

Mom's head would likely split down the middle if I had sex hair for my wedding.

In other words, that got me moving.

I nodded but I couldn't help it. Not in that moment. Not because, in five minutes, we were about to begin building our lives legally, spiritually, emotionally and indelibly connected.

Not after the way Jacob had just looked at me.

So I took my chances, leaned into him, put a hand on his chest, got up on my toes and tipped back my head.

Jacob didn't touch me but he did bend his neck and give me his mouth.

I pressed my lips to his.

His tongue slid out, my mouth opened, and he gave me a light stroke that felt amazing and tasted unbelievably sweet.

When he was done, against my lips, he whispered, "Go, baby."

I nodded, my nose sliding against his as I did, and pulled back. I gave him a trembling smile and headed to the door.

"Emmanuelle?" he called when I had my hand on the knob.

I turned to him.

"When we get to the Brown Palace tonight and you see the box the staff are putting on your nightstand for me, I'll tell you the story about how I tracked down an old guy and told him what I wanted. I'll also tell you how, until about two minutes ago, I thought he was a total whackjob when he laughed for five minutes before agreeing to make you a kaleidoscope and insisting on doing it for free."

My hand went from the knob to lay flat on the door as my knees went weak, my heart slid into my throat and the vision of Jacob started swimming.

"Go, baby," Jacob urged gently.

Hearing his gentle words, seeing his tall frame, it would only be Jacob who could look beautiful even through tears.

"I really, really, *really* like you, Jacob Decker," I whispered.

"I know," he whispered back.

The smile I sent him was seriously trembling before I dashed out the door.

*　　　*　　　*

Deck

Putting the kaleidoscope to his eye, pointing it at the window, Deck turned the dials and his vision was accosted with nothing but beauty.

It was extraordinary to witness.

But by then he was used to it as he had it every day.

As the lights and colors danced, he heard a sharp knock on the door before he heard Chace calling, "Deck. It's time."

Deck watched the miraculous dance Emme gave him another long moment before he took the kaleidoscope from his eye, carefully laid it in its box and closed the lid.

He moved to the door and he did this ignoring Chace grinning huge at the box.

He didn't have time for that shit.

It was time to marry his Emme.

*   *   *

Harvey

Three years, two months later…

Harvey Feldman moved through the grocery store, his mind on other things, so when he found himself in the aisle with the magazines, an aisle he never needed anything in, he was surprised.

This was happening with more and more frequency.

Then again, he was getting old.

He focused on his list then started moving down the aisle quickly in order to get what he needed and get home.

Now focused, it was a flat miracle that he turned his head and his attention caught on something he would never normally look at, and even if he did, he wouldn't see.

But since it was a miracle, he saw it.

A magazine on architecture, the cover an aerial shot of a

very large home in the mountains with a sweeping front drive, a gracious pool to the left and a lush terraced garden at the back.

At the top of the sidebar, the magazine noted, *"Mountain Gem Restored: How the Canard Mansion was brought back to life."*

Harvey stopped and stared at the picture, the words, then he snatched up the magazine, threw it in his cart and whizzed through the aisles, getting the bare necessities, paying for them and getting home.

He left the groceries in the car and took only the magazine with him when he went into his house. He didn't delay in sitting at his kitchen table and flipping it open, slapping page after page aside until he stopped and caught his breath.

Slowly now, with utter care, he moved through the pages of the article.

Then he went back.

Then he flipped the pages again, slower, studying the pictures.

And finally, he allowed himself to go back.

The title of the article and photo spread was at the top of a full-color, full-page picture. But Harvey didn't look at the title.

Instead, he looked at the picture of the man, woman, child and dogs standing among the gleaming wood and dazzling crystal of an extraordinary, regal entryway.

Emme and her man, standing close, sides tucked tight. His arm was around her shoulders. His other arm was tucked under the tush of a dark-haired toddler who was straddling his side. A hound was sitting on his behind, resting against the leg of Emme's man. A Rottweiler was sitting by Emme's leg but the dog wasn't leaning into her, though it was close.

Jacob Decker had on jeans and a nice tailored shirt.

But he needed a haircut.

Emme Decker had on a stylish but casual dress that went to her ankles and fit close to her body. She also was wearing high-heeled sandals that were even more stylish than the dress.

And last, the dress didn't disguise the fact that she was more than a little pregnant.

They looked perfect together. Strangely perfect in that they looked like they belonged in the mountains, with the healthy glow of their tans, their dogs and Decker's jeans (and need for a haircut), but they were standing in a majestic entry, the kind that would launch a million dreams.

Then again, they looked like they belonged there too.

Harvey looked down to the bottom of the picture to read the caption.

Jacob and Emmanuelle Decker, with their son Chace and dogs Buford and Daisy Mae in the famous starburst entry that they stunningly refurbished in the Canard Mansion in Gnaw Bone, Colorado.

Harvey's eyes went back to Emme to see her smiling, carefree and bright, at the camera.

So bright, it was nearly blinding.

He took one last long look, closed the magazine and finally, *finally*, he felt it.

Redeemed.

He looked to the ceiling.

Then he whispered, "Thank you."

After that, he went out to get his groceries.

*   *   *

Deck

"That is not gonna happen," Emme declared, and Deck turned his head from watching Chace in his highchair somewhat eating, mostly throwing his food to the black-and-white-diamond-tiled floor, and looked at his wife who was standing in front of her six-burner Viking range.

"I didn't say it was going to happen tomorrow," he told her, fighting a grin.

"Of course it isn't going to happen tomorrow. He's not even two. But I'll just point out, honey, it's not going to happen *ever*," she retorted.

"Yeah it is. I'm thinking when he's twelve," Deck replied.

She threw up her hands. One had a wooden spoon in it that luckily, with the force of her action, was clean.

"It's not happening at all!"

Daisy Mae, lying on her belly four feet from Emme, picked up her head and looked at her mistress. Always on the alert, even as often as this happened.

Buford, on the other hand, with more experience, was moving around under Chace and Deck, cleaning up Chace's mess.

"It's just a BB gun," Deck stated.

"I don't *care* if it's just a BB gun. A gun's a gun!" she shot back.

"No one can get hurt with a BB gun," he declared, her eyes got huge and she was so damned cute, he was finding it harder to fight his smile.

"No one...no...no one..." she spluttered. Then she slammed her fists on her hips, which wasn't easy to do with a spoon in her hand and their baby daughter who would come into this world in about a month taking most of the space of her middle, and she hissed, "Haven't you seen *A Christmas Story*?"

At this ridiculous question, Deck stared at his wife.

She was very pissed, very pregnant, very beautiful, and very cute. She was also standing in her expensive, flawless kitchen in their rambling no-longer-a-wreck mansion with her dog at her side, her son throwing food and her man in her sights.

He took all that in, he did it for a good long while and he enjoyed every second as he realized, with Emme, the kaleidoscope that was their life just kept on spinning.

Then he burst out laughing.

For Nina Sheridan, a desperately needed vacation turns into the biggest risk of her life...

Please see the next page for an excerpt from

The Gamble.

CHAPTER ONE

Time-out

I LOOKED AT the clock on the dash of the rental car, then back out at the snow.

I was already twenty minutes late to meet the caretaker. Not only was I worried that I was late, I was also worried that, after I eventually made it there, he had to drive home in this storm. The roads were worsening by the second. The slick had turned to black ice in some places, snow cover in others. I just hoped he lived close to the A-frame.

Then again, he was probably used to this, living in a small mountain town in Colorado. This was probably nothing to him.

It scared the hell out of me.

I resisted the urge to look at the directions I'd memorized on the plane (or, more accurately, before I even got on the plane), which were sitting by my purse in the passenger seat. There was no telling how far away I was and what made matters worse was that I was doing half of what I suspected, but wasn't sure, was the speed limit.

Not to mention the fact that I was exhausted and jet-lagged, having been either on the road, on a plane, or in a grocery store the last seventeen hours.

And not to mention the fact that yesterday (or was it the day before? I couldn't figure out which in changing time zones), I got that weird feeling in my sinuses that either meant a head cold was coming or something worse and that feeling was not going away.

Not to mention the *further* fact that night had fallen and with it a snowstorm that was building as the moments ticked by. Starting with flurries now I could barely see five feet in front of the car. I'd checked the weather reports and it was supposed to be clear skies for the next few days. It was nearing on April, only two days away. How could there be this much snow?

I wondered what Niles was thinking, though he probably wasn't thinking anything since he was likely sleeping. Whereas, if *he* was off on some adventure by himself, or even if he was with friends (which was unlikely, as Niles didn't have many friends), *I* would be awake, worried and wondering if he made it to his destination alive and breathing. Especially if he had that niggling feeling in his sinuses that I told him I had before I left.

I had to admit, he didn't tell me he wanted me to ring when I got to the A-frame safe and sound. He didn't say much at all. Even when I told him before we decided on churches and dates that I needed a two-week time-out. Time to think about our relationship and our future. Time to myself to get my head together. Time to have a bit of adventure, shake up my life a little, clear out the cobwebs in my head and the ones I fancied were attached (and getting thicker by the day) to every facet of my boring, staid, predictable life.

And, I also had to admit, no matter where I went and what I did, Niles didn't seem bothered with whether I arrived safe and sound. He didn't check in, even if I was traveling for work and would be away for a few days. And when I checked in, he didn't seem bothered with the fact that I was checking in. Or, lately (because I tested it a couple of times), when I *didn't* check in and then arrived home safely, sometimes days later, he didn't seem bothered by the fact that I hadn't checked in.

The unpleasant direction of my thoughts shifted when I saw my turn and I was glad of it. It meant I was close, not far away at all now. If it had been a clear night, I figured from what it said in the directions, I'd be there in five minutes. I carefully turned right and concentrated on the ever decreasing visibility of the landscape. Making a left turn, then another right before heading straight up an incline that I feared my car wouldn't make. But I saw it, shining like a beacon all lit up for me to see.

The A-frame, just like it looked on the Internet, except without the pine trees all around it, the mountain backdrop, and the bright shining sun. Of course, they were probably there (except the sun, seeing as it was night); I just couldn't see them.

It was perfect.

"Come on, baby, come on, you can make it," I cooed to the car, relief sweeping through me at the idea of my journey being at an end. I leaned forward as if that would build the car's momentum to get up the incline.

Fortune belatedly shined on me (and the car) and we made it to the postbox with the partially snow-covered letters that said "Maxwell," signifying the beginning of the drive that ran along the front of the house. I turned right again and drove carefully toward the Jeep Cherokee that was parked in front of the house.

"Thank God," I whispered when I'd stopped and pulled up the parking brake, my mind moving immediately to what was next.

Meet caretaker, get keys and instructions.

Empty car of suitcases and copious bags of groceries, two weeks' worth of holiday food—in other words, stuff that was good for me, as per usual, but also stuff that was definitely not, as was *not* per usual.

Put away perishables.

Make bed (if necessary).

Shower.

Take cold medicine I bought at the grocery store.

Call Niles if even just to leave a voice mail message.

Sleep.

It was the sleep I was most looking forward to. I didn't think I'd ever been that exhausted.

In order to make the trips back and forth to the car one less, I grabbed my purse, exited the car, and slung my bag over my shoulder. Then I went to the boot, taking as many grocery bags by the handle as I could carry. I was cautious; the snow had carpeted the front drive and the five steps that led up to the porch that ran the length of the A-frame and I was in high-heeled boots. Even though it was far too late (though I *had* checked the weather forecast and thought I was safe), I was rethinking my choice of wearing high-heeled boots by the time I hit the porch.

I didn't get one step across it before the glass front door opened and a man stood in its frame, his front shadowed by the night, his back silhouetted by the lights from inside.

"Oh, hi, so, so, so sorry I'm late. The storm held me up." I hastily explained my easily explainable rudeness (for anyone could see it was snowing, which would make any smart driver be careful) as I walked across the porch.

The man moved and the outside light came on, blinding me for a second.

I stopped to let my eyes adjust and heard, "What the fuck?"

I blinked, focused, and then I could do nothing but stare.

He did not look like what I thought a caretaker would look like.

He was tall, very tall, with very broad shoulders. His hair was dark, nearly black, wavy, and there was a lot of it sweeping back from his face like a stylist had just finished coifing it to perfection. He was wearing a plaid flannel shirt over a white thermal, the sleeves of the shirt rolled back to expose the thermal at his wrists and up his forearms. Faded jeans, thick socks on his feet, and tanned skin stretched over a face that had such flawless bone structure a blind person would be in throes of ecstasy if they got their fingers on him. Strong jaw and brow, defined cheekbones. Unbelievable.

Though, in my estimation, he was a couple days away from a good clean shave.

"Mr. Andrews?" I asked.

"No," he answered, and said no more.

"I—" I started, then didn't know what to say.

My head swung from side to side. Then I looked behind me at my car and the Cherokee, back around and up at the A-frame.

This *was* the picture from the website, exactly it. Wasn't it?

I looked back at him. "I'm sorry. I was expecting the caretaker."

"The caretaker?"

"Yes, a Mr. Andrews."

"You mean Slim?"

Slim?

"Um..." I answered.

"Slim isn't here."

"Are you here to give me the keys?" I asked.

"The keys to what?"

"The house."

He stared at me for several seconds and then muttered, "Shit," and right after uttering that profanity, he walked into the house, leaving the door open.

I didn't know what to do and I stood outside for a moment before deciding maybe the open door was an indication that I should follow him in.

I did so, closing the door with my foot, stamping my feet on the mat to get rid of the snow, and looking around.

Total open space, all shining wood. Gorgeous.

Usually, websites depicting holiday destinations made things look better than they really were. This was the opposite. No picture could do this place justice.

To the left, the living area, big, wide, long comfortable couch with throws over it. At the side of the couch, facing the windows, a huge armchair two people could sit in happily (if cozily) with an ottoman in front of it. Square, sturdy, rustic table between the chair and couch, another one, lower, a bigger square, in front of the couch. A lamp on the smaller table, its base made from a branch, now lighting the space. Another standing lamp in the corner of the room by the windows made from another, longer, thicker branch with buffaloes running across the shade, also lit. A fireplace, its gorgeous stone chimney disappearing into the slant of the A-frame; in its grate a cheerful fire blazed.

A recessed alcove to the back where there was a rolltop desk with an old-fashioned swivel chair in front of it, a rocking chair in the corner by another floor lamp, its base looked like a log and was also lighting the space.

A spiral staircase to a railed loft that jutted over the main living space and there were two doors under the loft, one I knew led to a three-quarter bath, the other one, likely storage.

The pictures of the loft on the website showed it held a queen-sized bed, had a fantastic master bath with a small sauna and a walk-in closet.

To the right I saw a kitchen, perhaps not top-of-the-line and state-of-the-art but it wasn't shabby by a long shot. Granite countertops in a long U, one along the side of the house, the other, a double top, a low, wide counter with a higher bar, both sliced into the open area, and the bar had two stools in front of it. A plethora of knotty pine cabinets that gleamed. Midrange appliances in stainless steel. Another recess at the back where the sink was, the fridge to the left. And a six-seater dining table at its end by the floor to A-frame windows, also in knotty pine, with a big hurricane-lamp-style glass candleholder at its center filled with sage-green sand in which was stuck a fat cream candle. Over it hung a candelabra also made from branches and also lit.

"You got paperwork?" the man asked, and I was so caught up in surveying the space and thinking how beautiful it was and how all my weeks of worries if I was doing the right thing and my seventeen hours of exhausting travel was worth getting to that fabulous house, I started. Then I looked at him.

He was in the kitchen and he'd nabbed a cordless phone. I walked in his direction, put the grocery bags on the bar, and dug in my purse to find my travel wallet. I pulled it out, snapped it open, and located the confirmation papers.

"Right here," I said, flicking them out and handing them to him.

He took them even though he was also dialing the phone with his thumb.

"Is there a prob—" I asked. His eyes sliced to me and I shut up.

His eyes were gray, a clear, light gray. I'd never seen anything like them. Especially not framed with thick, long, black lashes.

"Slim?" he said into the phone. "Yeah, got a woman here…a…" He looked down at the papers. "Miss Sheridan."

"Ms.," I corrected automatically, and his clear gray eyes came back to me.

It had also dawned on me, at this juncture, that he had a strangely attractive voice. It was deep, very deep, but it wasn't smooth. It was rough, almost gravelly.

"A *Ms.* Sheridan." He cut into my thoughts and emphasized the "Ms." in a way that I thought maybe wasn't very nice. "She's lookin' for keys."

I waited for this Slim person, who I suspected was Mr. Andrews, the absent caretaker, to explain to this amazing-looking man that I had a confirmed two-week reservation, prepaid, *with* a rather substantial deposit in the rather unlikely event of damage. And also I waited for this Slim person to tell this amazing-looking man that there obviously was some mistake and perhaps he should vacate the premises so I could unload my car, put away the perishables, have a shower, talk to Niles, and, most importantly, *go to sleep.*

"Yeah, you fucked up," the amazing-looking man said into the phone. He concluded the conversation with, "I'll sort it out," beeped a button, and tossed the phone with a clatter onto the counter. After doing that, he said to me, "Slim fucked up."

"Um, yes, I'm beginning to see that."

"There's a hotel down the mountain 'bout fifteen miles away."

I think my mouth dropped open but my mind had blanked so I wasn't sure.

Then I said, "What?"

"Hotel in town, clean, decent views, good restaurant. Down the mountain where you came. You get to the main road, turn left, it's about ten miles."

He handed me my papers, walked to the front door, opened it, and stood holding it, his eyes on me.

I stood where I was and looked out the floor-to-A-point windows at the swirling snow; then I looked at the amazing but, I was tardily realizing, unfriendly man.

"I have a booking," I told him.

"What?"

"A booking," I repeated, then explained in American, "a reservation."

"Yeah, Slim fucked up."

I shook my head; the shakes were short and confused. "But I prepaid two weeks."

"Like I said, Slim fucked up."

"With deposit," I went on.

"You'll get a refund."

I blinked at him, then asked, "A refund?"

"Yeah," he said to me, "a refund, as in, you'll get your money back."

"But—" I began, but stopped speaking when he sighed loudly.

"Listen, Miss—"

"Ms.," I corrected again.

"Whatever," he said curtly. "There was a mistake. I'm here."

It hadn't happened in a while but I was thinking I was getting angry. Then again, I'd just traveled for seventeen-plus hours. I was in a different country in a different time zone. It was late, dark, snow was falling, and the roads were treacherous. I had hundreds of dollars' worth of groceries in my car, some of which would go bad if not refrigerated and hotels didn't have refrigerators, at least not big refrigerators. And I was tired and I had a head cold coming on. So I could be forgiven for getting angry.

"Well, so am I," I returned.

"Yeah, you are, but it's *my* house."

"What?"

"I own it."

I shook my head and it was those short, confused shakes again.

"But it's a rental."

"It is when I'm not here. It isn't when I'm home."

What was happening finally dawned on me fully.

"So, what you're saying is, my confirmed booking is really an *unconfirmed* booking and you're canceling at what is the absolute definition of the very last minute?"

"That's what I'm sayin'."

"I don't understand."

"I'm speakin' English. We do share a common language. I'm understandin' you."

I was confused again. "What?"

"You're English."

"I'm American."

His brows snapped together and it made him look a little scary, mainly because his face grew dark at the same time. "You don't sound American to me."

"Well, I am."

"Whatever," he muttered, then swept an arm toward the open door. "You'll get a refund first thing Monday morning."

"You can't do that."

"I just did."

"This is . . . I don't . . . you can't—"

"Listen, *Ms*. Sheridan, it's late. The longer you stand there talkin', the longer it'll take you to get to the hotel."

I looked out at the snow again, then back at him.

"It's snowing," I informed him of the obvious.

"This is why I'm tellin' you, you best get on the road."

I stared at him for a second that turned into about ten of them.

Then I whispered, "I can't believe this."

I didn't have to wonder if I was getting angry. This was because I knew I was livid and I was too tired to think about what I said next.

I shoved the papers into my purse, snatched up my grocery bags, walked directly to him, stopped, and tilted my head back to glare at him.

"So, who's going to refund the money for the gas for my car?" I asked.

"Miss Sheridan—"

"*Ms.*," I hissed, leaning toward him and continuing. "And who's going to refund my plane ticket all the way from England where I *live* but my passport is *blue*?" I didn't let him respond before I went on. "And who's going to pay me back for my holiday in a beautiful A-frame in the Colorado mountains, which I've spent seventeen-*plus* hours traveling to reach? Traveling, I might add, to a destination I paid for *in full* but didn't get to enjoy *at all*?" He opened his mouth but I kept right on talking. "I didn't fly over an ocean and most of a continent to stay in a *clean* hotel with *nice views*. I did it to stay *here*."

"Listen—"

"No, you listen to me. I'm tired, my sinuses hurt, and it's snowing. I haven't driven in snow in years, not like that." I pointed into the darkness, extending my grocery-bag-laden arm. "And you're sending me on my way, well past nine o'clock at night, after reneging on a contract."

As I was talking, his face changed from looking annoyed to something I couldn't decipher. Suddenly, he grinned and it irritated me to see he had perfect, white, even teeth.

"Your sinuses hurt?" he asked.

"Yes," I snapped. "My sinuses hurt, *a lot*," I told him, then shook my head again; this time they were short, *angry* shakes. "Forget it. What do you care? I'm too tired for this."

And I was. Way too tired. I'd figure out what I was going to do tomorrow.

I stomped somewhat dramatically (and I was of the opinion I could be forgiven for that too) into the night, thinking this was my answer. This was the universe telling me I should play it safe. Marry Niles. Embrace security even if it was mostly boring, and deep down if I admitted it to myself, it made me feel lonelier than I've ever felt in my life.

Paralyzingly lonely.

Who cared?

If this was an adventure, it stunk.

I'd rather be sitting in front of a TV with Niles (kind of).

I opened the boot and put the bags back in. When I tried to close it, it wouldn't move.

This was because Unfriendly, Amazing-Looking Man was now outside, standing by my car and he had a firm hand on it.

"Let go," I demanded.

"Come back into the house. We'll work somethin' out, least for tonight."

Was he mad? Work something out? As in him *and* me staying in the A-frame together? I didn't even know his name, and furthermore, he was a jerk.

"Thank you," I said snottily. "No. Let go."

"Come into the house," he repeated.

"Let go," I repeated right back at him.

He leaned close to me. "Listen, Duchess, it's cold. It's snowing. We're both standin' outside like idiots arguing over what you wanted in the first place. Come into the damned house. You can sleep on the couch."

"I am *not* going to sleep on a couch." My head jerked and I asked, "Duchess?"

"My couch is comfortable and beggars can't be choosers."

I let that slide and repeated, "Duchess?"

He threw his other hand out, his gaze drifting the length

of me as he said, "Fancy-ass clothes, fancy-ass purse, fancy-ass boots, fancy-ass accent." His eyes came to my face and he finished firmly. "Duchess."

"I'm American!" I shouted.

"Right," he replied.

"They don't have duchesses in America," I educated him.

"Well, that's the truth."

Why was I explaining about aristocracy? I returned to target.

"Let go!" I shouted again.

He completely ignored my shouting and looked into the boot.

Then he asked, what I thought was insanely, "Groceries?"

"Yes," I snapped. "I bought them in Denver."

He looked at me and grinned again, and again I thought it was insanely, before he muttered, "Rookie mistake."

"Would you let go so I can close the boot and be on my way?"

"Boot?"

"Trunk!"

"English."

I think at that point I might have growled but being as I was alarmed at seeing only red, I didn't really take note.

"Mr. . . ." I hesitated, then said, "Whoever-you-are—"

"Max."

"Mr. Max—"

"No, just Max."

I leaned toward him and snapped, "*Whatever*." Then demanded, "Let go of the car."

"Seriously?"

"Yes," I bit out. "Seriously. Let. Go. Of. The. *Car*."

He let go of the car and said, "Suit yourself."

"It would suit me if I could travel back in time and not click 'book now' on that stupid webpage," I muttered as I slammed the boot and stomped to the driver's-side door. " 'Idyllic A-Frame in the Colorado Mountains,' not even *bloody* close.

More like Your Worst Snowstorm Nightmare in the Colorado Mountains."

I was in the car and had slammed the door but I was pretty certain before I did it I heard him chuckling.

Even angry, I wasn't stupid and I carefully reversed out of his drive, probably looking like a granny driver and I didn't care. I wanted out of his sight, away from the glorious yet denied A-frame and in closer proximity to a bed that I could actually *sleep* in and I didn't want that bed to be in a hospital.

I turned out of his drive and drove a lot faster (but still not very fast) and I kept driving and I didn't once look into my mirrors to see the lost A-frame.

Adrenaline was still rushing through my system and I was still as angry as I think I'd ever been when I was what I figured was close to the main road but I couldn't be sure and I hit a patch of snow-shrouded ice, lost control of the rental, and slid into a ditch.

When my heart stopped tripping over itself and the lump in my throat stopped threatening to kill me, I looked at the snow in front of my car and mumbled, "Beautiful." I went on to mumble, "Brilliant."

Then I burst out crying.

*   *   *

I woke up or at least I *thought* I woke up.

I could see brightness, a lot of it, and a soft, beige pillowcase.

But my eyeballs felt like they were three times their normal size. My eyelids actually *felt* swollen. My head felt stuffed with cotton wool. My ears felt funny, like they were tunnels big enough to fit a train through. My throat hurt like hell. And lastly, my body felt leaden, like it would take every effort just to move an inch.

I made that effort and managed to get up on a forearm. Then I made more of an effort and pulled my hair out of my eyes.

What I saw was a bright, sunshiny day out of the top of an A-frame window through a railing. I could see snow and lots of it and pine trees and lots of those too. If I didn't feel so terrible, I would have realized how beautiful it was.

Cautiously, because my stuffed up head was also swimming, I looked around and saw the loft bedroom from the A-frame website.

"I'm dreaming," I muttered. My voice was raspy and speaking made my throat hurt.

I also needed to use the bathroom, which I could see the door leading to one in front of me.

I used more of my waning energy to swing my legs over the bed. I stood up and swayed, mainly because, I was realizing, I was sick as a dog. Then I swayed again as I looked down at myself.

I was in a man's T-shirt, huge, red, or it had been at one time in its history. Now it was a washed out red. On the left chest it had a cartoonlike graphic of what looked like a man with crazy hair madly playing a piano over which the words "My Brother's Bar" were displayed in an arch.

I opened up the collar to the shirt, peered through it, and stared at my naked body, save my still-in-place panties.

I let the collar go and whispered, "Oh my God."

Something had happened.

The last thing I remembered was bedding down in the backseat of the rental having covered myself with sweaters and hoping someone would happen onto me somewhat early in the morning.

I'd tried unsuccessfully to get the car out of the ditch and, exhausted and not feeling all that well, I'd given up. I'd decided against walking in an unknown area to try to find the main road or happen onto someone who might just be stupid enough to be driving in a blinding snowstorm. Instead, I was going to wait it out.

I also suspected that I'd never get to sleep. Not in a car, in a ditch, in a snowstorm after a showdown with an unfriendly but insanely attractive man. So I took some nighttime cough medicine, hoping to beat back the cold that was threatening, covered myself with sweaters, and bedded down in the backseat.

Apparently, I had no trouble getting to sleep.

Now I was here.

Back at the A-frame.

In nothing but panties and a man's T-shirt.

Maybe this *was* My Worst Snowstorm Nightmare in the Colorado Mountains. Weird things happened to women who traveled alone. Weird things that meant they were never seen again.

And this was all my fault. *I* wanted a time-out from my life. *I* wanted an adventure.

I thought maybe I should make a run for it. The problem was, I was sick as a dog and I had to go to the bathroom.

I decided bathroom first, create strategy to get out of my personal horror movie second.

When I'd used the facilities (the bathroom, drat it, was fabulous, just like in the photos) and washed my hands, I walked out to see Unfriendly, Amazing-Looking Man—otherwise known as Max—ascending the spiral staircase.

Like every stupid, senseless, idiotic heroine in a horror movie, I froze and I vowed if I got out of there alive I'd never make fun of another stupid, senseless, idiotic heroine in a horror movie again (which I did, every time I watched a horror movie).

He walked into the room and looked at me.

"You're awake," he noted.

"Yes," I replied cautiously.

He looked at the bed, then at me. "Called Triple A. They're gonna come up, pull out your car."

"Okay."

His head tipped to the side as he studied my face and asked, "Are you okay?"

"Yes," I lied.

"You don't look too good."

Immediately a different, stupid, senseless, idiotic feminine trait reared its ugly head and I took affront.

"Thanks," I snapped sarcastically.

His lips tipped up at the ends and he took a step toward me. I took a step back.

He stopped, his brows twitching at my retreat, then said, "I mean, you don't look like you feel well."

"I'm perfectly fine," I lied.

"And you don't sound like you feel well."

"This is how I sound normally," I lied yet again.

"It isn't how you sounded last night."

"It's morning. I just woke up. This is my waking-up voice."

"Your waking-up voice sounds like you've got a sore throat and stuffed nose?"

I kept lying. "I have allergies."

He looked out the windows, then at me. "In snow?" I looked out the windows, too, and when he continued speaking, I looked back at him. "Nothin' alive in the ice out there that'll mess with your allergies, Duchess."

I decided to change the topic of conversation; however, I was becoming slightly concerned that I was getting light-headed.

"How did I get here?" I asked him.

His head tipped to the side again and he asked back, "What?"

I pointed to myself and said, "Me"—then pointed to the floor—"here. How did I get here?"

He looked at the floor I was pointing to, shook his head, and muttered, "Shit." He looked back at me and said, "You were out. Never saw anything like it. Figured you were fakin'."

"I'm sorry?"

He took another step toward me and I took another step back. He stopped again, looked at my feet, and for some reason grinned. Then he looked back at me.

"I waited a while, called the hotel to see if you'd checked in. They said no. I called a couple others. They said no too. So

I went after you, thinkin' maybe you got yourself into trouble. You did. I found your car in a ditch, you asleep in the back. I brought you and your shit to the house. You were out like a light, dead weight." His torso twisted and he pointed to my suitcase, which was on a comfortable-looking armchair across the room; then he twisted back to me. "Put you to bed, slept on the couch."

I was definitely getting light-headed, not only because of being sick but also because of what he just said. Therefore, in order not to fall down and make a right prat of myself, I skirted him, walked to the bed, and sat down or, if I was honest, more like *slumped* down.

I looked up at him and asked, "You put me to bed?"

He'd turned to face me. His brows were drawn and he didn't look amused anymore.

"You're not okay," he stated.

"You put me to bed?" I repeated.

His eyes came to mine and he said, "Yeah."

I pulled at the T-shirt and asked, "Did you put this on me?"

The grin came back. It was different this time, vastly different, and my light-headedness increased significantly at the sight.

Then he said, "Yeah."

I surged to my feet and my vision went funny, my hand went to my forehead, and I plopped back down on the bed.

Suddenly he was crouched in front of me, murmuring, "Jesus, Duchess."

"You took my clothes off," I accused.

"Lie down," he ordered.

"You took my clothes off."

"Yeah, now lie down."

"You can't take my clothes off!" I shouted, but I heard my loud words banging around in my skull, my head started swimming, and I would have fallen backwards if my hand didn't come out to rest on the bed to prop me up.

"I can, I did, it ain't nothin' I haven't seen before, now lie down."

I started to push up, announcing, "I'm leaving."

He straightened and put his hands on my shoulders, pressing me right back down. My bottom hit the bed and I looked up at him, suddenly so fatigued I could barely tilt my head back.

"You aren't leavin'," he declared.

"You shouldn't have changed my clothes."

"Duchess, not gonna say it again, lie down."

"I need to go."

I barely got out the word "go" when my calves were swept up and my body twisted in the bed. I couldn't hold up my torso anymore so it also fell to the bed. Then the covers came over me.

"You had medicine in your groceries. I'll get that and you need some food."

"I need to go."

"Food, medicine then we'll talk."

"Listen—"

"I'll be right back."

Then he was gone and I didn't have the energy to lift my head to find out where he went. I decided to go to my suitcase, get some clothes on and get out of there. Then I decided I'd do that after I closed my eyes just for a bit. They hurt, too much, and all that sun and snow, I had to give them a break. It was too bright.

Then, I guess, I passed out.

*　　*　　*

"Nina, you with me?" I heard a somewhat familiar, deep, gravelly voice calling from what seemed far away.

"How do you know my name?" I asked, not opening my eyes, and I would have been highly alarmed at the grating sound of my voice if I wasn't so very tired.

"You're with me," the somewhat familiar, deep, gravelly voice muttered.

"My throat hurts."

"Sounds like it."

"And my eyes hurt."

"I'll bet."

"And my *whole body* hurts."

"You've got a fever, Duchess."

"Figures," I murmured. "I'm on holiday. Fit as a fiddle through my boring bloody life, I go on holiday, I get a fever."

I heard a not in the slightest unattractive chuckle and then, "Honey, I need to get you up, get some ibuprofen in you, some liquids."

"No."

"Nina."

"How do you know my name?"

"Driver's license, credit cards, passport."

My eyes slightly opened and that was too much effort so I closed them again.

"You went through my purse."

"Woman sick in my bed, yeah. Figured I should know her name."

I tried to roll but that took too much effort, too, so I stopped trying and said, "Go away."

"Help me out here."

"Tired," I mumbled.

"Honey."

He called me "honey" twice. Niles never called me "honey" or "sweetheart" or "darling" or anything, not even Nina most the time, which was my bloody name. In fact, Niles didn't speak to me much if I thought about it, which, at that moment, I didn't have the energy to do.

I was nearly asleep again before I felt my body gently pulled up, then what felt like my bottom sliding into a man's lap and what felt like a glass against my lips.

"Drink," that somewhat familiar, deep, gravelly voice ordered.

I drank.

The glass went away; then I heard, "Open your mouth, Duchess."

I did as I was told and felt something on my tongue.

The glass came back and then, "Swallow those down."

I swallowed and jerked my head away. The pills going through my sore throat hurt like crazy.

I ended up with what felt like my forehead pressed into someone's neck, soft fabric against my cheek.

"Ouch," I whispered.

"Sorry, darlin'."

I was moved again back between sheets, head on pillow, and before the covers fully settled on me, I was asleep.

*   *   *

I woke up when I felt something cool, too cool, hit my neck.

"No," I rasped.

"You're burnin' up, baby."

I wasn't burning up. I was cold. So cold I was trembling, full on human earthquake.

"So cold." The words scraped through my throat and I winced.

The cool left my neck and was pressed to my forehead.

"Nina, do you have travel insurance?"

I tried to focus but couldn't and asked, "What?"

"This doesn't break soon, I gotta get you to the hospital."

I stayed silent mainly because I was trying to concentrate on getting warm. I pulled the covers closer around me and snuggled into them.

"Nina, listen to me, do you have travel insurance?"

"Wallet," I told him. "Purse."

"Okay, honey, rest."

I nodded and pulled the covers closer but I couldn't get warm enough.

"I need another blanket."

"Honey."

"Please."

The cool cloth stayed at my forehead but I felt strong fingers curl around my neck; then they drifted down to my shoulder.

I heard the word "fuck" said softly and the covers were drawn away.

"No!" I cried. It was weak but it was a cry.

"Hang tight, baby."

The bed moved and I fell back as substantial weight came in behind me.

Then his body was the length of my back, fitting itself into the curve of mine. I nestled backward, deeper into his solid warmth as the tremors kept quaking my frame. His arm came around me, his hand found mine, and the fingers of both my hands curled around his—hard, tight, holding on.

"So cold, Max."

"Beat it back, Duchess."

I nodded against the pillow and said, "I'll try."

It took a while, the trembling keeping me awake, him holding me tight, his body pressed to mine.

What felt like hours later, when the tremors started to slide away, I called softly, "Max?"

"Right here," came a gravelly yet drowsy reply.

"Thanks," I whispered.

Then I slid into sleep, so exhausted it felt like I'd fought an epic battle.

*   *   *

The cool cloth was again against my brow, sweeping back across my hair.

"Max?"

"Fever's broke."

"Mmm," I mumbled, falling back to sleep.

The words, "Work with me, Nina," stopped my descent.

"Okay," I whispered, and I was moved to my back and my upper body was pulled up.

"Lift your arms."

I did as I was told and the T-shirt came off.

"You sweated it out, Duchess. You're in the home stretch."

"Okay."

"Keep your arms up."

"Okay."

I felt another T-shirt come down over my arms, over my head. I felt it yanked down at my belly, my sides. I fell forward and felt my forehead resting against something soft and hard. The material was soft and it covered what I figured was a hard shoulder.

"You can drop your arms."

"Okay."

I dropped my arms and slid them around what felt like a man's waist. Then I cuddled closer. It felt like arms came around my waist, too, and it also felt like a hand was trailing gently up and down my back.

"You're sweet when you're sick."

"I am?"

"Hellion when you're riled."

"Yes?"

"Yeah."

"Mmm."

Then he muttered, "Not sure which I like more."

I had no reply. Mainly because I'd fallen back to sleep.

Fall in Love with Forever Romance

I'VE GOT MY DUKE TO KEEP ME WARM
by Kelly Bowen

Gisele Whitby has perfected the art of illusion—her survival, after all, has depended upon it. But now she needs help, and the only man for the job shows a remarkable talent for seeing the real Gisele...Fans of Sarah MacLean and Tessa Dare will love this historical debut!

HOPE RISING
by Stacy Henrie

From a great war springs a great love. Stacy Henrie's Of Love and War series transports readers to the front lines of World War I as army nurse Evelyn Gray and Corporal Joel Campbell struggle to hold on to hope and love amidst the destruction of war...

Fall in Love with Forever Romance

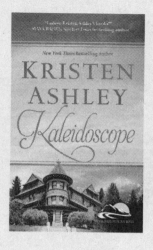

KALEIDOSCOPE
by Kristen Ashley

When old friends become new lovers, anything can happen. And now that Deck finally has a chance with Emme, he's not going to let her past get in the way of their future. Fans of Julie Ann Walker, Lauren Dane, and Julie James will love Kristen Ashley's *New York Times* bestselling Colorado Mountain series!

BOLD TRICKS
by Karina Halle

Ellie Watt has only one chance at saving the lives of her father and mother. But the only way to come out of this alive is to trust one of two very dangerous men who will stop at nothing to have her love in this riveting finale of Karina Halle's *USA Today* bestselling Artists Trilogy.

Fall in Love with Forever Romance

DECADENT
by Adrianne Lee

Fans of Robyn Carr and Sherryl Woods will enjoy the newest book set at Big Sky Pie! Fresh off a divorce, Roxy isn't looking for another relationship, but there's something about her buttoned-up contractor that she can't resist. What that man clearly needs is something decadent—like her...

THE LAST COWBOY IN TEXAS
by Katie Lane

Country music princess Starlet Brubaker has a sweet tooth for moon pies and cowboys: both are yummy—and you can never have just one. Beckett Cates may not be her usual type, but he may be the one to put Starlet's boy-crazy days behind her... Fans of Linda Lael Miller and Diana Palmer will love it, darlin'!

Fall in Love with Forever Romance

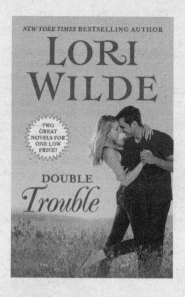

DOUBLE TROUBLE
by Lori Wilde

Get two books for the price of one in this special collection from *New York Times* bestselling author Lori Wilde, featuring twin sisters Maddie and Cassie Cooper from *Charmed and Dangerous* and *Mission: Irresistible*, and their adventures in finding their own happily ever afters.